The UNTHINKABLE

D1637165

OTHER BOOKS BY MONICA

Regency:
Taming the Rake

Scottish:
Highlander Untamed
Highlander Unmasked
Highlander Unchained
Highland Warrior
Highland Outlaw
Highland Scoundrel
The Chief
The Hawk
The Ranger
The Viper
The Saint
The Recruit
The Hunter
The Knight (novella)
The Raider
The Arrow

The UNTHINKABLE

New York Times & *USA Today* Bestselling Author

MONICA McCARTY

ALL RIGHTS RESERVED

THE UNTHINKABLE Copyright © 2015 Buccaneer Press
LLC
Excerpt from TAMING THE RAKE Copyright © 2015
Buccaneer Press LLC
Cover Design: © Seductive Designs
Photo: Woman © Novel Expressions
Photo: Landscape: © Depositphotos.com/ianwool
Photo: Ship: © Depositphotos.com/Elenarts
Photo: Letter: ©Depositphotos.com/ estudiosaavedra

This is a work of fiction. References to real people, events,
establishments, organization, or locales are intended only to
provide a sense of authenticity, and are used fictitiously. All
other characters, and all incidents and dialogue, are drawn
from the author's imagination and are not to be construed as
real.

All rights reserved. No part of this novel may be reproduced
without prior written permission from the publisher, except
for brief quotations for purposes of review.

ISBN:978-0991210428

ACKNOWLEDGMENTS

I need to go back quite a few years to give proper thanks to some of the people involved with this book from the beginning. Bella Andre and Jami Alden, I'm looking at you! As my early critique partners, I don't even want to think about how many times you read this book (Jami, thanks for reading it yet again after about a ten year lapse), but thanks to you both for your collective brilliance, sage advice, and ongoing encouragement in (finally!) seeing this book to publication. A huge thanks to Carrie at Seductive Musings for this gorgeous cover, Shona McCarthy for her extremely helpful copyediting, Anne Victory and Cyrstalle for their eagle-eyed "oops" detecting, and Lisa Rogers for the ebook formatting. I also want to give a very special thanks and shout out to Isobel Carr who generously offered to help me format this novel for print only to be caught in word processing program hell. It wasn't pretty, and the fact that it was last minute made it even worse. A huge thanks—I owe you big time.

If thou remember'st not the slightest folly
That ever love did make thee run into
Thou hast not lov'd.

—William Shakespeare, *As You Like It,* Act II, scene iv

CHAPTER ONE

Carlton House, June 19, 1811

THE SOFT GLOW OF THE gaslights cast ominous shadows across the coach as it crept along Pall Mall. But not even the black curtain of a starless night could relieve the oppressive heat of the sweltering London evening. The air inside the luxurious carriage had passed beyond stagnant over an hour ago, turning the once-delicate mingling of the ladies' fine French perfumes to pungent and cloying. The normally loquacious occupants of the coach had been silenced by darkness and shared discomfort. The short journey from Berkeley Square to Carlton House that should have taken a quarter of an hour had already extended to an excruciating three.

The interminable wait would try the patience of a saint. And Eugenia Prescott had long ago forsaken her chances for sainthood. Tension knit with excitement balled in her gut. With what was at stake tonight, each minute of delay was pure agony.

After years of pain and heartbreak, Genie stood poised on the verge of triumph. If all went according to plan, tonight would be the beginning of the end of her long quest to secure the life that was denied her five years ago.

The coach lurched forward then jerked to another abrupt stop. Stop and start, like the erratic pounding of her heart. Yet each step, no matter how infinitesimal, brought her closer to the realization of her dream.

She sank back against the silken walls, closed her eyes, and slipped into the shadows, hiding her impatience from the watchful eyes of her companions. She drew a deep breath, both to steady her nerves and to give herself a moment to absorb the significance of all that she had accomplished.

She'd journeyed from the doorstep of hell to the very pinnacle of elite society. Miss Eugenia Prescott, the prodigal parson's daughter, who'd fled ruin and disgrace, surviving hardship her provincial upbringing never could have imagined, had returned as the soon-to-be fiancée of an earl. Accomplishment enough to be sure, but there was more. Tonight Genie would make her entrée into high society at one of the grandest events ever to befall the fashionable world.

Much rode on her success this night. Acceptance by the ton would secure her future and enable her to finally put the darkness and bitter memories of the past behind her.

Resisting the urge to look outside the small window yet again, Genie adjusted the bodice of her gown, giving only momentary relief from the biting pinch of her stays. Though beautiful, her ensemble was not particularly comfortable in even the most agreeable of circumstances. After hours of confinement in the stifling coach, the diaphanous ivory column gown clung to her lean body as if she'd dampened the skirts, as was the fashion of the more risqué members of the ton. Still, despite her discomfort, Genie had never looked more beautiful. It was a fact, thought without conceit. She had long since taken any pleasure in her beauty. What she'd thought a blessing had turned out to be anything but. Now her face and body were all she had to ensure her survival—and her future.

"Finally," Lady Hawkesbury, one of her companions and chaperone, broke the silence. "It's almost our turn."

Too nervous to respond, Genie instead concentrated on calming her racing heart. Trepidation nibbled at the edges of her consciousness. Everything she had battled and scraped for was so close she could almost reach out and grab it.

Almost. But not quite.

The coach clattered to its final stop. A moment later the blue and gold liveried coachman opened the door, releasing the stale air with a gentle cleansing swoosh. Accepting the proffered white-gloved hand, Genie alighted out of the carriage and into her future.

Temporarily blinded, it took a moment to digest the vision before her. Hundreds of gaslights illuminated the evening sky, turning night into day. Astonished, Genie gazed around at the Prince Regent's wonderland. She'd never seen anything like it, and for a moment, she was an awestruck young girl from Gloucestershire again.

"Dear Prinny will never be criticized for restraint."

Genie clamped her mouth shut, reminding herself that sophisticated soon-to-be countesses did not gape. She pulled her gaze from the pink and silver draperies and mirrors adorning the trellises of the garden walkways to look up at the handsome man who had appeared at her side. Though not accustomed to seeing him in such dandified evening attire, the jaunty grin and sparkling blue eyes were comfortingly familiar.

Edmund.

An aura of peace settled over her as it always did when she looked upon his handsome face. Genie had sworn never to trust a man again, but Edmund St. George, the Earl of Hawkesbury, had chipped away her resistance with his irrepressible chivalry and nobility. Nobility might be conferred at birth, but being noble was earned—not passed along as part and parcel of a title. Lord Hawkesbury, Edmund after all that they had been through, was a truly noble man. And there had been precious few of those in Genie's life since she'd been forced from her home.

As much as Genie could trust any man, she trusted Edmund.

She met his bemused smile with one of her own. "I've never seen anything like this." She shook her head. "If this is just to celebrate the prince's regency, I can't conceive what the coronation will be like."

Edmund took her kid-gloved hand and placed it in the crook of his arm. "I dare not fathom, but whenever that illustrious event takes place, I'll not wait three hours just for the privilege of descending from my carriage. A more miserable journey I cannot recall."

"Don't be ridiculous, darling," Edmund's mother, the Countess of Hawkesbury, chided from his other side with an emphatic snap of her ivory fan to his arm. "Of course you will."

Genie laughed while Edmund grumbled fondly at his mother. But the countess was indubitably correct, Edmund could be depended upon to do what was right. And attending his king, future or otherwise, certainly qualified—three-hour wait to descend his carriage or not.

They stood unmoving near the entrance to the spectacular Gothic conservatory, held captive as much by the sheer extravagance of the decoration, as by the crush of the throng around them. With two thousand of the crème de la crème of polite society milling about, the crowd inside wasn't any easier to navigate than the long procession of carriages that lined the Mall.

"It's both incredible and outrageous," Edmund said, a touch of recrimination in his voice.

Genie agreed. The Prince Regent's "Grande Fete" (ostensibly to honor the exiled royal family of France, though in truth a celebration of his regency), was both magnificent and appalling. It was impossible not to be awed by the grandeur of the decoration, but it was an exorbitant expenditure of money for a man already sharply criticized for his excesses.

"My word," the countess exclaimed. "Look at that table!"

Genie followed the direction of the countess's fan. Her eyes widened. "Who could possibly have conceived such a thing?"

No one spoke; they were all too transfixed. The dining table had to be at least two hundred feet long. And running down its entire length, from an ornate silver fountain at its head, was a stream, replete with moss, tiny bridges, and silver and gold fish.

The opulence of this celebration would strike even the most jaded of the haut ton with wonder. Everywhere Genie looked were riches beyond her imagination, from the elegantly dressed guests in their finest evening dress and jewels to the gold and silver ornamentation that appeared to adorn every surface. The spectacle, the theater of the Prince Regent's fete, was a long way from the Kington House rectory.

Overwhelmed by the thought that she could soon be a part of this closed society, her façade of confidence knew a fleeting moment of panic. Nothing in her past could have prepared her for such a lavish display of wealth and power. Certainly not the country balls and assemblies she frequented as a girl, or even the elegant intellectual salons of Boston that she'd enjoyed over the past year with Edmund and his mother.

Could she actually do this? Would these people accept her?

"There are so many people," she said, almost to herself. Turning back to Edmund, she hesitated. "Are you sure this is the best time?"

Instinctively, Edmund pulled her closer to his side. *Always the protector. A veritable knight in shining armor.* Genie felt a stab of guilt, knowing that she had taken advantage of those propensities. But tonight she truly needed his stalwart conviction and strength.

"If you wish to cause a sensation, there is no better time. The ton will all be gathered in one room tonight. At one table for that matter," he said wryly, indicating the enormous table. His hand moved over hers, giving it a comforting squeeze. "There's nothing to be scared of, Genie. You're incomparable. They'll love you, as I do."

Scared? Her back straightened. She wasn't scared. She was no longer a frightened country mouse, but a woman hardened by life's disappointments. She'd faced far more difficult challenges than navigating the perilous pitfalls of society. Edmund was right. This would work. She would be accepted. Genie would not allow herself to be intimidated by rank again. That naïve country miss was gone forever. She was older now, a woman of three and twenty. Five years, well four at least, of suffering had changed her forever. It had been almost a year since Edmund had found her. If only he could have saved her before...

She blocked the memory. Genie refused to dwell on the past when her future, a secure future, was laid out before her.

And ready for the taking.

Genie knew what she wanted and more important, she knew what she had to use to get it—no matter how much playing the coquette went against her natural disposition. The sweet, innocent girl she'd been had been a lamb in a pen of lions. But now she knew better. Men—even decent ones like Edmund (she'd seen the way his eyes devoured her body when he thought she wasn't looking)—only wanted one thing from her.

So she gave it to them.

Her composure recovered, Genie caressed the hard bulge of Edmund's upper arm with her thumb. She wobbled a brave smile and peeked up at him from beneath her lashes. Years ago the innocent, vulnerable look might have been done unthinkingly. Now she understood its effect.

Heat warmed Edmund's gaze.

He really was extraordinarily handsome, with his coal-black hair, piercing blue eyes and ruggedly masculine features. Rakish looks without the profligate behavior to go along with it. Genie was fortunate to have him, and she knew it.

She fought the stab of conscience. Was it really so horrible to give him what he wanted? Edmund *liked* to be the knight in shining armor. What did it matter if she had to pretend a little to be the innocent maiden in need of rescue?

She nudged a little closer, allowing her breast to brush against his arm and said, "With you by my side, my lord, how could I fear anything?"

His eyes lingered on her bosom for a moment before his face grew suddenly earnest. His voice dropped. "You don't need to do this, my love. Say the word and I'll shout from the rooftop that you have agreed to be my countess. I don't care whether we rusticate in the country all year long, as long as we're together."

She was half-tempted. Before, Genie might have let him do just that. She would achieve the security of wealth and position just by marrying him—with or without society's approval. But over the past few months, she'd grown to love him. Not in the soul-encompassing, uncontrollable way she'd loved before—*shudder*—but in a safe, manageable way.

Dear Edmund. Always gallant, always noble. Even if that nobility could lead to his own social ruin. Though she wanted the protection that marriage to Edmund would afford, she would not destroy him needlessly. The taint of scandal once given could never be undone. A woman with a shadowed past was vastly different from the woman of mystery she hoped to portray.

Genie just had to make sure the ton accepted her, or rather the respectable widow Mrs. Ginny Preston. Miss Eugenia Prescott, parson's daughter from Thornbury, was a distant memory.

Although there was one person who might remember.

She quickly discarded the thought. He probably had forgotten all about her—just another notch in his bedpost. And if he hadn't...

He could be persuaded to remain silent.

Genie scanned the crowd for familiar faces, though it was unlikely that she would know anyone. The exalted circles of the haut ton did not often overlap with that of a country parson. She knew that her family would eventually hear that she had returned from America, but she couldn't face them just yet. She told herself she would go to them and explain once she was established. Once they had reason to be proud of her. Once she was a countess and the threat of scandal was behind her.

For now, she was simply Mrs. Prescott, the widow of a soldier, recently arrived from America. There was no reason to suspect anything else. A carefully constructed web of lies would pave her way to happiness. A brittle bed, perhaps, but it was all she had to sleep on.

Edmund knew her secrets, or those that mattered, and was still willing, even anxious, to marry her. Indeed, since she'd revealed her true name to him a few months ago, his desire to marry her had taken on an almost frantic urgency.

Edmund dared the unthinkable: a *misalliance*—an inferior marriage in the eyes of the ton. After all that he'd done for her, she owed it to him to try to not make it a costly decision.

"Nothing would make me happier than to announce our betrothal," she said truthfully. "But it's better this way. We've already agreed. I'll win them over first then we'll announce our engagement in a few weeks."

Then she could relax.

If her past didn't find her first.

THREE HOURS LATER, GENIE COULD breathe more easily. The night was progressing well. At supper she'd found herself inexplicably seated between Edmund and the charming old Earl of Clarendon—much too high on the table for a mere soldier's widow. Edmund's doing she suspected. She'd been introduced to the highest peers in the realm and had acquitted herself well. She'd even, at his request, been presented to the Prince Regent.

But her real achievement came earlier in the evening. Lady Hawkesbury had presented her to five of the seven grandes dames of society, the famed Patronesses of Almack's, and Genie had secured a "stranger's ticket" as Lady Hawkesbury's guest for next Wednesday's ball from the friendly Lady Cowper. A mixture of joy and relief surged through her. If she could win over the dragons of Almack's, her success was virtually guaranteed.

They'd finished the lengthy meal and had moved into the gardens where a temporary courtyard had been set up to accommodate the two thousand guests. The evening's entertainment of dancing and gaming would begin shortly. The band of Guards played under the portico while the guests enjoyed the temporary promenades that had been erected for the occasion.

Edmund leaned over to whisper in her ear.

The countess playfully rapped Edmund's knuckles with her fan. "Stop that whispering immediately. You've drawn enough wagging tongues already." Motioning to Genie she said, "Come along, my dear, move away from your vicious guard dog's side." She turned to frown at her son. "And you, my boy, should know better. It's not the thing at all, monopolizing her like this. Why you've barely let any other man near her. I thought for one horrible moment that you might refuse to present her to the prince."

A decidedly petulant scowl descended across Edmund's handsome features. Genie hid her smile behind her hand. He looked at any moment like he might thrust out his lower lip and pout like a naughty schoolboy.

"That lecherous old cur! Did you see him? I thought he might drool down the front of her dress—"

"Shush," the countess scolded, rapping him harder this time, but still smiling. "Do you want someone to hear?" She turned her cheerful smile back to Genie. "And can you blame him? It's a remarkable bosom." Genie blushed, but the countess didn't seem to notice. "You've created quite a stir, my dear. Why that harpy Lady Jersey is just positively twittering with curiosity." The countess preened. "You'll be the talk of the ball tonight, I can feel it. You look exquisite." She studied Genie over the top of her fan. "Simply exquisite."

"I feel like a princess. This dress is beautiful. You've been so generous, I can't thank you—"

"Oh, posh," the countess said cutting her off. "I've enjoyed every minute of it. It's great fun giving the ton something to talk about. And I know you must think it difficult to believe, but I caused a minor sensation in my day."

"I don't find that difficult to believe at all," Genie said honestly, giving her a fond peck on the cheek. With her dancing eyes and vivacious smile, Lady Hawkesbury was still a beautiful woman.

Lady Hawkesbury was another reason for Genie to feel fortunate. The countess cared not that her son was to marry an inconsequential widow of no standing and without five pounds to her name. Edmund loved Genie and that was enough for his mother. Lady Hawkesbury's support and friendship tonight had been just as important as Edmund's, perhaps more so.

If only the rest of the ton were as easily persuaded.

But Genie knew she should feel pleased. So far the evening had gone exceptionally well. The ton was intrigued. And there hadn't been any unwelcome vestiges of her past to fend off. It was more than she could have hoped for.

She turned back to Edmund to tell him she would see him for their dance later when she noticed him scanning the crowd behind her. Strange, she thought. She'd caught him doing the same thing many times throughout the evening. He appeared to be looking for someone. Though Genie had refused to tell Edmund *his* name, perhaps he, too, was concerned that *he* might be here.

Now that she thought about it, there was a distinct edginess to Edmund tonight. Genie bit her bottom lip, feeling guilty. She'd been so preoccupied with her own thoughts, she hadn't realized that this night might be difficult for him as well. They both had much riding on her success.

She touched his arm and gave him a tender smile. There was no need to feign this time. Her eyes dropped to his mouth and she ran her tongue along her upper lip, thinking about how she would thank him later for all he had done tonight. She'd come to enjoy kissing Edmund. Though it didn't create the heart-pounding frantic craving from her youth, Edmund's kiss was like him: warm and secure.

Not dangerous and destructive.

"Your mother's right," she said, disengaging her hand from his arm. When Edmund looked like he might argue she continued, "I'll be fine. Don't worry."

"But I do worry," he said in a tone that was far too serious than was warranted by the situation. There was a tense moment where it seemed like he might refuse, before he sighed. "I'll go for now, but I'll be back if you need me." He paused meaningfully. "For anything."

Genie watched him make his way through the crowd. Even his carriage seemed odd. Though graceful, there was a predatory slant to his movements tonight. It was almost as if he were stalking something... or someone.

Whatever was bothering him—and she was sure something was—it was getting worse as the evening drew on. Perhaps Edmund was more jealous than she'd realized?

She was prevented from thinking about the matter any further as the dancing began and she was led into the ballroom by the first in a steady stream of partners.

DISMOUNTING, THE MAN CARELESSLY TOSSED the reins of his horse to the waiting footman and hurried up the walkway, barely noticing the outrageous extravagances of tonight's fete.

He was late. Very late. Prinny would be furious, though he'd been fortunate to make it at all. A last-minute trip to Surrey to attend to an emergency for a friend had taken him from town yesterday. He'd only arrived home an hour ago, leaving him barely time to change before rushing to Carlton House to put in the obligatory appearance.

He felt around for his watch fob but realized that in his haste he'd forgotten it. Instinctively his fingers dug around in the small pocket on his waistcoat that lay right below his heart. Relieved, he exhaled. It was there. The slide of cool silk slipping between his fingertips was strangely comforting. A corner of the blue ribbon, frayed and worn with time, peeked out from the opening of the pocket for a moment before he quickly stabbed it back down out of sight.

Such sentimentality was not like him. But like some wretched talisman, he carried the damned thing with him everywhere.

It was all he had left of a past that he could not forget.

For it seemed nothing would ever bring her back.

MUCH LATER, BREATHLESS AND FLUSHED from the heat of the ballroom, Genie decided to take a turn on the promenades. Catching sight of Edmund outside in the courtyard, she started across the room.

She stepped outside Carlton House and paused for a moment, shocked by the drop in temperature. It had taken until well past midnight, but the sweltering heat had finally dissipated. She closed her eyes, allowing the cool breeze to wash over her.

A startled gasp drew her attention to the man coming up the walk. He stood perhaps ten feet in front of her, dressed in a black cape and tall beaver hat. She tilted her head to one side in question. There was something familiar...

Their eyes met and her heart stopped.

Time stopped.

The music and dancing, the din of conversation around them slipped away. Unbidden, the memories rushed back in a chaotic montage: the first time she'd seen him, the first time he'd held her in his arms on the dance floor.

The first time they'd made love.

Heat stained her cheeks as if he could know her thoughts. The memories were so strong, so clear, as if five years of recrimination and tribulation had never happened.

But it had.

Other memories, much darker memories, blotted out the fond ones, breaking the spell. Her gaze shifted.

He, however, continued to stare at her in shocked

silence.

She'd known it was bound to happen, seeing him again. And she'd realized that there was a good chance it would be tonight. Perhaps a small part of her had hoped it would be so, when she undoubtedly looked her best. She wanted him to see what he had forsaken. She wanted him to know regret. As she did.

Genie studied him. He'd changed so much she was surprised that she recognized him. There was nothing left of the lean young man she remembered. His shoulders were unfashionably broad and muscular; his legs thick and powerful. Unusually tall, perhaps standing four inches above six feet, his frame with the added bulk seemed infinitely larger. He looked more like a blacksmith or common laborer than a vaunted peer of the realm. Even his elegant court attire did nothing to civilize his appearance.

Undeniably he was still incredibly handsome, but he'd changed more than just from the passage of time. There was a hard edge to his face that had not been there before. As if chiseled from stone, his once softly sculpted features had sharpened from those of a boy to a man. The wide, arrogant mouth she recognized, but now it sat atop a cynical jaw that was both square and uncompromising. Where before there had been only dimples, now she noticed tiny cruel lines around his mouth. His hair was darker—no longer blond but golden brown—and longer, but still thick and straight with a slight wave that framed his face. His striking blue eyes shone as hard as glass, no longer sparkling like the sun upon the sea.

Though changed, it was still the face that had launched hundreds of hours of tears and regret. Yes, she thought with relief, she could finally feel regret behind all the bitterness and recriminations. Behind the cold dull edge of hatred. Regret for the suffering, regret for the anger. But most of all, regret for the loss of love.

When she looked at him and saw how changed he was, she felt something that she had not anticipated: a poignant longing for the innocence of youth.

An innocence that he had taken from her.

She was connected to this man by a past that should no longer matter. But it did. Perhaps it always would. He'd taken something from her that could never be returned. He'd forced her to open her eyes to the real world, where people are imperfect, where people break your heart and your trust.

He'd once meant so much to her. Yet, oddly, Genie felt detached. She was not that same young ignorant country girl. He did not have the power to affect her any longer. That part of her life was gone forever. Seeing him again had finally solidified it.

She might grieve for the innocence of youth, but she would never forget what had come after her cruel disillusionment. She would never forget what this man did to her.

Lord Fitzwilliam Hastings.

The man who'd nearly destroyed her.

She'd given him her soul and he'd sent her into hell. Alone.

The echo of her childhood ringing in her ears, Genie remembered. How he'd failed her. For refusing to do the unthinkable...

CHAPTER TWO

Thornbury, Gloucestershire, July 1806

"GENIE!" LIZZIE PRESCOTT SHRIEKED AS she raced up the oak staircase, her slipper-clad feet pounding as loud as a coach-and-four across a ballroom. "It's true, it's true."

Genie lifted her head from the letter that she'd been composing and wondered what all the ruckus was about this time. Probably something to do with a young man, Genie thought. At sixteen years of age, Lizzie could barely think of anything else. She grinned. At only two years her senior, Genie hadn't quite outgrown the fascination herself.

She turned her head in the direction of the clamor just in time to see her younger sister appear at the entry to her bedchamber, dramatically framed in the doorway, white-blond ringlets bobbing against flushed cheeks, her large bosom heaving from the short burst of exercise.

Genie slowly put down her quill, giving her sister a chance to compose herself. "What's true, dearest?" Genie asked calmly.

Lizzie hardly took a breath before blurting out, "I've just heard it from Susan, who heard it from Jane, whose mother heard it from Lady Buckingham directly." She clapped her hands together excitedly. "The Duke of Huntingdon has let Peyton Park."

The arrival of a peer of such distinction was exciting news to be sure in the provincial village of Thornbury, but Genie could tell from Lizzie's near-bursting-with-excitement expression that there was more. She quirked her brow. "And?" she asked patiently.

Lizzie lowered her voice, her luminous deep blue eyes wide and shining. "And the duke intends to stay until the spring."

She paused, a broad self-satisfied smile spread across her cherubic face, clearly eager to impart the final *coup de grâce*.

Genie knew what was required of her. "And?" she asked dutifully.

"And he intends to bring his two eldest sons with him." Lizzie folded her arms across her buxom chest, enormously pleased to be able to pass on the latest *on-dit* to her *older* sister.

Genie feigned indifference. She picked up her quill and turned back to her letter. "Oh, that is very interesting."

"Oh, that is very interesting?" Lizzie echoed incredulously. "Is that all you have to say. How can you be so calm, how can you go back to your letter as if—"

Genie's smothered gurgle of laughter stopped her.

Lizzie stomped her tiny foot. "Eugenia Prescott, how dare you tease me like that! For a horrible moment I thought you were serious."

Their eyes met and both girls broke out into fresh peals of laughter. Genie enjoyed gossip—especially concerning young eligible gentlemen—nearly as much as her sister. When their laughter died down, Genie patted the small bench next to her chair. "Come. Sit down and tell me the rest. What else did Jane say?"

Lizzie took the proffered seat and bent toward Genie, a conspirator in arms. "It was Susan who told me, Jane told her—"

"And Jane heard it from her mother who heard it from Lady Buckingham," Genie finished.

Lizzie beamed. "Precisely. And the Marchioness of Buckingham is reportedly great friends with the Duchess of Huntingdon so it must be true. Susan didn't know too many details; just that the duke has let the place while the family seat, Donnington Park, in Leicestershire is undergoing some improvements." In a clearly reverent voice she added, "Mr. Capability Brown himself is said to have designed the gardens. The family will stay at Peyton Park through the hunting season until the beginning of the London season. None of the daughters are out yet, but there are two older sons." Lizzie gasped, as if the most astonishing thing had just occurred to her. "Genie, do you think they might attend your coming-out ball?" Her words tumbled out even faster. "Maybe they'll ask you to dance. Maybe they'll both fall in love with you and they'll fight a duel to decide who can win your hand. Maybe—"

"Hold on, hold on. I think I may have told you one too many romantic tales." Genie laughed, knowing that she was responsible for putting all those silly notions into Lizzie's head with her stories. But Lizzie's enthusiasm was definitely contagious. As much to rein in her own burgeoning excitement, Genie said cautiously, "I'm sure our annual ball is not grand enough for a duke's family, Lizzie."

Lizzie frowned, taking umbrage at the suggestion that there was anything lacking in one of the great country traditions of Thornbury. The harvest festival race-week ball had come from the old Lammas Day feast, which the village had been celebrating for hundreds of years. "The Marquess and Marchioness of Buckingham always attend. It's grand enough for them."

"We are fortunate; Lord and Lady Buckingham have always been most gracious to the local gentry." Gracious, but aloof. They've never invited anyone, including her parents, to dine at Thornbury Castle, but Genie kept that thought to herself. "Lizzie, you must realize that country society is vastly different from the circles of a duke."

"Well, they'll have to do something for entertainment for the next few months," Lizzie said stubbornly. "And the annual ball is the best that Thornbury has to offer."

Lizzie was right. Perhaps they *would* come. "Even if the duke's sons do attend, it's highly unlikely they'd be fighting duels over a parson's daughter with less than five hundred pounds."

"Why, you're the sweetest, most beautiful girl in Gloucestershire," Lizzie dismissed with a short wave of her hand. "What's not to fall in love with?"

"I think you are hardly the most objective critic, my sweet, as you and I look more like twins than sisters separated by two years."

Lizzie shrugged, grinning. "After you break his heart, perhaps the loser of the duel will console himself with your younger sister."

"Naughty scamp!" Genie laughed, swatting Lizzie's hand playfully with her feather quill. "Better not let mother hear you say such things. You still have two years before your coming-out. Besides, we know nothing about the duke's sons. Perhaps they are more frog than prince?"

"Oh, balderdash. A duke's sons are invariably handsome."

Genie quirked her brow. "I think you've been listening to Susan for too long." It was no secret that Mrs. Andrews would do anything to secure a title for her precious daughter. And with her fifty thousand pounds courtesy of the family shipping business, the pretty Susan just might grant her mother's wish.

Lizzie ignored her, caught up in her own reverie. "Once you are married, you'll go to your spectacular townhouse in Mayfair for the season. Of course you'll invite your beloved younger sister to share in your good fortune, and I'll have a real season with the most beautiful gowns..."

Genie shook her head, listening to the fanciful ramblings. Lizzie's imagination, once freed, was impossible to harness. So rather than try to stop her, Genie just sat back and allowed herself to be swept along for the ride.

A duke's son. A sharp thrill shot through her. To wed the son of a duke was almost like marrying a prince—with a coronet instead of a crown. What a wonderful story it would make, to be whisked away into the privileged, exciting world of the beau monde. Was such a thing possible?

Hardly. She grinned. It was about as likely as Lizzie

sitting still long enough to finish her sampler.

But it was certainly fun to dream about.

AFTER MONTHS OF PREPARATION, NOT to mention countless trips to her mother's mantua maker, the eagerly anticipated day had finally dawned. The week-long horse races held at Thornbury's prized racetrack were over, and tonight, Genie and three other girls, including her dearest friend Miss Caroline Howard, would be presented to society tonight at the ball held in the town's hall on High Street.

The town was abuzz with excitement. And not just on account of the annual harvest festival race-week ball. The Duke of Huntingdon and his family had arrived at Peyton Park a few days ago, though no one seemed to be sure whether they would attend the ball tonight. After four weeks of Lizzie's outrageous imaginings, Genie hoped they would show if only to put an end to all the speculation.

Genie had been giddy with excitement all day—all week for that matter. She'd begun her preparations for the ball hours ago and was finding it difficult to sit still while Patty, her mother's lady's maid, put the finishing touches on her elegant coiffure.

Genie couldn't believe the difference in her appearance. The elegant woman reflected in the mirror was in sharp contrast to the excited young girl twittering inside.

The pearl encrusted bandeaux that matched the delicate pearl earrings, necklace, and bracelet borrowed from her mother, had been secured on the crown of her flaxen head. Her long hair was bound up in the back into a high cascade of ringlets. More silken curls had been artfully arranged along her temples. What in the end was meant to appear simple and uncomplicated had thus far taken over an hour and a half to arrange. All that was left was to weave fresh pink flowers through the bandeaux to match the satin trim of her gown..

"Sally," her mother called anxiously to one of the harried

chambermaids darting in and out of the room. "Where is the pink satin ribbon? Did you find the flowers for the bandeaux? Oh, where is my cashmere shawl? And find someone to help Miss Prescott get these kid gloves on."

"I have the ribbon and the flowers right here, ma'am. Your shawl is on the bed. I'll send Kitty right up to help with the gloves." The poor girl was barely coping with the frenzied demands of her nervous mistress.

It seemed that all four of the female servants had been in her room at some point today. Indeed, the entire household of Kington House, from her father down to the daily scullery maid, had been on edge all week long.

Expectations ran high. Despite her rather insignificant dowry, Genie knew that her family hoped that her "angelic beauty and sweetness of character" would enable her to make a good match. The entire family would benefit. The son of a wealthy squire or perhaps even the son of a nearby baronet could aid her eldest brother, Charles, in securing a good parish and help advance William and John with more desirable commissions.

Critically, Genie studied her reflection as Patty began to weave the tiny flowers through the bandeaux. Her father called her and Lizzie his "two little Rubens cherubs." Genie supposed it was an apt description with their pale, baby-soft blond hair, tiny turned-up noses, round pink cheeks, red bow lips and big blue eyes. Both girls also enjoyed their sweet cakes and tended toward a curvaceous figure. Pleasing enough, Genie supposed, but the big question was whether she would prove popular tonight.

She dearly hoped so. What girl didn't dream of having a swarm of handsome beaux to choose from at her first ball? And maybe from those beaux she would find her one true love. Like Lizzie, at her heart Genie was a romantic, though she was a tad more sensible than her oft impulsive sister.

Genie yearned to be swept away by love and happiness like that which her parents had found. A husband whom she loved, a comfortable home, and a dozen children were everything Genie could wish for.

But she'd yet to meet a man who came close to fitting her dreams. With only a few thousand people in the parish, she was already acquainted with most of the eligible young men in Thornbury. But tonight, many of the gentry from the surrounding countryside would join in the celebration. Perhaps her true love would be amongst them?

The last flower secured in place, Genie stood to view the culmination of months of planning. Otherwise unadorned, the white crepe gown was trimmed at her high waistline with a thin pink satin ribbon to match the delicate pink satin petticoat. A moderate train, which would be pinned later for dancing, fell in small gathers down the length of her back. A rounded neck, tight bodice, and short sleeves completed the fashionable Grecian-style gown. Genie and Lizzie had pored over the latest sketches from their aunts in London to achieve just the right design. Thrilled with the result, she twirled before the looking glass.

"Oh Eugenia," her mother exclaimed, her eyes misting with tears. "You are loveliness itself. You've always made your father and me so proud, always such a good, sensible girl. Now look at you, all grown up..." She trailed off, dabbing her eyes with a lace-trimmed piece of linen she'd pulled from her reticule.

"Truly, I've never seen you look so beautiful, Genie. The men will be falling at your feet. I do wish I could be there to see you tonight," Lizzie said from her forlorn perch on Genie's bed. "It's not fair. Why must I wait until I'm eighteen?" She scowled at their mother. "Susan is coming-out with Genie and she has only just turned seventeen."

Sly puss, Genie thought. Lizzie's nagging magically lightened the sentimental mood.

"That's only because Mrs. Andrews can't wait to catch a title," Mrs. Prescott replied briskly. "Your father and I harbor no such ambition. Though I wish we had more for you girls."

Genie could hear the silent apology in her mother's voice. Although her father's advowson of seven hundred and fifty pounds a year under the patronage of the Marquess of Buckingham was considered substantial for a rector, after providing for her brothers and supporting her two maiden aunts there was not much left for the two girls.

"But you are both beautiful and accomplished," Mrs. Prescott continued firmly, convincing herself. "It will be enough." She sighed. "Before I know it both my girls will be gone with homes and families of their own."

"That will be some time yet, Mother."

"Especially for me," Lizzie piped in glumly.

"It will be your turn soon enough, young miss." Mrs. Prescott gazed at Lizzie thoughtfully. "Perhaps it is the bane of the youngest to always want to be the eldest." Gently, she lifted Lizzie's chin with her finger. "So impatient, always afraid that you'll miss something." Leaning down, she placed a light kiss on Lizzie's cheek. "Try not to grow up too fast, my love."

Empathizing with her sister's impatience—a feeling she understood only too well at the moment—Genie offered what consolation she could. "I promise to tell you everything, including every boring detail about the duke's sons—*if* they deign to make an appearance."

"Boring?" Lizzie laughed. "You don't fool me, Genie Prescott. You are as curious as I am. But I'll hold you to your promise. I want to hear every detail." She sighed dramatically. "I just know something wonderful is going to happen tonight."

Any trepidation Genie may have harbored vanished in the first few minutes after her arrival when she was immediately surrounded by a throng of very enthusiastic gentlemen vying for her introduction.

Never had she had such fun. Dancing, laughing, even her first foray into a little innocent flirting. It was perfect. She wished the night would never end.

Awaiting refreshment, Genie stood with her friend Caroline at the back of the large hall next to the wide doors that opened to the patio, fanning herself with the cool breeze of the starry summer night. Along with her first ball, she was also experiencing the unbearable heat of a crowded ballroom lit by hundreds of candles. Genie welcomed the rare moment of peace, content to merely observe the dancers for a while. A sea of white and pastel silk swirled by, the ladies' gowns shimmering in the soft flickering candlelight.

"It feels like I've been caught up in a pink and violet whirlwind."

Genie turned to Caro, taking note of the bright eyes and flushed cheeks that surely matched her own. Fortunately, Caro had not lacked for suitors either. As the only daughter of the baronet Sir John Howard, Caro was guaranteed a certain modicum of success by her connections alone, but her vivacious *joie de vivre* immediately enraptured all around her. Her otherwise ordinary features transformed to beauty by the force of personality alone.

"I know what you mean," Genie agreed. "The night has flown by. Everything has happened so fast I can barely remember any of it."

"You better," Caro warned, "or Lizzie will never forgive you."

They shared a smile. Bereft of a sister, Caro loved Lizzie as her own. Thinking of her last conversation with Lizzie, Genie said, "She'll be disappointed that the duke and his family have chosen not to attend. She was in quite a sulk when I left. I only pacified her by promising details."

Caro nodded, understanding. "I suppose it is to be expected, but a disappointment all the same. I've never seen a duke before."

"Most in this room have not."

Above the din of the music, a wave of whispers rippled through the hall. Genie glanced toward the entry. A shiver of excitement ran up her spine. A distinguished older gentleman and an extremely thin woman of indeterminate age, wearing the most extraordinary turban she had ever seen, were being welcomed by the Marquess and

Marchioness of Buckingham. Their unmatched elegance and haughty disdain alone proclaimed them as the Duke and Duchess of Huntingdon. Not to mention the giant diamond broach that secured a plumed feather that must have been two feet high to the turban. Genie could see the large sparkling gem from across the room.

"Perhaps Lizzie will not be disappointed after all?" Genie said, peering through the crowd that had gathered around the new arrivals but unable to see whether their sons had accompanied them.

"Her gown is magnificent."

Genie nodded. It was true. The intricate design, the elaborate beading in a room of simply adorned gowns, the workmanship, and the bold purple color were unrivaled. The Duchess's sophisticated ensemble exemplified rare wealth and power. Even the formidable Marchioness seemed provincial in comparison.

Their dancing partners, amiable young men from Tewkesbury, reappeared with the promised ratafia, drawing their attention away from the ducal party. She was led back onto the dance floor and the opportunity to apprize the sons from afar was lost.

LIZZIE WAS GOING TO KILL her. The ball was almost over and she had yet to catch a glimpse of the duke's sons. She'd managed a few discreet searches, but thus far, no luck. Perhaps they had decided not to join their parents? Perhaps they were too proud to partake of humble country society? She tried not to be disappointed but failed.

The dance ended and her partner led her back toward the circle of women that included her mother and Mrs. Andrews. Though some in the room might look down on the Andrews' trade connections as inferior, Mrs. Prescott was not so small-minded. "There's no shame in doing a hard day's work," was her gentle refrain.

Before Genie could rejoin her mother, an animated Caro

intercepted her. "They're here," she whispered.

"You've seen them?"

Caro nodded; a broad smile on her face.

"Then tell me," Genie asked impatiently. "Are the duke's sons more frog or prince?"

Caro's eyes widened to enormous proportions. "See for yourself," she whispered.

Genie's eyes narrowed quizzically. She turned to find her eldest brother Charles at her side, looking as if he'd just swallowed a horse.

A lump of dread formed in the pit of her stomach. *Please, don't let the duke's sons be standing right next to me.*

CHAPTER THREE

HER PRAYER WAS ONLY HALF answered.

"Sister," Charles said tightly. "May I introduce Lord Fitzwilliam Hastings."

Genie finally glanced at the young man at his side; though how she could have missed him, even for a moment, was incomprehensible. Her breath caught. Surely her eyes rounded with shock? He was tall, with dark blond hair and blue eyes, and quite simply the most handsome young man she had ever set eyes on.

Stunned into a temporary stupor, but eventually rote training took over and Genie curtsied. "A pleasure, my lord."

He seemed to be alone, but she took little relief that there were not two handsome duke's sons to witness her dreadful gaffe.

Beautifully white teeth gleamed from behind an amused grin. He bowed and an oh-so-tempting lock of dark gold hair fell forward across his cheek.

A single thought invaded her mind: She wanted to touch it.

The highly improper response succeeded in jolting her back to reality.

A reality where she might have just committed a horrible faux pas. Had he heard her compare him to a frog?

"Miss Prescott," he said.

Two little words. But enough to hear the laughter in his voice. Oh, he'd heard her all right.

She'd certainly have something to tell Lizzie about now, only the single most embarrassing moment of her life.

Yet, the charming twinkle in his sea-blue eyes disarmed her. Mirth was not what she expected from a gentleman of his distinction and rank.

"I hope more prince than frog, Miss Prescott?"

The color slid from her face. Mortified, Genie wanted to crawl beneath the nearest table and hide. "Though you might not agree once you meet my brother Henry." He laughed. His obvious good humor lifted the blanket of uncomfortable tension that had descended upon the small group. Even her staid brother Charles smiled.

Genie blushed at his gentle teasing. Lord Fitzwilliam Hastings was certainly not the too-proud man she assumed. Perhaps only a few years older than herself, she decided that he must be the second son. The elder had a title, Viscount Loudoun. Still too embarrassed to meet his gaze, she did manage a small smile in return. "Then I'll reserve my judgment, my lord, until I have had the pleasure."

Surprised by her own playfulness, Genie stole a quick glance.

From the way his dimples deepened, she could tell that he admired her pert reply. "If I promise not to croak too loudly, will you do me the honor of a dance?"

Her pulse raced. She hoped her voice sounded less eager than she felt. "Of course."

He took her hand and led her to the dance floor. Even through the leather of her gloves, she could feel the firm strength of his hand and the hard muscle of his arm as he placed her fingers in its crook. She seemed to be aware of everything about him, from the overwhelming strength of his tall, lean build to the hypnotic clean scent of sandalwood that surrounded him.

It was strange. She'd never had this reaction with her other dance partners. She glanced at him from under her lashes. Though she supposed none of her other dance partners looked like they stepped straight off the pages of a fairy tale.

The Country Dance began and the next half hour was interspersed with only the occasional snippets of conversation.

He was enjoying his time in Gloucestershire thus far. He found the long stretches of farmland near the river Severn crossed by the old stone walls particularly beautiful. Peyton Park seemed a fine country house and was more than sufficient while Donnington Park was undergoing improvement, thank you.

Conversation might have been limited, but Genie had never enjoyed a dance more. When the divergent movements of the dance prevented speech, he communicated with her in other ways. Just by the way he stared at her, his interest was clear: the intensity of his gaze, the subtle lifting of a brow, the irrepressible charm of his roguish smile.

Genie couldn't help but bubble with pleasure. She knew she was probably smiling too broadly, her eyes too bright, her cheeks too flushed, but she bloomed under his appreciative gaze.

She wanted to stare at him, to memorize his glorious features, but she kept her gaze down-turned and properly demure. Each time she managed to catch a glimpse of him from under her lashes, he was staring at her—improperly, boldly even.

Genie felt light-headed.

Unfortunately, the dance had to come to an end. He took a circuitous route to return her to her mother who was watching them with unabashed interest. As were most of the women in the room. He was amazing, and he'd singled her out. She couldn't prevent the smile, but she forced herself to repress the companion sigh.

They'd nearly reached her mother, but were still far enough away for a few last moments of private conversation. "And what do you do with your days in Gloucestershire, Miss Prescott?"

She sensed something lurking behind his pleasantry, but she answered him matter-of-factly. "I enjoy the countryside, my lord. Long walks, picnics along the river as the weather permits, and of course, riding."

"Hmm. Sounds delightful. Would you recommend any spots for walking in particular?"

"The path around the park of the castle is a great favorite of mine. My younger sister, Lizzie, and I take our morning constitutional there a couple of times a week."

He seemed pleased with her response.

They were almost within earshot of her mother when he said, "Well, Miss Prescott, have you found the answer to your question?"

She blushed and didn't bother pretending not to understand. "I am still as yet undecided, my lord," she said primly.

"Hmm," he considered. A naughty grin played upon his lips. "There is always another way..."

Genie looked up and their eyes locked. Her heart lurched, overwhelmed by the sheer charisma that radiated from him, sucking her in. She couldn't put her finger on it, but there was something more powerful at work than the simple attraction of his incredible good looks. He was stunning—if that term could be used to describe a man: the classic bone structure of a perfectly shaped nose, high cheekbones, square jaw and wide forehead; a wide sensual mouth; dark blond hair streaked with strands of gold; and striking blue eyes.

No, there was more. He seduced her with the charm of his twinkling gaze and naughty smile punctuated with dimples. When she looked at him she saw something that definitely wasn't good for her, but which proved impossible to resist. Like the sweet cakes and chocolate cream puffs that she devoured. In the back of her mind, a voice urged caution. But Genie was drawn to him like a magnet.

How could she ever think him a frog? He was the prince of her dreams. Knowing she shouldn't, she found herself asking nonetheless, "There is?"

"Indeed." The huskiness of his voice sent chills down her spine. "You could always kiss me to find out."

HASTINGS RETURNED GENIE TO HER mother, bowed, thanked her graciously, and excused himself. Rendered temporarily mute, Genie could only nod like a simpleton.

She *should* have upbraided him for such a shocking, highly improper statement. She *was* shocked. But not in the way that she should have been. Genie was shocked by the thrill that shot through her, by the thought of how much she would like to kiss him. Once formed, the image of his mouth on hers could not be undone. Would his lips be hard or soft? Warm or cool? How would it feel to have those lean, muscular arms wrapped around her in a crushing embrace?

She jerked upright. What was happening to her? Had she taken complete leave of her senses? Proper young ladies did not think about, let alone discuss, exchanging kisses with gentlemen. Whatever must he think of her? No doubt he thought her a wanton for not immediately taking him to task for his untoward suggestion. She should have been offended. She should have been appalled and asked him never to speak of such indecorous things again.

She resolved to do exactly that the next time they met.

Which of course begged the question... would there be a next time?

HE DIDN'T CALL.

A week had passed since the night of the ball. It was clear from the number of gentlemen morning callers at Kington House that despite her lack of fortune, Genie had been a resounding success. Many of her suitors seemed in earnest, including the son of an important squire from Tetbury and the eldest son of the baronet Sir John Thurston from Tewkesbury. Genie knew she should be excited by the prospect of having so many acceptable—more than acceptable, really—suitors to choose from, but try as she might, she could not muster any enthusiasm.

Not when the person that she most wanted to see had yet to cross the threshold. Despite the obvious barrier of rank, even Charles and her parents seemed surprised. Genie knew that she had not imagined his interest.

She feared that her initial conclusion could be correct—he thought her wanton and uncouth. Surely he must realize how shocked she was by his suggestion of a kiss? A feeling of dread and dismay swept over her. What if he'd guessed the truth? That she'd actually considered it.

How could a man that she'd only met once have such a profound effect on her? Perhaps it was because he so resembled the fairy-tale prince of her dreams. Tall and handsome, charming, and kind. He'd soothed her embarrassment with his humor and wit, flirted with her, admired her, and he was the son of a duke. All she could think about was whether she would see him again.

It seemed not.

Disappointment rang acute, and not just for Genie. Even Lizzie seemed unusually subdued. There was no more talk of duels and London seasons.

This morning, for the first time since the ball, Genie and Lizzie decided to take their favorite walk through the castle's vast surrounding park. Thornbury was unusual in that it could boast two grand country houses, Thornbury Castle and Peyton Park—though Peyton Park had once been part of the neighboring parish of Alveston.

The magnificent castle was built by the third Duke of Buckingham during the reign of Henry VIII—the same King Henry who later took possession of the castle when the unfortunate duke was beheaded for treason. Queen Mary returned the castle to the Stafford family in whose hands it remained to this day.

Genie's home, Kington House, a comfortable brick family home of classical design, was situated not far from the castle, and just down the road from the church of St. Mary's with its impressive tower pinnacles, where her father was rector under the esteemed patronage of the Marquess of Buckingham. The Buckinghams were the current holders of Thornbury Castle and until recently the only peers in the vicinity.

"It doesn't make any sense," Lizzie said, breaking the silence.

They'd come upon a favorite resting place, an old tree trunk carpeted with bright green moss and shaded by the giant oak trees circling the pond. Some distance behind them, but not visible through the band of trees, stood the old stone Tudor Castle.

Seated on the stump, Lizzie had tucked the yellow skirts of her muslin walking dress up beneath her, revealing an improper display of her shapely calf. She tossed a stone; it skipped three times before sinking into the dark, murky water. Genie could see the frustration screwed on her sister's lovely face beneath the rim of her straw gypsy hat. Lizzie yanked the pink ribbon under her chin, whipped off her hat and carelessly tossed it next to her, completing the indecorous picture.

"From everything you've said," Lizzie continued, "from what mother has said, from what Susan has said, I don't understand. Why has he not called on you?"

"Isn't it obvious?"

Lizzie's eyes narrowed. "There's nothing wrong with being a parson's daughter."

"There is if you're the son of a duke," Genie quipped. Noticing Lizzie's pressed lips, she softened her tone. "Come now, Lizzie. You know as well as I that such a pairing is highly improbable, if not impossible. You and I were carried away, that's all." She forced a gay smile to her lips that she did not feel. "It's no use worrying over something that cannot be. Let's talk about something else."

Lizzie ignored her. "Tell me again what he said to you after the dance."

Genie felt her cheeks burn despite the fact she had omitted the kissing comment from her retellings. "If I tell you, will you promise to put it aside for the remainder of our walk?"

"Very well," Lizzie agreed distractedly. "I promise."

Genie nodded. "Fine. He asked me what I liked to do in Gloucestershire. I told him walk, picnic by the river, and ride. He asked me if I had a favorite path, I mentioned—"

"That's it! How could I have been so obtuse?"

"Obtuse about what?"

"I knew we should have gone walking a few days ago," Lizzie said crossly.

"What are you talking about?"

"Don't you see?" At Genie's blank look, Lizzie shook her head. "Of course you don't. Genie, sometimes for an otherwise sensible girl you can be unbelievably green." It was not said unkindly, so Genie tried not to take offense. "He wanted to know where you walked so that he could happen upon you."

Genie's brow furrowed. "But why? Why would he not just call at the rectory?"

Lizzie wasn't listening to her. She was looking over Genie's shoulder at the path directly behind her that led to the castle. A huge smile lit her face.

"Don't look now, but I think your prince approaches." She tossed in a cheeky smile. "Though he seems to have misplaced his trusty steed."

Genie forced herself not to crank her head around like a wrung chicken.

Instinctively, she gazed down at her simple ivory muslin walking dress. She groaned softly. Why couldn't she have picked a more elegant gown? There was even mud around the hem. Of course there was nothing she could do about it now. She consoled herself that at least she was wearing her finest silk spencer in a flattering periwinkle blue. "Is my bonnet straight?" she asked anxiously.

"It's fine." Lizzie jumped off the stump, knocked out her skirt, and hastily plopped her hat back on her head. "But you might want to wipe the smudge of chocolate off your cheek."

"What!"

Lizzie giggled. "Only teasing. You look beautiful, Genie. Don't fret."

A few moments passed. Although Lizzie was making a show of appearing not to notice them, Genie could tell by her sister's expression that something had changed. "What's wrong?"

"There is a young woman with him."

"Oh." Crestfallen, Genie tried not to let it show. Lizzie indicated that they were now close enough for Genie to turn around. Genie plastered what she hoped was a carefree smile on her face and looked.

It was him. And he was with a woman. A beautiful young woman no less. Lord Fitzwilliam Hastings was everything she remembered... and more. The brilliance of his smile could rival the sun god Apollo. He seemed so happy. She felt her mouth quiver trying to maintain her smile in the face of disappointment that curdled her stomach like bad beef. As they drew closer, Genie could see that the woman was young, very young. Probably even younger than Lizzie.

Hastings spoke first. "Miss Prescott, what a pleasant surprise."

"It is indeed, my lord," Genie replied, proud of her blithe tone.

"Would you do me the honor of introducing me to your companion, your sister, I presume? The likeness is uncanny."

"My younger sister, my lord, Miss Elizabeth Prescott."

"A pleasure, Miss Prescott. I am sorry that we did not have the opportunity to meet at the ball."

"I am not yet out, my lord," Lizzie said, unable to keep the resentment from her tone.

"Neither am I," his companion piped in, equally resentful.

Hastings scowled at her fondly. "And that is precisely why, brat. Your manners are deplorable," he chastised, but with a smile. "Misses Prescott, may I present my sister, Lady Fanny Hastings."

Genie brightened. His sister. Of course. How could she not have guessed? Despite their different hair color—Lady Fanny's was a rich, chestnut brown—the beautiful young woman greatly resembled her brother. Lizzie was visibly pleased with the new development as well. "Do you walk here often, my lord?" she asked politely.

"No—" he started.

Rolling her eyes, Fanny blurted out at the same time, "We've walked this same path for six straight days."

Hastings shot his sister a venomous look that promised brotherly retribution. When he turned to Genie, she noticed telltale red blotches on his cheeks. His boyish embarrassment charmed her like nothing else. Her handsome prince wasn't quite as confident as he appeared.

She felt a jump of excitement in her chest. He did like her. He had been hoping to meet her. Lizzie shot her a smug "I told you so" grin.

Genie felt like such a fool. How could she not have realized why he'd inquired into her habits? She could have avoided six days of torturous waiting. But she still didn't understand why he had not called at the rectory.

Though replying to his sister, Genie looked at Hastings's flushed face and teased, "It is a favorite walk of mine as well, my lady."

"May we join you? We don't want to intrude," he asked.

"We'd love the company," Lizzie replied a shade too eagerly. She immediately engaged his sister in conversation and they moved off ahead, leaving Genie and Hastings a discreet distance behind them.

"I'm afraid that didn't go quite as smoothly as I had planned," he said sheepishly.

"Younger siblings have a way of upsetting even the best laid plans, don't you think?"

He grinned. "That they do. Especially that one," he said indicating Fanny. "She can't keep a secret for longer than five minutes."

Genie shook her head. "I have a feeling your sister and

mine will get along famously because Lizzie loves nothing more than to convey secrets."

"Should we be worried?"

Genie laughed. "Probably."

They walked along in pleasant silence for a minute or two, enjoying the sunshine. "I feared that I had misunderstood you," he said.

Heat rose to her cheeks. He obviously wondered why she had not walked before today. "I'm afraid I *did* misunderstand you. I didn't realize..."

He peered at her questioningly for a moment then seemed to understand. "Ah. So you weren't avoiding me?"

She shook her head.

"I thought I might have offended you."

Her cheeks flamed. She peeked at him from under her lashes. He looked like a downtrodden puppy with his troubled frown and soulful eyes. Now would be the time to upbraid him for his improper suggestion, but he looked so worried she didn't have the heart. "Shocked perhaps, but not offended. Though you should not say such things, my lord."

He raked his hair back from his face, clearly at a loss. "I'm not sure what provoked me; I offer no excuse for my deplorable conduct except to say that I was bewitched by your beauty."

Genie tried to look stern. "That is no excuse."

"Perhaps not," he said. "But it is the truth. You are beautiful, you know. The most beautiful girl I have ever seen."

Embarrassed and at the same time enormously pleased, Genie stared at the tops of her half boots just visible beneath the slightly higher front hem of her walking dress. "When you didn't call at the rectory, I thought..."

"I planned to later today. I'd hoped to get the chance to renew our acquaintance under less formal circumstances. I wanted to talk to you, really talk to you. We wouldn't have that opportunity in a crowded reception room. And I've heard just how crowded your reception rooms have been this week."

Good gracious! He sounded jealous. Genie couldn't believe it. This handsome gentleman, the son of a duke, was actually jealous of her country suitors. Didn't he know that they could not possibly compare? Was it possible that beneath the charming, lighthearted exterior he was just as uncertain as she?

"Not so crowded that I wouldn't have welcomed you, my lord."

He beamed. "I shall call this very afternoon then. But first tell me something about you, Miss Prescott. Other than catch frogs, what do you like to do?"

Her breath caught. Was he referring to himself? Genie felt like her dreams were unfolding right before her eyes. This was how falling in love was supposed to be: instant attraction, instant camaraderie, instant understanding with no cause to feign disinterest. "The usual pursuits, my lord: pianoforte, embroidery, and singing."

She glanced up to find him staring at her. His gaze intensified. She seemed to be caught in a whirlpool, drowning in the azure depths of those gorgeous eyes.

"All fine pursuits for a young lady," he dismissed. "But what do you *really* enjoy?"

She warmed under his earnestness. He truly wanted to know more about her. The *real* her, not the accomplished young woman presented to society. Shyly, looking back and forth between him and her feet, she took a deep breath. "I'm afraid that I'm a simple country girl at heart. I'd rather be outside, walking, fishing, or riding than doing anything else." She peeked again to gage his reaction. "I even, on occasion, hunt when I can persuade my brothers to let me accompany them."

"I knew it. A girl after my own heart. What else?"

"I love children, my young cousins often visit. I read to them, sometimes we make up stories and act them out."

"A budding playwright?"

She giggled. "I'm afraid nothing quite so formal, my lord. More like a displaced governess." Had she really just said that? Her cheeks burned at the unfortunate slip of tongue. Good gracious, he probably thought her a silly country mouse. Fashionable young ladies did not compare themselves to governesses.

"If I had been fortunate to have a governess like you, I'd venture to say that I would have been a very devoted pupil. And a much better student. Shall I let you in on a little secret?"

Forgetting her embarrassment, Genie nodded.

"I consider myself a displaced farmer."

She thought he was jesting, but he looked at her in earnest. "It's true. I enjoy the labor, the sense of accomplishment. But promise not to tell anyone or I'll be laughed out of Brooks and Whites."

Genie grinned. "I promise. My lips are sealed."

"Now that you know my deepest secret, I should like to hear some of your stories sometime."

"I couldn't."

"Why not?"

"I'd be too embarrassed."

He made a small wave with his hands. "Nonsense." He stopped behind a tree where their sisters wouldn't be able to see them, took her hand, and gazed into her eyes. "I have a feeling you and I, Miss Prescott, like our young sisters over there are going to get along famously." He brought her hand to his mouth and pressed his lips against the thin leather of her glove. An improper gesture, but she would remember that later. Melting under the heat of his gaze, Genie felt a tide of warmth ripple through her body. He lowered his voice, a sultry whisper that sent chills down her spine. "Very *close* friends, indeed."

CHAPTER FOUR

"WHAT SHALL IT BE TOMORROW, my little princess? A ride around the countryside or a chance meeting in the park?" Lying on his side, perched up on one elbow, Hastings lazily tossed a small white flower into the water. The delicate bloom drifted gracefully along the surface for a long, deceptive moment before being dragged downstream by the indomitable flow of the river Severn.

Lounging on the grassy bank of the secluded cove that she discovered with her brothers many years ago, Genie sighed with contentment. This is how it had been for four idyllic weeks: intense, heart-stopping courting interspersed with magical moments of stolen privacy. He'd pursued her with a singularity of purpose, distinctly at odds with the lighthearted young man she'd grown to admire and esteem above all others.

He was so different from what she'd expected of a man of his rank. Blessed with wealth, position, and incredible good looks, rather than inspire envy, he wore his largess as one deserving of such gifts, benevolently bestowed rather than entitled. The good humor that she'd admired from their first inauspicious meeting had not waned, but rather seemed to permeate every corner of his character.

And this amazing man was courting her: singling her out at the weekly assembly balls, attending the same small soirées as she, calling at Kington House every day. Everyone knew. Though only a few knew just how intently. She was floating on air. How could anyone be this happy? It was perfect. He was perfect. There was an ease of conversation with him that she'd never experienced with another man, not even her brothers. It felt as though she'd known him her entire life.

As promised, he'd called the very afternoon of their first "chance" meeting along the footpath of the castle's park. Even her parents, initially hesitant because it had taken him so long to call, had begun to consider the possibilities.

With Lizzie and Fanny's assistance (it hadn't taken long for the sixteen-year-old girls to become fast friends), there had been many more chance meetings on the country lanes of Thornbury. The girls delighted in the romantic intrigue and they fancied themselves quite the matchmaking mamas. Even now, the two little scamps were off "foraging berries" (out of season no less), while Genie fished and Hastings relaxed in the sun.

She'd never had so much fun; the clandestine meetings only heightened the excitement. Yet a twinge of uncertainty niggled her conscience. Being alone with him was highly improper. Her parents would be horrified. But, she reminded herself, she and Hastings weren't doing anything *wrong*. Hastings was the perfect gentleman. He'd never even attempted to kiss her, though she knew he wanted to. But Genie had never done anything that might cause her parents displeasure before, and the guilt chafed uncomfortably at times. It was all for a good cause, she reminded herself. Soon he would ask for her and her conscience would be blissfully unburdened.

The sun beat down on his fair head, his discarded hat and cutaway coat strewn in a heap along with her gloves, bonnet, and spencer. He lay stretched out on a blanket amongst the remains of their picnic. He'd rolled up his shirtsleeves, revealing tanned, muscular forearms covered by a thin layer of fine golden hair.

She never tired of looking at him, memorizing every detail no matter how infinitesimal. Savoring each day as if it could be the last. He looked so peaceful, so young and handsome, basking in the unexpected warmth of a sun-drenched day.

Despite the unusual patch of dry weather, the days were getting shorter. Summer's last hurrah was upon them, and Genie desperately wished she could halt its determined march. She never wanted this dreamlike existence to end. Too soon, the cold gray rain would descend, and there would be no more picnics along the bucolic banks of the river Severn.

"Hmm." She put her finger to her chin and tapped, contemplating his question. "Since your parents are hosting a soirée tomorrow evening for your house party, it must be a quick walk about the park. I shall need time to prepare; I want to make a favorable impression."

"They'll be enchanted," he said softly, his eyes lingering on her face. "What's not to love?"

Genie's heart jumped to her throat. She tried not to show how affected she was by his careless use of the sentiment that she felt so strongly. Like a moth to the flame, she was irresistibly drawn to this vibrant man. But the deeper her attachment grew, the more she worried about their difference in rank. "Your brother does not approve of me."

Hastings frowned, something that did not occur very often. "That's not true. Henry is just reserved and so damnably serious. He feels the pressure of being heir." He shrugged. "He merely envies my freedom."

Genie remained unconvinced. It was more than that. The somber viscount, so like his brother in looks if not in temperament, looked at her strangely, like he pitied her. It made her distinctly uncomfortable.

"After Oxford we should have had our Grand Tour, but with the war..." He stopped. "There has not been much time to... how shall I say... enjoy the foibles of youth. Much is expected of him, he will be responsible for the ducal holdings. I'll have the lands from my mother, but it's not the same."

As the second son, Hastings was more or less free to choose his own path. He often spoke of the lands that would come to him from his mother's family, the plans he had for developing the land in an effort to make it more productive. Genie could see herself running the household surrounded by adoring children and reveling in the attention of a loving husband.

How could this be happening so fast? How could she have fallen in love so quickly?

In many ways, Genie and Hastings seemed destined for each other. Both romantics at heart, they were the perfect complement: his natural charm and good humor, her tender heart and trusting nature. With him, Genie knew she would have the security of a loving home. She felt it deep in her gut.

Though the hurdle of their difference in station concerned her, it did not seem insurmountable. He was the second son after all, not the heir. "It was kind of your parents to invite my family."

"Not kindness, your father is the rector." He held her gaze. "Besides, I think they are interested to discover why I have spent so much time at Kington House."

"And why have you spent so much time at Kington House, my lord?" she asked with wide-eyed innocence.

He grinned—that heart-stopping, crooked, dimpled grin that sent butterflies fluttering in her stomach.

"Because I've been bewitched by a beautiful princess who's cast a spell on me."

Genie giggled. "I think you've listened to one too many of my fairy tales."

He laughed, resting his head on his arms crossed behind his neck. After a minute, his eyes closed. Thick, long lashes curled against his cheek, shimmering in the sun like the tips had been dipped in gold dust.

A gentle breeze ruffled her skirts and tossed a few flaxen ringlets across her nose. Pushing them aside, she turned her gaze from the dozing Hastings back to the water in time to notice her line sway then dip. The fishing pole jerked in her hands.

"I think I've caught something," she said excitedly.

Hastings popped up, a bit groggy at first then jumped to

his feet, pulling on the taut line.

"It feels like a big one. Can you handle him?"

She nodded, her arms already straining against the pull. "I think so." Despite the pain surging through her hands and forearms, she grinned. This was the biggest fish she'd ever hooked.

Finding strength she did not realize she had, Genie battled for a good ten minutes, fighting to control her line. Hastings watched anxiously from her side. Not used to such exertion, her arms started to shake. "I can't hold it much longer..."

"Here, let me help." He started to reach for her pole when the line suddenly went slack.

"Oh no!" she moaned. She'd lost him.

Genie collapsed back on the blanket in utter exhaustion and burst into laughter. "Devil take it. After all that, I can't believe the blasted thing got away." Her hand covered her mouth in horror. She'd hooked one big fish and now she cursed like a sailor.

Hastings appeared not to notice her colorful vocabulary, he leaned over her prone figure, studying her flushed face with particular intensity. "You still have me."

Still laughing, she stared into his eyes. Something shifted in his expression, causing her giggling to stop and her chest to squeeze with longing. His gaze flickered to the rise and fall of her chest then back to her face. His eyes burned with unbridled desire, raw and hungry. Genie glimpsed a sliver of steel behind the lighthearted exterior that she'd never seen before.

"You're so beautiful," he whispered, his voice rough and solemn, devoid of its usual teasing lilt. "Like an angel."

So was he. His handsome face poised above hers, dark blond hair slumped forward across the chiseled lines of his cheeks and jaw, blue eyes stormy as the sea.

With one finger, he gently traced the side of her face. Genie's heart thumped wildly in her chest. Wordlessly, she watched him, eyes wide, waiting. She knew what he was going to do; she'd yearned for it from almost the first moment they'd met. The pad of his thumb ran across her bottom lip. Her breath caught high in her chest. She couldn't move.

Finally, his head dipped and his lips touched hers, so achingly tentative it almost hurt. Shocked by the unfamiliar sensation, she froze, not sure what to do. She should push him away and feign offense that he would take such liberties, but she couldn't. She wanted this; she would not deny it. Part of her was actually relieved. She'd worried that he might never kiss her. That he might never show her that he desired her as a man does a woman.

His lips were soft and gentle, brushing over hers like the wisps of a feather. Genie felt helpless, drunk with an unfamiliar emotion that had been unleashed by the simple touch of his mouth to hers. Excitement and anticipation fluttered high in her chest. She could go on like this forever, luxuriating in the sensation of being worshipped by his adoring mouth.

But the feather-soft kisses stopped. He raised his head and peered deep into her eyes. Whatever sign he sought there he must have found because his head dipped again and this time he kissed her harder, much harder. The change from tentative and worshiping to hot and furious both surprised and emboldened her. Stripped of civility and decorum, this was a side of Hastings that Genie had never seen. A serious side. A commanding side. A dangerous side. Here was a man who boldly captured her lips with fierce determination and wouldn't let her go.

She'd never been more aware of him as a man. She could feel the smoothness of his skin marred only by the faintest hint of stubble as his mouth moved over hers, the soft wave of his hair tickling her cheek. Deftly, he pried her lips apart and deepened the kiss. Her body felt unfamiliar, buzzing with the exquisite sensations he aroused in her. She wanted to devour him, the sweet, heady combination of wine, spice, and molten desire.

Her eyes fluttered closed and she relaxed, awash in sensation. He'd been holding himself off of her, but slowly his chest lowered. The hard plane of his muscled chest pressed against the softness of her breasts, so close she could feel the excited pounding of his heart against hers. He was so much larger, she should have felt crushed, but she loved the closeness, reveled in the power of his weight on her. She'd never felt so feminine, so protected.

"God, you taste so good, Genie. Like those sweet cakes you love," he moaned against her mouth.

Self-conscious about her own lack of experience, she desperately wanted to please him. "Show me what to do," she whispered, circling his neck with her hands, raking her fingers through the soft silk of his hair.

He groaned, wrapping her in his arms as though he would never let her go. Pressed against the muscled, hard length of him, she felt the evidence of his arousal pulse against her thigh. Indeed, he wanted her; and Genie was getting an inkling of just how badly. A warm flood of desire spread over her and pooled low in her belly. Genie didn't know what was happening to her, but she knew that she desperately craved something more.

She craved his touch.

Of its own accord, her body stirred against him, shifting in innocent frustrated silence.

He pressed himself more firmly against her, steadying her, allowing her to grow accustomed to the magnificent power of his body. Gently, he settled his hips against hers, moving the thickness she'd felt on her thigh into the crevice between her legs. The sheer sensuality of the positioning sent a bolt of desire shooting through her. She wanted to rock her hips against him, to increase the pressure of his body on hers until they melted together.

Reading her mind, his hips circled against hers, driving the thick head of his staff against the top of her mound. Rubbing against her until the lips of her sex swelled with desire for...

At once she understood her part.

Before she could process the thought, his mouth slanted over hers again, forcing it open. She gasped when his tongue stroked the inside of her mouth. Her heart fluttered. His lips and tongue brooked no argument, demanding her cooperation with his sinful kiss. Cautiously, she met the thrust of his tongue with her own. He growled his approval as his mouth continued its ravaged assault.

As he stroked her mouth with his tongue, inciting a wicked dance with her own, his hand moved to cup her breast. Too far gone, no longer heeding propriety, Genie only knew how good it felt. His hands stroked her body, claiming her with a possession that made her weak. She burned where he touched; her skin warm and sensitive. Every nerve ending in her body screamed for release from the wicked teasing dance. Kneading her breast with his hand, his thumb circled her nipple through the thin muslin of her gown and fine linen of her chemise, teasing it to a tight point.

They were both breathing hard, the fervor of youthful passion a conflagration that was quickly burning out of control. She knew it was too fast, too dangerous. But she was powerless to deny him—or herself. His movements at first slow and confident had turned frantic and less controlled. He lowered his head to her bodice, his warm breath and hot kisses peppered her tingling skin.

Startled by the impropriety of his kiss, a coherent thought broke through the madness. This was wrong. She should stop. The virtue she'd been taught to treasure above all else hung by a tenuous thread. She would be ruined if anyone discovered them.

"Wait, we have to stop," she murmured against his mouth.

A thin sheen of sweat glistened on his brow as his face contorted in pain. He looked ready to explode as he fought for control. "No, we don't, sweetheart. I love you too much, Genie," he said tightly. "I want you to be mine forever. I *need* to make you mine forever. Do you understand?"

She nodded. He loved her! He wanted to marry her! A wave of euphoria spread over her at his declaration, stoking the fires in her still-smoldering body.

"Then trust me," he rasped, his jaw clenched with the exertion of reining in his passion. "It will all work out fine, I promise."

Trust me. Of course, she trusted him. He wanted to marry her. How could she deny him? But still, she knew it was wrong.

He read her hesitance. "Do you love me, Genie?"

"Yes," she said shyly. "I love you very much."

Clearly in agony, a half smile crossed his tortured face. "Then there is nothing to fear."

"But—"

"No buts. Let me show you. Oh God, Genie, please let me show you." His whispered wooing turned into a soft, pleading kiss. Something primitive in his voice called out to her deepest desires, making her yearn to please him. She loved him and her body cried out to prove how much.

Reading acceptance in her expression, he kissed her again, quickly rousing her passion as if there had never been a momentary lapse. Genie forced the doubts aside, refusing to heed the warning in her head that told her she was making a horrible, irreparable mistake.

A mistake as old as sin.

The lessons of a lifetime dissolved in an instant. She couldn't explain it, but this felt right. Why attempt to justify actions that could never be justified? She was young and in love—nothing else mattered. Only the moment.

His mouth plundered hers as his hands caressed her body. Losing patience, his movements lost some of their finesse, becoming enchantingly fumbling. She could tell that they were swiftly moving beyond the realm of his expertise. Had he done this before? If so, he had yet to perfect his movements as he had his kissing. The realization thrilled her; they were experiencing the wonder of passion together.

When his hand settled over her breast again, Genie ventured a tentative exploration beyond his hair and neck. Given the intimacy of what they were doing, it seemed odd that he still wore his high starched cravat and white waistcoat. Her hands roamed over the fine linen of his shirt, following the curve of his wide shoulders down the long muscles of his arms. He flexed at her touch, the long cords of his muscles played under her fingertips.

He'd managed to lift her skirts and chemise. She tried to question him, but he covered her mouth with a kiss. His hand brushed the length of her thigh above her silk stockings and garter to come to rest between her legs. Shocked, she thought to protest, but when his finger entered her she lost the ability for coherent thought. Perhaps sensing her shock, he slowed his movements, allowing her a moment to grow accustomed to his hand in the most intimate of places.

"Close your eyes, my sweet," he murmured in her ear, sending a shiver down her spine. "Don't think, just feel. Feel my finger touching you, making you wet for me."

Gently, he stroked her, his finger dipping inside her as the palm of his hand rubbed against her mound. Unconsciously, her hips lifted against his palm seeking the sweet pressure that made her tingle with sensation. He drove her to the edge of oblivion then inexplicably removed his sinful hand. Her head rolled back and forth on the blanket, frustrated with the agony of burgeoning desire.

He fumbled with his breeches, releasing his manhood from the tight constriction of his breeches. She was too embarrassed to look—even to satisfy her bold curiosity.

"I wish we had more time, but they might return at any moment. It will only hurt this once," he promised through clenched teeth. His shoulders shook with tension, perilously close to losing control. Beneath his shirt Genie felt the dampness of his skin. He moved over her, positioning his hands on either side of her shoulders and wedging the thick tip of his shaft between her legs.

Reality hit her then. But it was too late. In one swift motion he sheathed himself in her, cleaving her in two, and smothering her bloodcurdling scream with his mouth.

She froze, stiffening with pain.

He cupped her face with one hand, running his thumb

across her cheek to smooth a tear. "I'm sorry, love. The first time can be painful for a woman, but the worst is over. From this point on there will only be pleasure. I promise."

Betrayed, her eyes shot daggers at him. She didn't trust his promises right now.

"Try to relax."

Was he a bedlamite? Her whole body clenched at his brutal invasion. She pushed against the wide shoulders that she'd admired only minutes ago. But like a wall of stone, he wouldn't budge.

Their eyes met. If it was any consolation (which it wasn't), he looked to be in as much pain as she was. He kept himself perfectly still—apparently no small feat if the bulging veins in his neck were any indication—allowing her body to adjust to him. And surprisingly, it did. After a few minutes he asked cautiously, "Better?"

She thought about it, wanting to disagree. Instead she answered honestly. "Yes." Her body had seemed to soften around him, gently stretching to accommodate his substantial girth. And though unfamiliar, it no longer hurt. The painful throbbing had been replaced by a gentle tingling of awareness—a tingle that extended from low in her belly up to the sensitive tips of her breasts.

With the realization that the pain had dulled, Genie began to grasp the beauty, the wonder of what they were doing. They were truly connected, joined together in a way she never could have imagined. Her heart soared with the knowledge that this was the man who was meant for her. Her one and only true love.

"God you're beautiful," he whispered.

He kissed her then with such depth of feeling that Genie ached, no longer from pain, but from the pure tenderness of his caress. He soothed her with his mouth. He worshiped her with his tongue. And Genie couldn't get enough, returning his kiss with equal fervor. His hands caressed her body, cupping her breasts and gently teasing her nipples, enticing her passion until the heat of desire spread over her body once again. Until she yearned for more. She yearned to feel his mouth on her skin, to shed the clothes that separated them and feel the hot press of his skin on hers. His mouth drove her crazy with need and her body responded, growing damp with desire. The yearning became too much. Writhing with anticipation, she moved her hips against him.

"Now?" he asked, his voice rough with pent up desire. "How do you feel now, my love?"

Genie felt strange, confused by the wave of sensation crashing over her. She was reaching out in the darkness for something, though she didn't know what it was. No longer did his entry feel like a brutal invasion. Now it felt right. Like he filled her. Completely. And Genie was amazed at how the sensation of his thick, long erection pressed deep inside her, aroused her to the point of frenzy. "I feel... I feel like I want more."

He groaned deeply, obviously relieved. As if the restraint he'd been demonstrating was more than he could bear. Eyes half-lidded, he threw his head back and thrust. Slowly at first, then increasing in speed and intensity. Instinctively, Genie sought more. She lifted her hips to meet his thrust, matching him stroke for stroke. The enthusiasm of her response seemed to drive him mad. He was perilously close to losing control.

And she loved it.

Her body cried out with pleasure as he pushed deeper inside her and she found the fulfillment that she'd unknowingly craved. Her heart raced as the frantic rhythm of their joining crested to its highest peak. It was quickly spinning out of control, but she didn't care. She'd lost the ability to think. All she knew was the force of the exquisite pressure building inside of her. She wanted it harder, faster, deeper. She wanted as much as he could give.

A deep guttural sound broke her from her trance. She glanced up just in time to watch the emotion traverse his face, a strange mix of agony and ecstasy. The magnitude of his passion overwhelmed her. And Genie felt something quicken inside her, a tightness that was building in intensity that she did not understand. The tingling was now throbbing, the elusive craving that something magical was just beyond the edge of her consciousness. She wanted to cry out.

"I'm sorry, love," he whispered. "I can't hold back any longer. Next time, it will be longer." His strange words made sense moments later when suddenly he jerked, crying out his release as he sank deep inside her. A warm rush surged through her and the sheer intimacy of the moment made her heart catch. Their eyes met and Genie felt as if she was looking into the depths of his soul. She would never be connected to anyone like she was to this man. He possessed her completely.

He reached out to stroke her cheek, seemingly as moved as she. "That was not very well done of me."

Her brow furrowed, not understanding. "I thought it was wonderful."

He laughed softly, sending a strange tickle through her body where they were still joined. "Believe me, it gets even better." He dropped a soft kiss on her lips. "I would show you right now, but this is already too dangerous. Fanny and Lizzie could return at any moment."

He kissed her again before reluctantly rolling off her, severing the connection. And with the loss Genie knew a pang of disappointment. The departure of his warm body chilled her, making her at once conscious of her exposed legs. Genie knew a long moment of gut-checking panic, as the enormity of her actions struck. As apparently it had him.

"Bloody hell," he muttered.

That about summed it up, she thought. She turned her head to look at him. If anything, he appeared equally as astonished by what had just transpired between them.

"That's never happened to me before," he said almost to himself, before turning to face her. "I'm sorry, Genie. I never meant for this to happen."

The blood drained from her face. Did he regret this? Did he not love her?

Sensing her fears, he smiled—that roguish grin that belonged on the face of a far more experienced man. He bent over and tucked a stray curl behind her ear. "Don't fret, goose. I meant that I've never been so clumsy. You made me lose control like an untried lad before I could bring you pleasure." His obvious embarrassment charmed her. Inwardly she smiled, realizing that he probably was close to being an untried lad. He dropped a soft kiss on her lips. "Everything about you overwhelms me."

Her heart burst with happiness. Everything would be fine. True, it would be better to be married before making love, but the passion between them could not be denied. She loved him and he loved her. Still, she needed reassurance. "Did you mean what you said before?"

His eyes twinkled with emotion, immediately sensing her need for reassurance. "Of course." He brushed a kiss across her forehead. "I can't wait for my parents to meet you."

Genie sighed with relief. Her dreams were coming true.

Reluctantly, he got to his feet. "I would stay like this forever, but we better get you cleaned up."

Genie blushed, noticing the dampness tinged with streaks of blood between her thighs. The harsh reminder of what they'd done confronted her again. Ignoring the stab of fear, she moved to lower her skirts, but he stopped her.

"Don't. You'll get blood on them."

Quickly adjusting his own clothing, Hastings picked up a napkin from their picnic and ran to the river. Returning, he knelt down next to her and tenderly washed between her legs with the cool, dampened cloth. Mortified to have his gaze on her in the stark daylight, Genie studied the trees.

When he finished, he pulled her to a stand and helped smooth the wrinkles from her clothing as best he could. Folding up the blanket splotched with blood, he bent down and picked up a pale blue satin ribbon that had fallen loose from her hair.

"Ah. A favor from my lady?" He knelt again and bowed his head like a knight at tournament.

Genie smothered a smile behind her hand. The effortless ability to ease an awkward situation was one of the things she most admired about him. One of the many reasons she loved him. Taking the ribbon from his hand, in mock seriousness she tied it around his shirtsleeve. "And how will you prove your devotion, Sir Knight? There is no battlefield on which to demonstrate your prowess."

Hastings glanced meaningfully to the grass where the blanket had rested only moments ago, and lifted an arrogant brow. "Is there not?"

Genie giggled; he was incorrigible.

"What would you have me do then, fair maiden, to win your heart?" he implored dramatically.

"Hmm." She pretended to consider. "I think slaying a dragon or two will suffice."

He took her hand and brought it to his mouth. His face turned grave. Instead of the flippant reply she expected, he said, "For you, my love, I would slay a hundred dragons."

Her heart squeezed. He sounded so sincere, she had to believe him. How could she not with him kneeling before her, an endearing, romantic expression cast across his handsome features, the sun shining on the shimmering strands of gold in his hair. This amazing man could do anything.

She wanted to hold on to this moment forever. The splendor, the vitality, the promise of young love seemed ripe with endless possibility. The magic of what they'd just shared filled her with happiness. At that moment, everything she ever wanted seemed to be at her fingertips.

But a scurrilous thought burrowed into the hidden recesses of her mind, casting a dark shadow across their fun. Were the dragons only in her imagination or did they lurk somewhere beyond the veil of paradise, preying in the darkness ready to pounce on their happiness?

"OH, LIZZIE, HE'S PERFECT," GENIE said dreamily. She yawned, stretched out her arms above her head, and fell backward, sinking into the downy softness of her bed. The

Prescotts had just finished receiving their afternoon callers
and the two girls had retired to Genie's room to converse in
private. Genie would have liked nothing better than to take a
nap, but this was the first opportunity she'd had to talk
privately with Lizzie since returning from her momentous
fishing escapade this morning.

In fact, this was the first opportunity Genie had to
consider what had happened this morning at all. She and
Hastings had declared—and then made—love. It seemed
impossible that Miss Eugenia Prescott, the proper parson's
daughter, could have done such a scandalous thing. How
had it happened? Even now, she couldn't explain it other
than to say that at the precise moment of truth, she wanted
to please him. The battle between her conscience versus
love and passion had never really been a contest.

The sheer magnitude of her physical response to him had
been completely unexpected. Never could she have
imagined the passion lying dormant inside her, awaiting
only his touch to erupt. She'd never felt like that before, like
she'd been swept up in the current of a powerful river of
sensation, unable to break free. She'd *needed* his touch,
needed the closeness of his body on hers.

It had been amazing.

But most of all, she'd loved watching the ecstasy
transform his face as they made love. She, Genie Prescott,
had made him lose control. For the first time, Genie knew
the exquisite power of her womanhood.

Nonetheless, she realized that it could not happen again
until they were married. It was far too dangerous. If anyone
should discover...

The thought was too horrible to contemplate. She'd be
shunned by polite society, shaming herself and her family in
the process. She'd be ruined.

Genie didn't want to feel as though she'd made a
mistake succumbing to temptation, but there was a
tenacious, sensible voice in the back of her head that would
not quiet. Hastings was young and inclined to
lightheartedness. His *joie de vivre* was one of the things she

loved about him, but it did not inspire constancy. Genie trusted him to do the right thing. A man of his rank and position, a true gentleman, would do so. And he had made his intentions known.

She had to share her exciting news with her sister. But Lizzie, who had still not responded, was looking at her strangely.

Sitting at the foot of the bed, Lizzie gave Genie a soul-searching stare; an unreadable expression on her face. Now that Genie thought about it, Lizzie had been acting odd since their return from the river this morning. Could she have guessed? Genie had been unable to prevent the blush when Lizzie asked her why she walked with such a strange gait on the way home.

"No one is perfect, Genie. Not even the handsome son of a duke," Lizzie said uneasily.

Lizzie's sudden reticence shocked her. Was this the same person who eagerly plotted their secret meetings with the adroitness of a born conspirator? It felt like the sisters had switched roles. Lizzie, the voice of caution and Genie the one running headstrong into... disaster? She chilled. Whatever made her think that, she wondered, burying the unwelcome premonition.

Genie had heard the underlying concern in her sister's voice. "I know that, dearest. I meant that he is perfect for me. Truly, he is everything I've ever dreamed of. Aren't you happy for me?"

"Of course, I am," Lizzie assured her. She paused, obviously searching for the right words. "I just don't want you to be too disappointed if—"

Genie cut her off. "I won't be disappointed."

"How can you be sure?"

Why had Lizzie's excitement about Hastings suddenly soured? Had Lizzie seen them on the riverbank? The thought was too mortifying to contemplate. What would Lizzie think of her? She had to explain. Genie lowered her voice and checked the doorway. "You must not say anything yet, but Hastings intends to ask for me."

Lizzie appeared visibly relieved. "He told you as much?"

Genie thought about it for a moment. He hadn't actually said those precise words, but he'd inferred by his actions and words that he intended to... hadn't he? She pushed aside the traitorous uncertainty. Genie trusted him. "He made his intentions known this very morning," she said confidently.

"Then that explains..." Lizzie's voice drifted off and she stopped whatever she'd been about to say. But Genie was now certain that Lizzie suspected that something had happened between Genie and Hastings on the riverbank.

Smiling, Lizzie threw her arms around Genie and hugged her enthusiastically. "I'm so happy for you."

Lizzie's heartfelt embrace covered Genie's temporary embarrassment and unleashed all the emotions bubbling so close to the surface since Genie and Hastings had unexpectedly made love this afternoon. Genie clasped Lizzie's hands, happiness bringing tears to her eyes. "I love him desperately and the more amazing thing is that he loves me. I think I'm the happiest, most fortunate girl in all of England."

Lizzie peppered her with excited questions: How did it happen? Why hadn't they said anything earlier (after all she and Fanny had done for them!)? When would he send the formal letter to father requesting a betrothal? Would they marry in the spring or the summer? Where would they live?

Genie answered the best that she could, given that she did not have the answers for most. Noticing the returning wariness on her sister's face, Genie explained, "I'm sure we shall discuss all the details after I am properly introduced to the duke and duchess tomorrow evening. Hastings must secure their approval first before approaching father."

Now Lizzie looked very worried. "Then the duke and duchess are not yet aware of his intentions toward you?"

"No, not as yet. But there is no reason to suppose that they will object—"

"Genie," Lizzie interrupted vehemently. "You said yourself before that a duke's son does not marry the daughter of a rector. It just isn't done."

"Hastings is not the heir, only the second son," Genie reminded her.

"But he will still be expected to make a good match," Lizzie said doggedly.

"I don't understand, Lizzie. Where is this coming from? I thought you wanted me to marry Hastings." Genie felt the happiness seep out of her. She needed Lizzie's support.

Lizzie chewed on her lip. She seemed reluctant to explain, but Genie knew there was a reason for Lizzie's sudden reticence, beyond what had occurred today. "What is it Lizzie?" she prodded. "If you know something, you must tell me."

"It's just something the viscount said to me yesterday, that's all." Lizzie tried to sound dismissive, but Genie experienced a growing sense of alarm.

"What did Loudoun say?" Genie asked cautiously, dreading the answer. Hastings's brother had made no secret of his disapproval.

Lizzie shrugged. "Just that although Hastings might choose to ignore his obligation, the duchess was counting on Hastings to make a good match."

Lizzie fidgeted with the laces on her boots. She was holding something back.

"What else, Lizzie?"

"That Hastings might seem carefree and irresponsible, but in the end he would do his duty."

"This is different."

"Why?"

Genie couldn't tell her what they'd done. "It just is—that's why." She lifted her chin stubbornly. "We love each other." And now he had a duty to her.

Lizzie grabbed her hands, holding her gaze. Genie wanted to look away, she didn't want to hear what Lizzie had to say, didn't want to acknowledge her own fears. Acknowledging her uncertainty made her somehow feel disloyal. But what if Lizzie was right? What if the duke and duchess did not approve of a match between them?

"Genie, promise me you'll be careful."

"Of course I will, goose," Genie assured her. But, of course she hadn't been careful at all. Indeed, the painful raw throbbing between her legs was a constant reminder of her lack of care.

Suddenly angry at herself, Genie vowed to halt the flow of distrustful thoughts. She was wrong to doubt Hastings, to allow Lizzie's fears to betray their love. They were bound together now; Hastings would do what was necessary to ensure that they would be together "forever" as he had promised.

Genie would find her happily ever after. Hastings would take care of his parents' objections and if necessary, defy his family. He'd taken her virginity. A mere social impediment would not stand in the way of a match between them now.

But Lizzie was at least partially correct: Genie had to be careful.

Such folly would not, could not, happen again.

CHAPTER FIVE

NOTHING HAD HAPPENED THE WAY Genie thought it would. How she, the daughter of a rector, came to be in this predicament, she could not explain any better today than she could two months ago. The twinge of trepidation that she'd experienced that afternoon with Lizzie was nothing compared to the horror that she felt today.

It had started out innocent enough, as all great falls from grace do, with one mistake. And then it happened again. And again. And again. Along the bank of the Severn, in the secluded greenhouse of Thornbury Castle, anywhere they could find. Her grand intention to not repeat her folly was all but forgotten with the silver of his tongue and the haunting tenderness of his embrace.

It was a vicious circle from which she could not wrench free. The further she fell from respectability, the more her body craved his touch. She no longer had the pain of the first time to viscerally remind her that she sinned. And after the second time, when she'd shattered in his arms and touched a sliver of heaven, she'd found the temptation of making love all but impossible to resist. As he'd promised, it had only gotten better. Now her body craved him as deeply as her soul. He'd awakened her passion, and it would not graciously retreat.

In truth, she didn't know that she would wish it away even if she could. The intimacy, the closeness, they shared was incredible. If she thought she knew him before, it was nothing compared to now. Genie didn't just know that he liked roasted potatoes but not roasted carrots, she knew the way his jaw clenched when he drove deep inside her, and the way he liked to look deep into her eyes as he exploded in release. Her heart squeezed just thinking about it.

She couldn't get enough of him even as she realized what they were doing was wrong.

Genie swore each time that it would be the last, but when he kissed her—touched her—the wicked cravings of her body took over, and she lost all manner of decorum and rationality.

Yet each time he took her in sin, she hated herself—and him—a little more.

Shame had tainted their love. Since that fateful sun-drenched September morning, Genie had learned a painful truth about the inherent fragility of virtue. Virtue, once taken, could not be restored. It was a lesson that had been instilled in her since birth, but which she had so easily forsaken for the gratification of a moment. Without virtue, Genie was ruined. No one else would marry her now. The fate of a woman without fortune was inextricably tied to marriage. Unmarried, she would become dependent on the charity of her father and later, of her brothers.

She'd been such a fool. Seduced by the oldest lure of all... love.

And may God forgive her, she still loved him—but with increasing desperation. He had to marry her, not only to restore her lost virtue, but because she couldn't imagine life without him. In a little over three months, he'd wormed his way around her heart. The immediate connection between them had blossomed into a true friendship. Hastings made her pulse race, her smile bright, and made her more comfortable than she'd ever imagined with a man.

But the moment she left him all comfort fled. She wanted to feel secure again, and that would only come with a formal proposal.

He'd dragged his feet for months. She'd hinted and danced around the topic of their understanding since it had become apparent that his parents would not happily welcome her into the family. The much-anticipated soirée at Thornbury Park had been a miserable affair. The duke and duchess had not cut her directly, but the cold manner of their greeting left no doubt as to their wishes on the matter.

Two months after they'd first made love, two months after that disastrous first meeting with his parents, and Hastings still had not offered for her. Indeed, he steadfastly avoided the topic of engagement at all, so much so that Genie had begun to wonder whether Lizzie had been correct. Had he ever intended it at all? But what else could "make you mine forever" mean? His vow of love was often repeated, but usually in the hazy, dreamy moments after they made love.

It was time to stop hinting. She'd learned over the past two months that Hastings did not like confrontation, but she had to do something. What they had was worth fighting for, he must realize that.

The front parlor of Kington House with her mother on the other side of the room might not be the best place for this conversation, but the opportunities for privacy had grown scarce with the increasing rain. And when they did have the occasion to meet in private, there was usually not much time left for conversation. With a laugh and a smile, he'd tell her not to worry before kissing her into oblivion, making her forget everything but the feel of his body on hers.

"What's wrong, love? Don't you like the cakes? I had the chef make them especially for you." Disappointed by the unenthusiastic reception of his gift, Hastings waited anxiously for her reply.

She hated to look at him. Even now, from his seat beside her on the couch as they took tea, Genie felt her heart tug. She desperately wanted to believe the adoration, the love he offered in his guileless blue gaze. "They're delicious. It's not the cakes."

"Then what is it? Something has been bothering you all morning."

Something has been bothering me for months. "I thought

you hadn't noticed."

"I notice everything about you," he murmured suggestively, in that husky voice that sent chills up her spine.

Ignoring her body's instinctive reaction, Genie took a deep breath. No matter how unseemly it was to broach such an indelicate subject, he'd left her no choice but to press the matter. The temporary lull of gentlemen callers afforded her the opportunity; she could not guess when it would be repeated. "The situation with your parents has not improved. I cannot help but worry about their resistance." She spoke in a low voice, but it was unnecessary. Her mother was occupied by Fanny and Lizzie taking turns at the pianoforte.

Hastings stiffened and immediately leaned away from her. A mask of discomfort descended across his gregarious features. She'd obviously offended his sense of propriety, but to Genie's mind they'd forsaken propriety the first time they made love. But clearly, he didn't wish to discuss this subject.

"You are mistaken," he said brusquely. "They are not resistant. Do not concern yourself with the matter."

Genie chewed on her lip. Her teacup rattled as she placed it in the saucer. His cold response hurt, but she would not be put off this time. At moments like this when he seemed every inch the remote, humorless duke's son, Genie wondered whether she knew him at all. Behind the fun, lighthearted young man she loved, she glimpsed a hard, impenetrable—immovable—layer of steel to his character that frightened her. She saw the shadow of the man he might have been had fate made him heir.

Genie looked down at her fingers as she nervously fiddled with the delicate teacup handle. "But what if they never approve?" she asked softly.

"Nonsense. There is plenty of time before we leave for town."

At the mention of him leaving, Genie's stomach twisted. Her panic increased. It was still some time before the season, but she didn't like to be reminded that he might eventually leave.

He continued in earnest. "I am confident that before that time I can persuade them..." His voice dropped off leaving an awkward silence.

Genie realized that he did not want to make her any promises, and it stopped her heart cold. Had he ever made her any promises at all? The color drained from her face and she felt suddenly nauseated. Mute, she stared at him in horror.

He took his thumb and wiped the crease from between her brow. "Don't worry, Genie, trust me." His greatest charm was the uncanny ability to say exactly what she wanted to hear. But this time, she felt not the least bit reassured by his empty promises. She needed to hear more. And she feared that she never would.

Genie did not doubt that he loved her. But did he love her enough to defy his family?

A SHORT WEEK LATER BROUGHT such a change in circumstance Genie could have wept for the joy of it. She'd been wrong not to trust Hastings. He had indeed kept his promise. The previous day card arrived from the duchess informing Genie of her intent to call on Mrs. Prescott and her daughters the following morning. Genie's happiness knew no bounds. There was only one explanation: Hastings had informed his parents of their attachment. Such condescension in calling at Kington House could not be misinterpreted; the duchess had signaled her approval.

The entire household shared in Genie's elation. Even Lizzie, whose worry matched her own these past few weeks (though she was careful not to show it), initiated a lengthy discussion on bridal gowns. Lizzie decided they must write their aunts in London as soon as possible to ensure an adequate amount of time to review the sketches.

The much-anticipated day dawned gray and dismal. So relieved that all of her dreams would soon come to fruition, not even the persistent rain could dampen Genie's spirits.

She woke early, paying particular attention to her appearance. Striving for just the right balance between sophistication and youth, she donned her best morning gown of a delicate pink silk crepe. The square bodice and short sleeves were fashionably made, but modest. Her flaxen tresses were braided then wound into a tight chignon and secured with a matching pink ribbon. Satisfied with the results, Genie anxiously took her place in the front parlor. Kington House had two small sitting rooms, both cozy and comfortable with pretty floral wallpaper and soft pastel furnishings, but they were hardly elegant enough to impress a duchess. After much agonizing, Mrs. Prescott decided that the front parlor took better advantage of the view to the gardens, rain notwithstanding. A fire had been set and lit, the rugs swept, the furniture polished, the servants bathed and dressed in fresh clothing. Mrs. Prescott's prized silver tea urn and Worcester china stood proudly on the tea cart. Everything carefully readied for this grand occasion. It was not often that a country rector was called upon by a duchess.

At long last, the crested doors of the Duke of Huntingdon's magnificent gilded coach came into view. The liveried coachman and footmen in their scarlet coats trimmed with gold seemed painfully out of place as it clattered down the narrow lane that fronted the rectory.

In due course, Higgins—the Prescott's devoted manservant—announced the duchess. Casually, as if the arrival of a duchess was a regular occurrence, all eyes turned toward the doorway.

The Duchess of Huntingdon filled the small room with her presence. Though diminutive in stature, the nobility of her bearing created the illusion of a much larger woman. Unlike the previous two times Genie had seen her, the duchess wore a fine silk bonnet instead of an elaborate turban. Her clothes seemed a luxurious reflection of her exalted rank. Her morning dress and matching pelisse were of a deep rose silk trimmed with sable. Genie wished she'd seen her cloak before Higgins had taken it.

Though a handsome woman, the duchess was remarkably thin. This emphasized the sharpness of her features and caused the hollows of her cheeks to appear sunken. It also had the unfortunate effect of making her look tight and uncomfortable, like all the air had been sucked out of her.

The resemblance to her sons, if any, was forced.

Eagerly, Genie sought the turn of her gaze. For a fraction of an instant, their eyes met, causing a shudder to ripple through Genie. Instead of the warmth she expected to find, the cold disdain of the duchess's haughty regard recalled their last meeting all too vividly. Nonplussed by the aloofness of her manner, Genie soberly awaited the duchess's address as Mrs. Prescott welcomed her into the room, made the proper introductions and offered the obligatory remarks about the frightful weather.

A seat affording the best view of the garden was offered and accepted, though the duchess seemed to perch on the very edge of the chair, indicating her intention of not becoming too comfortable. In fact, no one was comfortable. The air of excitement that had once permeated the room had dissolved with her arrival. Thankfully, the timely arrival of refreshments temporarily lifted the blanket of tension.

The duchess spoke to her mother about the status of improvements to Donnington Park and politely asked Lizzie about her growing friendship with Fanny.

Pleasantries exchanged, finally, the duchess fastened her gaze on Genie, though speaking to her mother. "I should like a few words with your daughter, Miss Eugenia Prescott." *Alone* was the unspoken command.

One did not argue with a duchess, no matter how rudely requested. Genie's normally unflappable mother appeared utterly discombobulated. She tossed Genie an anxious look before quickly bustling out of the room, sweeping Lizzie along in her wake.

Seated in a small chair opposite the duchess, hands folded in her lap, Genie kept her eyes demurely downcast in proper deference to a woman of such superior rank.

"So what have you to say for yourself, Miss Prescott?"

Genie knew right then. A stab of despair knifed through her chest. The duchess's tone said it all. Her words were uttered with such naked contempt that Genie could no longer deny what she'd intuited from the moment the duchess glided into the room. Genie had been wrong about the reason for the duchess's visit; the duchess did not approve of a match between her and Hastings. In fact, from the look of abhorrence on her face, her disapproval could not be clearer. Hope fell in a puddle at Genie's feet. A dull sense of doom spread over her. In the space of a few minutes her emotions had swung from utter euphoria to disappointment and despair.

Genie willed herself not to be intimidated, but the formidable duchess did not inspire confidence.

The duchess had not expected a reply. "I will not stand by and allow my son to be drawn in by the machinations of a silly girl with inferior connections and no fortune to speak of." Her lips pursed together into a grim line. "You have set your cap for the wrong man, my dear. You will find that I will not allow my son to ignore his duty and toss away his future on youthful fancy."

Despite her nervousness, Genie bristled. Before she could stop herself she remarked, "Surely your son is a man full grown, capable of making his own decisions?" The duchess's eyes narrowed. Genie bit back her tongue, realizing that a pert reply was not the best way to impress the duchess. Fighting to maintain her composure, she continued more politely. "I'm sorry, Your Grace, to speak so plainly, but I cannot allow you to suffer under the false impression that I have in any way sought to 'draw in' or manipulate your son. Indeed, by all accounts it is your son who has hotly pursued me."

The duchess gasped, her eyes burned with indignation. She was not often contradicted, especially by a girl of just eighteen.

"So there is an understanding between you?"

Genie's cheeks pinkened. She had thought there was, but

now... "I didn't say that," she hedged.

A scornful sneer spread across the duchess's face, her first betrayal of emotion. Clearly, she smelled blood. If there was a formal agreement, Genie would have been quick to say so.

"So, my son is not a complete fool."

Genie lifted her chin, meeting her gaze, refusing to be cowed. "I love your son, Your Grace. And he loves me."

The grin slid from the duchess's face, her face darkened in anger. Hard, beetle-like eyes peered at Genie. "Romantic drivel. You obviously read too many novels, Miss Prescott. Love or not, you reach too far. The son of a duke and the daughter of a rector." She grimaced. "It is unthinkable." Her gaze intensified, Genie forced herself not to cringe under the duchess's calculating stare. "Are you with child?"

Genie reared back. "No!" she exclaimed vehemently, but her cheeks burned hot. Obviously, the duchess knew that they had made love. Genie swallowed, a lump of shame stuck in her throat.

Pleased, the duchess nodded. "Good. That would be an unfortunate complication." Seeing Genie's shock she said sharply, "Don't be missish with me, girl. I was young once. My son is a handsome young man. It is not the first time such a thing has happened, though it is not like Hastings. But just because you are foolish enough to succumb to the first man who courts you, don't think it means that he'll marry you."

A noose of dread slipped around Genie's throat and tightened. Her eyes burned with unshed tears. This couldn't be happening. She had to do something. "He *wants* to marry me, Your Grace, in that Hastings has been very clear. Is a gentleman's honor limited only to his word, but not in his intention so plainly given?"

"And where is the honor in your conduct, Miss Prescott?"

Genie flinched. There was none.

"Are you so sure of his intentions?" the duchess continued. "Hastings is young, just two and twenty and hardly seems ready to settle down with a wife."

Stop! Genie wanted to scream. She didn't want to hear anymore. But hadn't she had the same thoughts herself? One of the qualities she most admired in Hastings was his irresistible carefree, devil-may-care attitude. Paradoxically, it was the very trait that instilled doubt.

The duchess had had enough. She studied Genie coolly, a shrewd half smile played about her mouth, filling Genie with dread. The duchess was about to play her final card.

"Your parents enjoy a certain amount of respectability in Thornbury, do they not, Miss Prescott?"

Her breath caught sharply. *No, not that!* Stricken, Genie nodded.

"It would be unfortunate if a scandal were to cause your father to lose his patronage."

"No," Genie gasped. "You wouldn't—"

The duchess cut her off. "Never doubt what I would do to protect my family, Miss Prescott. The Marchioness of Buckingham and I are girlhood friends, one word whispered in her ear and I'm afraid... Well, I hope it does not come to that. I'm sure I can trust you to do the right thing for all involved."

"The right thing?" Genie echoed dumbly. If her father lost his patronage in a scandal, he would be ruined. The bile rose in the back of her throat. The walls closed in around her. Her eyes darted around, looking for an escape. But there was none. If she did not give up Hastings, the duchess would destroy her family. She knew it in her bones. Could the Prescotts weather the storm? Would Hastings stand by her even in defiance of his family? Or would he avoid confrontation again?

"I think it is best if you were to go on an extended holiday. A temporary separation will be the cure for what ails you."

"No separation will change my feelings. I won't give him up," Genie said defiantly.

The duchess laughed. It was not a pretty sound. "Hmm. But the question is: Will he give you up?"

Genie blanched. "What do you mean?"

"Time and distance have a way of making people see things differently. There is a ship bound for America that leaves Bristol on Monday next."

"America?" Genie exclaimed in shock. The duchess must be desperate to be rid of her—it was the other side of the world.

The duchess continued as if she hadn't interrupted. "I have made the necessary arrangements. I will have a coach waiting down the lane, just beyond the bend at midnight late Saturday night." Only five days, Genie thought. How could she leave in five days? "You will be provided with everything you need, the best cabin on the ship, plus two thousand pounds." Genie's eyes rounded. "A maid of course will join you."

Two thousand pounds! Dear heavens, it was a small fortune. "I can't just sail away to America." She'd never been out of Gloucestershire, for goodness' sake. But did she have a choice? "What would I tell my parents?"

The duchess gave a short, dismissive wave. "You shall tell them nothing, of course."

"I can't just leave."

"Write a note if you must. But say nothing of my involvement."

"Please," Genie begged. "Please. Don't force me to do this. There will be a scandal. I will be ruined."

"You are already ruined, you foolish girl. Do you wish your family to suffer for your stupidity?"

The pain in her gut was acute. Genie just wanted to bend over and curl up into a tiny ball. Where was Hastings when she needed him?

"Your brothers and sister will benefit, of course, by your good sense. I believe your brother Charles is looking for a living? There is a parsonage in Ashby-de-la-Zouch near Ashby Castle, our former ancestral seat destroyed by Cromwell. I will write at once. And as Fanny has taken to your sister, Elizabeth, perhaps she would join us in London for a season next year?"

Genie's dreams of happiness faded into nothingness. With such inducement, did she have any choice?

"How long?" she asked dully. It would take at least six weeks just to sail there—and that is if nothing went wrong. The journey would be long and uncomfortable at best, and miserable and dangerous at worst.

"A few months. We depart for town in the spring. You may return any time after that."

Cornered, Genie realized that she had to think of something. "If I agree to go, you will not object if Hastings offers for me when I return."

The duchess drew herself up to her full regal height. "You are in no position to issue conditions, Miss Eugenia Prescott."

Genie dug down deep and found a sliver of strength that she did not know she possessed. "I could stay and take my chances. My parents are well respected in Thornbury. There will be little scandal if Hastings and I marry. Are you sure that Hastings will not defy you?"

Genie held her breath.

The duchess's brows lifted. Genie had surprised her. Genie probably imagined it, but she thought a smidgen of respect glimmered in the duchess's eyes before she quickly dropped the blank, proud curtain back across her features. "I will never support such an unthinkable match. I will do all I can to dissuade him. However, if you do as I have instructed, I will not interfere by other means."

Genie nodded her agreement. The small concession was more than she expected.

The duchess rose, her business complete. "Saturday at midnight, Miss Prescott. Do not forget." And just like that she was gone, a plume of lavender and broken dreams in her wake.

Overwhelmed by what had just occurred, Genie sat there unmoving, unsure of what to do. America? Fleeing her family in disgrace? There had to be some way out of this horrible nightmare. Hastings couldn't know about the reason for his mother's visit. He did intend to marry her, she told herself. Their love would stand the test of time.

Genie had to see him. Together they would think of something.

She hadn't been wrong about his intentions.

THE NEXT FEW DAYS PASSED in almost unbearable agony. Hiding the reason for the duchess's visit from her family was hard enough, but explaining Hastings's absence from what had become a routine daily call was much more difficult. Explaining it to herself was impossible.

On Thursday morning, two days before the coach would arrive to take her to Bristol and three days after the duchess's visit, Genie could stand the wait no longer and took matters into her own hands. Though highly improper, she penned a short note to Hastings and had it delivered into his hands that same morning by the visiting Fanny.

My lord, Desperate circumstances have forced me to take the extraordinary action of contacting you. If there exists an attachment between us, I beg that you attend me in all due haste. Only by your immediate attendance can I trust in the ardency of your affection. Please, my lord, I need you. Do not fail me.

Yours, Eugenia

Through the omnipresent gray sheet of rain, Genie stared from her bedroom window for hours, eyes glued to the lane searching for his familiar bay. For two long days, she waited in vain for a prince who did not come.

GENIE PICKED A STRAND OF hair from her eyes, vowing not to dwell on those excruciating days of waiting any longer. She stood at the rail of the ship bound for America, her borrowed sullen maid at her side, watching the jagged coast of England fade into the distance. Her dreams fell away along with it.

Right up until her departure, she'd held out hope. She prayed there had been some terrible mistake. Hysterical laughter bubbled inside her. *Fool!* There had been no mistake. He hadn't come after her. There was only the letter.

She looked at the bit of parchment still clenched between her fingers. She hadn't wanted to accept the truth. But the truth could no longer be denied.

His response had arrived late Saturday afternoon. Not in the person of her prince, but of his sister. Her heart had leapt to see Fanny, hope flickering in her chest. He'd sent word! She knew he wouldn't let her down. She'd raced to the door, thrown it open, but the light of innocence within her was extinguished forever.

A bitter wind tore across the deck. She looked at the scrap of parchment in her hand one more time, but she didn't need to read it—the words were etched forever in her heart. Slowly opening her fingers, Genie allowed the offending letter to be carried away by the powerful damp gust. The parchment floated higher for a moment, before plummeting into the white foam of the sea, at last swallowing the damning words that had been his only reply:

Miss Prescott, I was most surprised to receive your correspondence. I regret that I am unable to do as you've requested. If you have misconstrued my intentions, I sincerely implore your forgiveness.
                              Lord Fitzwilliam Hastings

Had he used a sword, he could not have cut her any deeper than this formal, impersonal response from the man who'd known her so intimately. From the man who was the other half of her soul. She'd begged him to come to her and he'd responded as if he didn't know her.

Nothing could have prepared her for his betrayal. The despair she'd experienced from the duchess's outrageous demand paled in significance to the heartbreak of Hastings's defection. He didn't love her. He'd failed to honor his promise of marriage, and left her alone to face ruin. His betrayal had cleaved her in two, taking her innocence forever.

How could she have been so wrong?

Like a thief in the night, she'd snuck from her chamber that very night to meet the carriage, leaving a note to her parents that could never explain, but which she hoped would soften the blow. There would be no engagement, she explained. She couldn't bear to stay in Gloucestershire; she would return when the Hastings family left for town. Try not to worry. She went to visit a school friend. Make whatever excuses they deem necessary to avoid a scandal. She regretted the pain that her sudden departure might cause.

"Miss Prescott?"

Genie turned to find the porter standing beside her. She hadn't missed the disdain in his tone. Even with a maid, an unmarried young woman traveling alone was highly suspect. She glanced down at her dark gray woolen traveling gown. An opportune solution popped into her mind. She thought for a moment then made a decision—eager to disappear for a while.

Maybe then she could forget.

"No. There must have been a mistake. My name is Mrs. Preston. I am a widow."

CHAPTER SIX

Carlton House, June 19, 1811

IT WAS SO LONG AGO, a lifetime really. Yet here he was, five years later, staring at her as if they'd never parted. He even had the gall to break out into that charming crooked grin she so remembered. His clearly elated reaction gave her a momentary jolt. Why did he look so happy to see her?

If she were that hopelessly romantic country girl again, she would say that he was staring at her as if he'd spent every day since the moment she left searching for her. As if he had never written her the hateful note that cruelly rejected every precious moment they'd spent together.

But Genie wasn't that innocent young girl anymore. The heartbreak she'd experienced on the ship had been nothing compared to what had come after.

She shook off the memories and met his grin with a cool, haughty glare of disinterest. Some things were better left in the past.

Lord Fitzwilliam Hastings was one of them.

Genie had a future now. Edmund offered her everything she'd dreamed of with Hastings. This time, she would do whatever was necessary to protect her engagement.

A hand cupped her elbow. On cue, conjured from her very thoughts, Genie turned to find Edmund at her side.

His eyes locked on her, intently studying her face. "Are you well, my love? You look like you've seen a ghost."

❧

Transfixed, the man blinked repeatedly, not trusting the vision before him. But she wasn't a ghost or a figment of his wishful imagination. She was hauntingly real.

Dear God, Genie. After years of fruitless searching, he couldn't have been more shocked to find her here than if she'd walked up the stairs of Huntingdon House and casually knocked on the door.

And he'd nearly passed right by her. He'd been in a rush, knowing Prinny would be furious that he'd missed most of the big celebration, but he'd been unavoidably detained, called away at the last minute for an emergency at the bequest of a friend, who was currently out of the country on his behalf. He'd arrived at Carlton House in time to at least make an appearance, albeit a short one. At the last moment he happened to glance up. He'd frozen, rigid with shock.

Genie. It had to be her. He'd only seen eyes like that on one person. They were unforgettable. Big and round, framed by long dark lashes, set deep in her tiny heart-shaped face. They screamed out innocence and vulnerability. But it was the extraordinary color that truly startled: a flawless cobalt blue.

Everything else about her had changed. Gone were the soft, well-rounded curves of girlhood. The elegant woman before him was strikingly thin, her generous bosom and gently curved hips the only softness in an otherwise willowy figure.

She'd been a beautiful girl, the quintessential English boy's fantasy of a sweet country dairymaid with her lush curves, flaxen hair, milky skin, high pink blush and bowed red lips. She'd exuded sweetness and vulnerability. He'd fallen half in love with her the first time he'd seen her. He hadn't been the only one, he remembered with a sharp stab of jealousy. He'd been forced to move quickly to stake his claim. Too quickly.

If she was beautiful then, she was exquisite now. No longer the sweet country dairymaid, rather she reminded him of a fragile porcelain doll. So delicately beautiful she could almost break. Her flaxen hair had darkened to a shimmering honey blond. Those incomparable cobalt eyes still seemed hauntingly overlarge in her tiny heart-shaped face. The high pink bloom of her cheeks had faded to a soft, dusty rose; her milky soft skin so fair it seemed translucent. Her mouth, no longer curved in a perpetual girlish smile, looked harder, but promised untold sensual delights. The woman exuded a sensuality that was so distinctly at odds with the sweet innocent girl that he remembered.

Of course, he'd taken that sweet innocence and trampled where he should have treasured.

Seeing Genie again brought back all the memories—and all the guilt.

The dull ache in his chest, a constant companion for the last five years, sharpened. Not a day passed that he did not blame himself for what had happened. That he did not regret what he'd done to her. In many ways, the mistakes he'd made with Genie had been the defining moment of his manhood. His failure, his conduct, in Thornbury had haunted him ever since.

He wished he could blame his actions on the idiocy of youth. But there was more to it than that. Meeting Genie when he had had been a test in character that he failed. Miserably.

As the second son, he'd largely sauntered through life without any real responsibility. He played the "fun one," the "charming one," to his brother's stern fortress of duty and responsibility. Only twenty-two and fresh out of Oxford, he hadn't been prepared to fall in love, defy his family, and take a wife.

He hadn't intended to make love to her.

But with Genie his intentions and actions rarely meshed.

He still cringed when he recalled his ungentlemanly conduct. She'd been so soft and lush like a juicy, ripe summer peach just begging to be devoured. He'd had to taste her. It only took one kiss for him to lose control. He'd needed to possess her, with a gut-wrenching intensity that had never been replicated. To persuade her, he would have promised her the world. Instead he'd seduced her with an unspoken promise of marriage. It didn't matter that he'd meant it. He'd asked her to trust him and he'd let her down.

He'd been so damned weak. He'd had every intention of marriage, but he'd allowed himself to be persuaded by the prejudice of his parents and the jealously of his brother. "You are young, you lack proper comparison," they'd said. "She's taking advantage of you, don't be a fool." Their universal condemnation of the match as both unsuitable and foolhardy worked on his youthful insecurities.

Trapped between duty and desire when Genie pushed him to declare himself, unknowingly she'd exacerbated his guilt and resentment. Building to the point that when the letter arrived, he'd lashed out in anger like a cornered dog. He whipped off a terse reply to her heartfelt entreaty, never considering the ramifications of his actions. He'd just wanted the problem to go away.

For a little while.

When he discovered that Genie had fled, initially he felt relieved. He didn't realize then that a part of him had departed with her. Within days he knew he'd made a mistake.

It took far longer to realize how much of one.

Though he might not have intended to, he'd acted the cad. He offered no excuse for his conduct. The fault was his. But he was no longer the unreliable, carefree young man. Circumstances had forced him to change.

And now that he'd found her, he'd have the chance to atone for his sins. Finally, he could begin to chip away at the block of guilt and regret that had been strapped across his shoulders since she'd left.

He started toward her, a broad, benevolent smile on his face.

Before he could reach her, a man moved protectively to her side, halting him dead in his tracks. There was something possessive about the movement that made his blood run cold.

But only for a minute. When he realized who stood before him, he nearly sighed with relief. Pushing aside the moment of unease, he chuckled at his foolishness. It was only Hawk. His best friend. The very man he'd sent to find her.

Strange that Hawk hadn't notified him of his return. No matter. He owed Hawk a debt that he could never repay. How could he ever thank him? For Hawk had traveled half the world to find the girl who'd haunted his memories. The girl he could never forget.

GENIE GAZED FONDLY AT EDMUND. He'd said that she looked as though she'd seen a ghost. One corner of her mouth lifted with the barest hint of amusement. His heartfelt concern warmed the dank chill in her heart. She'd exchanged a frog for a true knight. "In a way, I suppose I have," she said wryly.

Edmund followed the direction of her gaze and flinched, immediately dropping her arm. The blood rushed from his face. No doubt from her reaction, he realized who the man must be.

But there was something else. Something was very wrong. Edmund was staring at Hastings and he couldn't look away. He looked guilty—almost ashamed. "Edmund?" She clutched his arm, shaking him. She hesitated. "Do you know him?" Genuine fear laced her voice.

"Edmund?" Hastings repeated incredulously. Her use of Edmund's given name rather than his title had alerted him to the intimacy between them. Among peers, given names were rarely used—usually by siblings. Perhaps it wasn't surprising that Genie had never called Hastings "Fitzwilliam." The divide had always been there between them, even if she hadn't recognized it.

She ignored Hastings and turned to Edmund. Her question seemed to have snapped him out of his trance. His gaze drifted down to her, anxiety etched across his handsome features. "We've been friends for years. We were at Eton and Oxford together."

"You never told her?" Hastings demanded.

"Told me what?" Genie's brow creased with worry. She braced herself, instinctively knowing that she would not like his answer. But Edmund ignored her and turned back to Hastings.

He bowed. "Now is not the time to discuss this, Your Grace."

Bewildered, Genie rounded on Edmund. "Your Grace?" she echoed dumbfounded.

Edmund hesitated. "Mrs. Preston, may I present the 12th Duke of Huntingdon."

"But..." Her voice trailed off with disbelief.

His voice replied. "A carriage accident three years ago. Both my father and Henry." The husky honey-filled voice that sent chills down her spine had deepened to a sinful dark molten chocolate. The memories of his voice sent a feathery twinge across her heartstrings. The haunting voice of her past stirred up the buried memories. At one time she'd have given her life to hear that voice again.

"I'm sorry," she offered unthinkingly. Loudoun dead? It was unthinkable, all that youthful vitality snuffed out.

He acknowledged her condolence with a shrug. "It was a horrible shock to us all. My mother most of all; she is quite changed. She has quite forsaken town society and resides permanently in the country now."

The mere mention of his mother acted like a bucket of icy water, dousing all thoughts of sympathy. She schooled her features into the blank emotionless wall that tragedy had painstakingly perfected.

He was a duke. How horribly ironic after all his mother had done to prevent an unsuitable match when he was only the second son. What would the duchess be willing to do now? Genie thought with a bitter laugh. Ship her off to the Orient? She was almost tempted to find out. For years, all she had thought about was revenge. Revenge had protected her, giving her a purpose to survive, when nothing else did.

But then she'd met Edmund and forced it aside.

Coming face-to-face with the man who had stolen her virtue had awakened it again.

But even if Genie had harbored some inkling of making him regret what he'd done, Huntingdon—nee Hastings—was even farther beyond her reach. And there was no reason to think that he'd have any more interest in her today than he had five years ago.

No, revenge no longer consumed her. Not now that she'd found Edmund. Instinctively, she drew closer to his side. Edmund wrapped her carefully under his arm, shielding her. She lifted her face to his and smiled. Edmund would give her the security that she craved and she, in turn, would give him what he craved. What all men craved. Men wanted a woman like her for one reason only. She'd learned the harsh truth of that many times over. Dear Hastings had been her first instructor. It was a fair bargain, she told herself, assuaging any guilt.

Hastings—no, she corrected herself—Huntingdon had watched Genie's instinctive, intimate movement toward Edmund with disbelief. He turned to Edmund, looking for an answer and apparently found one.

One that was completely unexpected.

Huntingdon looked as if he'd been struck, as if he couldn't believe what he was seeing. The joyful, welcoming smile disappeared, replaced by one of horror. He had the look of a man whose best friend had just plunged a knife into his gut and twisted it.

And Edmund looked like a man who'd wielded the traitorous blade.

Genie's blood ran cold. Something was very wrong. This whole situation was making her extremely uneasy. She lifted her hand to cradle Edmund's bloodless face. "Edmund, we should leave."

But rather than defuse the situation, her thoughtless gesture only seemed to make things worse. Huntingdon seemed to snap. His jaw hardened, his eyes blazed with barely contained fury. Edmund straightened his back, squared his shoulders and met the duke's rage straight on. A silent battle was being waged that Genie didn't understand. Genie couldn't fathom what would cause Huntingdon to be so angry, except that it was not directed at her but at Edmund.

"Strange that I did not hear of your return," he sneered caustically at Edmund. When Edmund didn't reply he turned to Genie. "And how do you know Hawk?" His voice had turned dark and dangerous.

It took Genie a moment to realize that he referred to Edmund. Sensing her confusion, Edmund explained, "My friends call me Hawk." Huntingdon snarled his disavowal. The two men were no longer friends. Edmund stepped forward, shielding her from the duke as if he knew the reaction his words would effect. He took a deep breath, seeking strength. "Although it has not yet been announced, Mrs. Preston has agreed to be my wife."

Huntingdon froze at the unexpected announcement. He gazed at Edmund as if seeing him for the first time. It seemed to take him a minute to understand. But when he did, the words only inflamed his already burgeoning anger. Now almost murderous with rage, his muscles bulged; his entire body seemed to shake with the effort it took to restrain himself.

Genie read the raw clash of emotions that crossed his face—hurt, anger, betrayal... and rage. It was rage that won out. He flew at Edmund, his cape a black wing behind him. "You bloody bastard. How could you do this? I trusted you."

HUNTINGDON'S FIST SLAMMED TOWARD HAWK'S jaw. He had never wanted to kill someone as much as he did at this moment. To finally find the woman he'd been searching for, only to discover that the man he'd sent to find her had betrayed him. And the betrayal was made all the more crushing because it was delivered by the man he'd considered his closest friend. Tonight, he'd been sent on a fool's errand by this very "friend." Now he knew why.

At the last minute Hawk ducked, avoiding the blow. Hawk caught Huntingdon's arm midair, holding him back.

"Not now, Huntingdon," he cautioned through clenched teeth. "I promise you, we'll deal with this later. In private," Hawk added meaningfully.

Huntingdon looked around, realizing a small crowd had gathered along the walkway. A duke brawling with an earl at Carlton House was sensational enough to entice even the most cynical of the ton to gawk. Hawk was right, this was not the place. As it was, the rumor mongering ton would be atwitter for days.

He lowered his arm, but did not stand down.

Genie glared at him, disgusted, as if she didn't know him. Obviously, she blamed him for what she thought was an unprovoked attack. If only she knew.

But she didn't, he guessed. He'd seen Hawk's face. He'd seen the guilt. And fear. Emotions he'd never before seen on Hawk's face.

With effort, Huntingdon collected himself and backed off Hawk. But the heat of battle still pounded through his veins. "I'll expect you at noon." He lowered his voice, "Consider yourself fortunate, Hawkesbury. Only the present rather public nature of our circumstances prevents me from calling you out right now."

Genie did not miss the implied threat. He might not be so lucky tomorrow. "You have no right," she whispered angrily.

"Don't I?" he sneered, looking at Hawk. "Would you care to explain to her what *right* I have, Hawk?"

Face grim with understanding, Hawk turned to Genie. "Don't worry, love, I'll take care of this," he soothed. Face tense he glanced at Huntingdon. "Tomorrow then," Hawk agreed, dismissing him and immediately turning his overly solicitous attentions back to Genie.

Again, Huntingdon's gaze seized on that once beloved face, no longer familiar but even more beautiful—achingly so. In profound disbelief he watched Hawk's thumb trace the curve of her cheek.

Something primal in him revolted at the thought of anyone touching her but him. Time, he realized, had not softened his possessive streak. Had he once been privileged to stroke that porcelain skin? If he closed his eyes, he could almost remember how it felt to hold her in his arms and slide deep into her body. Did she still gasp and utter those sweet little moans of pleasure as she fell apart? He tried to picture her face as she gazed at him adoringly, full of love, the pink blush of her orgasm spread across her cheeks, her mouth bruised from his kiss. But the details were frustratingly fuzzy.

It was so long ago.

But not long enough to forget the powerful surge of desire that had made him rock hard whenever she was near. Time might have blurred the details, but his body remembered.

After all these years he still wanted her. For himself. Alone.

Holding himself back, watching Hawk's intimate ministrations was nearly unbearable—made worse by the bitter betrayal of the man touching her. The same strange urge to possess that had lain dormant for five years, now awakened, had not diminished in intensity. Despite the inappropriate venue, Huntingdon had to force himself not to attack Hawk again. Watching him put his hands on her was bloody torture, when he'd dreamed of nothing else for the past five years.

She on the other hand seemed to have forgotten Huntingdon existed. Once he'd been able to read her every emotion simply by watching the sparkle in her lively eyes or the naughty twitch at the corner of her mouth. No longer. The cool, self-possessed young woman standing before him guarded her thoughts well.

He searched for a connection, an indication that she remembered, but her face betrayed nothing. It was as if they were strangers and she'd obliterated him from her memory.

He pushed away the empty feeling in his chest. Guilt, he told himself. It was no more than he deserved.

He turned away from the intimate scene playing out before him. He could not watch any longer.

She moved and her gown shimmered in the moonlight. Now that the shock of seeing her after all these years had finally dissipated, the bitter irony of the situation did not escape him. For years he'd tortured himself with a hair shirt of guilt, while Genie had moved on and—if her elaborate and expensive gown was any indication—done quite well for herself.

Genie Prescott, the country rector's daughter had certainly come up in the world. Her fiancé was one of the wealthiest men in England. Wealthier even than him.

A fist of rage socked him in the gut when the second realization hit him. Hawk had introduced her as Mrs. Preston.

She'd married.

It was nearly inconceivable.

Though she must be widowed, why did the knowledge that she'd found someone to do what he would not feel like such a betrayal? What had he expected? That she would share the torch that he carried?

And now she was engaged to his best friend. Double betrayal.

The thought of Hawk and Genie together, the realization that she'd been married before, caused Huntingdon to turn some of his burgeoning wrath toward her.

The crowd, sensing that there would be no further spectacle, began to disperse. When it looked as if Genie meant to follow them, Huntingdon stopped her. "I shall look forward to renewing our old acquaintance," he mocked suggestively. Her back stiffened; she had not missed the sexual innuendo. He continued, unable to stop himself. "I'm eager to hear what you have been doing in the intervening years since last we met. You've obviously done well for yourself, *Mrs. Preston.*" He held his expression impassive, but he could not completely hide the biting sarcasm of his words.

She flinched. For a moment, he thought he saw a shadow of pain cross over her before the cool emotionless curtain dropped back into position. She lifted her chin and met his mocking tone. "As have you, *Your Grace*."

He couldn't conceal his rabid curiosity. "And what of *Mr*. Preston?"

The small smile she gave him did not reach her eyes. "A soldier, Your Grace. He fell at Vimeiro, not two years after we married," she parried, wielding her sword with pinpoint finesse, pinning his heart with the tip of her blade.

"My condolences," he murmured as the air squeezed from his lungs. The Battle of Vimeiro was in August of '08, meaning that she must have met and married her soldier soon after she'd fled Thornbury in November. Perhaps on the very ship that had carried her away from him. He fought to breathe normally. Clearly, she'd spared little time "getting over" him. Huntingdon held his expression even, but the load of guilt he'd been carrying for so many years combusted in his chest.

Their eyes met and held one last time. Hostility sparked between them like a vicious lightning storm. He was in no danger of romanticizing their past now. The past was gone. He didn't even have the memories to cherish any longer.

This time when she and Hawkesbury moved away, he let them go.

GENIE HELD HER BREATH AS Edmund steered her away from the duke. If she'd been forced to stand there one minute longer, biting back all the accusations she yearned to fling at him, she would have been in danger of screeching like a madwoman. That would certainly make a lasting impression on the ton.

Fortunately, Genie recalled what was at stake and maintained her façade of disinterest, an impressive enough performance to convince even the most curious that she was not a part of the disagreement between the two esteemed peers. Nothing would interfere with her debut, she vowed. Not even the blasted 12th Duke of Huntingdon.

Despite her forbearance in curtailing her temper, inwardly Genie seethed with indignation. How dare he assault Edmund then direct his venom toward her! Blaming her for his failures. Though his face retained its granitelike composure, she could not miss the brittle sarcasm of his conversation. He thought she'd benefited from her forced exile. She wanted to laugh at the irony. If he only knew how wrong he was.

He'd made her so angry, Genie had been unable to resist taunting him with her supposed hasty marriage. His self-righteous attitude had egged her on. The new Duke of Huntingdon was the same arrogant man she remembered, without the good humor. The irrepressible charm that had drawn her to him had turned stern and malignant.

She glanced up at Edmund, his mouth pressed into a thin line. Loss of good humor seemed to be a common affliction this night. Edmund had never looked so grave.

"What was that all about?" she asked Edmund as soon as they cleared the crowd.

"Unresolved issues."

"I gathered as much," she said wryly. "Will you not tell me the reason that you and Huntingdon nearly came to blows?"

Edmund met her gaze. Worry casted his handsome face in a gray, sickly light. "I fear what I have to tell you may change your good opinion of me."

"Nothing you do could alter my esteem and love for you," she said earnestly. "After all, you have restored my faith in honorable men."

Rather than console him, her praise only served to heighten his discomfort. "That is a heavy mantle for any man to bear. I fear I may disappoint you."

"Never," Genie said with conviction. "I could never forget everything you have done for me."

"I don't want your gratitude," he said angrily.

"But you shall always have it." She put her hand on his. "Though that is not why I love you. You are a good man, Edmund St. George. The best. Any woman would be a fool not to love you. And I am no fool. Whatever it is you have done, you can tell me."

Edmund raked his fingers through his hair, weighing his words with obvious precision. "I should have told you sooner. I meant to," he mumbled distractedly. Looking around he said, "Tomorrow I will explain everything. This is not the place for private conversation."

"Very well. It all sounds so tantalizingly mysterious. But I will not press... until tomorrow." She had her own problems with which to attend.

When Prinny finally departed, the Countess of Hawkesbury was found and the small party quit the waning delights of the magnificent fete to call for the earl's carriage. With so many guests having reached a similar conclusion, the wait again proved interminable.

Conversation lulled to a welcome halt. The evening had proved an exhausting one for all, each for very different reasons. Content with her own thoughts for company, Genie welcomed the opportunity to consider all that had occurred.

All in all, the evening had been a success. The ton had embraced her, she had secured the coveted invitation to Almack's, and she had acquitted herself well in the face of potential disaster.

She had almost lost control but had managed to hold her tongue. Though Huntingdon's appearance at the fete was not unexpected, Genie clearly had not been as prepared as she thought to see him. But now it was behind her.

His joy at seeing her had disarmed her. As had his sudden anger first directed at Edmund then at her. One thing was certain, his behavior could hardly be termed "indifferent" as she had hoped. But what significance did that have for her plans with Edmund? Would he interfere?

His odd reaction still niggled at her. Why had he seemed so happy to see her? Perhaps he regretted his harsh treatment of her all those years ago?

Did it matter?

No. She realized that it didn't. All the regret in the world could not return what she had lost. His feelings were immaterial. She was relieved to discover that she no longer cared. All she wanted now was to protect her future, and for that she needed a plan to secure his cooperation.

She had to find out whether the duke would maintain discretion regarding their prior connection. There was no reason to suspect that he would have any interest in rehashing the past, but she had to make sure that he did not hint at what had transpired between them. Surely people in Thornbury must have speculated about the reasons for her swift departure, but she had no idea of how far afield those suspicions might have traveled. In any event she did not want to be connected with Huntingdon. It might provoke more questions about her past than she had answers for.

Her thin veil of respectability had to be protected at all costs. She knew the knife's edge upon which she walked.

That the duchess resided in the country was admittedly a welcome boon. Would that all her problems proved as simple. Fanny and Lizzie, for example, might both be in town. How she longed to see her sister. She'd made a few discreet inquiries, but without explaining the connection, obtaining information on Lizzie proved difficult.

But her primary concern was the duke.

The young man she'd fallen in love with had changed, and not just in rank and appearance. No, the change was more elemental; his character had changed. The youth that had been quick with a smile and a jest, had transformed into a hard man, quick to temper. A man who no longer shied from confrontation. More important, Genie sensed that he might not be so easy to persuade as she had anticipated. She'd assumed he would be eager to forget the shame of what he'd done. But he didn't seem embarrassed or ashamed at all.

No matter, Genie had also changed and she was well prepared for whatever challenge he could muster.

Confined once again within the silken walls of the

carriage, Genie relaxed. All the excitement and nervous energy that had accompanied her on her arrival had fled along with the oppressive heat. She closed her eyes, allowing the gentle sway of the carriage to ease the storm of worries in her mind.

The night that began with a bang of promise, then fizzled to an abrupt end with the slow break of dawn. Though she had achieved her objective this night—her debut into society had been a resounding success—Genie couldn't help but feel that her appearance at the prince's fete had opened a Pandora's box.

CHAPTER SEVEN

THE DUKE OF HUNTINGDON HUNCHED over his desk and swirled the viscous amber liquid in the cut crystal glass before draining the contents in one deep gulp. Another followed. And another. Soon he lost count. The sun had risen hours ago, at last putting an end to a night that he wanted to forget. Closeted in his private study, heavy velvet curtains closed to block the offending light, the memories of all that had transpired stuck. Not even inebriation could dull the lingering emotion still smoldering in his chest, kindled by disappointment and betrayal.

Sweet, innocent Genie had betrayed him as surely as Hawk. That it was undoubtedly deserved did not lessen the pain. Nor make him feel less of a fool.

He'd romanticized a youthful liaison, relegating it to such enormous proportions, he was bound to be disappointed by reality. He just never expected the truth to be so painful. Had he honestly meant that little to her?

After so many years shouldering the blame for the disastrous end to their affair, it felt strangely traitorous to contemplate ulterior motives on her behalf. Could she have had a different purpose all along? Could she have entered into a love affair with him knowing that his family would buy her off rather than see him marry so far beneath them? He couldn't believe it of her. It didn't fit with his memory of the sweet, naïve country girl.

But it did seem more in line with the cool beauty who stood on the walkway of Carlton House and acted as if she

.

barely knew him.

At least he had one answer. Genie's sudden marriage explained why she hadn't returned to England. Why she hadn't come back to fight for him as she'd vowed to his mother.

What a damned idiot he'd been. He was embarrassed for all the times that he'd thought about her over the past five years, for the pedestal on which he'd placed her, for the comparisons to other women who had always fallen impossibly short of her perfection.

He'd spent the years since they'd parted chasing after something that had never been. The way he'd agonized after she'd left, the years of searching all seemed laughable now.

Five years ago he'd loved her with all the unfettered passion of youth. The intensity of his feelings had terrified him. It was too strong, too fast. Too much. And he'd been too inexperienced to realize that he had stumbled onto something worth fighting for.

As intensely as he'd loved, he suffered doubly when she left. He'd tortured himself for months trying to find her, but she'd disappeared without a trace.

He took a deep breath, clearing the painful memories. That was a long time ago. Thankfully, he'd put those dangerous feelings behind him. He would never give himself up to a love like that again; it was far too destructive. The guilt, the suffering, the frustration of not being able to find her, was something he never cared to repeat.

Unfortunately, her quick marriage did not erase the fact that he'd acted dishonorably; Huntingdon could not be absolved that easily. But the insatiable drive to redeem himself no longer burned quite so intensely. He'd lived with guilt for so long, he acknowledged that the burden might prove difficult to relinquish.

He'd always felt that something terrible had happened to Genie in America that prevented her from returning to her family, if not to him. What else would explain her silence all these years? He'd made it his personal crusade to find her, to convince himself that she was unharmed. And because he never seriously contemplated marriage, it had never occurred to him that she would.

Fool.

The door opened and the Earl of Hawkesbury strode in unaccompanied. Apparently Huntingdon had neglected to instruct Grimes that his former best friend should now be announced like any other stranger.

Hawk took one look at him and said, "You look like hell. Haven't you slept?"

Huntingdon glared at him with bloodshot eyes, taking in Hawk's equally bedraggled appearance. He, too, still wore his evening clothes. The rage he'd felt last night at Hawk had diminished. Though he was not as drunk as he'd like to be for this conversation, his temper had cooled. He wanted answers. "Have you?" he returned.

Hawk's mouth curved into something that vaguely resembled a smile. He bowed and tipped his hat as if to say touché.

Though the duke had not given him leave, Hawk sank down in a chair opposite him. He reached across the desk and helped himself to a generous pour of Huntingdon's best brandy.

They stared at each other, both unsure how to approach the insurmountable barrier erected between them. A lifetime of friendship desecrated by one unforgivable act.

Huntingdon tapped the empty glass in his hand with his fingertips, the dull clink resonating in the silence. Finally, he spoke. "Does she know?" His voice sounded sluggish, rough from drink and lack of sleep.

"Know that you sent me to America to find her?"

Huntingdon nodded.

"No," Hawk said tightly. "Though she will later today."

Huntingdon raised a brow. "No excuses?"

Hawk sighed wearily. "Would it make a difference?"

"It might. I should like to think that my oldest friend did not set out to betray me."

"I didn't." Hawk stopped, searching for the right words.

"There are things I can't discuss, but I can tell you that I did not know who she was when I found her. She is much changed from your description..." He looked to Huntingdon for confirmation.

"Yes, she is," Huntingdon acknowledged reluctantly. "I barely recognized her."

Hawk nodded and continued. "When I first met her she was going by the name of Mrs. Ginny Preston. She only revealed who she was a month ago, by then it was too late. I was already in love with her. She trusted me. I couldn't risk losing her."

Huntingdon gritted his teeth. The litany of accusations he'd been holding back shot forth. "Your losing her? You of all people know what I have gone through to find her. How I searched for her that first year without any trail to be found. How I drowned my shame and disappointment in drink and women. You were there. You pulled me out of the gutter. You know how much I have blamed myself for her being forced to leave her home, how much I've wanted to rectify my conduct. How relieved I was when my mother finally broke her silence and gave me a place to search. It was you who offered to go in my stead when Prinny wouldn't allow me to leave England last year and I was about to commit treason and go anyway, throwing my political aspirations to the wind." He stood up, yanked the curtain open to gaze out the window, turning his back to Hawk. His voice shook. "How could you?"

"If you knew the circumstances..." Hawk began then stopped himself. "I know it seems insufficient, but there are reasons. And as I said, they are not mine to divulge. Suffice it to say that she is not the same girl you remember. I believed then, as I do now, that she was irretrievably lost to you."

Some of the duke's rage returned. "How dare you presume to judge. You are in no position—"

"I know," Edmund agreed pitifully.

"And last night? Was the 'emergency' that took me to your estate in Surrey part of your plan?"

Edmund shrugged abashedly. "I admit to desperation, though there was nothing so formal as a plan. Of course, I knew you would eventually discover the identity of my betrothed. I just hoped to formally announce our engagement beforehand. But Genie has proved more obstinate in that respect than I anticipated. She has an unreasonable desire not to see me hurt." He laughed without amusement at the irony. "She wants to ensure her acceptance by the ton."

Huntingdon understood. Genie feared that their former liaison might come to light and create a scandal. "There is little chance that our former connection would become known. Our families did a fair job of limiting speculation. It was a long time ago."

Hawk seemed pleased. "Then there is no impediment to our betrothal. Except for you." He paused, appearing to brace himself. "I ask that you stand down and not interfere."

Huntingdon crossed his arms and peered down his nose at Hawk. "Why should I do that?"

"Because she loves me and I will make her happy."

Huntingdon's eyes flared for a long moment. Reining in his anger, he chuckled dryly. "Are you so sure? The lady's love has proved rather inconstant. How do you think she will react when she finds out about your role in all of this?"

"I don't know." Hawk's voice sounded strained. "But it is my problem. You had your opportunity five years ago when you refused to do right by her and marry her. Why would you want her now when you don't make any pretense of loving her? You don't need to make the sacrifice to assuage your guilt; I will do it for you, happily. I hope you will not let pride get in the way of doing what is right."

"You are hardly in a position to lecture me on what is right, my dear Brutus." Huntingdon warned in a dangerous voice. But Hawk was right. Huntingdon didn't love her. The lovesick fool had drowned many years ago in drink, gaming hells, and between the loose thighs of too many women. But he still wanted her. Maybe if only to erase the importance of their interlude in his mind.

"Will you stand down?" Hawk repeated.

Huntingdon sank down in his chair and stretched his legs out lazily before him, the whole time intently studying his former friend. Only someone who had known him for as long would realize that Hawk was nervous. Very nervous.

Good. "Afraid of a little competition, my boy?"

Hawk's jaw twitched at his patronizing tone. "Hardly. Genie despises you."

Huntingdon ran his finger around the rim of his glass as if deliberating, but really only toying with the impatient Hawk. Huntingdon had already decided what he was going to do. A slow, lazy smile curled his lips. "I'm told there is a very thin line between love and hate."

GENIE COULDN'T SWALLOW, A BALL of hot tears lodged in her throat. Her eyes burned. But she would not cry; not over yet another man who disappointed her.

"Why didn't you tell me?" she asked softly, her words conspicuously strangled.

And why did it matter as much as it did? Because she had let him in and he had lied to her. A lie of omission, but a lie nonetheless. And Edmund knew how significant even the most insignificant of lies was to her.

She'd thought him different. She'd *trusted* him as much as she'd thought to trust anyone again. But he, too, had lied to get what he wanted: her. Even dressed in shining armor he was still a man.

Edmund had arrived at Hawkesbury House on Berkeley Square hard on the heels of the departure of their last morning caller. Genie was relieved to see him, knowing that he had come from Huntingdon House, and could barely hide her impatience to speak with him in private. Understanding, the countess discreetly bowed out of the elegant sitting room under the pretense of getting ready for the Duchess of Devonshire's "intimate" soirée for a hundred guests that they were to attend later that evening.

His dark, tousled hair still damp from bathing, Edmund appeared utterly exhausted. Weariness tugged around his eyes. He probably hadn't slept at all last night. Genie was afraid the duke might have made good on his threat of a challenge. Edmund promptly allayed her concerns on that matter, sat her down on a small silk upholstered settee, and without further ado blurted out his damning confession.

Genie took a deep breath, allowing the tears to abate. Eyes glassy but composed she turned back to face Edmund.

"You lied to me," she said, her voice hollow. How could she have let it happen again?

Her accusation drew blood. Strong, confident Edmund seemed strangely deflated as he tried to explain. "At first, I didn't realize who you were. You were so ill; my focus was only to make you well. Later, when you recovered and confided some of your history, I began to suspect that I had accidentally stumbled upon the very woman I'd been sent to discover. My suspicions were finally confirmed when you told me your real name." Exasperated with the feeble excuse, he tossed up his hands. "I don't know why I didn't tell you. I knew how you despised him. I suppose I was afraid."

"Afraid of what?" Genie scoffed. "You couldn't possibly believe that I would catch the next ship back to England at the snap of his fingers, merely because his guilty conscience had caught up with him. You couldn't have thought that. Not with everything you knew."

"You loved him," he said simply as if that fact explained everything. "And this was not a whim; he'd searched for you before."

She ignored this new tidbit of information, though it stopped her for a moment. Huntingdon's actions after she fled were irrelevant. "I loved a boy. A boy who failed me. You are a man, I expected honesty from you."

"I know it sounds ridiculous. I started to tell you so many times, but I could never quite get the words out. Perhaps I was reluctant to dull the shine of my armor. I loved the way you looked at me. But no man is perfect,

Genie. Certainly not me."

"I am well aware of that," she snapped.

"Are you? At times I wonder..." His eyes raked her face, looking for something. "I realized that it was a losing battle. You would eventually find out that Huntingdon was searching for you. I just wanted you safely beyond his reach before you did. He is not the same boy you knew, the man can be very determined."

"You should have trusted me. I have never been anything but honest with you, Edmund." Her voice broke to a whisper. "I've told you things I've never told another living soul."

The truth of her condemnation struck the fatal blow. He knew he had violated her trust and how much it meant to her. Stricken with shame and remorse, Edmund appeared on the verge of being ill.

"I did trust you. I just didn't trust myself. Or him," he muttered as an afterthought.

She stared at him blankly.

"I erred horribly. I should have told you the truth as soon as I suspected. Please tell me you can forgive me?"

Could she? Genie thought about it. It was her fault, really. She never should have let her defenses down. Did she have to be beaten over the head repeatedly for it to sink in? Men would say anything to get what they wanted. Even a man as wonderful and honorable as Edmund. He was all that, she realized. Perhaps that is why his lie hurt so much. She gave him herself, and in the end, her knight, like everyone else, had let her down.

She could forgive, but she would not forget.

"Of course, you are forgiven," she said firmly. "We will not speak of it again."

He took her hand and brought it to his mouth, relief bringing a joyous shine to his eyes.

Fundamentally, she realized, Edmund's lie did not change anything. She would still marry him. Now, however, she would not suffer under any delusions.

Perhaps she should thank him for allaying any guilt she

might have in using any artifice or feminine wiles to encourage his suit.

Genie hadn't forgotten the debt she owed him. No matter how he came to be there, Edmund had rescued her from hell. Edmund St. George, the 8th Earl of Hawkesbury, would get what he wanted, and so would she. With his name and wealth, she would never find herself at the mercy of a man again.

CHAPTER EIGHT

"I'D HOPED TO FIND YOU alone."

The deep, silky voice startled her out of her reverie. Genie swung around to find the Duke of Huntingdon at her side. Locked in the tumult of her thoughts, she hadn't heard him approach. For such a muscular man, he moved as stealthily as a cat.

His face was partially hidden in the shadows of the soft garden moonlight. Hard, blue eyes pierced the smoky veil, glowing unnaturally. Not a cat, more like a panther, she thought. Sleek, dark, and dangerous.

Genie tensed at the intrusion, but held her ground. He stood closer than was proper which she assumed was intentional. Heat radiated from his body. She fought the urge to step away, refusing to let him think his closeness bothered her.

But it did.

It was impossible not to be aware of him. His size alone demanded her attention. The cast of his shadow seemed to have doubled in size over the years. The bulky muscles and broad shoulders were so different.

Good. She had enough reminders already.

She lifted her chin and met his stare. Again, the change in his demeanor took her aback. The jaunty grin and twinkling eyes had vanished to the point that he seemed to have lost the ability to smile. Even his posture had changed. The relaxed, lackadaisical young man now stood straight and inflexible. This improved her spirits considerably.

Change pleased her; it wrought unfamiliarity. The more he seemed a stranger, the less chance there was for her memories to blur the space of time and confuse her.

Genie steeled herself for the inevitable; she'd known she could not evade him forever. Huntingdon, the man, no longer shied from unpleasantness.

"I desired a breath of fresh air and Edmund is engaged at the gaming tables." Her gaze flickered over his blank expression that still managed to convey arrogance by the square set of his jaw and the firm line of his mouth. "But I suspect you know that. You've had a remarkable habit of turning up everywhere I've been this week." Every soirée, every ball, every assembly. Even Almack's. Fortunately, until now, he had not sought to approach her. She'd almost convinced herself that he meant to leave them in peace. She'd almost grown accustomed to seeing him again. Almost.

Genie had done her utmost to avoid him, keeping close to Edmund and the countess. Until now. She screwed her lips together, annoyed that he'd found her alone in Lady Jersey's garden. After refreshing herself, and using the necessary, she'd slipped out onto the garden path from a side door, trying to escape his constant predatory stare. Like him, it followed her everywhere.

He shrugged noncommittally, neither admitting nor denying. "I looked for you."

"Apparently, I'm not too difficult to find," she quipped dryly.

"That's not what I meant. I looked for you when you disappeared five years ago."

She clamped her mouth closed, biting back the scathing retort that he only had to look as far as his own mother. It didn't matter.

"I never meant for things to turn out the way they did."

"You didn't?" she said blandly. "I received your letter. I think things turned out precisely as you intended."

A crack of chagrin appeared in his arrogant façade. "That letter was a mistake. I should never have written it. I felt so much pressure at the time, like I'd been backed into a corner. I reacted. Horribly, I know, but I didn't know what my mother had planned. I was young and foolish."

Genie flinched, disappointment surprisingly acute. Part of her had always wondered whether there was some chance that he hadn't written that horrible note. She'd harbored the tiniest hope that it had all been some atrocious misunderstanding. *Fool.*

"We both were," she finished for him, not wanting to hear anymore on the subject. "There is no need to explain."

"I'd like to try."

Anger mounted at his conceit. As if words could make a difference. "Don't bother. I know why you're really here. You should know that you're wasting your time."

"I'm afraid you have the advantage." His mouth curved into a lopsided grin. "You'll have to explain my motives as I myself am not certain." He took a seemingly innocuous step closer.

But Genie felt the threat. She couldn't stand it a moment longer. The nearness of his body, the heat, the subtle spicy scent, combined to overwhelm her senses with his raw masculinity. He affected her much more than she wanted to admit. It was natural, she knew, after what they had once shared. She'd lain naked in his arms for God's sake. But still, it infuriated her. She broke away, moving a few feet toward the warm, candlelit glow of the ballroom before turning to answer him. "Edmund explained that you refused to back down graciously. He warned that you might try to interfere with our engagement. I don't know why it should possibly matter to you, but be assured that I have no interest in reliving the past." The memories were painful enough.

He smiled as if amused by a private joke, but there was no warmth in the sentiment. "Edmund," he began sarcastically, "shows surprising candor for someone so proficient at holding his tongue about other things."

Genie flushed with resentment, keenly aware that she had shared those same thoughts. But how dare *he* malign Edmund. Edmund's dishonesty paled in comparison to his own. "No more surprised than I in the divergent choice of friends of an *honorable* man like Edmund."

His gaze narrowed, but otherwise he gave no indication that he understood the disparagement in character that was intended. "I'm no longer a foolish boy, Mrs. Preston." He took an intimidating step toward her. "Edmund is not the only man whose intentions are *honorable*."

Genie sucked in her breath. He couldn't mean marriage? Did he expect her to weep with gratitude and jump at the chance to marry him after all that he'd done? She'd laugh in his face if his continued conceit didn't infuriate her so greatly.

But marriage did hold a singular charm. For a brief, tantalizing moment, the image of a supplicant duke brought to his knees, begging for her to marry him flashed before her eyes. Impossible, of course, but the potential for revenge wrought by marriage tempted for a long moment before she pushed it aside.

She remembered that Huntingdon's definition of "honorable intentions" could be subject to creative interpretation. Genie had no interest in being mired in the cesspit of his intentions again.

Genie didn't know what game he was playing, but she wanted nothing to do with it. "What will it take to get you to leave us alone?" she asked, throwing down the gauntlet.

He cocked a brow. His eyes raked her body, pausing suggestively on her mouth, then lowering to her breasts. A dangerous grin spread across his features. His teeth gleamed white in the smoky darkness. "What are you offering?"

THE WORDS LEFT HIS MOUTH before he could stop them.

Genie recoiled as if he'd slapped her. Huntingdon swore he saw a trace of hurt in her eyes before they turned to hard, black pebbles. The sensual mouth that he'd watched move between a pout and a smile all week—depending on whether she was getting her way—narrowed into a thin line.

Damn, Huntingdon swore. Why had he said that? Huntingdon might not know what he wanted from her yet, but whatever it was he wouldn't achieve it by lewd propositions. He raked his fingers through his hair, irritated by the turn in conversation. He meant to apologize, not besmirch her virtue. But she'd provoked him by comparing him to Hawk and finding him lacking. It rankled, so he'd struck back—cruder than warranted no doubt, but heightened by pent-up frustration.

And Huntingdon was a frustrated man.

For the better part of the week, he'd bided his time, patiently waiting for the perfect opportunity to confront her. Alone. It had taken far longer than he'd anticipated; she hovered close to her stalwart protectors. Forced patience only intensified his desire. As did the cool detachment that she presented whenever he was near. Her indifference goaded him. He craved the attention she'd once bestowed so freely. Genie was aware of him, he knew, but it was as a horse is aware of a fly.

He wanted more. He wanted to shatter that cold mask of indifference and see her eyes burn for him... again. He wanted her to remember his mouth on hers, his hand cupping the velvet skin of her breast, his cock plunging deep into her tight flesh, catapulting her to peaks of shattering ecstasy.

Because he could think of nothing else. Would the enchantment between them still be there? Had it ever truly existed?

Would she still be hot and tight, making him ache to come as soon as he entered her?

But as the week wore on, instead of attending him, her devotion to Hawk became strikingly obvious—and increasingly difficult to endure. They presented as a well-matched pair, he thought sardonically, like his prized chestnut bays.

And the ton couldn't get enough of them.

Hawk had always been sought after, but Genie's beauty and subtle air of mystery irresistibly sweetened the pot, placing them on the top of every hostess's list. Genie moved through the ton with a grace and ease that he'd never expected, though perhaps he should have. At times he wondered whether he had ever really known her at all.

How ironic. If he'd had the guts to defy his family all those years ago, he would have been proud to call her his duchess. He'd underestimated her. He acknowledged it, and added it to the long list of failures where she was concerned.

She had refinement and beauty, impeccable manners, and an ease of conversation fostered by an unusual proclivity toward kindness. She also exuded a sensuality that made men fools. As a girl she'd been completely unaware of the power of her sexual charms. This woman was very aware, and moreover, wasn't afraid to use her considerable beauty to get what she wanted. He couldn't help but wonder how far she would be willing to go to protect her engagement to Hawk. And how far had she gone before with him to get what she wanted?

The thought chilled him.

His suggestive taunt had at least cracked her icy indifference. Boldly, her sultry blue eyes returned his hungry gaze, sliding down his body, lingering for a moment at the broad expanse of his chest then lowered to the substantial bulge in his fitted silk breeches. Blood surged with the weight of her eyes on his manhood.

One side of her mouth quirked in a mocking half smile. "Offer? Why should I offer you anything? Except for silence, you have nothing that interests me. As I recall, you have very *little* to recommend you." She raised her eyes from his crotch and met his stare full force, so there could be no mistaking her meaning. "Edmund more than fulfills my every desire."

Huntingdon saw red. Not from the slur on the size of his manhood—he was more than confident in that regard—but to the thought of her and Hawk together. The picture of Genie in Hawk's arms ate like acid at his insides. It had been haunting him, and having it confirmed stung.

She turned to flounce away, but his hand whipped out to

grab her arm. A sharp jolt shot through him at the contact. Touching her opened floodgates that he'd desperately battled to keep closed. His fingers clutched the small expanse of skin between the short sleeve of her sheer evening gown and the top edge of her glove. Through the dark haze of jealousy, he noticed the firm muscle beneath the velvety skin. Skin that was even softer than he remembered.

He bent his mouth to her ear. "It seems you have a short memory. It hasn't been that long. Should I remind you of all that I have to offer?" The coarse threat was tempered by the huskiness in his voice.

Taking advantage of her shock, his hand wrapped around her waist, and he pulled her into the protective shield of his chest. The unmistakable truth of his words stood between them; his long, thick, very substantial erection pulsed against the slim contour of her stomach.

Heat flushed her cheeks and her eyes burned with indignation. She was clearly furious. Yet all he could think about was the lush rose of her lips raised in protest mere inches below his.

Lust and anger converged, his body raged with indecision. Never had he experienced such a primitive craving to take, to overwhelm a woman with the sheer power of his body. He wanted to kiss her, to brand her with his mouth. To force her to acknowledge that she belonged to him. To dare her to deny the heat that still crackled like wildfire between them.

Bloody hell, he sounded like some sort of animal.

But he couldn't help it. The mouthwatering lure of her lips was too great.

Before she could utter the words to stop him, he lowered his head, capturing her startled gasp with the force of his kiss.

Something caught and tightened in his chest at the first taste of her. It had been so long. The memories washed over him. He groaned, feeling like a glutton, eager to sate the hunger that had gone unfed for five years. Her mouth was achingly sweet, a sweetness that had lingered in the farthest reaches of his mind, a taste that he'd never been able to completely erase.

With a tenderness that belied the savage urge to ravish coursing through his veins, he moved his mouth over hers, wooing with a bittersweet plea for remembrance of all that had once existed between them. Love, passion, friendship.

For a moment he thought she responded. Her hand pressed against his chest, fingers splayed out over the wide ridge of muscle. Her mouth softened, her lips parted. For one glorious instant she succumbed.

Or so he thought.

He pulled her closer in his arms, pressed her firmly against his body and deepened the kiss. Lust overtook sensation. His demands turned frantic. He wanted her under him, legs wrapped around his waist, hips raised to meet his deep, primal thrust. His tongue flicked out to plunder her mouth, but her lips, so soft and pliable, closed, refusing entry. The hand that had once seemed content on his chest braced against him. She tried to break free, fluttering like a bird in the steel cage of his arms.

Refusing to accept that she might not want him, that the same wild abandon was not heating her blood, his kiss hardened. He pried her lips apart, and swept her mouth with his tongue. She stilled. His ears buzzed and his heart pounded with excitement. He mimicked the rhythm of lovemaking with the thrust and swirl of his tongue. The carnal kiss intensified, firing his raging lust. *Yield to me,* he wanted to roar, but instead commanded it with his mouth.

Her lips opened.

Thinking he'd won, he growled, heady with masculine pride.

Just before her teeth clamped down on his tongue, her foot smashed down on his instep, and her knee made a brash attempt at sending his bollocks to his chin. Only the cumbersome skirts of her evening gown prevented his near gelding.

Pain cleared his head. He released her with a loud curse.

Tasting blood, his hand moved to cover his mouth.

Breathing hard, chest heaving with the force of her fury, Genie moved far away from him. Except for the anger, she seemed unaffected by the passion that had just strangled his senses.

From her position of safety, she eyed him warily, as the lamb watches the fox. "How dare you," she said coldly. "Along with your charm, you seem to have lost much of your subtlety."

"I thought..."

"What? That I would welcome your kiss?" She laughed, an ugly sound loaded with scorn and mockery. "That we might pick up where you left off? I despise and loathe you. I am no longer a green country girl excited to folly by an inconsequential kiss or the slobbering gropings of a randy boy, *Your Grace*. I have learned much from my mistakes, including never to repeat the same one twice."

What had he thought? To overpower her good sense with sensation? Shamefully, he realized yes. Foolishly, he'd hoped to break down her resistance with passion. For a moment he'd even thought that it had worked. "Nothing between us has ever been inconsequential, including that kiss."

"I fear the sentiment was one-sided. I seem to have lost my taste for charming scoundrels." The flashing in her eyes hardened. "Though I believe you no longer qualify as charming. As to what was once between us, I also believed differently, until you so conclusively proved the fallacy of those beliefs."

She was right. He had been the one to debase what had once been between them.

Collecting himself, he bowed slightly. "I'm sorry. It seems I erred in judgment once again." His tongue still throbbed and his arch felt like it had flattened. "Though I must say that your ability to rid yourself of an unwanted suitor is quite admirable. And an unusual accomplishment for a society lady."

A shadow crossed over her face. Clearly exasperated she

asked, "What do you want from me?"

One corner of his mouth lifted. "I would have thought that was obvious."

If he'd embarrassed her, she hid it well. She looked down her nose at him mockingly. "You've had that. You don't even know me now. I'm not the same girl who left Thornbury five years ago."

"And I'm not the same boy who let you go." Genie's disappearance had forced him to take a hard look at his character. He hadn't much liked what he'd seen. The unexpected death of his father and brother, and the responsibilities appurtenant, had completed his transformation.

They stood staring at each other in the moonlight, the memories an ethereal but surprisingly strong bond between them. The connection would always be there, but not in the way it had been in the past. For the first time, Huntingdon realized the truth. He could not go back. No matter how much he wanted to do it over again and make things right, he couldn't. It was too late. For a man accustomed to getting what he wanted, failure was a bitter pill to swallow.

But where did that leave him? What did he want from her?

"If that is all then, I bid you good night." She turned to leave, but he stopped her—this time with words.

"Wait." He'd cornered her for a purpose. He needed answers, but first he owed her something. Something that was long past due. "You're right. I do want something from you." She eyed him cagily. He took a deep breath. "I want to apologize for what happened in Thornbury—all of it. I cannot regret making love to you, but it was wrong. As was my failure to offer you the proposal of marriage that you deserved. The letter was..." He winced as if with pain. "My behavior was appalling. I offer no excuse. I was wrong, terribly wrong. It was the biggest mistake of my life. I can only ask for your forgiveness."

Her eyes widened with surprise. And something else... pain? "It was a long time ago. We've both moved on."

His eyes locked on her face, searching for a sign of hesitation. Regret? Sorrow? Anger? Any sign of doubt. A faint blush still stained her cheeks and her lips were swollen from his kiss, but emotion, even anger, had fled under the mask of cool serenity. He knew better than to ask, but he had a perverse need to know. Had she truly moved on? "Do you love him?"

"Yes," she said without hesitation. "I do."

He felt like the air had been knocked out of him, leaving a dull pain in his chest.

That was that then.

Or was it?

He still wanted to know what had happened to her, why she hadn't returned as she'd promised. Had she ever loved him?

But most of all, he needed to know the one thing that had plagued him since his mother had first voiced the possibility. The one thing for which he could never be absolved.

Clearly determined to have done, Genie turned and started back to the ballroom.

"Eugenia. Mrs. Preston," he called after her.

She looked back. Her face seemed a perfect mask of alabaster carved by a soft beam of moonlight.

Their eyes met.

The importance of the question he was about to ask gave him pause, but he had to know. "Do I have a child?" he asked softly, though he knew immediately that she'd heard him.

She paled, utterly horror-struck. The façade of cold detachment collapsed. She seemed to almost cower like a wounded animal cornered and being beaten with a stick. For a moment, beneath the serene beauty, he glimpsed a different woman. A woman that had known pain. A woman that life had not treated so kindly. He saw a girl cruelly aged by hardship and misfortune.

Taken aback by the sudden transformation, he didn't think she was capable of replying. But her voice, when it

114 | *Monica McCarty*

came, resonated in the cool night air like the hard crack of a whip. "You did."

Before he could react, she turned and fled into the protective embrace of Lady Jersey's crowded ballroom.

CHAPTER NINE

OVER AND OVER, THE WORDS reverberated in her head, unrelenting, as she slipped in and out of consciousness. "Trust me... trust me..."

I do! Her heart cried. But where are you? I need you.

His face floated above her, smiling, the bright sun in the midst of darkness. She reached out, frantically grasping at emptiness. Her voice found strength. "Please. Come to me, help me...," she begged. Not in a letter this time, but from the terrified throes of torture.

Her body ripped apart in excruciating agony, sweat poured off her skin, as she writhed in a sopping blanket trying to break free from the invisible chains of delirium.

The ship rolled, tossing against the waves in a dangerous dance with a torrential storm. Nausea turned her stomach, but she'd long passed the relief of retching. Something cool pressed against her brow, but still she burned.

Other voices, softer voices invaded her dreams. Fever. Too much blood. Dying. And something else.

No! Not that! Her body twisted free. She screamed. Sheer terror provided a fleeting moment of lucidity.

Please God, don't punish my child for my sins. I promise I'll make it right. I'll crawl back to England on my knees. I'll swallow my pride and force him to marry me. I'll do anything. Please, don't take my child.

A knife of pain sliced through her abdomen in harsh response. She curled up into a ball, trying to escape the twisted knot of cramps burning in her belly.

Hastings, where are you? I need you...

She closed her eyes, trying to block out the excruciating agony—the violent purging of her sins.

But still the damning words pounded in her ears. Trust me...

Until at last, the haunting voice faded away as she slid into merciful blackness.

Genie woke from the dream with a start. Wide-eyed, she popped straight up, gasping for breath, fighting the suffocating panic that squeezed her chest. Her pulse raced wildly, sweat dampened her linen chemise. Suddenly, heavy bile rose in her throat. Knowing she couldn't stave it off, she leaned over the side of the bed and emptied the paltry contents of her stomach into an ivory porcelain chamber pot.

The sight of porcelain where she expected tin jogged her fully awake.

For a moment Genie didn't know where she was. Ravaged by the force of her memories, she felt like she was reliving a nightmare. She looked around trying to place her surroundings. In the darkened room she could just make out the soft floral wallpaper and fine mahogany furniture that lined the walls of her large sleeping chamber. A beautiful silver candelabrum rested on the table beside her bed. Rather than a wooden sleeping berth, a gracious velvet canopy hung over her head. She loosened her grip on her coverlet, her fingers clutching fine silk, not rough wool.

Her heart slowed. She was safe at Hawkesbury House, the pampered guest of the Countess of Hawkesbury, and not imprisoned by delirium on a ship bound for America.

It had been horrible. The sickness, the storms that had turned six weeks into ten, the unfathomable loss...

Incapacitated from the start of the voyage by nausea, it took Genie weeks to realize that she was pregnant, not seasick. And by that point, almost four months along. If it were possible, she would have returned to England immediately and demanded that Hastings marry her. For her child she would have risked anything. Her pride, her reputation, the formidable duchess... anything.

But then came the blood. So much blood and the decision was wrested from her control. The fever that followed had lingered for days. When she regained consciousness, the ship had docked in Boston Harbor and her sullen, "borrowed" maid had disappeared, absconding with her fortune. Leaving Genie alone and destitute; at the mercy of a cruel world that she had not known existed.

Only the kindness of two elderly sisters had saved her. Temporarily at least.

Trust me.

Her heart twisted.

She had. Even then, on the ship in the middle of the ocean with nothing around but the endless indigo vista of the wide-open sea she thought: He must realize his mistake, surely he would sense her agony and would come for her. Their connection was strong enough to bridge an ocean.

Irrational? Probably.

Foolish? Undoubtedly.

Genie could only depend on one person and that was herself. Never again would she trust a man. Controlled by lust, men only sought one thing from a beautiful woman. And if she was not willing, they simply took. Huntingdon had demonstrated that well enough tonight with his suggestive taunts and unsolicited embrace.

He'd taken, without care for her wants or wishes. His were still the self-indulgent actions of an arrogant man. After all that had passed between them, did he actually believe that she would fall into his arms overwhelmed by something as fleeting and unreliable as passion?

As if she could be persuaded by the mere favor of his kiss.

Thoughts of that kiss stopped her mental rampage.

She hadn't been as indifferent as she pretended, or as she wanted to be. When his lips touched hers, the years had magically slipped away. She was an innocent young girl again, heart fluttering uncontrollably in her chest. The soft pressure of his mouth teased and seduced with the same heart-wrenching intensity. His arms felt achingly familiar. He even tasted the same. Spice laced with a tinge of claret. And he still smelled cozy and warm; she wanted to burrow deep into his embrace and sleep in blissful ignorance forever.

Her blood had pounded with honest desire for one brief moment. It had been so long she'd almost forgotten what it felt to have every nerve in her body on end. To drown in sensation and heat.

Until her hand had pressed against rock and her cheek was scraped by the heavy stubble of his jaw.

This was not the Hastings of her youth; this was a stranger. A man. A duke. Suddenly, everything felt different, no longer familiar, and the span of five years seemed infinitely longer. She couldn't escape his kiss quickly enough.

Genie wrapped her arms around her waist, rested her forehead on her knees and, for the second time that night, wept. Shoulder-racking sobs that shook her core, but could not rid her soul of the emptiness that had haunted her for years. She wept for the memories dredged up by a kiss and a question. She wept for the loss of the child that she would never know.

She wept, she swore for the last time, for the loss of her golden prince. The prince who in those rare moments of weakness slipped into her dreams and made her remember what it was like to love. Dear God, how she yearned for that charming boy who'd stolen her heart before everything had gone so horribly wrong.

When the sobs subsided, she wiped her burning eyes with the sleeve of her gown and sucked in great gulps of air, trying to catch her breath. She felt silly. Crying never seemed to help; it only intensified the feeling of loneliness. But it had helped her reach a decision.

This time she was determined to have him out of her life forever.

Huntingdon owed her. She'd paid a heavy price for their

sin. She alone had shouldered the tragedy begot from their brief affair. Surely he would acknowledge his debt and leave her and Edmund to their future.

If not, Genie knew that she would fight him with everything she had. From the arsenal of tricks that life had so cruelly taught her.

THE NEXT MORNING, A KNOCK on Genie's door interrupted her morning correspondence. "Come in," she answered.

One of the young housemaids scrambled in and bobbed an unnecessary and painstakingly deep curtsey. The countess's bevy of servants seemed intent on treating Genie like nobility; she'd given up trying to correct them. Genie wrinkled her nose and tried to make out the features nervously turned to the floor and half hidden by a large white cap.

She placed her quill back in the well. "Yes, Sarah, what is it?"

The girl bobbed again, her plump cheeks pink with pleasure at the personal greeting. "The countess requests your immediate presence in the south sitting room, my lady." Seeing Genie's expression she corrected herself. "Er, ma'am. There is a gentleman waiting." Her eyes stayed firmly planted on the floor. "A duke, ma'am," she said in hushed, reverent tones.

Genie's heart sank. She should have known he would call on her first thing in the morning after what she'd revealed last night. She drew a deep breath, preparing herself for the inevitable questions that were sure to follow such a disclosure. She'd never meant to tell him about the baby, but she couldn't lie. She could never deny her child. But how had he known to ask? How had he guessed? And why couldn't he have thought about the consequences of their illicit affair five years ago?

Not bothering to glance in the looking glass, she shook out the skirts of her robin's-egg-blue muslin morning gown, tidied her loose chignon with an indifferent pat of her hands, and followed the eager maid through the vast corridors of the palatial Hawkesbury House. Though she'd been here for a few weeks, Genie still had trouble navigating the endless maze of rooms and halls.

The modern-built house was situated on the north side of Berkeley Square adjacent to Lansdowne House and within a stone's throw of Devonshire House and the Jersey residence. Built by Edmund's late father in the last century with no expense spared, the grand public rooms of Hawkesbury House took some getting used to—as did the luxurious private rooms for that matter. The countess had stayed on after the passing of the earl—with Edmund insisting that his bachelor lodgings in St. James's suited him perfectly for the time being—but when Genie and Edmund married, this house would be hers. The prospect of being mistress of such a place was daunting, to say the least.

But, she reminded herself, Hawkesbury House represented wealth and security for her future. That and the small country manor in Gloucestershire she would purchase after the wedding. Edmund had never asked what she intended to do with the money that he insisted be hers upon their marriage. One day, when she finally felt safe, she would tell him.

The duke stood with his back toward her as she entered the room. For the first time since their confrontation at the Prince Regent's fete, Huntingdon was dressed casually in buckskin trousers and a dark green morning coat. The informal garb suited him, much more so than the elegant evening attire she'd grown accustomed to seeing him in. His broad shoulders and muscular legs were more apropos of a country sportsman than of one of the highest ranking peers in the realm. Though Genie still thought he could pass for a common laborer—if he could somehow manage to lose the omnipresent arrogance of rank he wore like a heavy mantle across his broad shoulders. The confidence of supreme authority was another change that took some time getting used to.

The countess was seated on a small settee and shot Genie a curious glance, promising further inquiry at the first opportunity.

"Here she is now," the countess said brightly, rising from her seat.

The duke turned and bowed stiffly, his expression at once formal and severe. "Mrs. Preston."

Genie curtsied brusquely. "Your Grace," she said, mimicking his curt manner.

The countess looked back and forth between them, clearly troubled. Finally, her gaze settled on Genie. "The duke has requested that he speak with you in private about a personal matter." From the censure in her voice, Genie could tell she did not approve. "I was not aware that you were acquainted with the Duke of Huntingdon?"

Genie fought the heat that threatened to rise in her cheeks. How dare he put her in this position! She greatly admired Edmund's mother and did not relish lying to her. But what other choice did she have? The truth? Even the open-minded countess was not so liberally inclined to welcome a daughter tainted by ruin, with the shadow of scandal hovering close behind her.

Huntingdon apparently sensed her discomfort and answered for her. "A passing acquaintance many years ago, Lady Hawkesbury. I would not even trouble Mrs. Preston to remember it, but it has recently come to my attention that she may be in possession of some information that may help a member of my family locate an old friend." He lowered his voice to a conspiratorial whisper. "I hope I can count on your discretion in this matter, my lady."

The request, and the charming wink that accompanied it, seemed to pacify the countess. Apparently, he had not lost all of his boyish charm, Genie thought, though it did seem manipulative and not as naturally disposed.

But perhaps it had always been so and Genie had just not realized it.

"Yes, of course," Lady Hawkesbury replied. "I'm sure there is nothing improper in a few minutes of conversation while I attend to some refreshment. Edmund should be here soon," she added as an afterthought, but Genie recognized the polite warning.

As did Huntingdon. He smiled knowingly. "Of course."

The countess looked to Genie for affirmation and Genie nodded her approval. "I don't know what information I could have that would possibly be helpful to the duke," Genie started, "or to his family. But of course I shall endeavor to provide whatever assistance I may." She hoped it didn't sound as sarcastic as she thought.

The countess took one last long look at Genie before exiting the room. There would be some explaining to do on that front later, Genie knew.

Before the doors had closed firmly behind the countess, Huntingdon was upon her. He grabbed her elbow and pulled her harshly to his side, releasing the pent-up tension and anger that he'd barely kept under control while Lady Hawkesbury remained in the room.

Genie felt like she was being smashed against a wall of granite. Everything about him was hard. His chest, his arms, even the square jaw fixed in an uncompromising block mere inches from her face.

He wasted no time. "Where is my child?" The dangerous edge to his voice sent a chill up her spine.

Despite the warning in his tone, Genie bristled at his audacity. *His* child! Of all the unbelievable gall. He'd forsaken that claim long ago. She could laugh like a madwoman.

Furious by his rough handling of her person after his brutish behavior the night before, Genie said scornfully, "A strange question, Your Grace, to pose to such an inconsequential, 'passing acquaintance.'"

"I was trying to do you a favor. Would you have me tell her the truth?"

"I'd rather you hadn't brought our previous association up at all."

"You made that impossible by running away from me last night. I'll have my answer," he hissed. "Now." His mouth threateningly close to her ear.

Genie's lips pressed into a flat line. She wrenched her arm free from his grasp. She wouldn't be manhandled—even by him. "Your boorish behavior grows tiresome, Your Grace. Kindly refrain from such improper displays of familiarity. Your touch, in all of its forms, is repugnant to me. Nor do I appreciate an armful of bruises."

He glanced at her arm, obviously shocked to realize that he'd been hurting her. His hands fell to his side. "I'm sorry, I didn't realize..." He raked his fingers through his oh-so-charmingly disheveled hair. One heavy lock immediately fell back across his forehead. Genie felt a momentary pang. A flashback of lying in the grass along a bucolic riverbank mesmerized by that errant lock made warm and shiny in the bright autumn sun.

Would she never escape the past? she thought hopelessly.

Just as quickly, the unbidden recollection hardened her heart. She owed him nothing. Not even kindness. She yearned to hurt him as much as she'd been hurt. "*Your* child, Your Grace, lies at the bottom of the sea."

IT TOOK A MOMENT FOR the words to sink in. "Dead?" he posited inanely. The finality of the word hung between them for a long, agonizing moment.

The haunted, vacant look in her eyes returned. All the fight seemed to seep out of her. She nodded then sighed deeply and said in a much softer voice, "He never had a chance to live."

Huntingdon felt like he'd been knifed in the gut. "He?" his voice strangled with emotion. The anxiety he'd experienced all night wondering whether he had a child was replaced by the sudden knowledge that he did not. And the impossible knowledge of what might have been had he acted with honor. He would pay with guilt for the rest of his life with that knowledge.

She nodded. Her mouth quivered, and her eyes filled with tears. She looked away.

"I didn't know," he said hoarsely.

"Neither did I. If I had, nothing would have persuaded me to leave. Not even your formidable mother or the possible disgrace of my family."

Huntingdon grimaced. But he understood. His mother had relayed the entirety of her ugly threat.

"Why didn't you send word when you discovered you were with child?"

"To what purpose? The babe was lost at sea. There was no way to reach you, no passing ship on which to send a message. Afterward, I was too ill—" She stopped herself, cleared her throat and said, "There was no reason. If you recall, I had sent you a note before. You had made your choice plain enough."

"I regretted that letter immediately and came to see you, but you had disappeared. I had no idea what my mother had done. It was only last year that she confided her part in your disappearance and where she'd sent you. Before that I never thought to look as far away as America. I was furious when the prince wouldn't let me leave, which is why I sent Hawk in my stead. If it is any consolation, my mother has paid many times over for her actions. I'll never forgive her interference."

Genie shrugged indifferently. "It doesn't matter. Hers was not the only blame," she pointed out.

"No. You're right. I let you down. I let our child down."

She wobbled a little. He reached out to steady her, but stopped himself before touching her, remembering her request. She dropped to the seat vacated by the countess. Composing herself, she folded her hands in her lap and serenely met his gaze. "Now that you have your answer, I trust you will leave me in peace."

Now that he had his answer, he didn't know if he could. The guilt for not honoring his unspoken promise to marry her was dwarfed in comparison to the knowledge that he'd failed her when she'd been with child. Instead, he asked,

"Why didn't you return to England?" *To me.*

"My circumstances changed rather suddenly," she said carefully. "And as I said before, you had made your intentions very clear."

"You refer to your marriage." He could barely say the word, the thought alone so distasteful.

She looked puzzled. "No." Suddenly, she caught herself. "I mean yes, of course, my marriage."

She sat still, too still, waiting for him to say something. Huntingdon noticed the nervous twisting of her hands in her lap. She noticed the direction of his gaze and her hands clenched the fabric of her skirt.

Though she'd tried to cover it up, he'd heard her mention that she'd been ill after she'd lost the child. Now she forgets her husband. Something about this was not right. "I would like to hear more about your husband. When did you first meet?"

She stood up and moved to the window overlooking the garden, avoiding his eyes. "Why is this important to you? What reason could you possibly have for being interested in a common soldier?"

He moved beside her, careful not to get too close. Her face looked pale, even under the warming glow of sunlight. Her bottom lip trembled ever so slightly.

"I'm curious about the man to whom you would give your heart. About the man who did what I have regretted not doing for five years," he said quietly.

She stood perfectly still. He could tell that she was engaged in a fierce battle to control her emotions. What he didn't know was what she was trying to hide: sadness at the memory of her dead husband or at him for his betrayal.

She lifted her chin defiantly. "It's easy to make such claims now."

"No," he said with a crooked smile. "It isn't." She looked so vulnerable, he ached to reach out and touch her. But he didn't, knowing it would not help his cause. "My conduct back then is not something I'm proud of and not something I like to remember. But neither can I forget. You see, inexplicably, I find myself very curious about one thing."

She turned to face him, eyeing him cagily. "Yes?"

"If you loved me, how could you have married someone else within weeks of leaving England?"

GENIE DIDN'T KNOW WHAT TO say. She hadn't married someone else, but she could hardly tell him that. It was a foolish mistake to claim she'd married so quickly, but he'd made her so angry, she hadn't been able to resist. It was clear that he questioned the ardency of her affection. She'd laugh if it wasn't so painful. If he only knew how long she'd held out hope.

No, the constancy of her heart was never the issue.

She'd desperately wanted to return to her family, but she'd been left utterly destitute by the treachery of her borrowed maid.

Rather than answer the question, she hedged. "People marry for many reasons, most of which have nothing to do with love."

"So, you didn't love him?" *Or you didn't love me?* She heard the unspoken question.

"I didn't say—" She stopped. "Perhaps I married him for money?" she said provokingly, noticing the erratic pulse in his jaw. She held his gaze. "Or perhaps to give a child the protection of a name." He flinched at that and Genie suddenly felt cruel. She didn't want to get into this. Accusations, drama, emotion. She wanted to stay comfortably detached. "And what of yourself, Your Grace? Surely, a man of your position must have been tempted to take a wife?"

White lines appeared around his mouth. "No," he replied stonily.

Genie remained silent.

He stood so close she could hear the harsh unevenness of his breathing. Gazing out the window, warmed from the gentle heat of sunlight, she could smell the faint hint of sandalwood that lingered from his soap.

His voice deepened. "I was tempted... once."

A pit dropped in her stomach. "Oh?" She hadn't been expecting that. She should have, but hadn't nonetheless. Sadness swept over her. A dull ache resounded in her chest, born of disappointment and something else. Jealousy. Why? It shouldn't matter. She was marrying someone else, wasn't she? But it did. Matter, that is.

"What happened?" she found herself asking.

He thought for a moment. "I was a cad and a fool. I promised to marry her, I wanted to marry her, but in the end I betrayed her. She went to America and she didn't come back."

Me. He means me. She relaxed her shoulders, not realizing that she'd been holding her breath. Relief filled her chest. He hadn't wished to marry someone else. She hadn't been completely wrong in his intentions all those years ago. Possibly he had even loved her...

But not enough, she reminded herself.

Genie couldn't stand this anymore. Couldn't stand the feeling he was arousing in her. The awareness of him that she'd tried to snuff out, but which apparently would never be completely extinguished. Huntingdon the man was infinitely more dangerous than he'd been in his youth. Without the carefree charm to moderate his pursuit, he attacked with a fierce single-mindedness, with such forthright determination that it was difficult to withstand the onslaught. She'd successfully put the past behind her, but he wanted to force her to remember. To reopen a part of herself that had been locked away for a very long time.

She looked down at her hands, curled into tight fists at her side. "Why are you speaking like this? Why tell me this now? After what I just told you, surely you understand that it is far too late—I would never wish to relive the past, even if it were possible."

Slowly, so slow that she could stop him if she wanted to, he brought his fingers to her chin and gently tilted her face up to meet his gaze. She read the turmoil there that surely matched her own. Possibly, he was just as confused as she by the heavy fog of emotion that seemed to encircle them.

"If I could, Genie, I would do it differently. I'd do anything to make it up to you." His callused thumb swept the side of her cheek in a heart stopping, loving caress. Her heart skipped unwillingly. "Are you sure that it is too late?" he asked.

Her skin tingled under the gentle stroke of his fingers. His question echoed in her head. Was it too late? She studied his face. Older, harder, but still incredibly handsome. The blue eyes, straight nose, square jaw, wide sensual mouth. Handsome enough to plummet her to the deepest bowels of hell again. If she were fool enough to let him.

"Yes," she said adamantly. "I'm sure. If you truly wish to make amends, leave me be," she pleaded. "Allow me to marry Edmund in peace. Your pointed interest in me has drawn enough speculation. Someone is bound to put it together."

He hesitated.

She could tell he was not ready to give up. She sensed a dogged determination in him that would never let go if she gave him reason to hope.

Genie debated her next move. She knew that he had political aspirations, a cabinet post according to Edmund, and that she could threaten him with scandal—ruin worked both ways. Though he would not suffer as much as she, it would not be pleasant for him. But somehow she sensed that such a threat might have the opposite effect with Huntingdon. No, she'd discovered his weakness. If he agreed, it would be from guilt.

"You owe me," she whispered. It wasn't necessary to mention their lost child. "Stand aside and pay the debt you owe me." He understood what she meant.

His expression shuttered. His fingers fell from her chin, leaving her cold. The tiny, cruel lines around his mouth became more pronounced. "Very well, Mrs. Preston. You shall have your wish."

And with that, he turned on his heel and was gone. Leaving Genie feeling emptier and more desolate than she had in years.

CHAPTER TEN

THIS TIME, HUNTINGDON KEPT HIS word. And his distance. Genie no longer felt the heat of his predatory gaze stalking her around London's ballrooms. Although she'd seen him arrive at Almack's that night, after a polite nod to her and Edmund, he'd completely ignored her. As he'd done every time their paths happened to cross since the emotional confrontation in Lady Hawkesbury's drawing room one short week ago.

Genie was relieved, but not as much as she should have been. She'd achieved her goal: He would not reopen the past by recalling Genie Prescott, parson's daughter from Thornbury, to the ton. The questions that could tumble her into ruin and disgrace—about his prior courting of her, her sudden unexplained disappearance, the dead husband—had been avoided. In keeping his distance, he'd given her a chance.

You got what you wanted, she told herself. Peace. Acceptance.

Why then did she feel such disquiet? Restless and on edge, she navigated the treacherous path of high society night after night with a brittle smile forced on her face and an anxious ache in her heart.

She should be ecstatic. It was clear she had been accepted, welcomed even, by the all-important "grande dames" of the beau monde. Even the formidable Lady Jersey had pronounced her "beautiful" and "charming," notwithstanding her lack of fortune and "misfortune" of birth.

No one had connected the former Genie Prescott with Mrs. Preston, soldier's widow. She and Edmund could announce their engagement without fear of reprisal. Though there might be rumblings and murmurings about her lack of rank and fortune, Edmund could be excused because of his superior wealth and her exceptional beauty. The ton would forgive much for a fat purse and pretty face.

Scandal had been averted.

She'd triumphed. She would have wealth beyond her imagination and security for the rest of her life. She could return to her family without shame.

Why then did she feel like she'd failed? Memories constantly accosted her, stirring feelings and emotions that she'd thought long buried. No more so than when she noticed Huntingdon dance twice with a beautiful dark-haired woman who effortlessly teased a smile from his grim countenance.

And why did her nerves prickle with apprehension as the date for Lady Hawkesbury's ball approached? The much-anticipated night when she and Edmund had agreed to formally announce their betrothal.

Edmund caught her gaze across the dance floor. An apologetic smile flickered across his face as he carefully made his way back to her. The promised ratafia had taken some time to procure.

Guilt gnawed at her. The strain of the last week showed plainly on Edmund's face. He seemed as uneasy as she with the precarious truce forged with Huntingdon. Accepting her explanation that Huntingdon would not interfere, Edmund hadn't questioned her about what took place that morning, but he knew that it had upset her. He was giving her time to confide in him, but it was costing him. He'd lost some of his easy, swaggering confidence. He was worried and Genie knew it, but couldn't bring herself to speak of what had occurred—the kiss, the confessions, and her subsequent confusion.

Confusion exacerbated by Huntingdon's continued

presence amongst the ton. Why was he here? Tonight, at least, she'd thought to be free from his infernal presence. Most unmarried men avoided the "marriage mart" like the plague.

Of course, there was one explanation that Genie had refused to heed. Could the rumors be true? Genie had heard the whispers upon the duke's arrival that he had finally decided to take a duchess.

Was the beautiful dark-haired woman the chosen one?

The very thought turned her stomach.

The gorgeous couple sliding across the dance floor distracted her from Edmund. A third dance. Huntingdon was as good as declaring his intentions. Although Genie hadn't been able to see the woman's face, her exquisite profile was enough to attest to her great beauty.

His head fell back and he laughed.

A sharp stab sliced through Genie's chest.

The indifference she'd brokered from him was peaceful, but surprisingly painful.

Stop it! she scolded herself, dragging her eyes away from the laughing couple. She was being ridiculous, allowing him to affect her. Even if she accepted that he'd once loved her, that he'd looked for her, that he'd changed from the feckless young man to the determined, hard man who attacked without pretense, too much had passed between them. Too much had happened to forgive and forget.

Why was she acting like a jealous, lovesick fool?

The truth unsettled her. She was not as immune to Huntingdon as she wanted to be. He still had the power to affect her. She must acknowledge it. Only by acknowledging her weakness could she find the strength to defeat it. And Genie would not be turned from her course.

It was time to look to the future. Paying no heed to the tightness in her chest, she tilted her chin and turned back to find Edmund fast approaching, looking more worried than he had only moments ago.

Genie pasted a lighthearted smile on her face. "I thought you'd forgotten all about me," she said playfully.

Taken aback by her sudden change in attitude, Edmund nonetheless recovered quickly. A dazzling smile warmed his troubled features. "Unhappily delayed, but never forgotten. My mother waylaid me, claiming a surprise, and dragged me halfway across the ballroom before I could tell her of my important quest for refreshment. Reluctantly, she agreed that the surprise could wait."

Genie laughed. "Well, apparently it couldn't wait too long because here she comes now." The countess plowed through the crowd, heading directly for them, an excited smile transforming her face to youthful mischief.

Genie stilled.

The countess was not alone. She led a very reluctant Huntingdon and his jubilant dark-haired dance partner along with her.

The time for Genie to confront her weakness had arrived.

THE COUNTESS OF HAWKESBURY SHOULD be a politician. The woman did not seem to comprehend the word no. Somehow, Huntingdon found himself being dragged across a ballroom to confront the person he *should* be trying to avoid.

It had only been a week, but Huntingdon already regretted his promise.

He realized, of course, that Genie had manipulated him into not interfering with her engagement to Hawk, but after learning about the dire circumstances he'd left her in, he'd felt guilty enough to accede to her emotional blackmail.

He owed her. For the life of their child. For the perfidy of his mother. For not keeping his word.

But staying away from her was the last thing he wanted to do. The disclosure of the fate of their child had only exacerbated his guilt. Every bone in his body cried out for the chance to do something about it.

And something else bothered him. The explanation of her past did not ring true. The timing of her marriage just didn't make sense. He'd had one of his contacts in the foreign office looking into Mr. Preston and found no one matching his name in the army at that time.

Genie was hiding something. Before Huntingdon could accept her marriage to Hawk, he had to find out what it was. But he didn't have much time. The announcement of their engagement could come at anytime.

Lady Hawkesbury quickened her pace. They were almost there.

He never should have come tonight. His attempts to put the past behind him this week had failed miserably. He knew he had a duty to marry, but for so many years he'd been unable to forget the one that he'd let get away.

Now that he'd found her, he didn't want to let her go. Not yet at least.

She might have changed from the girl he once loved, but he still wanted her.

It was not often that Huntingdon willingly backed down from something he wanted. And Lord how he wanted her. The kiss had only increased his hunger.

Her tongue flicked out to nervously wet her pouty lips and a bolt of desire shot right to his groin.

He hoped he hadn't made her another promise that he would be unable to keep.

HEART BEATING ERRATICALLY, GENIE WATCHED the countess approach with her striking charges. Trepidation and jealousy churned uneasily in Genie's stomach. She should be relieved that he'd moved on and found someone else to bestow his attention upon. So what if the woman was beautiful, elegant, and positively sparkled with life?

There was something familiar...

Recognition dawned when the woman, eyes fixed solely on Edmund, unable to contain her pleasure, burst out with exuberance, "Hawk, you've returned!"

The dark-haired beauty who'd inspired such jealousy by

making Huntingdon laugh was none other than his sister, Lady Fanny Hastings. For the second time, Genie had nearly made a fool out of herself with misplaced jealousy over his sister. She'd laugh if she wasn't so miserable.

In the five years since Genie had last seen her, Fanny had grown even more beautiful. Of age with Lizzie, Fanny was one and twenty and at the height of her bloom. The resemblance to her brother was marked, especially around the eyes and mouth. The same sea-blue eyes sparkled in a face almost Grecian in its sublime beauty. But the rest was pure Fanny: slim nose, tiny pointed chin, high cheekbones, and wide, sensuous lips set off by a creamy peach complexion and chestnut hair that shimmered with flecks of gold in the candlelight.

Her refined, classical beauty seemed at odds with the vivacious expression that transcended her features. Everything about Lady Fanny Hastings exuded warmth: her coloring, her smile, her animated personality. Like the countess she was frank in manner, but open rather than blunt. Every emotion portrayed vividly and candidly on her face. A face that stared at Edmund with unconcealed joy, admiration, and...

Genie's heart sank. Adoration.

A moment was all it took for Genie to realize that Fanny loved Edmund—or at least thought she did.

Edmund was obviously happy to see her, but there was something unusual in his expression, almost quizzical. Carefully, he took in the elegant form fitting gown, the low curved neckline and high rounded bosom displayed to bounteous perfection. Fanny's body was near perfection, and she wasn't hiding much of it. He frowned rather severely, resembling a disapproving older brother.

"Fanny, you look different. That gown..." He paused, looking discomfited for having said too much. "You look older," he finished brusquely.

Fanny blushed, but was saved from having to make a response to the odd observation by the countess's timely intervention. "Of course she's older," she chided. "Lady

Fanny has been out for two years. If you'd bothered attending a ball or two, you would know that."

Edmund recovered his manners quickly. He grinned, taking Fanny's hand and bowing. "Forgive me, it seems more time has passed since last I saw you than I realized. You'd just come home from that school."

Fanny grimaced and finished for him. "Mrs. Peniwithe's Academy for the Proper Education of Young Ladies in all Manner and Decorum. And that was three years ago. But my brother has kept me apprised of your travels. When did you return?" Fanny asked excitedly. She turned to her brother. "Why didn't you tell me that he was back from America?" Then back to Edmund. "Did you find out anything about—"

Huntingdon interrupted before she could say too much. "Fanny, I should like to introduce you to someone."

Fanny took her eyes off Edmund long enough to finally look at the woman hovering so close to him.

Already uncomfortably warm in the crowded assembly room, perspiration gathered on Genie's hands and brow. Fanny's feelings for Edmund had just complicated things immensely. Fanny knew everything—well, almost everything—about her past relationship with the duke. Could Fanny be persuaded to keep their secret?

Genie watched as recognition slowly dawned.

Fanny's jaw dropped. "You found her!" Incredulity echoed in her voice.

Noticing the countess's puzzled expression, Edmund grabbed Fanny's elbow before she could do more damage. "Fanny, do me the pleasure of this dance." Not waiting for a reply, Edmund unceremoniously yanked her off toward the dance floor.

The countess's eyes narrowed at Edmund's quickly retreating back. She turned a suddenly distressed gaze upon Genie and Huntingdon. "I think I'm beginning to understand." Her steady gaze fell upon Huntingdon. "Edmund went to America to attend to some business at your bequest, did he not?"

Huntingdon's face betrayed none of the tension that Genie knew lie just below the surface. "He did indeed, my lady."

"I seem to recall you were looking for someone."

"Why look who's here, Hyacinth," came a booming, cheerful voice. Lady Hawkesbury's recollections were interrupted by the raucous entry of the Viscount and Viscountess Davenport into their small circle. Of middling age and portly stature, the Davenports seemed the epitome of jovial companionship; never far from each other's side. Genie had admired their unusual proclivity for demonstrative affection from afar. A great rarity in the ton, they were a married couple who enjoyed each other.

She would welcome them if only for their timely interruption, but she was also looking forward to an introduction.

Lady Davenport with her heavily rouged cheeks wore the powdered hair and wide hooped gowns of the previous century. Lord Davenport had the ruddy cheeks of a seaman with a long white mustache that drooped down on either side, reminiscent of a walrus. A very happy walrus at that, Genie thought.

"Fitzie, my boy," Lord Davenport said, swatting Huntingdon affectionately, if a tad exuberantly, on the back, causing Huntingdon to stumble forward a few steps. Fitzie? Genie had to smother a gurgle of laughter at what was obviously a childhood nickname. Not even Fanny called him that. "Never thought I would see the day that you willingly cross the threshold of the marriage mart twice in one month. Mayhap the rumors are true and you've decided to end your prized bachelor days? Every man's duty to beget the heir, eh, my boy?" The old man needled Huntingdon forcefully with his elbow in the ribs. "Though the begetting part is not all bad," he said with a leer to his wife, guffawing loudly at his own ribald jest.

The familiarity and manner of Lord Davenport's address to Huntingdon suggested a long-held acquaintance. Probably a contemporary of his father's, Genie thought.

Though she could hardly reconcile the memories of the cold, humorless old duke with this brash, inelegant but thoroughly likable man.

"Leave the poor boy alone, Nigel," said Lady Davenport, with a fond swat of her fan. "I for one am glad to see his handsome face." Genie wouldn't have believed it if she hadn't been standing right there, but Lady Davenport actually reached over and pinched the Duke of Huntingdon's cheek. "Always were a pretty one, even as a child. Oh, your mother would be so pleased to see you married," she said. "Perhaps she might come out of seclusion for such an occasion."

"Now who's teasing the poor boy, pet," Lord Davenport chided. "And men aren't pretty," he said with exaggerated affront.

Genie glanced at Huntingdon and was surprised to see a hint of redness in his cheeks. Obviously, he cared a great deal for the Davenports to stand there silently enduring the embarrassing display of affection.

Genie for one found this greatly amusing. To see the proud, arrogant duke reduced to a blushing schoolboy was well worth the discomfort of having been abandoned to his company. Her spirits improved considerably.

Lord Davenport extended no mercy to Huntingdon's proud sensibilities. "Now look, my dear, you've embarrassed him in front of this beautiful girl that he can't keep his eyes off of. Not that I blame him." He laughed heartily. He took Genie's hand and, despite his barrel-shaped belly, executed a spry, gallant bow over her hand. "If you ever tire of pretty, my dear, I can still lead a merry turn around the dance floor. Perhaps a waltz...?"

Despite Lord Davenport's misunderstanding of the situation, Genie couldn't help but be charmed. She laughed and mimicked his bow with a courtly curtsy. "It's an honor, my lord, my lady."

"Nigel, don't tease the poor girl," Lady Davenport reprimanded at the same time. "You know the waltz is scandalously improper." Lady Davenport took Genie's arm and nestled it firmly between her arm and bosom. "Don't listen to him my dear, he'll stomp all over those tiny toes of yours."

Rather than be offended by her gesture, Genie found strange comfort in the motherly hold. Although affectionate, Lady Hawkesbury was a typical aristocrat and not physically demonstrative. Genie's mother had been more like Lady Davenport, always free with a hug and a squeeze. Genie didn't realize how much she'd missed the easy exchange of affection. She rarely allowed herself to think about how much she missed her mother.

"Mrs. Preston is a guest of mine for the season," Lady Hawkesbury explained.

Lady Davenport lifted an eyebrow at that, glancing back and forth between Huntingdon and Genie. "Oh. I thought... Well, never mind." She waved her fan excitedly, turning toward a young dandy who had just joined them. His cravat was starched so high, Genie was surprised that he could move his neck. But he managed to lift his chin and stare down his nose at her well enough.

Though not unpleasant of countenance, his expression was one of great boredom and disdain well beyond his years. He couldn't be much older than her three and twenty. "There you are," Lady Davenport said. "I was wondering where you'd disappeared to. Mrs. Preston, this is our son, Percy."

Genie had to close her mouth to prevent a startled gasp. The Honorable Percival Davenport could not have been more dissimilar from his parents if he'd tried. Noting the haughty expression extended to his parents, Genie thought that perhaps that was the point. He did not appear to value his parents' rustic charm.

Percy greeted Lady Hawkesbury, nodded to Huntingdon and lifted his monocle to study Genie with great condescension. He could have taught Prinny a thing or two, she thought.

Huntingdon didn't bother hiding his dislike of the younger man. "Percy," he said simply, but his voice was full of the patronizing scorn affected by an older playmate. The dislike was apparently mutual. "I'm surprised to see you here, Fitz. A confirmed bachelor like yourself gracing the assembly rooms of Almack's? Finally done scouring the countryside for that little country mouse of yours?" Percy mocked.

Genie gasped, not believing what she'd just heard. The ton knew about her. If not by name, then as a "country mouse." What other rumors were floating about? Fear of discovery mixed with humiliation. Tense, every hair stood on end praying for the conversation to take a different course.

Her prayers were not to be answered.

Unaware of the pain and embarrassment he was causing, Percy continued on. "You were fortunate to get out of that horrible blunder without irreparable social disaster. Couldn't have an *esteemed peer* like yourself marry a little nobody. Think of the precedent," he exclaimed sarcastically. "Though it was great fun to see you make a fool of yourself over a little 'dairymaid,' wasn't that what you called her? Wonder what ever happened to the silly chit? I'd wager she found herself a nice farmer somewhere, has a dozen brats, and rues the day she let a duke slip through her grasping fingers."

Genie felt her cheeks burn with mortification. She didn't know what was worse, being referred to as a nobody or as a grasping nobody. She couldn't look at Huntingdon. He'd called her a dairymaid? Humiliation ate at her insides. She waited for him to say something, to right the degrading manner in which Percy referred to her, but Huntingdon said nothing to defend her—or himself.

The poignant silence rang cruelly in her ears.

When she couldn't stand it any longer, she dared to glance at Huntingdon. He looked thunderous, but was trying not to show it. His mouth set in a firm line with tiny white lines etched around his lips. His eyes burned nearly black with fury. His fists were curled into tight balls and he looked as though he fought to restrain himself from punching Percy in the nose.

Say something!

Nothing.

He wouldn't even look at her.

Genie felt something inside of her flicker then go out. Why would she think, even for a moment, that he'd changed? She still wasn't good enough for him.

"Hush now, Percy," Lady Davenport scolded. "You've teased the poor boy enough. Look how you've shocked poor Mrs. Preston. She'll want nothing to do with our dear duke now."

Truer words had never been spoken.

Finally, Huntingdon looked at Genie. Their eyes held. A harsh sneer curled his top lip. "There was not much danger of that was there, Mrs. Preston?" No doubt aware that he'd said too much, he didn't give her time to answer. "Percy, I can see your years at Oxford were wasted. You still have the manners of a guttersnipe and the tongue of an asp. If you don't want those fancy clothes of yours mussed, you'll do best to remember that I am no longer the tolerant playmate that I was when we were lads. Learn to curb your tongue, or you'll no longer find yourself welcome in my presence."

Genie watched the younger man flush. The threat was unmistakable. The duke had put Percy in his place and firmly reminded him of his rank and power. Important considerations for an ambitious young dandy.

But Huntingdon had said nothing to defend her.

How did he still hold the power to disappoint?

Into this already awkward gathering, Fanny and Edmund returned. It was immediately obvious that Edmund had confided in Fanny about his relationship with Genie. Fanny wouldn't look at her. Strain lined her pale face. It seemed as if all that joyful spirit had been flogged right out of her.

It was just a schoolgirl's fancy. Fanny will get over it, Genie told herself, looking away and trying to quiet the guilt.

Just like you got over it?

Even in her own mind, the truth could not be denied. She

hadn't completely gotten over Huntingdon, perhaps she never would. But she'd learned to survive without him—in spite of him.

It was better that Fanny learn the truth about men now. Before disillusionment stripped away all of her youthful idealism like petals from a flower of her innocence, and left a withered, thorned stem in its place.

The Davenports seemed happily oblivious to the awkward surroundings and to Fanny's obvious turmoil. They enfolded Fanny in a crushing hug and regaled her beauty.

"Oh, we're so happy to see you, my dear," Lady Davenport said. "How you've grown," she exclaimed, looking Fanny up and down. "In all the right places, I dare say," she added with a teasing wink.

Fanny managed a wan smile. "It's good to see you too," she said, returning the embrace and planting a fond kiss on Lady Davenport's cheek.

"How is your dear mother? You've just returned from Leicestershire?"

Fanny shot a nervous glance to Genie at the mention of the duchess. Genie felt her blood rise, but held her expression impassive.

"I only returned to town yesterday," Fanny answered cautiously. "Mother is well."

"Still won't come to town, eh?" Lord Davenport asked.

Fanny shook her head.

"Ridiculous," Lady Davenport muttered. "This self-imposed exile must come to an end. I'm of half a mind to go and fetch her myself."

"I'm sure she would welcome your company," Fanny replied kindly. "But she is quite determined—"

"My Hyacinth won't be gainsaid, not if she puts her mind to something," Lord Davenport said with an affectionate squeeze of Lady Davenport's plump arm. "She could stand down Wellington."

The black patch above Lady Davenport's lip twitched with unshed laughter. "Balderdash." She preened.

"Napoleon perhaps, but never our esteemed Wellington."

"If the duchess will not travel to London, maybe we could bring a bit of London to her?" Lady Hawkesbury suggested.

"A house party!" Lady Davenport cried, taking up the reins. "What a fabulous idea. With the season nearly ended that will be just the thing."

"Capital. Capital," Lord Davenport added.

Edmund looked as though he wanted to strangle his mother. "Aren't you forgetting the ball, Mother?"

"No, no, of course not," the countess said with a meaningful glance at Genie. "After the ball of course. That is if the duke has no objections?" Lady Hawkesbury eyed him intently, almost daring him to do so.

Huntingdon bowed. "I shall write to my mother at once."

"It's settled then," Lady Davenport said, clapping her hands.

Genie shot a look of plea to Edmund. *Do something.* She couldn't go to Donnington Park. The Duchess of Huntingdon was the last person she wanted to see. She could ruin all her plans with one word. And the hatred for what the duchess had done, for what she had taken from her, still burned too bright. Genie didn't trust herself to hide it. There was no confusion where the duchess was concerned, unlike Huntingdon, Genie had never loved his mother.

Edmund moved closer to her side. "I'm afraid I'll be unable to get away from London for some time."

He'd intended to exclude Genie and his mother from the invitation, but Lady Hawkesbury ignored his obvious ploy. "Perhaps you'll join us later then, dear?"

Good gracious, Genie thought. If there was anything worse than being fed to the lions, it was being fed to the lions without a shield.

The Davenports chattered on enthusiastically about the plans now set in motion for the sojourn to Leicestershire. With the exception of Percy, who appeared simply bored, the rest of the group was noticeably subdued.

She and Edmund would think of something, Genie

vowed. Nothing could persuade her to go to Donnington Park.

Even if it meant confessing the truth to Lady Hawkesbury.

HUNTINGDON WAS WORRIED ABOUT HIS sister. Fanny had suffered quite a shock. Apparently, her childhood attachment for Hawk was more significant than he'd realized.

He should have warned her, but there hadn't been an opportunity. So focused on his own problems, he hadn't recalled Fanny's infatuation with Hawk until it was too late.

Side by side brother and sister stood on a balcony off the assembly room, silently peering out over the railing to the gardens below. He needed time to let his blood cool. Fury still pounded in his ears. Percy had always been a nuisance, even when they were boys, but never had Huntingdon so yearned to pummel him. To wipe that condescending sneer into the ground.

The only thing that stopped him from violence was the realization that defending himself or Genie might somehow give her away. He knew Percy. If Percy sniffed a scandal, especially one that involved his childhood nemesis, he would not rest until he uncovered it.

Huntingdon had wanted to explain to Genie, but noticing Fanny's pallor, he'd sought to remove her from the unpleasant situation at the first opportunity.

But not before he'd agreed to that damned house party. How had that happened? And what was Lady Hawkesbury's purpose in suggesting it?

How could he be expected to maintain his distance with Genie living under his roof? And with his mother no less. This spelled a perfect combination for disaster.

"You can't let this marriage happen," Fanny said, panic rising in her voice. "You must do something."

"What would you have me do?" he said, exasperated.

"I've tried to apologize, but after what happened, Genie wants nothing to do with me. Do you blame her?"

Tears glistening in her eyes, Fanny turned to him and shook her head. "No, I don't blame her. I've told you for years that you behaved abominably. You broke her heart. But to marry Hawk? Your best friend?"

"My former best friend," he corrected. "But she didn't know that until recently."

Fanny's eyes rounded with horror. "Do you mean that Hawk knew who she was?"

"Not initially," he said grudgingly. "But he's known for some time."

"And Genie was married?"

"So she says. A soldier."

"When?"

"Not long after she left for America."

Fanny's gaze narrowed at that. "I don't believe it."

Huntingdon shrugged. He'd come to much the same conclusion himself. Too many things didn't make sense.

Fanny was silent after that, again leaning over the stone banisters, intently studying the couples strolling in and out of the shadows along the moonlit garden paths.

Huntingdon felt impossibly stuck. As a brother, he naturally wanted to protect his sister. But he'd also made a vow to Genie not to interfere. A vow that he'd been manipulated into. A vow that he already deeply regretted. And now, a vow held at the expense of his sister's heart.

If Huntingdon thought there was a chance for Fanny, it might provide the excuse he needed to step in. But Hawk had never shown Fanny any interest beyond that of a tolerant older brother. Even if Hawk's heart wasn't otherwise engaged, Fanny was probably doomed to heartbreak.

Just as he was doomed to watch the woman he couldn't forget marry his best friend.

Was allowing Genie to marry Hawk the way to atone for his mistakes? And could he let her go... again?

He heard a sharp intake of breath and followed the

direction of Fanny's gaze. Like two players on an intimate stage, Hawk and Genie stepped out of the shadows and into a small circle of light.

Neither he nor Fanny moved. With painstaking slowness, the farce unfolded before the captive audience of two. Although Huntingdon couldn't hear what they discussed, both seemed upset. Genie appeared to be pleading with Hawk. Consoling her, Hawk pulled her under his arm and gently kissed the top of her head.

Huntingdon's heart pounded, knowing what was going to happen next, but trying to stave it off by sheer force of will. His fingers gripped the unyielding stone until his knuckles turned white. Incapable of speech, his lungs constricted as he held his breath.

Hawk led Genie farther into the shadows. But not far enough. Silhouetted against the moonlight, Hawk pulled her into his arms, tipped her chin and kissed her. Not with mindless passion, but with infinite tenderness.

Tenderness that seized Huntingdon's chest in a vise.

The kiss lasted only for a minute, but it was long enough to alter his good intentions. His reaction was swift and unequivocal. He knew exactly what he had to do. For Fanny.

No, he admitted, for himself.

His attempts to put the past behind him were finished. The past was not over. He knew it with every inch of his body, a body that now shook with a primal rage. He would not stand aside and let her go without a fight. And maybe not even then. He would do whatever it took to win her.

Even if she hated him for it at first. He told himself in the end it would be all right.

With a soft cry of utter despair, Fanny turned and ran.

Before Huntingdon chased after his sister, he stole one last look at Genie. Fanny's cry must have carried across the still night air, because both Genie and Hawk had turned their surprised faces up toward the balcony. But it was only Genie who interested him. Their eyes met and held. His uncompromising stare burned into hers, promising one thing and one thing only: The Duke of Huntingdon, a man now revered for his trustworthiness, was about to break another promise to her.

CHAPTER ELEVEN

"BISCUIT?" THE COUNTESS OF HAWKESBURY offered, breaking the uncomfortable silence. She held the silver platter piled high with the mouthwatering morsels directly under Genie's nose. So tantalizingly close, Genie could almost taste the rich creaminess of the butter and the deep caramel of the warm sugar.

There was a time when Genie would have been unable to refuse. A time when she had delighted in food, especially in sugary cakes and pastries. No longer. Genie's body was a finely honed weapon of war with no room for indulgences.

"No, thank you," she answered, though her stomach rumbled with hunger. Hunger she'd learned to control ever since she'd known what it meant to truly be hungry. So hungry that you'd be willing to do *anything* for something to eat...

Still feverish, it had taken Genie some time to fully comprehend their meaning.

"Poor dear, you mean she has nothing?" A feeble high-pitched voice stirred her from a deep slumber.

"Nothing. The villainous maid took every last halfpenny, fleeing the ship as soon as we docked."

A man's voice, Genie realized. A voice of authority. The captain. That's right, they'd landed in Boston Harbor a few days ago. Why was she still on the ship? What had he said? Then she remembered. Her fortune. Her future. Gone.

Cold fear gripped her heart. She wanted to go home. She wanted her mother. What would she do? How would she survive when she couldn't even lift her head from the lumpy pillow?

"And to lose her child when she has just lost a husband, what a tragedy! Of course we must help her. She'll come home with us." Another high-pitched voice. Similar, but distinct from the first.

Two ladies. Sisters. Sisters who occasionally helped the ship's doctor with nursing his patients while in port. The kind, elderly spinsters had taken pity on a poor soldier's widow and brought Genie into their humble one-room home in a boarding house to recuperate. They'd tended her, cared for her, fed her, brought her back from death's door with their gentle ministrations. Without them Genie would have surely died.

Just as day by day she had been surely killing them.

Genie had to save them from their own kindness. Kindness that would have left them all starving. For each morsel of food that they put in her stomach was taken directly from their own mouths. The nursing, supplemented by the extra sewing and embroidery work that the sisters took on, was barely enough to support two. Three mouths stretched the meager income to a mere pittance.

Pride again had been Genie's downfall. She should have accepted their assistance while she got back on her feet. But she hated feeling helpless. Hated the knowledge that she was repaying their kindness with suffering. Surely, an educated woman of good breeding would have no problem finding employment as a governess?

And she hadn't. Especially, as her face and emaciated form, ravaged by sickness, did not provoke undue attention. So she moved from the boarding house to a comfortable private home in Harvard Square.

In the beginning, Genie had truly loved her work, welcomed the anonymity of her position and the obscurity of her destroyed beauty. Adored instructing her young charges. Lavishing the love and devotion on the two girls that she would have on her own child. Burying her memories in hard, honest work. Thoughts of home grew more distant. More filled with fear and shame. Should she write them? Would her family even want her? Questions that were irrelevant as she was still far too sick to travel on such a long, arduous journey.

As the months passed, her health returned. As did her voluptuous, flaxen beauty. The beauty that had at one time seemed such a blessing now became the source of her downfall. No longer could she take refuge in obscurity. Along with the bloom in her cheeks and extra flesh on her limbs, returned unwelcome attention from men. Attention that forced her to seek new employment again and again. Attention that quickly depleted her small savings.

Fending off unwelcome advances from her employers began a vicious cycle of hiring and discharge, with each new post a substantial step down the social ladder of respectability. Taking her farther and farther from her dreams of returning home.

Thinking to appear sickly, Genie starved herself. But it didn't work. Nothing worked. They kept coming after her...

She'd been utterly powerless. Genie had never understood precisely what it meant to be a woman in a man's world until she found herself alone in a strange country, without funds, and with no family or connections to protect her from the lasciviousness of men. Vile, base creatures who saw an unprotected woman alone in the world as nothing more than easy prey.

What choice did Genie have when there was none? Find work or starve. It was as simple as that. Strength of character did not put food in your belly. Moral righteousness did not prevent men from taking what they wanted. A slimy kiss here, a lewd grope there. They cornered her, used their physical strength to overpower her objections. She hated them. But most of all she hated *him* for putting her in this position.

Hatred had enabled her survival. Dreams of revenge had fueled her will to live.

Genie had learned by living the alternative that money and position were the only power that mattered. Everything else was illusory. As fleeting as innocence.

She'd vowed never to be without choices again. She controlled her own destiny. Money, land, position—those were the only things that mattered. Those that called such goals mercenary had never experienced the desperation of hunger and poverty.

"You know, dearest," the countess broke into the memory. "I've never asked you about your past."

There it was, Genie thought. Her worst fears voiced. Buying time to think of an appropriate response, Genie lifted the teacup to her lips and sipped. The hot liquid scorched a long path down her chest, plummeting like a burning river into the snake pit of nerves twisting in her stomach. But rather than calm her down, the bitter drink only fired her edginess.

The delicate porcelain cup rattled as Genie carefully placed it back in the saucer. Because she could do nothing else, Genie glanced up to face the countess who was staring at her patiently across a mahogany tea cart.

"Yes, my lady."

What else could Genie say? I appreciate your forbearance, because I do not want to lie to you?

Nothing good would come of this conversation.

A conversation that, after the revelations last evening, Genie had known was all but inevitable. The countess must know or at least suspect her true identity. And sure enough, before Genie had even broken her fast this morning, Lady Hawkesbury had wasted no time sending for Genie to join her in the conservatory.

Genie's fists nervously clenched and unclenched in the deep folds of her skirts. Her grand plans were about to be tested. This conversation with the countess was only the first.

Huntingdon would also prove a challenge.

If only he hadn't witnessed that kiss. A simple kiss that may have complicated everything.

The look on Huntingdon's face had terrified her. He looked like a half-crazed berserker poised to attack. And she was the spoils. Could she control him? Would he stand by his promise? She no longer felt entirely confident that he would.

But it was also the feelings that Edmund's kiss aroused in her that terrified her. Or rather, feelings that the kiss *did not* arouse. While not unpleasant, she could not stop comparing it to another. Could not help but feel that what she was doing was wrong. Her overactive conscience would not quiet. She didn't love Edmund the way he deserved to be loved. She knew that. But Fanny did. Fanny who had once been like a sister to her.

And when they'd been caught in an embrace, like two naughty children, she'd suffered a sharp twinge of guilt. Guilt that said kissing a man she did not love with all of her heart was wrong. Edmund was also affected. She'd read the shame of disloyalty on his expression. Disloyalty, for an honorable man like Edmund, would eventually eat away at his soul.

Stop. She had to stop this constant second-guessing.

She would not risk her future again.

Not on memories. Not on guilt. Not on a kiss. Not on anything.

The countess ignored Genie's obvious distraction. "But my dear, please do not confuse forbearance with ignorance. I've known for some time that your past was, how shall I say, complicated." When Genie opened her mouth to protest, Lady Hawkesbury held up her hand. "Please. I make no judgment. We all have our secrets, some more scandalous than others..." The countess paused, looking down at her skirt to smooth a nonexistent wrinkle from the yellow muslin of her morning gown as if she was remembering something acutely painful. Clearing the memories, she blinked her eyes and glanced back up at Genie. "Though you play the coquette admirably, you do not have your heart in it. Often, when you think no one is looking, a strange, haunted look comes over your face. A deep sadness that cuts to the bone." Perhaps sensing Genie's growing horror, Lady Hawkesbury smiled. "But, I digress.

I've said too much. I don't mean to cause you more pain or embarrassment. What I want you to understand is that your past has never really mattered to me. I love my son and I want him to be happy."

Relieved, Genie exhaled loudly. "As do I, my lady."

"I do not doubt that. And until recently, you have done so. But circumstances have changed, have they not?"

"I'm not sure I understand..."

"Mrs. Preston," the countess interrupted kindly. "May I be frank?"

Genie smiled at that. The countess was nothing, if not frank. "Of course."

"I can see the way the duke looks at you, I saw the recognition in Fanny's face when she saw you, I heard what she said—or rather what was left unsaid. I suspect you are the girl from Thornbury who Huntingdon has searched for over the past few years. The very girl my son was sent to find."

Genie couldn't help it—to hear her secret said out loud—she blanched, but said nothing.

Unperturbed, Lady Hawkesbury continued. "I have no intention of asking you about your past relationship with the duke. Nor would I ever voice my suspicions to anyone else. Ever. So, do not fear disclosure from me." Genie's relief was short-lived. "However, with the ball where you will announce your engagement fast approaching, I will ask you to think long and hard about your feelings for my son and for the duke—"

"I have no feelings for the duke," Genie quickly retorted. "If anything, I despise him."

The countess lifted a questioning brow. "Hmm. For my son's sake, I hope that is the truth. I learned long ago the pain of being trapped in a loveless marriage."

Shocked, Genie took a moment to respond. "But I thought... Edmund has always said that yours was a great love match."

"You could call it that, I suppose," Lady Hawkesbury said, a wry smile turning her mouth. "But I fear the love was rather one-sided. On my part."

"I'm sorry." And she was. Genie knew all about the agony of one-sided love.

The countess's smile turned bleak. "Not half as sorry as I. Unrequited love is not quite as romantic in real life as it is in novels. You'll understand, then, why I won't condemn my son to the same damnation. To the agonizing purgatory of loving without being loved in return."

As if a mask had been lifted, the countess's face, usually so sweet and cheerful, transformed. Her lively eyes were dull with heartache. Heartache that had taken years of suffering to perfect.

A haunting image of a morose and disheartened Edmund flashed before Genie's eyes before she forced it aside. *It won't get to that point.* She wouldn't allow Edmund to suffer.

But how could she prevent it?

"I love Edmund," Genie said firmly.

The countess leaned over and patted her hand. "Of course you do. He is a good man and has been a good friend to you. But friendship isn't enough. Do you *love* him with a gut-wrenching passion that permeates every fiber of your being?" Her voice turned thick, as if she was fighting off tears. "Is he the only man in the world for you? When he walks in the room, does your soul cry out for its other half?"

Lady Hawkesbury's voice laid bare sounded like a soul torn apart, ripped to shreds. In the face of such honesty, Genie couldn't speak. Because, of course, the answer was no. She would never love like that again. Never again allow a man that power over her. There was more than one man in a lifetime for her, there had to be. God would not be so cruel.

"Does Edmund love you like that, my dear? At first I thought he did, now I'm not so sure. He wants to protect you, but that isn't the same thing, is it?"

They both knew it wasn't. But instead of answering her question, Genie hedged. "I promise to consider what you have said."

"Very well, I have said my piece. Now I must attend the preparations for the ball. You will let me know whether there will be an engagement to announce?"

Genie nodded and quickly fled the room before her conscience overrode common sense.

So what if Edmund's kiss did not make her heart tumble, did not make her yearn to bare her soul to completion? She'd had that before and look what it brought her. Genie would not fall victim to love's painful grasp again. She would do her best to love Edmund as he deserved to be loved. And in marrying Edmund, perhaps she would protect herself from the countess's cruel fate.

The Duke of Huntingdon be damned.

CHAPTER TWELVE

THE DUCAL CARRIAGE ROLLED TO a clattering halt before Hawkesbury House. Eyes fixed straight ahead, focused on the task at hand, the Duke of Huntingdon barely noticed the festive grandeur of the house set ablaze with hundreds of torches, candles, and gaslights. Music, laughter, and the dull roar of a large crowd reverberated through the crisp autumn air. The Countess of Hawkesbury's much anticipated ball was in full swing.

Threading his fingers through the soft kid of his gloves, one by one the duke yanked the hem at his wrist and forced the snug leather down hard over his knuckles. His movements were impatient and rough. Tonight was not a night for finesse.

Tossing his black cape behind him, he alighted from the carriage and made his way up the staircase lined with rows of footmen dressed in vivid blue and gold livery. Cheerful greetings accosted him as he stormed through the crowd, but he barely acknowledged them.

He was a man on a mission.

The Duke of Huntingdon had made his decision, even if it would damn him in her eyes.

He would live with the consequences. The alternative was simply inconceivable.

He hated that it had come to this. But there was no time for wooing, for explanations, for convincing. Edmund and Genie planned to announce their engagement tonight. And he was there to put a stop to it.

There would be an engagement this night, but it would not be the one anyone was expecting.

WHEN HUNTINGDON ENTERED THE BALLROOM, everything around her seemed to stop. Genie's heart beat so furiously her entire body shook. Lulled by his conspicuous absence over the past few days, she'd nearly succeeded in convincing herself that she'd imagined his reaction to her kiss with Edmund.

But the moment he entered the room, his ice-blue gaze shot straight for her, piercing her with a cold, possessive intensity. A shiver of apprehension cut through her. Whatever his purpose there this evening, it did not bode well.

Lady Worthington, one of her companions, noticed the direction of her stare. "The Duke of Huntingdon is a very handsome man is he not, Mrs. Preston?"

Lady Worthington was a shrewd, exotically beautiful woman, perhaps in her mid-thirties, rumored to have had many paramours amongst some of the more distinguished members of the ton. Yet despite her reputation, Genie rather liked her. But Genie would have to be more careful. Controlling her blush, Genie arched a brow skeptically. "I suppose. I haven't paid him particular attention."

Lady Worthington laughed, a low, seductive throaty sound. "No. But it seems he has paid you quite a bit of 'particular attention.'"

Thankfully, Lady Thornton, an older woman who would never be called sharp, broke in. "He's remarkably large, don't you think? And appallingly muscular. Quite unfashionable, but irresistible nonetheless with those golden-god looks. He looks like he tumbled right off Mount Olympus." She sighed dreamily and fluttered her fan.

Genie made a small choking sound. He'd tumbled from Mount Olympus all right, straight to Hades. Lady Worthington's gaze intensified; those dark, feline eyes altogether too perceptive. "Where did you say you hailed from, Mrs. Preston."

Genie's heart raced. "Gloucestershire," she murmured, but was saved from further inquiry by the impending arrival of Huntingdon. She took one look at his face and suddenly she had a powerful urge to run.

He wore the devil's own black expression. Firelight flickered off his dark-golden head like some macabre halo. His mouth was drawn in a thin line of a man determined to act, though the task might prove distasteful. No, she had not imagined his reaction. He'd only been biding his time. But for what?

She was about to find out.

Quickly, he closed the distance between them with long, purposeful strides. Before she could make good a coward's retreat, he was at her side.

He made his bow to the other ladies in her group before turning his undivided attention to her. "Mrs. Preston."

"Your Grace."

She felt like a hare trapped in a hunter's snare. The heat of his magnetic gaze held her. She couldn't look away.

He wore black. Black that contrasted sharply with a stark-white waistcoat and cravat. The colorless garb suited his devilish demeanor. All he needed was a red cape and a trident and he could rival Hades for the throne of the underworld.

Despite his somber attire, every man around him paled in comparison. The thin, foppish peacocks of Brummel's set seemed ridiculously feminine. For once, his heavily muscled form did not seem out of place encased in such finery. The hard lines of the cutaway coat emphasized the wide set of his shoulders and narrow waist, and the tight breeches his powerful thighs.

The Duke of Huntingdon was a man and every woman in the room was aware of it.

Including Genie. Much to her irritation.

She lowered her gaze, trying to ignore her attraction, but even her nose fell traitor to the enticing male scent of soap and sandalwood. Damp locks of dark blond hair curled along his collar. The knowledge that he'd just come from his bath conjured up some rather explicit images. She swiftly forced the unwelcome picture aside before she did something utterly humiliating and blushed like a moonstruck schoolgirl.

He flashed a dazzling smile to the other ladies that surely sent quite a few hearts a flutter. "If you'll excuse us, Mrs. Preston has promised to show me Lady Hawkesbury's prized pineapple plants."

Pineapple plants? That was original.

"I'm afraid now is not a good time, Your Grace," Genie refused ungraciously to quite a few raised eyebrows. A soldier's widow did not countermand a duke. "Lady Hawkesbury is expecting—"

"I'm sure our hostess will not mind a few moments delay," Huntingdon interrupted smoothly. "I am most anxious to see them. I am thinking of trying to grow the fruit in my own greenhouse." Despite the deceptive pleasant tone, Genie heard the firm command underlying the request.

Boldly he met the obstinate refusal in her gaze, almost daring her to deny him. The silent standoff lasted only a moment before sanity returned. Genie pursed her lips together, biting back an unladylike oath. Unless she wanted to create a scene, she would do as he asked. Clearly, he meant to have this discussion and she supposed that now was as inconvenient as any other time. She lifted her chin and smiled icily. "Very well, I'm sure I can spare a few minutes."

He took possession of her elbow, a sizzling brand on her skin, and quickly steered her toward the door. In one last brilliant defensive maneuver, Genie turned around to ask Lady Thornton to accompany them, but he stopped her with a gentle squeeze. In a low voice meant for her ears alone, he warned, "I wouldn't if I were you."

She clamped her mouth shut. Before she knew it, they were outside in the rose garden headed for the greenhouse.

"I fail to see what could be so important that it can't

wait—"

"Trust me," he murmured near her ear, the deep husky burr sending a warm tingle down her spine. "It can't."

Genie jerked her elbow free and stomped into the greenhouse. An action made much less effective by an accompanying wince of pain. The thin soles of the slippers that she wore with her diaphanous silver ball gown permitted every sharp stone to pierce the soft skin of her feet. She glanced down at the elaborate Grecian-style ensemble. She hadn't noticed before, but the dress was remarkably similar in style to the one she wore to the harvest festival race-week ball all those years ago. Fitting somehow. But this time she was not the same naïve little innocent. She was a woman equipped for battle.

The room was hot and ripe with the pungent fragrance of flowers. Roses, ferns, and large potted fruit plants lined the narrow stone paths. She wished she'd thought to bring a lantern. The only illumination was the dim cast of flame from the torches that burned along the dark garden paths outside. The heat, the starlight, the delicate smells, the uncertainty of his intentions, all combined to heighten her senses.

Though he stood a few feet away, she could *feel* him around her, crushing her with the weight of his presence. It was insane, this feeling of a physical connection whenever he stood near. If only he didn't smell so good. The fresh, warm scent of sandalwood was almost hypnotic. She frowned. She needed to get out of there before she completely lost her mind and let sensation override her good sense.

"Well, there they are." She pointed to the large potted pineapple plants in the far corner. Ruse fulfilled, she spun around to leave. "Now if you'll excuse me—"

"Not so fast." He caught her waist and turned her back to face him, pulling her hard against his body.

Genie gasped at the intimate contact.

"Let me go!"

"You and I have some unfinished business." His head

dipped until his mouth was only a few tantalizing inches from hers.

Genie's temperature shot up a few hundred degrees. Enveloped in the heat of his embrace, awareness surged through her. Pressed against the muscled wall of his chest, her breasts rose and fell with the excited pounding of her heart. He gazed down at her low décolletage with such an expression of raw desire that her nipples grew taut, straining against the thin fabric of her bodice. Disconcerted by her body's reaction, Genie lifted her chin and mustered in her most prim governess tone. "We have discussed everything there is to discuss."

"I'm afraid not. Circumstances have changed."

"Nothing has changed," she said stubbornly.

He ran his fingers down the bare skin of her arm. She shivered, from fear or excitement she didn't know. All she knew was that her heart pounded furiously and she couldn't breathe, waiting for him to make his next move.

"*Everything* has changed."

That blasted kiss. All her plans undone by a simple kiss. There had to be irony in there somewhere, but Genie was too upset to see it. Why did he have to be on that balcony?

She was so close to achieving her goal, she would not allow the man who had once taken everything from her to interfere with her future. She wanted it all back: the promise of youth, the life that had been cheated from her by cruelties of fate. Security. Happiness.

But would Edmund make her happy? And what of his happiness?

She quieted the obnoxious voice of uncertainty that would not shut up. "You vowed to leave me be and I intend to hold you to your promise."

He shook his head. "I'm afraid that is no longer possible."

Genie's eyes narrowed, frustration and anger mounting. She nudged her pointed finger at his chest, stabbing him repeatedly to mimic the staccato of her voice. Though it was about as effective as trying to dent stone with a feather. "I thought you had changed. I thought you might have learned the word honor. But you are still the same selfish boy that you were five years ago. Breaking vows, taking without thought or care of others."

A shadow that looked like regret crossed his features. His hand pressed the small of her back, bringing her even closer to the hard wall of his chest. "I can't allow you to marry Hawk."

Squirming, she scoffed at his arrogance. "I don't need your approval. I will marry Edmund whether you like it or not." She cursed the breathlessness in her voice that weakened the impact of her words. If only he'd stop holding her so close. If only she couldn't feel every hard plane and ridge of his chest, every angle of his hips, and something else. Something that demonstrated the sheer magnitude of his attraction. Something that made her legs turn liquid from... It was such an alien feeling she almost didn't recognize it—lust. She'd no longer thought herself capable of that weakness.

His gaze darkened, a heady mix of anger and attraction. "I think not. It seems I have a strong aversion to seeing you kiss another man."

Jealousy. Possession. Lust. That was all that this was about. He wanted her and he was willing to destroy her to have her. How could she have thought even for a moment that he'd changed?

"You have no right," she said furiously, trying to pull free from his embrace.

His arms tightened. "I have every right." A wicked grin curved his lips. "You will be my wife, and my duchess will confine her kisses to me."

He took her dumbfounded open mouth as an invitation, smothering the startled cry of outrage by the force of his lips on hers. It was a kiss meant to show possession. A kiss to brand. A kiss to erase all thoughts of others.

And God help her, it did.

He told her with his mouth what she didn't want to accept, but what she instinctively knew: some things never changed. For her, no other man would ever compare. She wanted to cry, to rail at the cruel Fates for making her still want this man after all he had done to her. Why him and not Edmund? She choked on the bitter truth as he kissed her senseless and her body soared with the sheer perfection of the sensations leaping through her.

Heaven and hell. Huntingdon could bring her to both.

But right now, it was all heaven. She'd tried to forget the magic of being wrapped in the arms of a man who made her heart lurch with each seductive caress of his lips. A man who could ignite the ashes of her passion with a simple stroke. She wanted him to kiss her, to touch her, and she wanted to drown in the seductive warmth of his mouth and arms.

He kissed her with a raw hunger that should have terrified her with its intensity. There was no gentle buildup, but rather a spontaneous combustion of molten desire.

She should have banged against his chest like a madwoman and demanded to be released or bite his tongue as she'd done before. But she could no more deny his kiss than she could the breath that gave her life. Genie needed to feel alive again and Huntingdon was the only man who could awaken the dormant embers and make her burn. Again.

Her heart beat wildly in her chest, but behind the hazy fog of desire, she could not completely quiet the conflicting emotions battling in the dark recesses of her mind. Her pride hated the weakness, the very helplessness that made her melt into his arms. But the weak part of her yearned to succumb to the promise of pleasure in his tormenting kiss.

This time, she couldn't fight the pull, the attraction, the memories. A traitorous whimper escaped from between her lips, practically begging him for more.

And he gave it to her, sliding his tongue into her open mouth. He stroked and teased, taunting her with a carnal rhythm that promised untold sensual delights.

The man could kiss like the Devil.

And the Devil take her, she responded, matching the

movements of his mouth, entwining her tongue with his, sliding deeper into the kiss, allowing her body to sink into the warmth of his powerful embrace. The heavily muscled body of a laborer mixed with the suave elegance of an aristocrat was an impossibly attractive combination.

He was so big it should have terrified her, knowing that she was helpless against his dominant strength. But she knew—no matter what his other flaws—that he would never use that strength against her, only to protect her. Her insides uncurled with wicked delight as her tiny hands made him shiver with desire. She explored the expanded planes of his body, tentatively at first, but with burgeoning intensity. Her fingers splayed against his chest then gripped his broad shoulders, traced the firm muscle of his upper arms and back, admiring the impressive male strength of his form. The layers of hard muscle flexed instinctively under her fingertips and a gut-checking slice of lust cut through her. She wanted to rip his shirt off and place her hand on his bare skin.

He pulled her closer, pressing her hips firmly against him, slowly sliding up and down, allowing her to feel every thick inch of his heavy erection. He cupped her bottom and lifted her until she could feel the engorged head of his arousal against her shivering entry. Something hot and deep uncoiled inside her. Her body responded to the primal urge of desire, softening, turning her insides to mush.

Huntingdon felt her response and it nearly drove him mad with lust. The sensation of her hands on his body was like no other feeling he'd ever experienced. Her soft little moans tortured him, so he kissed her harder, silencing her, devouring her mouth with his lips and tongue. He couldn't get enough of her fast enough. He wanted to lift her skirt and plunge deep inside her, putting an end to her protestations once and for all. She was his, and he was going to prove it. He wanted her naked. He wanted her wet. He wanted her astride him, bare breasts bouncing as she rode him harder and harder until her head fell back in delirious ecstasy calling his name and flooding his cock with wave after wave of shuddering release.

He wanted to look deep into her eyes as she came and dare her to deny him.

He wanted to tell her exactly what he wanted to do to her, where he wanted to lick her, to suck her, but he didn't want to give her the opportunity to think. His hands roamed her body, molding her breast, cupping her bottom, savoring every inch of velvety exposed skin. But it wasn't enough. He wanted to see every naked inch of her. He wanted to tear her hair from its bindings, releasing the shimmering silk veil. He wanted her weak with passion, he wanted her to scream his name as she climbed the jagged pinnacles of a violent orgasm.

His mouth moved to the sensitive place below her ear as his hands loosened her gown and freed her breasts from the wretched confines of her gown, chemise, and stays.

He groaned at the vision before him. Her breasts were large and round, tipped with tiny pink nipples, rising high above the ivory contours of her belly. He reached out and cautiously slid his thumb across one sweet nipple. The helpless shudder that racked her shoulders nearly made him explode. Reverently, he weighed her breasts in his hands, lifting a delicate pink tip to his mouth for his kiss. Softly at first, then harder. He sucked and rolled the tip between his teeth until she moaned. Flicking his tongue and nibbling until she moved, circling her hips against his cock. She tasted so sweet, like honeysuckle laced with the faintest hint of salt. She was so hot, nearly ready for him, and just the thought of entering her, sinking into her full hilt as she wrapped her legs around him—he couldn't stand it.

Genie had lost all sense of pride and decorum. The sultry air of the greenhouse became an oasis. His fingers skimmed the inside of her thigh, teasing. She stilled. Relax, she told herself. *He won't hurt you.*

But Edmund had never done anything more than try to kiss her, and she wasn't sure...

His hand brushed the juncture between her legs and she gasped—with pleasure. Awash in sensation and desire, a trance came over her for a second as her body focused on the urge to find release for the pressure building inside her. A sweet rush of dampness spread between her legs as she imagined the deft stroke of his fingers and the hard thickness of his manhood driving inside her.

Nothing else mattered. For a moment lust overrode panic. The rush of blood surging through her body hummed in her ears. For a moment she thought she could forget. She thought the darkness wouldn't come.

Until he slid his finger inside her and she froze. Dark memories accosted her and a moment of panic set in. No, she fought silently, trying to shake the fear. She could do this.

But perhaps sensing her hesitation, Huntingdon stopped. So suddenly she nearly collapsed when he released her.

They stood staring at each other, breathing hard, both unsure of what had just happened. And why he had stopped.

After a few minutes he seemed to come to a decision. Genie fumbled with her gown and, silently, thankfully, he helped her dress.

Her cheeks burned. What must he think? She claimed to want nothing to do with him, but then he kissed her, and she nearly fell apart in his arms. She'd convinced herself that she'd changed, hardened. But she was still as susceptible to him as she had been five years ago. She was still a fool enslaved by the cravings of her body.

He lifted her chin with his fingers and looked straight into her eyes. "When I make love to you, it will be as man and wife."

The arrogance of his words grated against her shredded pride. Her chest heaved as she lashed out. "You must be daft," she spat. "I will never marry you."

There was a long, dark pause before he spoke. The jagged shadows of the greenhouse cast his features in a sinister light. His eyes still gleamed with the angry vestiges of unspent desire. His steely gaze did not flinch from her face. "You'll marry me, or I'll be forced to see to it that you have no other choice."

The words pelted her like ice. After what they'd just shared, what they'd nearly done, the coldness of his threat hurt. But Genie could not doubt that he meant what he said. She froze as the full impact of his words hit her. The blood drained from her face. He meant to ruin her. "You wouldn't," she whispered.

"To stop you from marrying the wrong man, I would. I've made some inquiries about your late husband."

Genie felt panic claw her chest. He knew. He knew she'd lied about being married.

"Strange, but there does not seem to be a record of him?" The knowing look on his face belied the feigned surprise in his tone. "When I make our previous acquaintance in Thornbury known, it won't take long for people to remember the mysterious disappearance of the county's reigning beauty. I'm afraid my ongoing attempts to find you are rather well-known. It won't take long for someone to figure it out." He lifted a brow. "If I'm not mistaken, Lady Hawkesbury has already done so."

He was right. But she was not ready to admit defeat. "Edmund would still marry me."

He smiled and shook his head, a patronizing movement that further bruised her damaged pride. "But would you marry him, knowing what it would cost him?" He gave her a long, hard look. "You have changed Genie, but not that much. Would you have Hawk shunned by polite society?"

Would she? Had she become that mercenary?

The iron resolve forged by disappointment and tragedy faltered. The realization that Huntingdon might know her better than she knew herself chafed. He'd played her well. She'd changed, but not as much as she wanted to.

She would not intentionally harm Edmund. Not after all he'd done for her.

Scandal had to be averted. "It won't come to that."

"Do you doubt me?" He smiled, but his voice turned hard. "Don't."

He would do it. He wanted her and he wasn't going to back down unless she did something. She felt the walls closing in on her. Her mouth went dry and her voice, when it came, broke pitifully. "Why?"

He shrugged. "I feel responsible for what happened to you. I want to do right by you. To do what I should have done all those years ago."

"So you seek to erase your shame, and you think forcing me to marry you will make it right?" She couldn't believe the insanity of his reasoning. "Did you learn such gentle persuasion at your mother's knee?"

He flinched, but did not back down. "Would you agree otherwise?"

She ignored his question. She had not agreed. "Why now? Surely, you can't claim to love me?" she asked incredulously.

His face shuttered. A wry smile curved his lips. "No. I want you. Let's leave it at that."

The truth stung. Even though she'd known his answer, the disavowal still managed to find a tender spot in her hardened heart.

"You want a possession," she challenged. "You only want me now because you can't have me. This is about lust."

He glanced meaningfully down at his breeches. The evidence of his arousal obvious in the tight, form-fitting clothing. "I can hardly deny that's a part of it."

"Passion eventually dies."

Amused, he quirked a brow. "Does it?"

Perhaps not. Five years hadn't dampened his any. Flustered, she tried a different tact.

"Why?" she asked hollowly. "Why do you want to ruin my life again?" The conflicting emotions of what had nearly happened between them and his cruel threat had shaken her defenses. "Wasn't once enough for you?"

Don't cry. Please, don't let him see you cry.

His tone softened. "Don't you see? I want to make it up to you. I'll give you everything you ever wanted. Name it and you shall have it. If I thought you truly loved Hawk, it would be different." He grasped her shoulders and stared deep into her eyes, daring her to deny his words. "I know you don't love him. I saw the way you kissed him. It was nothing like what just happened between us."

Her cheeks burned. He was right, but she didn't want to concede to it. But after Huntingdon's latest kiss, the comparison with Edmund was... well, there wasn't any comparison.

Genie grew frantic, trying to find a way out of the noose tightened around her.

She was scared. Scared of what he made her feel. She didn't know how long she could resist this insane pull to him—a pull that challenged her resolve whenever she was around him.

Genie realized that she'd been wrong. It wasn't the past she needed to worry about, it was the present. The man he'd become was infinitely more dangerous than the man he used to be. He no longer relied on charm. The charisma of power and confidence was infinitely more appealing. Ironically, Huntingdon had become the sort of man who inspired trust. She couldn't believe she was even thinking about trust and Huntingdon together. How long could she resist him? And resist him she must; his betrayal had run too deep.

She'd survived once, but she couldn't do it again.

The urgency of the situation made her contemplate something that she would never have thought possible: confiding a bit of the truth. The truth would put an end to his threat, but could she stand his censure? Could she stomach witnessing the disgust that he would try to hide when he looked at her? She would have to.

"You don't understand. You can't marry me. There are things about my past..." She sighed, calming the nervousness in her voice. "Things that could make your political ambitions impossible."

He spoke without hesitation. "I don't care."

But he would. Any man would. Even though she was innocent of wrongdoing, it would not matter.

"But a cabinet post is important to you?"

"Extremely."

She couldn't do it. She couldn't bear to see his disgust or, even worse, his pity. But he'd left her with no choice. She turned away. There was no other way, she could not destroy Edmund, and marriage to Huntingdon was unthinkable.

She hated him anew for forcing her to this.

"Ask Edmund where we met," she said dully.

"Why?" he asked, puzzled. "It won't change my mind."

But it would, she thought sadly. But said, "Just ask him."

Out of the corner of her eye, she could see his brow wrinkle. He turned pensive, searching for a clue in her expressionless face. "Very well, but you'll do something for me."

She eyed him warily, justly cautious of his ultimatums.

"You will call off the announcement of your engagement to Hawk tonight."

She started to protest, "But Lady Hawkesbury is expecting—"

"Lady Hawkesbury will understand." Noticing Genie's guilty blush, he smiled. "In fact, unless I am mistaken, I think Lady Hawkesbury will not be surprised."

No, she wouldn't. "Fine," Genie managed. "But it will be only temporary."

Huntingdon's hand reached out to tuck an errant strand of hair behind her ear. Her heart leapt to her throat. The hard, callused fingers singed a fiery path along the soft curves of her face. He gazed at her in a way that could only be described as loving. Her foolish heart actually had the gall to clench.

"We shall see about that," he said softly, an arrogant smile played about his mouth. "Marry me, Genie, and I will do everything in my power to make you happy. If it takes me a lifetime."

The tenderness of his touch and the huskiness of his voice chipped away at the ruins of her defenses. She wanted him to go on looking at her like that. She wanted to trust him again. For the first time since she'd returned to England, Genie actually considered the ramifications of surrender.

With the pad of his thumb he wiped an errant tear from the corner of her eye. Their eyes met and held. She ached for something deep in her chest with an intensity that took her breath away. Something that felt horribly like fulfillment.

"Trust me," he whispered.

The words jolted her back to reality. The familiar refrain that had haunted her darkest memories shattered the fragile moment of connection.

She laughed, a pitiful, slightly hysterical sound.

Furious with her capriciousness, Genie jerked her face from his hand and ran. Ran as if the very Devil were nipping at her heels.

And in a way, she supposed he was.

Huntingdon couldn't force her to marry him. He couldn't.

But in her heart she knew he could.

If it came to that, even if it took her a lifetime, she would make him regret it. She would have her revenge not only for what he did five years ago, but for forcing her into an unwanted marriage. And for something even worse: making her wish it could be different.

CHAPTER THIRTEEN

AFTER GENIE LEFT THE GREENHOUSE, Huntingdon made his way to the library to await the fallout. It wouldn't take Hawk long to track him down.

Huntingdon had visited Hawkesbury House many times over the years, but it had been some time since he'd ventured into the library. A lifetime ago, more times than he'd care to remember, Huntingdon and Hawk had been marched to this room—knees shaking—to face their punishment for some boyhood infraction. This room had represented the end of the road, when the transgression was grave enough to warrant the final arbiter.

The desk still stood in the same place, dominating the center of the dimly lit room like some great mahogany fortress. Despite the distance of years, Huntingdon shivered. He could still remember the late earl looming like a giant executioner behind his behemoth desk, a black scowl indicating his displeasure at the bothersome interruption, ready to impart some horrible punishment. As was often the case with youth, the imagined punishment usually eclipsed reality.

The room hadn't changed much in the ten years since the earl's death. Heavy furniture, plush dark fabrics, and endless shelves of leather-bound books lined the walls from floor to ceiling. A worn rug in deep colors with eastern designs covered the wooden floor. A decanter of brandy rested on the sideboard. Taking this as an invitation, Huntingdon helped himself to a generous pour.

He pulled the chair out from behind the desk and sat down to wait.

The irony of the place he'd chosen to have this conversation did not escape him. No doubt Hawk's anger, like Genie's, would be formidable.

Not that he blamed them.

Huntingdon wished there was another way. He reminded himself to focus on the ends and not the means. He'd gambled and won. He had her. He'd seen her hesitation when he mentioned Hawk. Genie would agree to marry him; it was just a matter of time.

If Genie had actually called his bluff, Huntingdon didn't know what he would have done—whether he would have actually gone through with his threat to ruin her.

But he did know that he wouldn't lose her. Not again.

He wanted her. Wanted her in a way he never had another woman.

His body still raged from that kiss. More than a kiss really. And moments away from being much more. No doubt after this latest disappointment his bollocks had turned a permanent shade of blue. He recalled the softness of her responsive lips beneath his, the feel of her silky skin under his palms, the weight of her breast in his palms, the honey taste of her tight nipple rolling between his tongue and teeth, and the sensuous press of her hips against his swollen cock. He shook his head to clear the vivid fantasy, raking his fingers through his hair in frustration. Cursing the semipermanent rise in his breeches, he adjusted himself as best he could when his body still demanded release.

For one sweet moment, he thought he'd had her. But something had made her hesitate, and it was enough to clear his mind. It was important that she realize that he'd changed. He didn't want their joining to be like before—illicit and dishonorable. He owed her the honor of his name. He owed her the proper order of things: marriage *then* passion.

A short engagement would be the most that he could manage. Otherwise, he'd be forced to take matters into his own hands, so to speak. The constant state of arousal she left him in was interfering with his ability to concentrate on anything else.

He didn't analyze his motives for marriage too deeply. It was time for him to take a wife. To have children. And he'd never wanted another woman the way that he wanted Genie. It was reason enough.

The door flew open with a crash.

Spitting the expected fire, Hawk stormed into the library, issuing an impressively creative string of colorful epithets. Huntingdon lifted his timepiece from the pocket in his waistcoat. Forty minutes. Not bad. Not even an hour had passed since he'd delivered his ultimatum to Genie.

"I should kill you."

Huntingdon chuckled, but it was without amusement. Lazily, he held his crystal glass up to the light, slowly rotating it in his hand, observing the subtle play of candle light flickering off the amber liquid. After draining the contents in one deep gulp, he glanced back to his seething friend. "You could try."

"I might succeed."

Huntingdon shrugged indifferently. "You might."

Hawk shook his head, disappointment etched across his features. "I honestly didn't expect this of you, Fitz. She wouldn't agree to marry you, so now you'll force her to it? Issuing crude threats like the lowest blackguard?" Hawk banged his hands down on the desk in front of Huntingdon with enough force to make his empty glass rattle. "You don't know what you do. You don't know how she'll hate you for forcing her." Hawk stared at him intently, his expression losing some of its anger. "I beg of you, as a friend, don't do this."

Uncomfortable with Hawk's earnestness where he'd expected only anger, Huntingdon ignored the sudden shiver of trepidation that shot up his spine. "It's already done."

"I could do the same, you know. Bring ruin down upon your heads if you go through with this."

"But you won't." It was not a question. Huntingdon

knew his friend too well. Hawk was noble to the bone—even if it meant he would lose something important. That was where they differed.

"No," Hawk murmured, clearly disgusted with himself. "But it doesn't have to be this way. It's not too late to walk away."

"Yes, it is." He wouldn't lose her again.

"Why?"

Huntingdon didn't answer.

"Do you love her?" Hawk persisted.

"I did."

"Then why are you doing this?"

Huntingdon stared at him mutely. Not really sure himself.

A glimpse of understanding appeared in Hawk's eye. He laughed dryly. "You're a fool. You're seeking some kind of atonement, but don't you realize if you do this you'll never find it? You're going to do what you should have done five years ago, and you think that magically the past will be corrected? It sounds more to me like you're repeating your past mistakes by taking what you want, without any thought as to the consequences."

Huntingdon had heard enough. Hawk would never understand. "I will make it up to her. You won't change my mind; I've made my decision."

"There are things you do not understand," Hawk warned. "Things that might interfere with your plans for a cabinet post. Things that could destroy your position in society."

Huntingdon's expression darkened, annoyed at being kept in the dark about Genie's mysterious past. "I'm getting tired of hearing the same refrain from you and Genie. Why don't you tell me what it is I don't understand? She said that I should ask you where you found her."

Startled, Hawk stood from his bent position over the desk. "She said that?"

Huntingdon nodded. There was clearly something wrong here and a twinge of uncertainty niggled at him. Exactly what was the mystery he was seeking to unlock? He had a strong premonition that it might be something he didn't want to know.

Hawk paced the room. Abruptly he stopped and spun around to face him. "Can't you just leave it be?"

"No."

"I want your word that you'll never speak of this."

"Don't insult me."

Hawk considered him for a moment, obviously debating whether to believe him or not, seemingly forgetting that they'd been friends for years.

"Very well," Hawk agreed, albeit reluctantly. "I don't know how to begin." Hawk pulled a chair out and sat down. But he kept repositioning himself, unable to get comfortable. "I searched most of Boston as you asked, with no luck. I visited many of the leading drawing rooms of Boston society, numerous employment agencies, theaters, workhouses, markets." He paused. "Every respectable place I could think of with no sign of her. No one had ever heard of Miss Eugenia Prescott and given your description of her, I figured that she was not one easy to forget. I nearly gave up. I didn't know where else to look."

As he spoke, Huntingdon started to feel vaguely uneasy, until the pit of dread that had settled in his stomach snowballed. Something in Hawk's face made him guess what was coming next. His gut twisted and the blood drained from his face. That ball of dread, so dark and twisted, rose, lodging in his throat. He could barely get the word out. "Except...?"

Hawk nodded, confirming a nightmare. "Except those places that are not so respectable." Hawk took a deep breath and met Huntingdon's agonized gaze with one of his own. "I scoured the waterfront and..." Hawk stopped and met his gaze squarely. "I finally found her in one of Boston's finest brothels."

"No!" he cried, though his voice barely broke above a whisper. Huntingdon's mind reeled. The world shifted. Everything he knew about good and bad, right and wrong, gone in an instant.

The innocent young girl he'd once loved had sold herself like a... He couldn't get the word out. A terrible blackness of rage, pain, and disillusionment washed over him. Stunned didn't even begin to describe how he felt.

Hawk continued to explain, but Huntingdon put his head in his hands, not sure he wanted to hear anymore. "It was only by chance that I found her at all. I'd asked around most of the houses of ill repute, but no one had heard of anyone matching your description. Finally, at one of the last stops on my list, one of the women overheard my questions and brought me to the room of a young girl who was very ill. I swear to you at the time I didn't know it was Genie. She was using a different name. Her appearance had changed drastically from your description. She was half-starved." He stopped and met Huntingdon's blank stare with true sympathy. "She'd been badly beaten."

Huntingdon flinched.

"The ladies of the house nursed her cuts and bruises as best they could, but her spirit was crushed. For a long time, even after her injuries had healed, I didn't think she was going to live. She'd lost the will of it." Hawk studied him. "You have to understand. My heart broke to see a young girl—any girl—so brutally treated. I didn't care who she was, I had to help her. I think I fell a little in love with her from the first time I saw her lying in that bed. She was like a little broken bird, so fragile, in such despair." Hawk's jaw hardened and took on a defiant tilt. "I would have done anything for her."

"But how?" Huntingdon asked incredulously. "How did she end up in a place like that? My mother sent her away with a small fortune."

Hawk's expression turned cold and accusing. "After she lost the child Genie became very ill. While incapacitated, the maid your mother so graciously provided stole her money, fleeing the ship as soon as they docked. Genie arrived in America ill, destitute, and alone."

Huntingdon felt ill. Bile soured his mouth. His mind was spinning in thousands of directions. He wanted to lash out.

To find answers that would explain the unexplainable. He'd wanted to know what she was hiding, but he'd never imagined anything like this.

"But as for how she ended up there," Hawk shrugged. "I don't know exactly. I've never asked her the details. I know that she worked as a governess, but that it became impossible for her to continue. I have my suspicions about why."

But to sell herself in a brothel? There had to have been another choice. *Anything* other than that. How could she have...? His stomach rolled.

He clenched his teeth together, holding back the bile. "Who beat her?"

"She never told me. Believe me, I did my best to find out. I was most eager to take care of the matter." Hawk gazed at him meaningfully. Huntingdon understood how "the matter" would have been handled. He felt the same way now—like he could kill the bastard. "But Genie said she didn't know."

Another horrible thought crossed his mind. He leveled a long look at Hawk. "Did you...?"

Hawk's eyes blared with fury. He drew himself up stiffly, every inch the honorable English gentleman. "No."

Huntingdon knew he spoke the truth. Hawk would never take advantage of a damsel in distress. He, on the other hand...

As if he knew what Huntingdon was thinking, Hawk explained. "She was hardly in any condition for that. It was many months before she'd recuperated enough for loving, and by then I knew I wanted her as my wife."

"But before you found her. Did she... had she?"

"I don't know." *And I don't care.* Huntingdon heard the unspoken censure. "Does it really matter?" Hawk asked.

Yes, unfortunately, it did. He was not as generous a man as Hawk.

Hawk must have read the answer on his face. He shook his head. "She was right then to tell you. You'll not force a marriage upon her now. I assume this means you will step aside."

Huntingdon put up his hand. "Not so fast. I'll hear the story from Genie first. Go. Rejoin your guests. I'll be along directly."

He needed to compose himself. To give his shock and anger time to abate. Edmund looked like he wanted to say something more, but deciding against it, left Huntingdon to his thoughts.

Suffocating in the small room heavy with emotion, he strode to the window. Fumbling with the latch, he managed to finally force it open. A cool breeze washed over him. He planted his hands on the wide sill and leaned out into the darkness, filling his lungs with long, deep breaths. The crisp air cooled the heat of his anger, but the twinkling stars seemed to taunt him with their celestial beauty. With their very purity.

Could he take a woman as his wife who had sold herself?

For the life of him, he didn't know. His reaction to Hawk's kiss had been visceral, extreme. What would the knowledge of her lying with another man, or God forbid, multiple men, do? Could he wipe the image from his mind?

What had driven her to such perdition?

Even if Genie had come to be in the brothel innocently—a hope that he clung to—if society found out she'd spent time in a house of ill repute, she'd be ruined. And he along with her. He hadn't thought a scandal would matter, but then he'd never imagined something like this.

A brothel. God in heaven, how had it happened?

CHAPTER FOURTEEN

AT TIMES LIKE THIS, GENIE thought morosely, the obligations imposed by society seemed particularly onerous. Rather than taking refuge in the cathartic solitude of her bedchamber as she wished to do, she laughed and danced as if she did not have a care in the world. As if everything she'd fought to achieve did not hang in the balance.

Looking at her, no one would ever know how dangerously close to the edge she hovered. How just one push might send her catapulting into darkness. She flirted harmlessly with her latest dance partner, a man old enough to be her father, executed the intricate dance steps with casual precision, and tried to keep her gaze from flickering back and forth to the entry. Her mouth ached from the effort to force a gay smile across her face. A smile that she hoped would mask the worry, and perhaps fear, clouding her eyes.

Edmund had been gone for some time now. At any minute...

Her dance partner stared at her expectantly.

He'd said something and she hadn't been listening.

"I'm sorry, Lord Chester." She swayed a little. "I feel a bit light-headed."

His weathered brow wrinkled with immediate concern, forgetting his unanswered question. "Allow me to find you a chair, my dear."

She gazed at him as if he was the most brilliant, most considerate man in the world. "That would be divine."

He ushered her to a cluster of armchairs in an adjoining

room. Genie took out her fan and fluttered it furiously.

"Is there anything I can get for you, my dear? Should I send for Lady Hawkesbury?"

"No, no. I shall be fine in a moment. But if you wouldn't mind, a glass of ratafia would be just the thing."

He hurried off to do her biding, eager to be of some use. Genie was grateful for the reprieve and for the moment of relative quiet. Aside from a handful of footmen, there were only a few people milling about and most seemed as eager as she to enjoy the solitude.

He would be coming soon and she wanted to be prepared.

But rather than Huntingdon, it was Fanny who found her first. Fanny, the girl who'd once giggled with her like a sister, but who now glared at her with something akin to hatred blaring in her lovely blue eyes. The constant none too gentle reproach was hard to take. She'd been doing her best to avoid Fanny, dreading this conversation nearly as much as Huntingdon's. Indeed, this was the first time she'd spoken with Fanny since that unfortunate episode in the garden.

"Where's Lord Chester? I saw him bring you in here?" Fanny asked.

"Fetching some refreshment." Genie motioned to the chair next to her. "He should be some time, it's quite crowded out there."

Fanny pulled the chair out and sat down. "Yes, Lady Hawkesbury's annual ball is always popular. It's become something of a tradition to mark the end of the season."

"So I see," Genie replied. They sat in uncomfortable silence for some time. Taking in Fanny's pale face, she asked quietly, "What is it Fanny? Is there something you want from me?"

Tiny white lines appeared around Fanny's mouth and brow. She met Genie's gaze with a flat stare that wasn't exactly a challenge, but more a look akin to betrayal. A look that made Genie distinctly uncomfortable.

Fanny appeared to brace herself and without further

preamble, she asked, "Are you going to marry Hawk?"

There it was. How like Fanny to come right to the point, no delicate sidestepping around the subject for her. Having care for Fanny's tender feelings, Genie said gently, "I've agreed to marry him, yes."

Fanny's face crumpled and Genie's conscience bit her soundly in the chest. She looked away, unable to bear the sight of Fanny's heartbreak. *It is just a schoolgirl's crush.*

"But why? You don't love him."

"Of course I do."

Fanny's jaw tightened. "Not in the way that matters. You forget, Genie, I know what you look like when you are in love. You don't look at Hawk the way you looked at my brother."

"That was a long time ago," Genie said sharply, intending to cut off any discussion of the past. "I was just a girl." *Like you,* she wanted to say.

"You still love him."

"I despise him," Genie replied fervently. Perhaps too fervently.

Fanny laughed, but it was with sadness not amusement. "I think you wish you did. And Lord knows he deserves your anger. He acted like the worst sort of cad. But I know he wanted to marry you. He made a mistake, a monumental one, confusing duty for honor. But you didn't see him after you left, believe me, he's paid for it. Many times over. My brother has changed, Genie."

Genie didn't want to discuss Huntingdon. She appreciated Fanny's sisterly loyalty, but Genie doubted Fanny knew everything about what had happened between them five years ago. "Perhaps he has changed, but not as much as you think," she said, thinking of his selfish attempts to force her to marry him and his broken promise to leave her alone. "In any event, it is five years too late. You can't change the past."

Fanny looked at her sadly. "No, you can't. But nor can you ignore it, no matter how much you might wish to. Don't make Hawk pay for your unhappiness, Genie. He deserves to be loved."

"And you think if I let him go, he'll fall in love with you?" she asked softly and immediately regretted it.

Genie heard Fanny's sharp intake of breath. Her lovely face twisted with grief. Genie felt cruel.

"No. I don't think that." Fanny's voice caught. "He doesn't think of me like that. But perhaps there will be someone else."

"I will make him happy," Genie said firmly, trying to convince herself.

Fanny stared at her for a long time, silently urging her to change her mind. But Genie stood firm. What choice did she have? Could she just give up on all of her plans? No. She had to marry Edmund. Apparently sensing that Genie would not be swayed, Fanny's glare hardened. "My brother is not the only one who is selfish."

Her words were loaded with pent-up emotion. Something other than Edmund was troubling her, Genie realized. "What are you talking about, Fanny? What have I done to make you hate me so?"

Fanny stood up. Back rigid and shoulders set regally she paraded to the door. Genie didn't think she was going to answer, but at the entry she turned. Pity and anger marred the beautiful planes of her face. Her voice shook. "Not once have you asked about your sister. Don't you care what has become of Lizzie?"

Startled, Genie rose and hurried after her into the ballroom, quickly losing sight of her. What about Lizzie? What had happened to her? Was she all right? Genie scanned the crowd for Fanny, but her eyes caught instead on Fanny's brother. And by the black look on his face, discovering what had happened to her sister would have to wait.

HE KNEW. GENIE COULD SEE it on his face. Disbelief, disappointment, anger... and perhaps the first seedlings of disgust. The sharp pinch in her chest told her that his reaction mattered much more than she wanted it to. It was foolish, of course, because she'd known what would happen by sending him to Edmund. She knew what he would think. Counted on it, in fact.

He was wrong. Yet in many ways, the truth was not much better.

Huntingdon picked his way across the ballroom, occasionally stopping to make brief remarks to the many who hailed him, but his destination was clear. Genie steadied her frantic nerves for the coming storm, telling herself that it would be worth it in the end. The truth—or partial truth—would free her from any further attempts from him to force marriage upon her.

He wouldn't want her, the threat of ruin would disappear and she would be free to marry Edmund. Forcefully, she pushed aside the memory of Fanny's agonized eyes and Lady Hawkesbury's heartfelt warning.

So intent on Huntingdon, Genie failed to notice Lady Hawkesbury's approach until she stood right beside her. She grasped Genie's hand and gave it a gentle, encouraging squeeze.

"I spoke with my son."

Genie hesitated, not sure what her reaction would be. "And he told you?"

The countess was visibly distressed, but nodded as if she'd expected it. "Yes, that you wish to postpone the announcement."

"I'm so sorry," Genie said, meaning it. Lady Hawkesbury had been nothing but kind to her, and she hated to disappoint her. "I had no choice." Genie's gaze traveled meaningfully to the duke, who was descending upon them like some dark, avenging angel.

Genie took immediate umbrage at his judgmental reaction. After all he'd done, his attitude stung. She thought she'd put aside the anger and resentment and moved beyond the need for revenge. But the dark emotions she'd suppressed threatened to explode. She felt a burning desire to make him pay for hurting her again.

Lady Hawkesbury took note of the direction of Genie's angry gaze and, despite the circumstances, smiled kindly. "No, if I know Huntingdon, I'm sure you didn't. He always was a willful child. But irresistible just the same." She nodded to the approaching duke. "Have care, my dear. Hatred corrupts in devastating ways. Make sure you know what you want before you make a decision that can't be undone." Startled, Genie's eyes widened. How did she know what Genie was thinking? Were her thoughts of revenge that transparent? Lady Hawkesbury continued, "Use my private drawing room. From the looks of it this is a conversation that is better held in private. No one will disturb you."

Genie nodded her gratitude and started to turn away. But something confused her. "Lady Hawkesbury?"

"Yes."

"There is something I don't understand. The other night, why suggest the house party?"

"Hmm." She brought a finger to her mouth, considering. "When I realized that you were the girl from Huntingdon's past... Well, I know something of the duchess's role in your disappearance. It is important to me that you be absolutely sure about marrying my son. The only way to do so is by fully facing your past."

"But isn't there a risk that forcing me together with Huntingdon might hurt Edmund?"

The countess gave her a long, thoughtful look and nodded. "Yes, of course. But if you and Edmund are meant to be together, you will survive the duke and his mother. True love can survive any obstacle, can it not?"

No, Genie thought, there were some things love could not survive. Like betrayal. Like the death of a child. Like the death of innocence.

Lady Hawkesbury continued, "In any event, the duchess will eventually hear that you have returned. You might not want it, but you will need her support—or rather her silence."

Huntingdon was almost upon them. "Go, now," Lady Hawkesbury motioned. "I'll tell him where to find you."

True to her word, not five minutes after Genie had dismissed the footmen, she heard the doors of the drawing room open behind her. She turned around only to see Huntingdon close the doors firmly behind him. A foreboding click and they were alone.

He approached her soldier's stance by the fireplace. A sudden chill swept over her and she shivered. Her delicate ball gown did not offer much protection against the drafty room. Although it was a cool evening, the coals had not been lit. As this was not one of the public rooms, it was not expected to be occupied during the ball. She dearly wished it wasn't occupied now.

He broke the silence. "Lady Hawkesbury is unusually accommodating," he noted dryly.

Genie met his gaze. His expression was strained, like he was fighting to stay calm, fighting the urge to hurl accusations at her. Genie shrugged. "She has her reasons."

Huntingdon looked at her questioningly, but did not pursue the matter. Instead he asked the question that hung like a giant albatross between them. "Why, Genie? Why were you in a place like that?"

He kept his tone careful, nonjudgmental, but Genie could hear the underlying plea. She steeled herself from the sudden urge to come clean. To tell him everything. Would he understand? Would he blame her? Judge her?

But she couldn't tell him the truth—not if she wanted to ensure that he left her alone.

Clearly, he was trying to be fair, giving her the opportunity to explain, but just as clearly he'd already damned her.

He would never understand. He was a man, used to taking what he wanted. Just like the others.

She squared her shoulders. "Didn't Edmund explain?"

He shrugged noncommittally. "Hawk said that you had been badly beaten." He took her chin and tilted her face up toward him, as if he was looking for any lingering evidence.

But the scars that remained were far too deep to see. Her skin tingled under his callused fingertips. Their eyes met and Genie felt that powerful connection. The awareness that could make her forget everything else—almost.

She could melt in the liquid warmth of his eyes, in the rugged handsomeness of his face.

"Who hurt you, Genie?" The soft caress of his husky voice made her eyes burn with longing. It was a voice that promised protection. The voice of a man who would defend her against the world.

If only he had been that man.

"A man." She wrenched her face free from his tender fingers. "It doesn't matter who."

"It does to me."

"Why? It was a long time ago. Don't worry, he has received his due." At her hand. No one had been there to save her but herself.

"Was he...?" He stopped, unable to finish the question. He cleared his throat and started again. "Was he a visitor to the house?"

He was my employer, she wanted to scream, *a man who'd hired me to care for his children. A man who refused to take no for an answer.* But instead she scoffed. "That's a rather kind way of putting it." She smiled coldly. "What you're really trying to ask is whether I was a whore?"

He flinched at her deliberate crudeness. "What am I to think? Was there another reason for you to be in such a place? Damn it, Genie. Help me understand."

She bristled; her back straightened. "Why should I? I don't owe you an explanation." Her eyes narrowed. "If anyone made me a whore, it was you."

His eyes sparked with fire, hearing in her response what he wanted. He grabbed her arm, furious. "Don't blame me for your choices."

"Shouldn't I?" The anger she'd been holding back for years finally burst free. "Who seduced an innocent, respectable young girl with a promise of marriage? Who refused to answer my letter when I begged you to come to me and honor that promise? Whose mother forced me from my home, my family, from everything I'd ever known? Who left me with child, a child whose death nearly killed me? Who left me alone to face the ugliness of the world, and men who only want—" She stopped herself, aware that she'd said too much. She was shaking from the release of emotion that had been kept bottled for too long. Her throat constricted with a knot of hot tears. Forcing herself to take deep breaths, slowly, stone-by-stone, she erected the wall of detachment back up around her.

Taken aback by the vehemence of her attack, he seemed honestly shocked by the level of her anger. And shamed. "I'm sorry," he said softly. "I know how horribly I wronged you. Forgive me, I never realized."

"No. Of course, you didn't. Why should you?" she asked bitterly. "As a man these are things you wouldn't consider. The 'choices' as you put it are not the same for a man. Tell me this, *Your Grace*, what choice does a woman alone really have? A woman without money, without connections, without protection, without useful skills other than a passable accomplishment at pianoforte or embroidery."

"You had other skills," he argued. "You are a bright, well-educated woman, surely there are many respectable professions other than being a wh—"

"Don't say it!" she warned through bared teeth. "Don't you dare say something you know nothing about. About the kind women who showed me the compassion and protection that you and men like you did not. Don't you think I tried to find employment? You know how I'd always loved children. I tried. Believe me I tried." She stood back, moving closer to the candlelight, allowing the light to fully capture the lushness of her form. "But look at me, Huntingdon. Really *look* at me."

He did. His brow creased, unsure of what she expected, as his gaze traveled up and down over her form, briefly lingering on her breasts and face. Unknowingly lingering. Unable to completely mask the accompanying desire that flared in his eyes.

"You're beautiful," he whispered, his voice rough with wanting.

It was what she expected him to say. She shook her head, disappointed nonetheless. "And that is all that anyone sees. I was told often enough that the only thing anyone would want me for was my beauty. Isn't that true, Huntingdon?"

HE COULDN'T TAKE HIS EYES off her. From the top of her golden head turned silver in the candlelight, to the pointed tips of her tiny satin slippers. Standing like a goddess in her ivory gown, the thin fabric hugging the rounded curves of her breasts and hips, skimming the long length of her lean legs. He looked at her, at the beautiful features that had haunted him for years, the tiny nose, wide cobalt eyes, plump pink lips and the tight lush body that screamed out her sensuality. He felt the familiar rush of blood and all at once understood.

The force of her accusation drove home with the increasing tightness in his groin. Like him, men would see her and want her. She could never fade into the background as a governess or servant must. No, she would be sweet temptation in any household. And completely, utterly vulnerable. He'd never thought of it like that before. Of the difficulties that a woman of quality would face when cast out with nothing. Women who had never been forced to protect themselves. No wonder she'd learned to defend herself, he thought, remembering her unique handling of him earlier. What else had she been forced to learn?

Huntingdon felt the first inklings of unease. That perhaps the moral righteousness he'd felt when Hawk told him where he'd found her, ought to have been something else. Compassion. Or guilt.

His own lust suddenly sickened him. It felt base and common. Had he really thought of her as just a beautiful face? Undoubtedly her beauty had attracted him, but there had been more to it than that.

"I will not deny that you are beautiful, Genie. But you are very wrong if you think that was the only reason I wanted you. I was just as attracted by your sweetness, to your kind heart and to your gentle manner. You were funny and warm, honest and playful. You enchanted me."

Her lips curved into a rueful half smile. "Well, I am none of those things any longer, Your Grace. So do not fear. I have no intention of holding you to your generous *offer* of marriage."

GENIE TRIED TO BITE BACK some of the sarcasm, but the bitterness once freed seemed to tumble out on its own accord. She was still furious at his attempts to force her into marriage with threats of ruin. He'd ravaged her hard-wrought pride with his high-handedness. She knew she was more than a beautiful face. She'd found strength within herself that she hadn't known existed. She'd survived so much in spite of his betrayal, and it infuriated her that he could take it all away with one well-placed whisper.

Or could he? She stopped for a moment to consider the ramifications of the errant thought. What was it that she really wanted? Security in the form of money and land. Security that would ensure she would not be vulnerable to the dictates of a man again. Social acceptance was just a means to an end because she did not want to hurt Edmund, but a place in society had never been *her* dream. She preferred the country to town on any day. A glimmer of an idea formed. One side of her mouth curved up. Perhaps there was a way of carving out her desires and settling old scores after all.

Did it really matter who she married as long as she had security?

But could she do it? She studied his face with new intensity. Even with what she'd just told him, Genie could see the conflict warring on his face. He wanted her, but still couldn't accept her place at a brothel. Would he honor his offer this time?

She waited for his response.

The silence rang loudly for a long time. Too long. Finally, he appeared to reach a decision. To her surprise, honor won out this time around. He drew himself up, every inch the duty-bound duke condescending to do something beneath him. "I have made you an offer of marriage. This changes nothing," he said stiffly. "I ask you again, Genie, will you marry me? It is your choice."

"Choice?" She laughed. "You speak of choice when you try to coerce me into a marriage that I do not want. And by the looks of it, neither do you."

He didn't bother to deny it, but she noticed his mouth tighten.

Genie was amazed. She wanted to laugh at the hypocrisy. He didn't want to marry her, but would go through with it out of some strange sense of honor. She had to give him credit, he'd changed enough not to turn tail at the first sign of difficulty. Despite the possible scandalous consequences, he would marry her, even though he thought she'd been a whore. She hadn't, but it wasn't by any moral superiority to the women she'd met at Madame Solange's. No, luck had been her morality. She hadn't become a whore because Edmund had found her before she'd been forced to make that particular "choice."

Edmund. She'd tried to ignore the truth, but hadn't been able to admit it to herself until this moment. Even without Huntingdon's high-handedness, the truth could no longer be denied. Marrying Edmund was wrong. She did not love him the way he deserved to be loved—and what's more, someone else did. After all he'd done for her, he didn't deserve that.

Maybe if she'd never come back to England, had never seen Huntingdon again, she could have gone through with it. Maybe if Lady Hawkesbury had not warned her of the devastation that unrequited love might bring. Maybe if there was no Fanny. But there were all of those things, and so she would not marry Edmund.

When she first met Edmund, Genie had been in the blackest period of her life. He'd been a light, something to hold on to. A way out of the darkness. But for a long time, she'd been holding so tight to something that never had a chance.

Her relationship with Edmund had begun with deception. She'd used her beauty and her body to tempt him into marrying her, tempting him with the promise of passion that would never bloom. She would have tried her best to love him, but it would have been a losing battle, one that would eventually have made him bitter. She loved Edmund, but as a friend, not as a lover. After what happened with Huntingdon, she feared how she would even manage that.

If she did not marry Edmund, where did that leave her? She glanced over at Huntingdon, still patiently waiting for her answer.

The answer of course was inevitable. What other choice did she have? None. She had no money and no other means of support. She could return home, but would her parents want her? Or would her unexpected return only bring them more embarrassment?

Her eyes raked his powerful form, calculating rather than admiring. He stood there so cocksure of himself, knowing very well that he'd left her without a choice. God, she was tired of arrogant men. His attempts to erase his shame by forcing marriage upon her, irrespective of her wishes, were the same selfish actions of the arrogant boy who had seduced her with a promise of marriage. The best she could do was ensure her own protection. And there would be some irony in tying herself to a man who thought her a whore. Rather a nice blade to hold over his head. The thoughts of revenge that she'd forced aside when Edmund came into her life had resurfaced and intensified with Huntingdon's latest maneuverings. She might have the last word yet.

But first she had to assure her future.

Stripping all emotion from her face, she said as indifferently as possible, "My requirements for marriage are quite simple, it matters little who the bridegroom is, as long as my terms are met. Will you agree to honor the terms of the marital agreement I have with Edmund?"

Only a slight tick in his jaw betrayed his shock at her crass words. "Yes."

Genie smiled knowingly. "Do you not want to hear the terms before you agree?"

"It matters not."

She ignored him. "Edmund has agreed to provide me with a separate residence of my choosing, placed in my name."

"What for?"

"It's not your concern."

"You can't expect to live there? You have duties as duchess—as my wife, damn it—which will require your presence by my side."

Genie stiffened at the none-too-subtle reference to what would be required of her. "I will fulfill my duties." She would not reside there—not at first, at least. "In addition, I will be provided with an annual income of two thousand pounds, again in my name only and held in a separate account." From the way his jaw tightened and his mouth turned white, she knew he'd understood the significance of the amount. The same amount his mother used to get rid of her. She paused, working up the courage to add the newest term, one that hadn't been necessary with Edmund. "The house and income shall be mine, whatever the state of our marriage. If you seek an annulment or a divorce, the terms of the agreement will still be in effect."

Huntingdon sputtered, unable to hide his shock this time. "That is simply not done, it is unheard of."

She arched a dainty brow. "Not completely unheard of. Am I not correct that many men make similar provisions for their mistresses?"

He blanched, discomfited by the truth.

Genie smiled, enjoying his discomfort. "I'll of course understand if you wish to reconsider, but I'm afraid my terms are nonnegotiable. My solicitor assures me that although unusual, it can be done."

He looked at her strangely, attempting to read the reasons for such terms in her expression. But her face betrayed nothing. Let him think her cold and mercenary. She cared not, as long as he agreed.

He nodded. "My solicitor will draw up the papers and send it over for your approval."

Genie relaxed. She'd done it. She would have her security and her revenge. Revenge that would assure her eventual freedom. "Then I will agree to marry you."

She watched his expression carefully, but if he was happy he did not show it. An unwelcome twinge of disappointment pinched her in the chest. What had she expected, to be swept into his arms and kissed? She'd been the one to treat his proposal like a business arrangement, and apparently, he'd taken a cue from her. Romance and love had no part in their agreement.

"I'll begin the arrangements for a special license immediately. If you have no objection, we can be married within a fortnight at Donnington."

Genie nodded, not questioning the urgency, indifferent about what she had once thought would be the most exciting day of her life. Five years ago it would have been.

Huntingdon frowned then ran his fingers through his hair. "I suppose I should be grateful to Lady Hawkesbury for one thing."

"What?'

"For suggesting the house party."

Puzzled, she looked to him for an explanation.

"It will suffice for a makeshift wedding party, and I suppose it will be as good a time as any to break news of our engagement to my mother."

Her heart stopped. The Duchess of Huntingdon. How could she have forgotten her nemesis, soon to be mother-in-law? The face she'd cursed a thousand times from the darkest corners of her nightmares.

SLEEP PROVED AN IMPOSSIBLE DREAM that night. Images, faces from the past, had lodged themselves firmly in her consciousness—and unconsciousness. Try as she might, Genie could not escape them. The cold visage of the duchess as she issued her ultimatum. The hard handsome features of her son as he issued his. When she closed her eyes their images blurred, the face she'd once loved with the face she'd hated, blue eyes over blue, until the faces became one, and her chest hurt with the force of trying to tear them apart.

Well into the small hours of the night, Genie paced the floors of her bedchamber. Her bare feet padded across the cold wooden boards like gentle slaps. Her heart still raced from the events of the evening as she tried to separate the conflicting emotions brought about by Huntingdon's unexpected play for her hand. As she tried to understand how she could hate a man and still respond to his kiss. As she tried to reconcile how the betraying face that had haunted her for years could still inspire an almost desperate longing.

A night that should have been the culmination of her dreams in the announcement of her engagement to the Earl of Hawkesbury had ended with her pledged to another. Five years ago the helplessness of the situation would have paralyzed her. But if Genie had learned anything from the cruel hand life had dealt her, she'd learned to adapt. To take the cards and turn them to her advantage. To survive. And if all went as planned, to win.

Land, wealth, security, she'd have them all. And something else.

Revenge. Just when she'd begun to soften toward him, he reminded her why she shouldn't. Foolishly, she'd begun to believe that he might have changed. He seemed so determined. So strong. So solid. So different from the charming, carefree youth that she remembered.

But at his core, he hadn't changed. He still thought of no one but himself. He no longer bothered to hide his manipulation under a veil of charm. He wanted her, and it didn't matter who he hurt to get her.

She still couldn't trust him. She'd seen his indecision. He'd considered withdrawing his proposal. Genie knew he would abandon her in an instant if there was a scandal. The truth wouldn't matter to him, just society's censure.

But for some reason he insisted on marrying her. Because he desired her? Or for some twisted belief that he could atone for his past failures? It didn't matter. Huntingdon would get what he wanted. She would marry him. But this time, he'd be the one to pay.

The answer how had come to her as she searched the ball for Fanny, seeking an explanation for her enigmatic comment about Lizzie. Fanny had vanished, but the remembrance of her unexpected anger had not. Anger that gave her the kernel of an idea.

Genie moved the single flame of the small lamp from her bedside table to her desk and sat down to write. The damning words flowed with surprising ease from her pen. When she'd finished her letter she climbed into bed and forced her eyes closed.

The fractured dreams of a simple country girl had finally been put to rest. There would be no fairy-tale ending for Eugenia Prescott. It was up to her to squeeze whatever she could from a deplorable situation. Huntingdon had made himself her only choice, so she'd take what she could before it was gone.

This time when the images assailed her she no longer tried to separate the emotions. Love. Hate. In this case, they were hopelessly entwined.

CHAPTER FIFTEEN

"OOH, MOTHER," THE YOUNG WOMAN whispered none-too-softly to her companion as they swept through the narrow entrance of Madame Devy's modiste shop on Bond Street. "Look, it's her! The one who's to marry the duke. Just wait until I tell Sophie, she'll be positively green with envy."

Genie, the object of such rude consideration, had to stifle a giggle as she watched the two women navigate their enormous ostrich plumed turbans through the treacherously low doorway. If the appalling manners had not given the girl away, Genie thought, the slightly garish ensemble pegged her as part of the rich new merchant class—the *nouveau riche*.

Genie winced at her own snobbery. Obviously, she'd been around the nobility for too long, she was beginning to think like one of them. It had only taken her a quick glance to recognize the subtle distinctions that branded the newcomers as of the merchant class: one too many accessories, jewelry better suited to the evening, gowns too bold in color and style. A little *too* everything.

It was the difference between arrogance of birth and arrogance of fortune. In America it had been different. Very different. Though she'd admired the way a man could improve himself irrespective of the class to which he was born, she'd missed the inherent protections offered by gentle birth and station. In Boston it had been what you know, not who you know, and Genie had suffered for it.

"Hush," quieted the second woman in an even louder

voice. "She'll hear you."

As she'd done hundreds of times that past week, Genie pretended not to notice the unabashed attention her appearance aroused. She couldn't go anywhere without speculative whispers and sly glances following her every move.

The small, inconspicuous announcement in *the Times* had not escaped the eagle eyes of the ton, or the middle class for that matter. Indeed, those who still remained in town for the little season could hardly speak of anything else. The betrothal of the relatively unknown Mrs. Preston to the Duke of Huntingdon—one of the highest-ranking bachelors in the land—rather than to the Earl of Hawkesbury as everyone had supposed, had even the most disciplined tongues wagging.

Speculation about her origins abounded. Genie had (mostly) turned a deaf ear to the rumors, but she knew it was only a matter of time before she was identified as Miss Eugenia Prescott from Thornbury. A girl who'd disappeared years ago under suspicious circumstances. Admittedly, after fearing discovery for so long, all the attention made her uneasy. If it wasn't for having to face the Duchess of Huntingdon, she might almost be relieved to be leaving for the country in a few days.

The prospect of marriage to the Duke of Huntingdon, and subsequent connection to the Duchess of Huntingdon, had become no more palatable one week later than it had been the day the ultimatum was issued. Genie still didn't know how she would handle seeing the woman who'd stolen so much from her.

Eager to escape the latest set of boldly prying eyes, she returned her attention to the fabric. Genie quickly made a decision, choosing the black braid rather than the gold. The selection of trim for her new riding habit completed her last-minute trousseau, such as it was. Before he'd left for Donnington, Huntingdon had opened accounts for her up and down Bond Street, insisting that she purchase at least a few gowns befitting a soon-to-be duchess. Always fond of fashion, Genie had hardly objected. She'd take her pleasure where she could. Running her fingers along the plush velvet of the outrageously expensive gown, the beginnings of a naughty smile curved her lips. For forcing her into this marriage, he'd be lucky if she didn't beggar him before she was done with him.

Genie suddenly frowned. Huntingdon had intruded on her thoughts far too often this week. She couldn't forget how he'd made her blood pound with desire. How his lips had felt on hers. How his hands had felt across her body. Nor could she forget his cruel ultimatum.

She had not yet set her plans in motion. The letter was tucked away in a safe place only waiting until the vows had been performed. But was that all that was holding her back? At times she wondered whether she was doing the right thing. She had much to lose. But then she remembered his reaction to her scandalous past, and her resolve strengthened. Enough remained of the boy who had abandoned her in the face of society's censure.

Straightening her back, Genie ignored the continued whispering behind her. Her companion, however, did not. Lady Hawkesbury's mild annoyance when the ladies entered the shop quickly turned to fury at their continued rudeness. With a regal turn of her head, she bestowed a withering glare upon the gossiping women that immediately halted all conversation.

As the ladies cautiously approached, Lady Hawkesbury turned her back in a direct cut and said firmly, "I think we're finished here." To Madame Devy she said, "We shall take the blue silk with us. Please have the rest sent to Hawkesbury House in the morning." Two choking sounds of horror emitted from the turbaned women as they realized the identity of the important woman whom they'd offended. Lady Hawkesbury continued as if she had not heard, but Genie noticed a small, satisfied smile turn her lips. "Will that be sufficient time, Madame?"

The tiny Frenchwoman flashed a shrewd look of understanding to Lady Hawkesbury. "Of course, my lady,"

Madame Devy assured her, her heavy French accent adding to her cache as one of the most fashionable modistes in town. "The other gowns are ready; Cosette will begin the trim for the habit immediately."

"Cosette" was no more French than she, Genie thought with amusement. Though she'd spoken only a few words, Genie had detected a trace of Yorkshire in the blond, pink-cheeked girl's speech. But despite the war with Napoleon, there was still a bias toward French-made fashion.

"Then we will take our leave. Thank you, Madame," Lady Hawkesbury said graciously. She motioned to Genie as if shuffling her under her protective wing, "Come along, dearest."

Genie allowed herself to be ushered to the door. Lady Hawkesbury's continued defense of Genie moved her greatly, especially in light of the recent turn of events. Disappointed but hardly surprised by the news of Genie's engagement to Huntingdon, more than anything, Lady Hawkesbury had voiced her deep concern. She seemed to truly want Genie to be happy. Perhaps due to her own experience, she sensed that all was not right between Genie and Huntingdon and it worried her. With good reason.

Telling Edmund had been far worse. A chill shivered along her spine with the memory. He hadn't argued, but listened to her explanation with a dreadfully blank expression on his face. It had been a terrifying side of him that she'd never before witnessed. It was the face of a man stripped of the social conventions that kept him civilized. Like an avenging warrior without the mantle of honor that kept him in check, he was left with the cold, dangerous fury of hatred and the urge to kill. In fact, he'd meant to. To prevent him from riding out to challenge Huntingdon, she'd been forced to remind him of his own foul play in this farcical drama playing out among them.

She winced. The guilt that had replaced the fury on his face had not been pleasant, but it had achieved the objective of cooling his anger.

Genie knew that she'd hurt him. Yet surprisingly, he too

seemed to almost have expected it. True to his honorable form, Edmund did not abandon her, insisting on traveling with her to Donnington in case she needed him or changed her mind. And in the end it was Edmund who suggested that Lady Hawkesbury stay on as Genie's chaperone. They would all make the trip to Donnington together.

Breezing past the two chastened magpies, they were about to exit when two more ladies entered the already crowded shop. Crammed together in the tiny vestibule there was no way to avoid a greeting.

The first woman was perhaps in her fiftieth year and quite rotund. In stark contrast to her well-lined face, her hair was tinted a rather unnatural shade of auburn and curled girlishly at the temples from under a wide gypsy bonnet. Unfortunately, her significant girth blocked Genie's view of her companion. Genie didn't know her, but the woman's eyes lit with excitement as she caught sight of the countess.

"Lady Hawkesbury, how good to see you."

Lady Hawkesbury visibly relaxed and returned the enthusiastic greeting in kind. "Lady Castleton, I had no idea you'd returned to town. I'd thought you were visiting your son at his estate in Scotland."

"We've only just returned," Lady Castleton explained. "I insisted that my new daughter accompany me to town." She lowered her voice conspiratorially. "It's not good for a young woman to be rusticating in the wilds of Scotland for too long. Heaven knows what might happen." Continuing in a louder voice she asked, "Do you recall my son's wife, the Viscountess Castleton?"

"Of course," Lady Hawkesbury said. "It's a pleasure to see you again, my dear."

The younger woman stepped forward and curtsied. "Lady Hawkesbury, how kind of you to remember our previous meeting."

It was the melodious sing-song of the voice that immediately gave her away. Genie gasped with sudden recognition.

The younger woman turned at the strangled sound and

204 | *Monica McCarty*

their eyes met.

Caro's hand went to her mouth, dumbfounded. "Genie?" she whispered hollowly. "Eugenia Prescott?" she repeated a little louder. "Is it really you?"

Before Genie had a chance to say anything, she found herself the recipient of a most exuberant embrace that cut off her ability to form a reply.

"But how?" Caro asked, bewildered. "When did you return?" She broke the bear hug and extended her arms, holding Genie away from her, staring as if she could not believe her to be real. "What happened to you? Where did you go?" Her lips pursed. "And why did you not write?"

Apparently taking note of the enthralled audience of two watching the reunion with blatant interest, Lady Hawkesbury interceded. "I see you are acquainted with Mrs. Preston, Lady Castleton?"

"Mrs. Preston?" Caro echoed, even more awestruck. Before Genie could alert her to hold her tongue, Caro blurted, "The Mrs. Preston who is to marry the Duke of Huntingdon?"

With a quick glance to the turbaned pair—who were still watching shamelessly—Genie wobbled a smile and nodded. She knew her time for anonymity had just run out. The news of her identity would be all over town before nightfall. The connection with her past had been made. Now the only question was whether the wall of lies she'd built would be strong enough to protect her? At least until she was married.

Caro finally noticed the furtive glances Genie took at the other occupants of the store and halted her steady barrage of questions.

Lady Hawkesbury took control of the situation. "Why don't you join us for tea at Hawkesbury House and we can discuss all that has transpired since you two lost touch? Shall we say four o'clock?"

Her explanation to Caro would have to wait, but Genie knew the damage was already done. The connection with Huntingdon and her disappearance from Thornbury would be made. And this time, she was not to blame.

CHAPTER SIXTEEN

DAWN BROKE JUST OVER THE horizon. Taking a jump across the ha-ha that bordered his estate, Huntingdon reined in his mount and paused, savoring the quiet beauty of the soft morning light cascading across the lands held by his family for centuries. Donnington Park, the country seat of the Duke of Huntingdon, loomed in the distance like a majestic fortress rising high above a grass-covered moat. The castle that had once stood on the same spot now faded into the mists of distant memory.

This picturesque approach from the south was his favorite. A magnificent stone arch marked the beginning of a long path that meandered through gracious woodlands, over a stone temple bridge, and up the rolling grass-covered hills of the broad carriage sweep. More than three hundred acres of gardens and parklands had been meticulously designed in the later half of the last century by Capability Brown to appear as nature—were it as talented as Mr. Brown—indubitably intended.

When his gaze turned back toward the house, his chest swelled with not a small amount of pride. With the renovations finally completed, Donnington Park was breathtaking. Of classical design and equal proportions, the house comprised the best of Burlington's and Kent's Palladianism. The clean lines of the limestone walls that flanked a large central portico formed a gracious façade interspersed with scores of large Venetian windows, pediments, and columns.

Most of the structural improvements were to the interior, but the crowning glory of the project was the domed conservatory opposite the south hall. It was an architectural masterpiece that complemented the existing building to stunning perfection. By any standard, Donnington was a grandiose estate fit for a king.

Satisfaction must have shown on his face.

"The house looks magnificent, lad. And the estate has never been more productive—or profitable."

Huntingdon turned to Mr. Stewart, his estate manager and his father's before him. He grinned sheepishly, feeling like he'd been caught admiring himself in a mirror. "Aye, it's magnificent," he agreed, lapsing into the comfortable vernacular of his boyhood. His father had shown a marked prejudice for hiring Scots. So much so that sometimes Huntingdon felt he had been raised in the wilds of the Highlands. Enabling him, at the very least, to turn a decent brogue.

"You've every right to be proud. I doubt the house looked this good even when it was first built. It was an enormous project to begin with and being forced into it in the middle... well, you proved your mettle in more ways than one. Not many about these parts thought you could do it." It was the old man's turn to look sheepish. "Myself included," he admitted ruefully. "But you surprised me and I'm glad of it. Your father would be proud of you," he added gruffly.

Coming from the taciturn Scot, this was high praise indeed.

At his father's death, in addition to management of his other lands, Huntingdon had assumed management of the massive improvements at Donnington. Undertaking the huge responsibility was a major turning point in his life. The drive to prove himself after his mistake with Genie had forced him to face the difficulties of unexpectedly inheriting a dukedom rather than delegating the responsibility away. He was all too conscious of failing again. He'd let Genie down horribly. He would not soon forget the feeling of self-disgust that went along with knowing you failed someone who had relied upon you.

Genie. His thoughts never strayed far from his soon-to-be bride. He couldn't help but wonder whether she would approve of her new home. And even more perplexing was the realization that her approval mattered. More than he wanted it to.

Nevertheless, right now, the old man's comments pleased him. Greatly. To cover his embarrassment at the uncharacteristic praise, Huntingdon joked, "I'd begun to wonder whether we should build a new wing just to house all the workmen. Now that they've gone—I can't believe I'm saying this—it seems almost too quiet."

"Enjoy it while you can, laddie. Once you and that bonny lass of yours start filling this place with a screeching brood of bairns, you'll long for a day of quiet."

Children. The thought struck Huntingdon cold. Of course, children were a natural consequence of marriage—especially for a duke. But after the discovery of the child they'd already lost, Huntingdon had avoided any consideration of a family. With four younger brothers and two younger sisters, he already had enough young people to worry about. The thought of a child of his own was far too painful and reminded him of just how profound were the consequences of his mistakes.

"It will be quiet for some time yet," Huntingdon evaded.

Stewart nodded in apparent understanding, though he had it all wrong. "You'll want to have some time alone. But bairns have a way of sneaking up on you. Like the plague," he murmured the last under his breath.

Huntingdon chuckled. "Said by the man with twelve—"

"Thirteen," Stewart corrected with his broad chest puffed out like a pigeon.

"Forgive me," Huntingdon bowed his head mockingly. "*Thirteen* children. With such a large number it's difficult to keep them all straight," he jested, though Stewart's brood was as familiar to him as his own siblings.

"Don't wait too long, lad. By the time I was your age I

already had three strapping lads and a couple of lassies nipping at my heels."

"You sound like my mother," Huntingdon said, shaking his head. "Or I should say, like my mother *used to* sound." Stewart frowned. He hadn't missed the bitterness in Huntingdon's voice.

Not waiting for a reply, Huntingdon dismounted. His feet sunk in the spongy grass, the ground still saturated from the heavy rains of the past few days. He took a deep breath, taking in the clean, fresh scent of summer falling all around him. "I think I'll walk the rest of the way."

Handing the reins of his mount to a young groom who had accompanied them on their rounds of the estate, Huntingdon started toward the stream.

Not so easily dismissed, Stewart trotted up next to him on his horse. "Your mother is expecting you. With the guests arriving in a few days, and her so long from society, well... she'd never admit it, but she's a mite uneasy."

"My mother can wait."

At Stewart's sharp look of reproach, Huntingdon sighed. "I won't be long."

"She's a stubborn woman, but your mother will come around, lad."

Would she? Actually, his mother had taken the news of his upcoming marriage with surprising equanimity. Her comments on his upcoming nuptials happily brief. "So the pert chit has finally grasped her brass ring. Humph. I'd begun to wonder whether I'd judged her incorrectly." He wondered what she meant by that but didn't follow up. Her only comment thereafter was the sweet sound of silence. But perhaps that said the most of all.

"It matters not," he said dismissively. The Duchess of Huntingdon's opinion had long ago ceased to be relevant. Huntingdon had learned in the years since Genie's ill-fated departure to make his own decisions—and more important, to hold to them. Yet, he couldn't shake the feeling that in this instance he'd made an ill-advised one. One that he couldn't explain, even to himself.

Scandal, or the potential for scandal, was not an insignificant consideration to a man in his position. And his place as one of the highest-ranking peers in the realm had surprisingly—considering his irresponsible youth—become important to him. It wasn't until he'd undertaken the responsibilities of Donnington and his six other estates that he'd fully understood what was required of him. He had a responsibility to his heirs and to the people who depended on him for their livelihood, to ensure the prosperity of the ducal lands for future generations.

Walking across the bridge, he began the long walk up the carriage sweep—doing his best to ignore the annoying clop of Stewart's horse a few paces behind him. His mother was not the only stubborn person at Donnington.

He stopped short and spun around. "Don't you have something to attend to?"

Stewart smiled, completely nonplussed. "Nothing that can't wait, Your Grace."

His brow jumped at that one. "Your Grace? Not lad or laddie? Since when do I merit 'Your Grace'?"

Stewart looked properly offended. "Humph," he grumbled. "With the house party and your new bride, I thought I'd do my best to make a good impression."

Huntingdon threw his head back and laughed. "You don't have a deferential bone in that mountainous body of yours. I thought men descended from kings didn't bow to any other man—especially *English* men?"

"You'll not mock the Bonnie Prince, lad," Stewart said in hollowed tones.

"I wouldn't dream of it. You'll have to explain to me someday how a good Tory like my father ever hooked up with a Jacobite Catholic Scot—second cousin twice removed from the 'Bonny Prince'."

Stewart shrugged. "We didn't discuss politics."

Huntingdon nodded. "Wise decision."

Nothing could ruin a friendship faster than politics. That's why the moderate position that he'd chosen to take was so precarious. He didn't fit neatly into one camp—so neither side completely trusted him. Nominally a Tory, nevertheless Huntingdon was sympathetic to many of the republican causes. He'd worked hard over the past few years to earn the respect of both Tory and Whig members of the Lords and Commons. He didn't want to lose it.

His own interests were varied. The increasing taxes to fund the war with Napoleon were an enormous burden to large landowners. Huntingdon had recognized the need to diversify his interests, to become less dependent on one source of income. So he'd begun to explore other alternatives to supplement his rental incomes. Mills, factories, and mines were the future. But recently there had been some unrest from workers in Nottinghamshire that concerned him. He nearly chuckled again, thinking about what his mother's reaction to his plans might be. News of his intention to go into "the trade" might be sufficiently alarming to distract his mother from the blow of marrying so far beneath him.

"Your father was never the politician that you are. He hadn't the stomach for it."

"I'm not sure I do either," Huntingdon admitted ruefully.

"You have an easygoing charm that he never had. People like you. It will serve you well." He paused, glancing at Huntingdon's broad grin. "Wipe that smirk off your face, lad. I didn't say that *I* think you're charming. I know you too well."

Huntingdon placed his hand over his chest. "You wound me."

Stewart scoffed and muttered something under his breath that sounded remarkably like "conceited fool" before he continued. "Mark my words, lad. You'll go as high as you dare climb. The only limit is your own ambition."

Right now, all Huntingdon wanted was a cabinet post. A position in Prime Minister Spencer Perceval's government would help ensure the future prosperity of his estates. And it was nearly his. But even the smallest whiff of scandal could crush his hopes.

So why Genie? His position demanded caution in his

choice of a wife. Why risk his future? He didn't know why—just that he had to. Despite the risks. He knew that the ton would discover that Genie was the same girl he'd courted all those years ago—at some point someone was bound to recognize her. He supposed it was too much to hope that his choice of bride would not be remarked upon.

But he'd make damn sure that the rest of Genie's past remain where it was, or his own ambitions, the future prosperity of his lands, the duty he owed to his heirs, could well be placed in jeopardy.

Ties he'd been fostering for years would be cut without thought.

It wasn't just his political future at stake. Truth be told, he rather liked his place in society and didn't relish living as an outcast—even if it was within the luxurious walls of Donnington Park. Walls that they were now approaching.

At last Stewart rode off toward the stables, leaving Huntingdon alone to face his mother. Bloody coward, he thought with disgust. Removing his hat and gloves, he started up the stairs. A line of liveried footmen suddenly appeared out of nowhere to greet him. A skill that never ceased to amaze him. As a boy he'd tried to surprise them, but the servants had a mysterious system that he'd never been able to unlock.

There was no mystery he'd rather unlock right now than the one of Genie. He'd gone over their conversation countless times in his head and knew he was missing something important. Genie had never really answered him about why she was residing in a brothel. Once they were married, he'd have the truth from her about what happened in America and do whatever was necessary to make sure all trace of her stay was erased. His own feelings on the matter, he would sort out later.

He wasn't proud of his conduct in forcing marriage upon her, but he didn't have time to find a more delicate alternative. The wisest course would have been to step aside and allow her to marry Edmund. For an instant, when Edmund had told him where he'd found her, Huntingdon had thought about it. But something—shame? guilt? remorse? passion?—prevented him from heeding his voice of caution. He'd searched for her for so long hoping for a chance to remove the stain upon his honor, that giving up had become unthinkable.

He'd just do his damnedest to ensure that the truth about her "husband" and her temporary residence in a brothel—whore or not—were never discovered.

Or Huntingdon would find himself ruined right alongside his reluctant bride.

Nothing like the intrusion of a little reality to shatter the perfection of a peaceful morning. He flipped his gloves to a footman and stomped into the house, barely heeding the trail of muddy footprints quickly mopped up behind him.

"I'VE BEEN WAITING FOR YOU," his mother rebuked the instant Huntingdon entered the blue drawing room. "I've just received a most informative correspondence from Lady Davenport."

The Duchess of Huntingdon stared at him expectantly, but Huntingdon didn't bite. Seated at a small writing desk, gowned head to toe in her usual black, his mother appeared very old and very frail. He ignored the unwelcome twinge of sympathy and poured himself a cup of strong coffee from the sideboard. He wouldn't feel sorry for his mother. Not after what she had done to Genie. To him. To their child. So pointedly, he took a seat on a small sofa with his back angled rudely away from her.

"Well, don't you want to hear what it said?"

Huntingdon shrugged, indifferent. "I'm sure you're going to tell me."

She made a small sound of annoyance. "Apparently the whole city knows of your plans to marry."

"I did post an announcement in *the Times,* Mother."

He heard the unmistakable rustle of silk skirts as she rose and walked toward him, placing herself in his direct line of sight.

"That's not all."

He took a long draw of the soothing black elixir, knowing very well that she was waiting. He forced himself to look at her. "I assumed it wasn't."

"Hyacinth writes that she cannot believe you did not tell her, but that she will hear the whole story from you when they arrive at Donnington for the house party."

Puzzled, he met her gaze. She had his attention now.

"It appears that everyone knows that Mrs. Preston is none other than the girl you have been searching for, Miss Eugenia Prescott, formerly of Thornbury."

"Damn," he cursed, dropping the cup on the saucer; it landed with a sharp clatter. He'd hoped to have some time, some peace before that particular connection was uncovered.

Nonetheless, he brushed aside the momentary displeasure. "It was to be expected. Genie is still an incredibly beautiful woman and someone was bound to remember her."

His mother stared at him, her eyes hard. "Yes, but the question is whether Mrs. Preston is ready with an explanation for why she left and why she did not return until recently. An explanation that you have not yet thought to give me."

"You know the answer to the first and didn't ask as to the latter."

The duchess looked pained. "I must admit I was reluctant to broach the subject."

"As well you should be. It is none of your business. Genie does not owe you—or anyone else for that matter—an explanation."

"I've apologized a thousand times for sending her away. I thought I was doing what was best. I was trying to prevent you from making an ill-advised match. I didn't realize..." Her voice dropped. "Will you ever forgive me?"

"I sincerely doubt that possible," he said harshly.

The duchess flinched and something that looked

remarkably like tears filled her eyes. Impossible. His mother never showed such pedestrian emotion. She waited a moment, seeming to collect herself, before saying anything else. "Perhaps, I do not deserve your forgiveness. The connection was obviously stronger than I realized. Maybe someday when you have a son of your own, you will understand that I was only doing what I thought best. What any mother in my position would do." *I might have had a son of my own.* When he did not respond, she continued. "Mrs. Preston might not owe anyone an explanation, but that will not stop the ton from demanding one. I realize that I am the last person that could possibly dissuade you from this marriage; I only ask that you have care. If there is anything in the girl's past, bury it well. Or it may well bury all of us—including your Mrs. Preston."

He held his mother's stare for a long moment and nodded. Despite her faults, the duchess was a shrewd woman. As the rest of the ton was bound to do, his mother had guessed that there was a mystery to uncover. A very destructive mystery. He wondered how the current duchess would react if she knew that his future duchess had spent time in a brothel?

He studied the sharp, patrician features of his mother. She'd probably be as horrified as he'd been. The realization annoyed him. He didn't like acknowledging any similarities to his mother, especially one that reeked of judgment and closed-mindedness.

But the duchess's point was well taken, bringing to a head the very issue that he'd been trying to ignore. Scandal would prove disastrous, and not just to his own interests. Genie would suffer, perhaps more so. An image of Percy's sneering face swam before him, multiplying, until there were hundreds of similar sneering faces joyously relishing the downfall of one of the most preeminent peers in the land.

Uncertainty had wormed its way into the snaking tunnels of his conscience. Once again, Huntingdon questioned his decision to marry her. Was he doing the right thing, knowing that in doing so it was bound to bring up the inevitable inquiries? Did he have any right to drag Genie through the gossip? To hurt her all over again? To destroy the newfound strength that he so admired, but which he sensed stood on a shaky foundation?

And for what? All for reasons that he couldn't articulate beyond the simple explanation that he wanted her. Because every bone in his body cried out to have her no matter what the cost. Trite, he acknowledged, but nonetheless true. Was it justification enough to risk so much?

He rose from his seat with a start, accidentally knocking the table with his knee. The mostly undrunk coffee sloshed over the side of the saucer and formed a large puddle on the tabletop. A footman quickly appeared to wipe away his mess. Would that all of his messes could be so easily cleaned up.

He didn't want to think about this. He was a duke, damn it, he could do what he wanted. Selfishly, he wanted to ignore the quandary of whether the determined duke used to getting what he wanted could jibe with the honorable man he strove to be.

Frustration at the untenable situation gnawed at him. He just wanted to make everything right, to right the wrong he'd committed all those years ago. Was that so wrong?

The answer reverberated in his head.

As if she guessed the torment she'd unleashed within him, the duchess quietly let herself out of the room, leaving Huntingdon alone to silence the nagging voices of his demons.

CHAPTER SEVENTEEN

THREE DAYS LATER, IT WASN'T guilt, but a very different demon that tormented him.

It was approaching midnight two days before he was to be married, and he was alone with his mother in the marble salon. The duchess peered up from her needlework, the soft glow from the fire pleasantly warming the ghostly gray of her complexion. She smiled, blissfully unaware of his agony. "I've never seen you so edgy. Wearing a path in the carpet won't make them arrive any sooner."

"I know that," Huntingdon snapped, then controlled his emotion. *She doesn't know,* he reminded himself. With uncharacteristic concern for his mother's feelings, he'd not told her just how late they really were. "I'm well aware of the delays imposed by traveling on wet roads." *And of the perils.*

That was what terrified him. To the point where he could no longer completely hide his disquiet. He scoffed. Disquiet, it was more like barely constrained panic.

The situation was laughable really. The cold, reserved duke brought to his knees by the simple delay of a carriage. But it was a very important carriage, with a very important occupant.

Anxiety, irrational or not, had swallowed him whole. He felt trapped, unable to concentrate on anything else.

The clock struck twelve. Like some wretched omen. Twelve long ominous booms, tolling each hour of delay with horrifying finality.

His heart raced and he felt his hands and forehead grow damp. He turned from his mother's prying eyes and resumed the only occupation he could handle at the moment, pacing. *Where are they?* The Davenports had arrived this morning, the other guests yesterday afternoon. But Genie and the Hawkesburys were nearly twelve hours late. Twelve agonizing hours. They'd traveled most of the one hundred and fifteen miles from London yesterday. After a night at an inn, they had been due to arrive at noon. As the afternoon hours passed into night, he'd grown steadily more frantic, his mind letting loose with all sorts of unspeakable horrors. From an attack on the road, to an accident, to wondering if she'd changed her mind. But it was the image of a carriage accident that struck him cold, recalling with poignant similarity the deaths of his father and brother.

"Didn't you say that they might stop for the night?" the duchess asked. "I thought you'd decided to retire for the evening."

As if he could sleep when Genie might be out there on the road, lying twisted in a bloody, muddy heap. Dear God, the grisly images would drive him mad. But he couldn't allow his mother to see how disturbed he truly was for fear that it would recall her own demons. So he'd lied.

For good reason. The death of his father and brother had nearly killed her. For the first time in recent memory, Huntingdon felt true compassion for his mother.

He forced himself to act nonchalant. "I couldn't sleep so I thought I'd come down to find a book."

"In the salon?" she asked with disbelief.

He shrugged. "I heard something and came to investigate. I didn't expect you to be up this late."

"Sleep is not as restful as it used to be," she answered. Again he felt a shock of sympathy. He'd lost a father and a brother, yes. But his mother had lost even more—he was only beginning to realize how much more. She studied his face and seemed to come to a realization. "You know, Huntingdon, you're not the first man to get married." The duchess dropped her embroidery ring in her lap and sunk back against the velvet cushions of her chair. "As I recall, your father was a bit nervous before our wedding."

Jitters. She thought he was suffering from something as benign as wedding jitters. The idea was so preposterous he could laugh outright if the reality wasn't so painful. Better that she thought he was a nervous groom than to have her relive the agony of their family tragedy: the seemingly inconsequential delay in arrival, the rain, the waiting, the increasing horror as time crept slowly by.

The roads were treacherous, carriage accidents common. But not twice, it couldn't happen twice in one family. But where were they? Why had they not sent word? He'd sent a couple of grooms out hours ago. They should have returned by now.

He forced himself to take a deep breath and managed to feign embarrassment. "I just want to make sure that everything is perfect for the wedding."

"You've thought of everything, what could possibly go wrong?"

Cold fear strangled his throat. *So many things,* he thought, but could not give voice to his greatest fear—that there would not be a bride.

The sound of footsteps approaching the salon drew his immediate attention to the door. The groomsmen? He froze, holding his breath in a moment of helpless purgatory as he waited to see who approached. Did the footsteps seemingly hesitate and falter, or were his ears playing tricks on him? Desperately, he craved news, but just as desperately he didn't.

He couldn't lose her again.

The solemn face of Grimes appeared in the doorway. "The Hawkesbury carriage has been spotted in town, Your Grace," he said matter-of-factly, not realizing the significance of his words, or how heavily Huntingdon weighed upon them.

Huntingdon exhaled long and hard. Relief washed over him like a torrential downpour. Hope. There was hope.

He tore from the room.

"Huntingdon, wherever do you think you're going at this hour?" his mother called after him.

But he didn't bother answering, already calling for his mount.

The tinkle of her amused laughter trailed behind him as he dove out into the night. But his mother's amusement at his supposed jitters didn't bother him. Fear had done what nothing else could—shattering the illusion of indifference. He cared all right. And it terrified him how much.

CONDENSATION FOGGED THE WINDOW OF the Hawkesbury carriage, Genie wiped at it furiously with the side of her hand. The cold dampness instantly seeped through the thin leather of her glove, turning the brown leather black. Anxiety, however, overrode discomfort. She barely noticed the added chill to her already frozen fingers. Their journey was near its end.

"Here, use this," Edmund said, pulling a handkerchief from his waistcoat and handing it to her. "But I don't expect that you'll be able to see much of anything this late."

Genie smiled her gratitude and attacked the persistent fog again, this time with the square of ivory linen. The window finally cleared, she peered into the darkness. High on a hill, still some distance before them, a shape began to take form.

No, it couldn't be.

But the truth dropped like a stone in her stomach.

"Is that it?" she asked Edmund hesitantly, pointing to the hazy patch of white nestled amongst the stars, floating above a blanket of shadowed treetops.

Edmund leaned forward to take a perfunctory look out the window and plopped back in his seat across from her. "That's it. Donnington Park in all of its regal splendor."

Genie tried to swallow, a knot of alarm closing her throat. "Regal" was right. The place looked to be the size of a small palace. Of a small kingdom for that matter. And in a matter of days, *she* would be responsible for the smooth running of that kingdom.

She would be a duchess.

Genie knew a long moment of panic. The great divide between the household of a duke and that of a country parson widened considerably with the first glimpse of her new home. Reality in this case had surely overreached her ambition. How would she ever manage such a place?

Yet wasn't this exactly what she wanted: wealth, position, security. Why did she suddenly feel so overwhelmed when she'd achieved more than she'd ever dreamed possible? Why did she feel like such a fraud? Like perhaps the duchess had been right all those years ago: She and Huntingdon were from different worlds and entirely unsuitable. Uncertainty twisted her insides. Was she equipped to preside over a duchy?

Fighting sudden queasiness, though unable to look away from the source, Genie kept her eyes glued out the window. Occasionally, she'd lose sight of the house as the carriage wound along the road, but slowly the blurred shape began to take solid form. With each passing minute her trepidation intensified. She'd never imagined anything so grand, so imposing...

So beautiful.

She hadn't realized just how much she would be forsaking. Or just how much Huntingdon had to lose.

Edmund patted her hand. "You'll be fine. It's just a house."

She made a dainty snorting sound of disbelief. And Versailles was just a small French country manor.

"Edmund's right," Lady Hawkesbury interjected. "Managing a household is much the same be it small or large. The duchess will be able to instruct you in all the particulars."

Genie stiffened at the mention of the duchess and straightened against the plush velvet cushions, which at the beginning of their journey had been comfortable.

The Duchess of Huntingdon no longer intimidated her. She's survived much worse. Heartbreak, the death of her child, poverty, near starvation, the vicious attack of a vile man.

One cruel, haughty duchess would not stand in her way. Edmund and Lady Hawkesbury were right. She could do this. For a short time anyway. This was what she'd fought for. With the help of a solicitor she'd already found a property in Gloucestershire just outside of Thornbury. She only needed to get through the ceremony and it would be hers. Nothing and no one would ever be able to take it from her—no matter what happened or what secrets were revealed in the future. Security had been ripped from her fingers before, this time she held a firm grip on her future.

"Oh look, dearest," Lady Hawkesbury said, pointing out the window. "Your bridegroom rides out to greet us. And at this late hour!"

Genie's pulse raced. Fighting the urge to look, she pinned her shoulders back against the cushions. Dear God, she was excited to see him. Like some lovesick fool.

Lady Hawkesbury squinted into the darkness. "My, he's riding fast." She turned to give Genie a sly wink. "I guess you're not the only one who is anxious." Her brow wrinkled. "Hmm. Perhaps we should have sent someone ahead explaining our delay? It took so much longer than we expected. Well, I do hope the dear boy hasn't been worried."

Ha! Genie thought contemptuously. The uncaring beast probably hadn't spared her a thought for weeks.

The dark silhouette of a rider appeared on the opposite side of the carriage, and Genie didn't need a torch to see that Lady Hawkesbury had identified the horseman correctly. The broad shoulders and muscular physique were unmistakable.

"Ho there." The familiar voice rang with authority. "Stop your horses, man."

Genie lurched forward as the carriage clattered to a bumpy stop.

"You there," he ordered brusquely, "open the door."

The carriage tipped again as the groomsman jumped to obey the duke's command and hopped down from his perch. The door was thrown open and Huntingdon came into full view. She tried not to stare, but her eyes seemed to have a will of their own. Astride a huge black horse, cloaked in a dark cape, his hair shimmered like a bright beacon across a moon-drenched sea.

He dismounted and approached the coach, motioning for one of the servants who accompanied him to move closer with a torch. The flames cast jagged shadows across his face as he carefully inspected the occupants of the carriage.

Edmund and Lady Hawkesbury leaned forward to investigate and blocked her view.

"Where is she?" Huntingdon boomed.

Genie pursed her brows, he was behaving quite oddly. Why did he sound so fierce? This was more than a simple welcome. He was upset about something. Was he angry with her?

"Now what's this all about, Huntingdon?" Edmund asked.

"Where is she?" Huntingdon repeated, ignoring the question. Something else laced his voice. Something that sounded like fear, or desperation. "Where's Genie," he croaked.

"I'm right here," Genie said, wedging her body into view.

Their eyes met. Her breath caught and she nearly gasped aloud. His gaze held hers with such tortured intensity, she could not break away. His eyes raked her face, drinking in every detail until he seemed to almost sag with relief. Clearly, he'd been worried about her. But why?

"You're well?" He spoke to her directly, as if Edmund and Lady Hawkesbury were not sitting there gawking.

"Quite well," Genie assured him gently, responding immediately to his distress.

The white flash of a grin broke across his features and Genie felt her heart tumble. He appeared so genuinely happy and relieved that Genie couldn't help but be moved.

They stared at each other for a long moment, both smiling, the connection between them taut and strong. The walls of distrust, built on disappointment and betrayal, for a short time forgotten. Genie thought that if Lady Hawkesbury and Edmund had not been blocking the way, he might have pulled her into his arms. For an instant, she fought the urge to rush into them.

The coachman cleared his throat, breaking the spell. All at once, Huntingdon recovered himself, he raised his gaze from hers and his expression shuttered.

He turned to Lady Hawkesbury. "Your journey is near an end, my lady. I welcome you to Donnington Park. If you'll excuse me, I shall receive you properly at the house." He looked up to the coachman. "Drive on." Then, with a bow and a rakish flourish he rode off into the night. Genie's gaze followed him until he slipped out of view.

"Oh, my! Now wasn't that the strangest thing?" Lady Hawkesbury murmured. "Whatever is the matter with the boy?"

Genie didn't know. But as Lady Hawkesbury did not seem to expect an answer, she slid back into the shadows and welcomed the obscuring sounds of the coach as it resumed its journey. Whatever had happened, it had been significant enough to put a large crack in his armor of indifference. He'd been worried about her, worried enough not to care who knew it. There was a rawness to the emotion that Genie wanted to hold on to, and never let go.

Huntingdon's sudden appearance and equally sudden departure had left Genie in a tangle of emotion. Why did her pulse still race and her chest still ache? Why did her heart leap in her chest and the heaviness that had weighed upon her the last few days suddenly lighten? Why was she so unabashedly happy?

These were not questions that Genie was prepared to answer. Not now. Not ever.

EDMUND WATCHED GENIE'S FACE AND felt disappointment burn in his chest. He recognized the complex emotions that crossed her face, even if she did not.

She gazed at Huntingdon as if he could give her the world... and take it away again in the same breath. She might hate the duke for all that he'd done to her, but deep down, beneath the bitterness of past disappointment, she still loved him.

The great tragedy for all of them was that it might not matter.

Love might not be enough to find happiness. Not unless Genie found the ability to forgive Huntingdon and learned to trust again. With what she'd been through, Edmund didn't know if that was possible.

Her fingertips cradled her face against the blurry pane of glass. Her erratic breathing evidenced by gentle puffs of fog clouding the window. The longing in her eyes as she gazed out at Huntingdon riding back toward Donnington was almost palpable.

Genie had never looked at him like that. Not once.

If she had...

Well, there might be something worth fighting for.

Edmund shook his head and dropped his gaze, feeling like he was intruding on a private moment.

What a mess. A broken engagement, an old friendship destroyed, a forced marriage, the specter of scandal casting a pall across everything.

And he was the odd man out.

Initially, when she'd broken their engagement, Edmund had been furious. Ready to charge out of Hawkesbury House and demand immediate satisfaction from his former friend. But then she'd reminded him of his own part in this tragedy and he'd reconsidered. He'd known the risk he took by not confessing who he was right away and why he was in America. Maybe he got no more than he deserved for deceiving Genie and betraying his friend. Although, he had to admit that a duel at dawn still didn't seem like such a bad idea if he could knock some sense into Huntingdon's thick skull.

When his anger had subsided, he was forced to accept her decision. Edmund held a place in Genie's heart, but it was only a place of friendship. He could see that now. It hurt, but perhaps not as much as it should have. The sharp ache had already begun to dull. He realized that if he'd ever really had her, he'd lost her a long time ago.

His gaze fell once again on Genie and his chest squeezed.

More than anything, Edmund felt profoundly sorry for Genie. His friend—or former friend—was determined to have her, even if he hurt her in the process. Edmund wanted to be there if she needed him. In case she changed her mind and decided that she couldn't go through with it.

This time as a friend, Edmund would be there to pick up the pieces.

FRESH FROM HIS RIDE, HUNTINGDON met them in the foyer and led them into the house, past the wall of liveried footmen, through the north hall and into the marble salon. Unsettled by the incident in the carriage, Genie didn't trust herself to meet his gaze again, so she concentrated on her surroundings. Her marvel at the stunning interiors, however, was interrupted by the elegantly dressed woman who rose to greet them.

"Mrs. Preston, welcome to Donnington Park. It's been quite some time since last we met."

Shocked speechless, Genie stared at the woman standing before her. At the woman who had at one time been imposing enough to bully Genie into leaving her home and family. The five years that had passed might well have been twenty, for the Duchess of Huntingdon was a mere shadow of her former self. Still frightfully thin, where before the duchess had exuded wiry strength, now there was unmistakable frailty. The sickly pallor of her skin was accentuated by the heavy black of her mourning. Her hair had grayed and deep lines covered her face. An air of sadness had replaced haughtiness, though Genie could still discern a subtle pride in the tilt of her nose and chin. Genie glanced at Huntingdon. Obviously a family trait.

She finally found her voice. And remembered to curtsey. "It's been five years, Your Grace," she challenged, making it clear that Genie remembered—even if the duchess chose not to.

The contempt, and anger that Genie had worked up over the past few years deflated in the face of her adversary's obvious downturn in health. Genie had suffered, but clearly she was not alone in doing so. For the first time it occurred to her that the duchess had also lost a child. And a husband (a husband who actually existed). Sympathy over a shared loss was not exactly what Genie had anticipated when coming face-to-face with her adversary after so many years. "Yes, I suppose it has," the duchess agreed. "So much has changed since our last meeting." Her voice drifted off, Genie suspected she was thinking of her lost husband and son. The duchess cleared her throat and continued. "In any event, the maids are busy lighting the fires and preparing your rooms, I'm afraid there will be nothing hot to eat as you were not expected until the morning."

"But—" Lady Hawkesbury began, surprised.

Huntingdon interrupted. "Actually, Mother, they were expected some time ago. At the noon hour."

Perplexed, the duchess started, "But you said—"

Huntingdon shuffled uncomfortably. "I didn't want you to worry."

"Oh, I hope we did not cause you undue concern," Lady Hawkesbury added, suddenly contrite. "We were unexpectedly delayed at the last carriage stop."

"A loose linchpin," Edmund interjected.

Obviously very put out by the experience, Lady Hawkesbury continued, "And after waiting a few hours for the linchpin to be fixed we had only traveled a few miles before the thill cracked. One of the footmen had to ride back and bring someone back to replace it."

The duchess's gaze never left Huntingdon. "I see. That explains my son's unusual behavior."

So Genie had been correct in her estimation. She turned to Huntingdon and lifted a brow in inquiry. "Worried, Your Grace?"

He looked charmingly embarrassed, making her heart do a strange twist in her chest.

He shrugged. "I feared that you might have had some mishap on the road."

The duchess paled and Genie realized the reason for Huntingdon's anxiety. Of course, how could they have been so thoughtless? His father and brother had died in a carriage accident.

"I apologize for not sending word, it took much longer to fix than we anticipated," Edmund explained, coming to the same realization as Genie. "But you can see that there is no reason to be concerned. We are all quite well."

Huntingdon looked at Genie, his gaze lingering and appreciative. "Very well, it seems."

She blushed. Awareness tingled down her spine. When he looked at her like that, the attraction was visceral... and gut-wrenching. The unmistakable connection that shadowed him, reining her in, had not weakened as she'd hoped. And by the amusement in this gaze, he was well aware of the effect he had on her—had always had on her.

His mother interrupted. "You all must be very weary after your overlong journey. If you are ready, Mrs. Mactavish, will show you to your rooms. I've arranged for a cold refreshment to be served." She glanced back to Genie. "I hope you will find everything to your liking at Donnington."

Genie's attention snapped back to the duchess. With every word she spoke, Genie listened for a double entendre. Every nerve ending in Genie's body stood at attention, poised for an attack. But if she intended sarcasm behind the pleasantry, Genie couldn't hear it. Genie searched, but the duchess's expression remained inscrutable.

Nonetheless, she couldn't help but feel defensive. Did the duchess expect Genie to be awed like a moonstruck country girl? Overwhelmed by the magnificence of the place?

Probably.

It embarrassed Genie that the duchess was right. But how could she not be? Her eyes swept the room, taking in the details of the salon. From the enormous carved marble fireplaces that flanked both sides of the room, to the ornate plaster work on the walls and ceilings, the exquisite paintings, the rich furnishings and ornamental figures, and the large Sèvres urns. In addition to the candelabras, Genie had counted at least three Argand lamps in this room alone. Genie's first impression had been correct. Donnington Park was as fine as any royal palace. The entire rectory would have fit in these first two public rooms alone.

Genie tried to keep her reply properly understated, but could not hide all of her enthusiasm. "The house is lovely. I'm sure I will be very comfortable."

Huntingdon, who had been hanging on her reply, beamed. Her approval of his home seemed to matter.

"If there is anything you require, you have but to ask." Huntingdon turned to his mother. "I'm sure you will do everything to assure Mrs. Preston's happiness, isn't that so, Mother?"

The room hushed at the blatant challenge.

The duchess's expression didn't move. Her true feelings on the matter remained blissfully hidden. "Of course," she said blandly. "Once you are married, I will remove to the dowager house—"

"No!" Genie interrupted unthinkingly then blushed. In a far calmer voice she continued, "I'm sure that is not necessary." Taken aback by her own words, Genie couldn't believe what she'd just said. But if the duchess left, Genie would be alone with Huntingdon and with the management of Donnington. She wasn't ready for such intimacy with the duke and she needed the duchess's help—even if it killed her to admit it.

The duchess's expression finally shifted, a slight lifting of her brow betraying her surprise. She gave Genie a long look, perhaps wondering at Genie's motives.

Uncomfortable by the close scrutiny, Genie tried to explain. "I mean, there is no need to make such arrangements right now. This is your home..."

Edmund seemed to understand and in typical fashion rode to her rescue. He put a comforting hand on Genie's arm and squeezed it for encouragement. "Of course, there will be plenty of time to make such decisions after Mrs. Preston has had a chance to settle in."

Genie gave him a small, grateful smile.

Never one to let an uncomfortable situation pass without comment, Lady Hawkesbury added matter-of-factly, "It wasn't so long ago that you were a nervous bride. I remember how imposing this all seemed to you at one time, Georgiana." The use of the duchess's Christian name was a none-too-subtle reference to their childhood friendship—and the fact that they were both only daughters of barons.

The duchess smiled weakly, a shadow crossed over her eyes. "I remember. Though it seems a very long time ago." Her voice had a far-off quality. It was clear to Genie that the loss of her husband still caused her enormous pain. The shadow cleared before she continued. "I will be happy to provide Mrs. Preston with whatever assistance she might need."

She sounded sincere, Genie thought. Her ready assent to help Genie came as a bit of a surprise. Apparently, the cruel duchess was not completely without feeling.

THE RELIEF HUNTINGDON FELT AT seeing Genie fled the instant Hawk touched her.

He'd known he acted like an ass—riding out into the night like some crazed bedlamite—but he'd never been more happy to see anyone in his life. Whatever embarrassment he'd suffered was surely worth it to see that she was unharmed. If he lived a thousand years he'd never forget how she'd looked when he'd first caught sight of her, glowing like the silvery moon in the black of night. Flawless, opalescent skin; honey blond hair that shone as bright as the sun; luminous blue eyes that pierced the veil of darkness.

When their eyes locked, he felt as though he'd been struck by a bolt of lightning. So severe had been his reaction. His chest had tightened with relief. And something more. Something he'd never thought to feel again. A wave of emotion so extreme, it felled him with a certainty that his happiness was inexplicably tied to this woman. Her suffering was his.

Ironically, it was at that moment—when he realized that she was safe—that he knew the answer to the question that had been haunting him.

He'd been agonizing for days. The conversation with his mother had sparked an ember of discontent that had been smoldering since the night of the ball. His recent conduct weighed heavily on him. Genie's accusations rang true. He'd pursued her with such a single-minded purpose that he'd lost sight of what was right and honorable. He wanted her, so he forced her to him by threatening to ruin her. Something he'd already done once.

He wouldn't make the same mistake again.

Fear of losing her had brought him unexpected clarity. The fog in his mind lifted, enabling him to take a hard, objective look at his actions. He'd become so focused on his goal, he'd lost sight of the harm he did in trying to achieve it. And harming Genie again was the last thing that he wanted to do.

For years he'd only thought to find her. To ease his conscience and assure himself that she'd come to no harm from his failings. But the moment he'd set eyes on her again, he'd wanted more. He'd wanted to make it up to her, to right the wrong he committed all those years ago. Failing a second time was unthinkable. So he'd done what was necessary to ensure that she married him.

But now, at the very cusp of the realization of his objectives, he knew that it would all mean nothing if he hurt the very person he wanted to protect more than anyone else in the world. It had taken the thought of losing her to make him realize that he had to let her go. He had hurt her enough; it was time for her to heal.

And to heal, he needed her trust. He wanted to prove to her that he was not the same boy who let her down all those years ago. He'd turned himself around and proved himself a worthy duke. Now he'd prove that he was a man worthy of her love. A man to whom she could confide the painful secrets of her past. Perhaps then he could soothe the pain and return the sparkle for life that she'd lost.

His good intentions, however, suffered a severe blow when Hawk touched her. A black haze of jealousy descended over him as he watched the easy interchange between his former friend and his bride. He fought the urge to rip Hawk's hand from her arm, the primitive possessiveness as unreasonable as it was inexplicable. He was a fool to be jealous of Hawk, but he deeply envied their closeness. A closeness that he'd squandered long ago. Every time she called him Edmund it reminded him of what he'd lost.

Huntingdon should be the one to offer Genie comfort. She seemed so confident and sophisticated; he was ashamed to admit that it didn't occur to him that she might be nervous about her responsibilities as a duchess. Or that Donnington Park might appear a bit daunting to its new mistress. He'd had no idea.

The duchess had summoned Mrs. Mactavish, the housekeeper, but Huntingdon couldn't let Genie go. He'd made a decision; he might not go through with it if he waited until tomorrow.

He stepped between Genie and Hawk. "Please, if you wouldn't mind, Mrs. Preston, I'd like to speak with you before you retire."

"I'm very tired."

The instinctive look that she gave Hawk before she replied burned in Huntingdon's chest. He kept his expression impassive, fighting a frown. "It will only be a minute," he insisted.

"Very well," she agreed, but with obvious reluctance.

Hawk looked like he was going to argue, but stopped himself when Huntingdon shot him a fierce glare of warning. It wasn't Hawk's place to interfere, and he knew it.

Huntingdon motioned to the footmen to follow the others out. He wanted privacy for this conversation. "Come," he said taking her arm. "I wanted to show you something."

She looked at him suspiciously. "Can't it wait until morning?"

He smiled. "No. I'm afraid what I have to show you can only be seen at night."

He led her across the marble salon and into the next room. Though a large fireplace provided warmth, the cavernous room was substantially cooler than the last and Genie shivered. He resisted the urge to fold her under his arm. He didn't trust himself to touch her.

Genie glanced around, her eyes stopping on the fine pianoforte and large golden harp. "The conservatory?" she asked. He nodded. "It's beautiful," she said.

"Ah, but this is not what I want to show you."

Her brows gathered above her tiny nose. "Then what?"

The blond curls peeking from beneath her traveling bonnet shimmered in the candlelight. His breath caught. Unable to resist the siren call of her beauty, he cupped her chin, his fingers stoking the soft velvet of her skin. He heard her sharp intake of breath. Her lips parted. God that mouth, he thought. He ached to taste her. But he couldn't. Not yet.

"I missed you." The words slipped out. He was surprised by the huskiness of his voice, by how fast his passion flared after only a moment in her company.

Standing so close, he could smell the sweet rose of her perfume and the subtle honey of her skin. He felt strangely alive, invigorated by her mere presence. Blood pounded through his body and his skin grew warm. The urge to kiss her was overwhelming.

She didn't answer, but her lips quivered as if she knew what he was thinking. As if she knew instinctively how badly he wanted to put his mouth on hers. To crush her body to him, and let their passion consume them. To kiss her mouth, her skin, to run his tongue down the sharp cleave of her breasts. To inhale her sweetness. To assure himself in the most primitive way that she was alive.

As much as he wanted to give free rein to his lust, even more desperately, he ached to hear her say something. To return the sentiment. To give him a reason not to offer her freedom. Her gaze fell to his mouth and his groin tightened at the unconscious response. Unspoken permission, but it wasn't enough. He wanted more than passion. He wanted her soul. He wanted everything.

Lust had always been between them. But unlike last time he would not let it control him. This time he had the maturity and the strength to do what was right. Before he could change his mind, he lifted her chin, forcing her gaze up to the ceiling. "I wanted you to see this."

He watched the wonder transform her face, giving him a glimpse of the girl that he remembered. For once she didn't hide her reaction. Her lips curved into a wide grin and her eyes sparkled. "Oh, my."

The heavens lay open above them. The stars twinkled brightly across the evening sky through the glass of the domed ceiling.

"Did you do this?" she asked.

He chuckled. "Not by myself."

"I've never seen anything like it. It's magnificent."

Her reaction pleased him. It was a masterful piece of architectural engineering and he was extremely proud of his accomplishment. He might be about to offer her her freedom, but he'd damned well use everything at his disposal to keep her here. Even if it meant regaling her with everything she'd be giving up.

Content to gaze at the stars, neither of them spoke. It was

a rare moment of peace, a painful reminder for Huntingdon of the times they spent together in Thornbury. When comfortable silence had communicated so much more than words. When he'd held her in his arms along the banks of the river, the weight of her body against his, when he'd buried his face in the sweet scent of her hair and known a happiness so complete it almost hurt to remember.

He sensed her returning impatience and reluctantly broke the silence. "I'm glad it pleases you. But that is not the only reason I wanted to speak with you." He indicated a small settee near the fireplace. "Please sit."

The temporary lull had lapsed. Genie raised her chin. "Thank you, I believe I'll stand."

He shook his head. *So we are back to that,* he thought. Was this how it was going to be? Stubborn defiance over even the smallest request? Argument for the sake of argument? Is this how he wanted her? Hating him? Distrusting everything he did?

The difference between the way it had been and the way it was now had never seemed so vast.

He dragged his hand through his hair and took a deep breath. "I was wrong."

She eyed him cagily.

Her continued distrust bolstered his resolve. "I was wrong to force you to marry me with a threat." He paused, still unsure of whether he would regret this decision for the rest of his life. Could he let her go a second time? He had to. This time he'd do the honorable thing even if it killed him.

He took a deep breath. "I want to marry you, Genie. But if you wish to break our engagement, I will not stop you."

GENIE COULDN'T BELIEVE WHAT SHE was hearing. For a moment she didn't understand. Why was he saying this? And then comprehension struck, and a sick feeling rose like bile in the back of her throat. Despair. Disbelief. An unmistakable hollow ache in her chest that could not be denied. He had heard. He was abandoning her again, at the first inkling of trouble.

She tried to contain the bitterness and hurt, the overwhelming pain that made her want to burst out into tears, but her words tumbled out harsh and caustic. "I see the gossip floating about town has reached you at Donnington?"

At first he looked puzzled, then genuinely shocked. "That's not why—"

"Do you deny it?" she practically spat, the betrayal too raw. "Do you deny knowledge of the fact that news of our previous connection is circulating amongst the ton? That everyone knows that I am the girl you courted who mysteriously disappeared five years ago? That people are speculating about why I disappeared and where I've been all these years? And you're having second thoughts because you know *exactly* where I've been."

He paled and shifted on his feet. The truth of her accusation was evident by his discomfort. "I admit that such news is not new to me, but—"

"Stop." She held up her hand. "Don't bother trying to explain." Anger and disappointment curdled any fleeting moment of happiness she'd felt when first she'd seen him riding out to greet her then when he'd shown her this heavenly conservatory. Fool. She thought he'd been reaching out to her.

Only moments ago she'd considered kissing him, melting against him and succumbing to a temporary bout of insanity. She'd actually believed him when he said that he'd missed her. How close she'd been to voicing her own secret, that she'd missed him too. A moment of idiocy that made this conversation all the more humiliating.

She forgot to feign indifference, forgot to control her emotions. She could feel her façade crack as the conflagration of emotion spewed forth. "I will most assuredly *not* call off the engagement." Her voice sounded suspiciously shrill. "You'll not break your word so easily this time."

"I have no intention of breaking my word," he said, clearly affronted. "You have it all wrong. I only wanted to give you a choice. I want you to marry me of your own volition, not because of a threat."

She scoffed. But when an additional explanation for his actions occurred to her, fear clutched her chest. "You are not thinking of trying to wriggle out of our agreement?"

His eyes narrowed at the coarse mention of the unusual marriage settlement she had wrested from him. He drew himself up stiffly, his eyes slitted. "The property you have chosen will be yours upon our marriage as well as the two thousand per annum. At our marriage you will become a very wealthy woman in your own right."

She let out her breath. "Very well," she said tonelessly. "Then the wedding will proceed as planned." And her letter would be dispatched soon thereafter.

How could he appear so strong and yet balk at the first sign of difficulty? But what other explanation was there for this sudden change of heart? Did he honestly expect her to believe that her feelings mattered to him?

He'd proved the fallacy of that belief many times over.

"In all honesty, I gave no thought to scandal. I only sought to right a wrong." His jaw tightened. "Why must you always believe the worst of me?"

Her mouth trembled and heat prickled behind her eyes. "Can you honestly ask me that after everything that has happened? If I believe the worst of you, it's because you've never given me a reason to believe anything else. What reason have I to trust you when you have never acted without selfish purpose?"

"Damn it, Genie! I'm trying to make it right."

"You're trying to protect yourself from scandal."

"If that were true I would never have asked you to marry me in the first place. I knew our previous connection would eventually be discovered. Admittedly, I'd hoped to have some time, but sooner or later, it was bound to happen."

He was right, Genie thought. But the timing of his offer couldn't be a coincidence. He'd not rid himself of her that easily. She fought for control and met his gaze, trying to mask the hurt. "Your conscience can rest at ease, Your Grace. Be assured, there is nothing more that I want right now than to marry you."

Perhaps you will suffer an ounce of the agony that I'm feeling right now.

Not interested in a reply, she spun on her heel and fled the room in search of a servant, praying that she could fight back the explosion of disappointed tears until she reached the haven of her chamber.

CHAPTER EIGHTEEN

"CONGRATULATIONS, DEAREST. I'M SO VERY happy for you." Caro's eyes shone bright with unshed tears as she enfolded Genie in an enthusiastic embrace. "We've certainly come full circle from that fateful harvest festival ball all those years ago." She sighed dramatically. "It's all so deliciously romantic."

Genie didn't have the heart to contradict her. News of her and Huntingdon's prior courtship, his parents' objection, and her disappearance had indeed been bandied about town. But thanks to the deft handling by Lady Hawkesbury, with a few well placed words, the "scandal" had been turned into a great romance. If the truth wasn't so painful, Genie might laugh.

She'd been a duchess for exactly an hour. They'd just returned to Donnington after a short, private ceremony at the parish church. She stood next to Huntingdon, his younger brothers and sisters, and the new dowager duchess, waiting to receive their guests. It was a small celebration, including the guests from the house party and a few of the local quality. But surprisingly, Caro had been first in line.

"I'm so glad you could be here," Genie replied and meant it, caught up in some of Caro's contagious excitement. Despite the less than happy circumstances of the occasion of her wedding, Genie was grateful for the presence of her old friend.

"It was all Huntingdon's idea," Caro gushed. "I didn't think it would be possible to get here in time—with the roads washed out from all the rain—but he arranged everything and here I am."

"He's thought of everything," Genie said dryly. And in truth, he had. Today had been as near to perfect as she could have imagined. Even the sun had cooperated, shining unusually bright and warm for a late summer day.

The day had been full of many other surprises. With Lady Hawkesbury's help, Huntingdon had secretly arranged for a special wedding gown of deep blue silk, precisely the color of her eyes, to be made by Madame Devy. Encrusted with hundreds of diamonds along the bodice, it was the most beautiful gown she'd ever seen. Then, right before they were to leave for the church, he'd sent a diamond tiara along with matching earrings and necklace. She sparkled from head to toe; even her slippers had jeweled buckles. She felt like a princess, though as a duchess she supposed that she was not that far off.

The smell of roses filled the air; the delicate blooms covered every surface not covered with food. Surely Huntingdon had raided every hothouse between here and London to find such a quantity at this time of year. The soft strum of the harp sounded in the background. It was magical. All the accoutrements of a fairy-tale wedding, with the exception of the happy bride.

But was she so terribly unhappy?

Admittedly not as much as she wanted to be.

Genie stole a covert glance at her new husband, who was pretending not to listen to her conversation with Caro. He'd surprised her with his thoughtfulness, secretly inviting Caro when he'd heard of their fateful meeting in the dress shop. Indeed, since their conversation in the conservatory he'd been nothing but thoughtful and kind. Almost wooing her.

Genie didn't know what to make of it, but it was all deeply unsettling.

As if he knew what she was thinking, he murmured in her ear, "A peace offering."

Genie tilted her head sideways to consider him. Seeing only sincerity in his expression, she said, "It was a very considerate gesture. I thank you."

He grinned, boyishly pleased.

Genie felt herself smile in return, hard-pressed to remain unaffected. Huntingdon seemed different these past couple days. Lighthearted. Happy. Playful. Not so serious. More like the boy she'd remembered than the hard, quick-tempered man she didn't.

Indeed, there had been so many moments of unexpected thoughtfulness these past two days, she'd wondered if perhaps he'd been telling the truth in the conservatory. Had she misjudged him? Had he truly been trying to do the right thing? The timing was just so suspicious.

What if he wasn't trying to avoid scandal? What if that strange episode with the carriage was the cause of his sudden change of heart? She couldn't get that incident out of her mind. Clearly, he'd feared an accident. Considering their long delay and the death of his father and brother in similar circumstances, she couldn't blame him for being worried. It was the magnitude of his worry that surprised her. He'd feared for *her*. Which meant he cared for her. Undeniably, from that moment on he'd behaved quite differently, seducing her with kindness.

She almost wished that he would go back to being angry and severe; it was far easier to hate him that way.

Huntingdon took Caro's hand and lifted it to his mouth. "I'm delighted that you were able to join us on such short notice. As you can see, it's a small celebration. I regret that Lord Castleton was unable to come, but I hope you and Lady Castleton will stay for the hunt."

"We'd be delighted," Caro answered on behalf of both women. "My husband is in Scotland, and he will be very disappointed to have missed meeting Genie, whom he's heard so much about." Caro looked about the room, her eyes narrowed slightly. "I was hoping that Lizzie might be here?" she asked gently.

Genie felt a sharp pang of sadness and shook her head.

Huntingdon slipped his hand around her waist. "The duchess and I hope to travel to Thornbury soon, and celebrate with her family at that time," he explained for her.

"Oh, I see," Caro said, though it was clear that she didn't.

The absence of her family was the most obvious indication that everything might not be as wonderful as it seemed. Huntingdon had of course written to her father with the news of their impending nuptials, but he hadn't pushed the matter of her family's attendance—somehow understanding that she wasn't ready to see them. She wasn't, but not for the reason he thought. It wasn't shame preventing her from reuniting with her family; she didn't want to have to lie to them again.

As for Lizzie, the mystery surrounding her had still not been explained to Genie's satisfaction. Unable to confront Fanny, who'd left soon after Huntingdon did for Donnington, Caro, on that afternoon at Hawkesbury House, had provided only the barest hint of what had happened to Lizzie. Immensely popular during her season in London with Fanny, Lizzie had nonetheless returned to Thornbury, never to be heard from again. As to why, Genie still did not know. She needed to speak with Fanny, but since Genie's arrival, Fanny had gone out of her way to avoid being alone with her. Apparently, breaking off the engagement with Edmund had not softened Fanny's opinion of her any. Genie couldn't blame her.

Caro reluctantly moved on and Genie felt Huntingdon tense at her side as the next group of well-wishers approached.

"So," Percy drawled. "What other secrets have you been hiding, Mrs. Preston? Or should I say, Miss Prescott?"

Genie fought to control her expression, but she knew she must have paled, because she felt Huntingdon's hand tighten protectively at her waist.

"Actually, it's Your Grace," Huntingdon corrected, his voice edged with steel.

Percy sneered. "Of course, how remiss of me, 'Your Grace'."

"Naughty scamp," Lady Davenport chided, swatting

Huntingdon with her fan. "Keeping all of us in the dark about the identity of your bride. Not that you fooled me. Didn't I tell you these two were in love, Nigel."

"That you did, dumpling." Lord Davenport swatted at Huntingdon, who, prepared this time, braced himself before he was knocked over. "You can't hide anything from my Hyacinth," Lord Davenport boomed, chest puffed out with pride. "Not to say that she hasn't been extremely put out, old boy. Keeping such details to yourself. It's not the thing," he said, shaking his head. "Not the thing at all."

"Just look at them," Lady Davenport cooed with her husband as if Huntingdon and Genie weren't standing right there. "Have you ever seen a more handsome couple? And so in love!" Genie's cheeks burned, but Lady Davenport went on, oblivious to the discomfort she was causing. "They can't keep their eyes off each other. Oh, to be young again," she said with a long, dramatic sigh. "I remember there was a time when you couldn't keep your eyes off me," she said to her husband with a playful pout.

Lord Davenport took her plump hand and brought it to his mouth. "I still can't, pet. You're still the most beautiful woman in the room."

"Nonsense," Lady Davenport chided, but she blushed like a schoolgirl receiving her first compliment. She turned back to Huntingdon and said starchily, "So what do you have to say for yourself, young man?"

"Yes," Percy interjected snidely. "We can't wait to hear the details of how this great romance developed across two continents. Why did you say nothing before of Miss Prescott's identity as Mrs. Preston at Lady Hawkesbury's ball? It's all tantalizingly mysterious."

"Nothing mysterious," Huntingdon said offhandedly, as if the question didn't bother him. "We knew the interest the ton would take in our marriage, we hoped to have some time to ourselves before the *vultures* began to circle." He stared at Percy, leaving no doubt for whom the emphasis was meant.

Despite the none-too-subtle warning, Percy did not back

down. "Hmm, sounds reasonable. But why do I have a sneaking suspicion that you are hiding something?"

Genie was shocked to hear the new dowager duchess intercede. "Why Percy, you dreadful boy," she said loud enough for everyone around to hear. "You always were such a quarrelsome child. Always trying to stir up trouble. I would have thought you were too old for such nonsense. My son had fond memories of our sojourn in Gloucestershire, and Mrs. Preston in particular, so it was only natural when she returned to England after the death of her husband for him to renew their acquaintance."

Genie knew her eyes must be as round as saucers. Even Huntingdon looked surprised. She couldn't believe it. The Duchess of Huntingdon had just come to her defense.

Lady Davenport finally seemed to comprehend that Percy was being rude. "Come along, Percy. You've made quite enough of a nuisance of yourself for one day."

"That's right, son," Lord Davenport guffawed. "Save some for tomorrow."

Red-faced and furious, Percy moved away. Genie relaxed, suddenly very conscious of the firm hand around her waist and the warmth of the powerful body pressed so close to her side.

Huntingdon leaned down. "Stay away from Percy," he warned, sending shivers down her neck with the soft tingle of his breath.

Genie nodded, ignoring his high-handed command, for once they were in agreement. Lord Percival Davenport was like an asp, coiled and waiting to spring.

But rather than just issue the order (as he usually did), Huntingdon surprised her by explaining further. "I'd hoped to curtail his interest in you at the Hawkesbury ball, which is why I ignored his snide remarks."

Genie's eyes widened. So that was why he'd not defended her.

"You see what he's like," Huntingdon continued. "Since we were children he's had an unreasonable hatred of me. When I became duke, even more so."

"He envies you."

Huntingdon looked at her hard. "Maybe. In any event, now that he knows you're the girl from my past, I'm afraid his suspicious appetite has been whet. He'll be insatiable, looking for anything to hurt me." He took her chin in his hand, and drew her gaze to his. "Including using you."

Her heart clutched at the huskiness in his voice. She was powerless to resist the blue sea of his eyes, stormy with emotion born of concern. When he allowed her a glimpse of what lay buried beneath the wall of reserve, it made her wonder whether it was possible to forget.

"I'll be careful," she promised—and meant it.

A shiver of apprehension slid down her neck. Whether a premonition of disaster or merely a response to the tone of his voice she didn't know. But one thing was for certain: The fact that her plans overlapped with Percy's bothered her. It smacked of cruelty. But she was different from Percy. Her revenge was justified. Wasn't it?

She squared her shoulders, subtly shifting her body away from Huntingdon. It was too late for second thoughts. The letter was posted this morning. All that remained was to see whether the recipient took the bait.

HER CONFRONTATION WITH FANNY HAD been put off for too long. Genie could handle the barely concealed venomous glances, but she needed to find out what Fanny's anger had to do with Lizzie.

Genie had kept her eye on Fanny during the long wedding breakfast, waiting for an opportunity. It wouldn't be too long, if the amount of champagne Fanny had consumed was any indication. When Fanny excused herself, Genie followed her and waited for her on a chaise in her bedchamber. Yet another of the incredible improvements made to Donnington were that many of the bedchambers were connected to a bathing room with hot and cold baths and Bramah water closets.

Fanny's surprise upon seeing Genie was not of the pleasant persuasion.

"What are you doing here?"

Genie smiled at the frowning girl, ignoring her rudeness. "I believe it's time we spoke."

Fanny lifted her chin defiantly. "Is that an order, Your Grace?"

Her question took Genie aback. She was a duchess. She took precedence over just about everyone, including Fanny. Genie *could* order her if she wanted to. How strange.

She shook her head. "No, it's a request. We were close as sisters once, now that we *are* sisters I should like to be friends again."

Fanny made a small sound through her nose. "I hardly think that is likely."

The girl was trying her patience. "What did I do to earn your contempt, Fanny? And what does it have to do with Lizzie?"

"So you *do* remember that you have a sister."

"Of course I do," Genie exclaimed, shocked. "How could you say such a thing? Lizzie and I were as close as any sisters could be."

"And yet you left without as much as a by-your-leave. Without explanation."

Memories of that painful time assailed her. She hated thinking about the days before she'd left for America. How weak she'd felt. How helpless. How impossibly hurt. Genie stood and walked to the window. "I had no choice," she said dully, feeling her throat tighten. "It was partly for Lizzie that I left."

"How can you say such a thing?" Fanny sputtered, aghast.

"Didn't you ever wonder why—after all that had happened—your mother agreed to sponsor Lizzie for a season?"

Fanny blanched, the red blush of anger slowly dissipating from her cheeks. "I never thought..."

"Didn't you?" Genie prodded gently. "Didn't you think

it odd that she would bestow such largess upon my sister and brother?"

Fanny shook her head. "It wasn't until much later that I found out what role my mother had played in your disappearance. I was never told the details. I thought it was for me that she brought Lizzie to London, though I suppose I did wonder about your brother getting the parsonage at Ashby. I should have known." She paused, having obvious difficulty in assimilating this new information into the pile of blame that she'd heaped at Genie's feet. Having a fair share of the Hastings pride, she refused to back down and pressed on. "What my mother did was abominable. But still, you could have confided in Lizzie."

Genie thought back, trying to remember what had been going on in her mind at the time. She hadn't exactly been thinking clearly. "I didn't want to put Lizzie in a difficult position with my parents. It was better if she knew nothing. Then she wouldn't be forced to lie."

"But don't you see? Lizzie was already involved. When you left, she blamed herself for what had happened to you."

"That's ridiculous. Of course Lizzie was not to blame. How could she think such a thing?"

"It's not such an absurdity. For a time, I blamed myself as well. If you recall we helped you and my brother meet in private, we encouraged you in a situation we knew was wrong. When you vanished under a cloud of suspicion, Lizzie felt like she'd let you down. She took your disgrace as hard as if it had been her own."

Genie recalled how involved the young girls had been, how excited they'd been to be part of the intrigue. "We never should have involved either one of you. I'm sorry. I never thought... Perhaps I should have told Lizzie. But believe me, Fanny, I never meant to hurt her."

"Well, you did."

Proud *and* stubborn, Genie thought, amending her previous description of Hastings character traits. "Tell me what happened in London," Genie urged. "Caro said Lizzie had a very successful season but never returned. Did you two have a falling out?"

"Of course not. I begged her to come year after year, but she refused." Fanny stopped, weighing how much to tell her.

"Please, Fanny, I need to know."

Fanny sighed—swayed if not convinced—then explained. "Despite the whispers about your disappearance, Lizzie was extremely popular that first season. She had many offers, but refused every one of them. Her heart was never in it. She changed after you left, she became sad and depressed. She said she would not be happy until you had returned and she could be assured that you were well. So she has lived in Thornbury ever since, rarely venturing out into society. And you," she accused, her voice increasing in intensity. "You could have freed her from the guilt years ago. But you never returned. You didn't even have the decency to write. Not one letter to tell her that you'd married and were well, living in America."

Genie fought back the denial that sprang to her lips. Fanny couldn't know the truth. Instead, she shook her head regretfully. She couldn't believe that her vivacious, sweet sister could have shut herself off from society all because of her mistakes. Lizzie had looked up to Genie, but she'd also been very protective of her older, "greener" sister. Perhaps Genie should have guessed that Lizzie would feel some responsibility for what had happened, but she hadn't. "Poor, dear Lizzie."

"Yes, poor Lizzie," Fanny retorted. "Like Edmund, another casualty of your thoughtlessness. Why, Genie? Why did you not write to her?"

Genie opened her mouth to defend herself, but quickly slammed it shut again. Better if Fanny continued to think the worst of her. But she couldn't just say nothing. "I was ashamed."

"Of what had happened with Huntingdon?"

"Yes." Amongst other things.

Fanny grimaced. "He behaved horribly. I told him he'd made a mistake, was acting like the worst blackguard, but he wasn't ready to hear it. He regretted his conduct almost instantly, but it was already too late. You'd disappeared. He loved you, Genie, but you never came back. My mother said you swore to return after we left for London, but you didn't."

She'd wanted to. But circumstances had conspired against her. But Genie couldn't tell her any of that.

When Genie did not explain, Fanny continued. "Any sympathy I had for you fled when I saw how you'd abandoned Lizzie, your family, and now Edmund. You've changed, Genie. The girl I remember loved her family. She would have written. She would have let her family know that she was alive. How could you treat them so cruelly? Lizzie's thrown her life away because of you."

Guilt tore at Genie's conscience. Somehow she would make it up to Lizzie.

Hands on her hips, Fanny stared at her, waiting.

Genie hated that Fanny thought so horribly of her. It pained her not to explain, remaining silent after such an onslaught was near impossible. But she did. There was nothing that she could say to Fanny that would explain why she'd cut herself off from her family. Shame, poverty, fear. Reasons that required far more of an explanation than she could give.

Disgusted, Fanny turned on her heel and stormed out of the room, slamming the door behind her.

FURIOUS, FANNY PRACTICALLY SPRINTED DOWN the hallways to return to the drawing room. Who was that woman? Certainly not the girl she remembered. How could Genie just sit there with that hard, expressionless look on her face and say absolutely nothing? Fanny turned the corner and nearly slammed right into Hawk.

"Whoa, whoa," he laughed, grabbing her shoulders to steady her. "What's all the hurry about?" When he caught sight of the expression on her face, he sobered. "What's wrong, Fanny? Has something happened?"

Concern for *her* on Hawk's face buoyed her lagging spirits. She almost smiled before remembering the reason for her anger. Her gaze narrowed. "It's Genie."

He paled, any concern for Fanny vanishing in an instant. "Genie? Did something happen? Is she hurt?" He looked over Fanny's shoulder, ready to vault over her if necessary. Disappointment burned in Fanny's chest. Genie. Always Genie.

"Nothing is wrong with Genie," she said, her voice tight. "We had an argument, that's all. She's changed so much I barely know her anymore."

Hawk sighed with relief, and then studied her no doubt petulant pout. A strange look crossed his face. Like he wanted to say something. "Be kind to her, Fanny. Things were difficult for her after she left Thornbury."

Fanny seethed with jealousy. She couldn't help it. "How can you defend her after what she did to you?"

Hawk sighed and tucked Fanny's hand into the crook of his arm to take her back to the party. "I was not without blame in what happened," he said.

Fanny didn't believe that for one instant. Hawk was kind, loyal, and above all—a gentleman. "Genie acted cruelly and selfishly." When it looked like he wanted to argue, she stopped him. "It's not only you, but Lizzie and Fitz too. I fear what she might do to my brother, he cares for her deeply."

One side of Hawk's mouth lifted. "Your brother can take care of himself." The decidedly avuncular expression in his eyes made her want to cry. "But your concern is sweet. You're far too protective of your friends and family, sometimes I think your emotions prevent you from seeing the whole picture. You're so young."

"I'm one and twenty," she said vehemently, managing not to stomp her foot in frustration.

"Practically ancient."

He thinks I'm a child. She wanted to cry. "Don't make fun of me," she said hollowly.

He seemed to take pity on her earnestness. "I'm sorry." He reached up to tuck a curl behind her ear. A brotherly gesture to him, but torture to her. Her breath caught as his finger swept the side of her cheek. She thought she might die with longing. For a brief instant she thought awareness flickered across his gaze. He smiled gently, perhaps reading her thoughts and dropped his hand, excusing himself.

Her hand covered her cheek, holding in the heat left by his touch.

But before she could consider what had just happened, someone came up beside her. Turning, she saw that it was Percy.

"Seems like I'm not the only one who is not enjoying myself," he said wryly.

"What do you mean?"

He indicated Hawk's retreating back. "Still pining after that one?"

Fanny didn't answer him, she didn't need to. No doubt her face probably said it all.

"Don't waste tears on Hawkesbury, Fanny," he said gently. "If he doesn't know your worth, he doesn't deserve your heart."

She shook her head. "It's not like that, he sees me as a sister."

"He's a fool."

He said it with such disgust she had to smile. Percy might be an unusual champion, but right now she was just happy to have one. Unlike her relationship with her brother, Percy and she had always gotten along quite well. She never understood why he hated Fitz the way he did.

"Not a fool. Only in love with someone else."

"Ah, the beautiful new duchess, conquering hearts wherever she goes?"

Fanny shot him a look of surprise. He knew about Hawk and Genie? Her heart sank, realizing Hawk's humiliation was common knowledge. It gave her all the more reason to be furious with Genie. "They met in America, but I don't think she ever loved him."

"Why do you say that?"

She shrugged. "I don't think she ever got over my brother."

"But she married?"

"So she says."

Percy's eyes sparked with something beyond brotherly concern. "What do you mean?"

Fanny bit her bottom lip, nervous. She'd allowed jealousy to loosen her tongue, giving voice to her suspicions that were based on nothing more than intuition. Despite Percy's kindness to her, she probably shouldn't be discussing this with him. But it was so nice to have someone on her side. "Nothing," she said quickly. "Don't mind me, I'm not making any sense right now."

He gave her hand a sympathetic squeeze. "He'll forget about her."

Fanny thought for a moment. "Yes, eventually, but it won't make any difference. He'll never see me as anything other than his friend's little sister."

He brought her hand to his mouth and gave her a courtly kiss. "As I said, he's a fool."

GENIE RETURNED TO THE CELEBRATION not long after Fanny had stormed out of the chamber.

She smiled and laughed, chatting amiably with the guests, but she couldn't stop thinking about Lizzie. How could Lizzie have blamed herself for Genie's mistakes?

Genie had never considered what her leaving would do to Lizzie. She thought she was doing the right thing, avoiding scandal, enabling her sister to have a London season. Instead, she'd left her sister to bear the brunt of the speculation and to shoulder the blame—wrongly—for Genie's mistakes.

Had Genie's mistakes ruined her sister's chances for happiness too? She remembered how anxious Lizzie had been to make her entry into society, how she couldn't wait to have a beau (or two), how the thought of a London season would have filled her to bursting with excitement. Could the sad, quiet girl that Fanny described be the same lighthearted, naughty sister she'd left five years ago?

Was it possible for someone to change that much?

Of course it was. All she had to do was think of herself.

Genie felt sick. How could her actions have had such unintended consequences?

A firm hand slid around her waist and she looked up to see Huntingdon at her side. Awareness and a warm sensation, not at all unpleasant, swept over her. *Unintended consequences.* Just like Huntingdon could never have guessed what would happen to her when he hadn't answered the plea in her note.

She shivered. Where did that come from? The situations were not at all the same... or were they? Thinking she was cold, Huntingdon lifted the shawl she wore low across her back and settled it higher over her shoulders. "I was beginning to worry about you." Huntingdon looked over meaningfully at Fanny who was speaking with Percy. "Is everything all right?"

It was so strange having a normal conversation with him. Her husband. One that did not involve anger and recrimination. Genie managed a crooked smile. "Fanny is very upset with me."

Annoyance darkened his expression. "If she is being impertinent or causing you any problems—"

She put her hand on his arm, stopping him. "Don't be upset with her. She has every right to be angry."

"Will you tell me what this is about?"

"Yes. Later."

He nodded, pleased, before he nearly fell over at her feet from a firm thump at his back.

"Delightful celebration, my boy," Lord Davenport said. "Capital, capital. But if I were you, I'd take my bride away before she's too exhausted to enjoy the rest of the wedding traditions," he boomed with an exaggerated wink. "If you get my meaning."

Genie stilled. The wedding night. She'd completely blocked it from her mind. Panic welled up within her. The cold sweat of fear broke out on her forehead. She thought that she could go through with it, but now that the time had come her confidence had deserted her.

CHAPTER NINETEEN

SHE LAY IN THE STRANGE bed like a trussed up goose waiting to be devoured. Her hair had been brushed until it shimmered in long waves down her back. She wore a silk chemise and wrap, which despite being chosen for their modesty, managed to cling to every womanly curve.

She yanked the bed coverings up to her nose and sank deeper into the feather mattress, trying to disappear. Her heart raced as the clock ticked and the fire crackled.

She could do this...

But it was the waiting that was the worst. Knowing what was to come, but being powerless to prevent it.

Just like in Boston.

Eventually, they'd worn down her resistance. Her employers, men who took her into their homes to teach their children, then tried to attack her in the hallways. Forced from one job to the next, she'd learned to let them grope. A graze of a finger on her breast, a squeeze of her bottom, a stiff kiss. She'd suffered the humiliation, knowing that each place of employment might be the last.

But sooner or later the greedy devils would want more than she could stomach and she'd be forced to leave. Until finally, ignoring the warning bells clamoring in her head, Genie was forced to accept a position in the house of a milliner and his family. A man with beady eyes and swarthy skin who made her flesh crawl.

Everything about it had felt wrong, but what choice did she have?

Work or starve.

And so she worked... and waited. Waited for the inevitable.

It didn't take long. One night not a month after her arrival, when the rest of the family was in bed, the milliner had snuck into her room. He'd refused to take no for an answer. She'd fought like a madwoman, his fetid hand over her mouth stifling her screams. He pulled up her dress and she felt his hard member against her stomach. Revulsion made her gag. She'd thrashed wildly and he'd hit her. Again and again. Until she stopped moving. He tried to jab his erection into her and she panicked—finding a burst of sudden strength through the haze of near unconsciousness. Her hand reached out toward her secretaire, groping in the darkness for anything, until her fingers curved around the handle of a letter opener. Without hesitation, she'd plunged the blade deep into his groin.

His screams still echoed in her head. Bloodcurdling shrieks that had brought his wife to her room. Despite the evidence before her, the horrible woman refused to believe Genie's claims of near rape. Worse, she'd actually accused Genie of seducing the vile bastard. "You flaunted yourself, begging for his attentions. You tease him with your beauty and then try to play the prudish miss." Threatened with a call to the constable, Genie fled into the night, barely able to stand after the vicious beating she'd endured at the hands of her employer.

Genie had saved herself from rape. No knight in shining armor had ridden to her rescue. She alone had fought off the milliner, nearly castrating him in the process. With the help of the ladies at Madame Solange's, she'd survived, but the memories of what had nearly happened would haunt her forever.

Now she feared they would ruin any pleasure she might have once felt in the act of lovemaking. She'd felt passion with Huntingdon, but only to a point, before the old fear returned and panic set in.

Time, she told herself. That was what she needed. Once

she felt safe, it would be different. But could she get Huntingdon to agree?

The door opened. And closed. Her heart pounded in her chest as the heavy footfalls approached the bed.

"I know you're not asleep, not with all these lights in here burning as bright as Hades."

She grimaced under the bedcovers. So much for subtlety. She'd definitely gone a little overboard with all the lamps and candles. But she'd wanted to discourage any thoughts of romance.

The bed tilted from the weight of his body as he sat on the edge of the bed, an enormous contraption that suddenly felt very small.

"I can see we'll need to discuss economy in seed oil," he said dryly.

Genie opened her eyes and met his amused grin with a sheepish one of her own. Seed oil for lamps was very expensive, even for dukes.

"I prefer a bright room," she said matter-of-factly, her voice steady. At least it was until she caught sight of him. Whatever else she was going to say died in her throat. He'd removed his jacket and loosened his cravat. His hair was charmingly mussed and one golden brown wave fell forward across his forehead. The comfortable state of dishabille was a poignant reminder of the intimacy of the present situation: They were man and wife.

"So I see," he said, indicating the four Argand lamps that she'd collected from around the house and scores of candles illuminating the chamber. Her things had been brought to the duchess's suite earlier. It was a large room, beautifully furnished and decorated. But it was the interior door that she'd noticed right away. The door that led to the duke's chambers.

"It's good for conversation," she replied, trying to explain her sudden preference for brightly lit rooms.

He chuckled. "Is that what you think we are going to do tonight?"

The huskiness in his voice set her nerves on edge. She

knew he was going to touch her. Wide-eyed, she watched him. Waiting, as the hunter stalked its prey.

He leaned down and scooped up a handful of her hair, mesmerized as the shimmering curls slid through his fingers to fall back onto the pillow in a pool of disarray.

She blushed. "I... no... I don't know," she stammered.

His gaze slowly traveled down the length of her body, lingering on the telltale curves and bumps. She pulled the covers tighter, feeling suddenly naked under the heavy bed coverings.

He smiled, no doubt at the futility of her efforts. The tighter covers only emphasized the lush shape of the body underneath.

"Perhaps you are right. A well-lit room has its benefits. For 'conversation.'" His grin turned devilish. "Among other things."

Genie gulped. Her silly attempt to ruin the mood for seduction had quite the opposite effect. She'd hoped to make him uncomfortable. To make him feel as awkward as she, but he was determined to have her. She could see it in his eyes.

Her hands gripped the edge of the sheet until her knuckles turned white. "Please..."

"What is it, Genie?" he asked, but he was already kissing her neck. Light kisses that tickled and teased. "Your pulse is racing." His tongue flicked gently over the beating spot. "Don't worry, sweetheart, there's no reason to be nervous." He chuckled. "It's not as if we haven't done this before."

He was right: they had done this before. So why was her heart fluttering like a bird in a cage?

She'd known what would be expected of her. She had to try to relax. *He won't hurt you...*

Her senses heightened, she took in every detail. He'd shaved. She could smell the soap on his skin, his chin smooth, with just the barest hint of roughness as he nuzzled her neck. The gentle caress of his mouth on her sensitive skin worked its subtle magic. She softened for a moment. The heat of his mouth and press of his body lulled her senses into a temporary stupor. Her eyes flickered, wanting to close. She could feel the haze of passion descending.

But she knew that it wouldn't be enough. "Wait!"

He lifted his head and studied her. She could see the questions forming in his eyes and knew she had to stop them. He was too perceptive. If she gave him an inkling of her fear, he would guess.

Genie fought the sudden urge to confide in him. Would he understand? Or would he jump to conclusions as he had about Madame Solange's? Would he be disgusted? Ashamed? Pitying? These past few days he'd seemed so different, she wanted to trust him. But to what avail? Her plans for revenge were already in motion.

"Please," she said more calmly. "I can't do this. Not tonight. I need some time." She scooted to a sitting position, putting some distance between them.

A mild look of annoyance crossed his face; he obviously hadn't anticipated having to persuade his new wife to his bed. "Time for what?"

"To grow accustomed to our new arrangement. To get to know each other better." It might have sounded reasonable if her voice wasn't shaking.

She sounded as if she was lying, and he heard it. His eyes narrowed. "We know each other well enough, intimately even. Much better than most new husbands and wives."

"Not anymore." She shook her head. "We've both changed."

His gaze fell to her mouth. "Some things never change. I had you in my arms not so long ago—I felt your passion for me."

Heat rose in her cheeks, recalling their last interlude. She had felt passion—for a while. But it hadn't been enough to erase all the memories. He thought physical intimacy would solve their problems. That the problems of the past would magically disappear under the bedcovers. If only it were that simple.

"What is this really about?" He studied her so intently,

she feared he could see right inside her. Her skin prickled when a hard glint of suspicion appeared in his eyes. "Does this have something to do with where Hawk found you?"

He couldn't even say the word brothel. Shame and disgust, that is what he would feel if she told him. She couldn't resist prodding him. "You mean about my being a whore?" From the way his face darkened, Genie knew she had made a mistake. Provoking him would not make him give her time. She took a deep breath and changed tactics. "This has nothing to do with that," she said honestly. "A little time, that is all I am asking for."

But his suspicion once roused would not be so easily dismissed. "Is this another negotiation ploy?"

"What do you mean?" she asked, genuinely confused.

"One of your conditions. Like the house and the annuity. What demands will you make of me now?"

"No! Of course not." She started to move off the bed, but it was clear he didn't believe her. He thought she was trying to manipulate him; the terms of the agreement she'd wrested from him were working against her. "This has all happened so fast, I need some time to get used—"

He grabbed her arm, stopping her. "Don't take me for a fool, Genie," he growled, his words clipped. "You made the bargain. I've kept my part, now you'll keep yours. You're my wife. And I assure you, I will not settle for a wife in name only. Nor will I give you the basis for an annulment. Your terms are beginning to make a lot more sense."

She felt the walls closing in around her, knowing a way out was slipping away from her. "I'm asking only for a few days, a week at most," she pleaded.

He was unmoved. "And if I give you this week, your trepidation will miraculously vanish, and you will come to me willingly?"

No. How could she explain that she might never be ready? But Genie knew one thing with certainty, if he pushed her now, it would be disastrous.

He saw the truth in her expression before she could think of a lie. "I didn't think so," he said. "I'll not be put off, my clever little wife. I intend to have you and consummate our vows tonight."

His voice left no doubt: he would not be dissuaded.

"You'll not force me." She tried to control the panic in her voice, but it sounded shrill.

HUNTINGDON STARED AT HER IN shock. Force? What the hell was she talking about? First she tried to manipulate him, and now she was casting him in the role of evil seducer?

A reticent bride was the last thing he'd expected when he entered the room. But if Genie thought he would let her wriggle out of their agreement with a few anxious pleas, she didn't know him very well. And if she thought she'd get out of this marriage with an annulment, she'd have to find another cause. Because tonight this marriage would be consummated.

Although at first he had wondered whether there was something else behind the request. There was something slightly frantic underlying her appeal. Almost as if she was scared. But it wasn't fear, it was just more of her scheming. Another way for her to try to control the situation—to keep distance between them.

But he wouldn't let her. Huntingdon had waited for this night for a long time. He would not be denied without good reason. Didn't she realize that tonight would be the final step in the long journey of bringing them together again?

Only when they'd made love would the closeness return, the closeness that had been missing from his life since she'd disappeared. The comfortable intimacy that he'd never been able to find with another woman.

He knew he could make her remember. And then they could begin to forget the past. He did not delude himself to think that forgiveness would come quickly, but sharing a bed would go a long way in reestablishing the closeness that they'd once shared. He believed it with every fiber of his being, and once she was in his arms again, she would see it, too.

Desire had simmered between them from the first moment they'd set eyes on each other again at Prinny's fete. She wanted him as much as he wanted her. How could she deny it after what had nearly happened in the greenhouse? He could have taken her then; her passion had burned as hot as his.

He'd learned much in pleasing a woman over the past five years. Enough to make her beg if he wanted to.

A slow smile spread over his face. "I won't need to force anything."

GENIE WATCHED THE ARROGANCE PLAY across his handsome features, so sublimely confident in his skills as a lover. How like a man to think that a few tricks in bed were all that it took to please a woman. Not realizing that there was something much more important missing between them—the connection that sparked true intimacy and love. Didn't he recall how happy she had been that first time, even though his "skills" were rather limited?

Lust had its limitations as she'd learned in the greenhouse. It would take more than passion to make her forget the visceral memory of that vile man trying to jab himself inside her.

Genie had accepted her fate. Huntingdon was determined to have her. Determined to make this a marriage in truth. She had not really expected to dissuade him. There would be no escape from her duty this night. Somehow, she'd have to find the strength to get through it. And not allow him to see just how damaged she truly was.

It was going to happen sometime; she might as well get it over with. And there was a small part of her—a very small part of her—that hoped his arrogance was deserved. That maybe he would be enough.

She slid back under the covers, silently praying for

strength.

He studied her face, but she held her expression impassive. Apparently satisfied that she'd come to her senses, he bent down and placed a tender kiss on her lips. "I'll take it nice and slow."

She didn't respond.

His finger traced the side of her face, almost lovingly. "If you want me to stop, Genie, I will. But give me a chance."

Something flickered in her. Perhaps a shadow of hope. She met his anxious stare. The partial capitulation surprised her. She did not doubt his word. If she asked, he would stop.

But she would not ask again. They were married and despite the terms of the marital contract, Genie knew it would be better if she gave him no cause to annul the marriage. Their marriage would have to be consummated at some point. And maybe, just maybe, she wouldn't want him to stop.

Not trusting herself to speak, she nodded.

He stood up from the side of the bed and perfunctorily began to remove his clothes. Her eyes widened. "What are you d-d-doing?"

He grinned. "I would think that was obvious."

She blushed, no doubt to her roots.

"We no longer have to worry about being interrupted, Genie. There is a certain freedom in being man and wife."

Despite her embarrassment, she could not look away. She'd never seen his bare chest before. She admitted being exceedingly curious as to how the broad shoulders and muscled chest that so gloriously filled a jacket would appear unadorned. Sensing her interest, his movements slowed, turning less mechanical. The makings of a sly smile curved his generous lips.

He started with his complicated cravat, untying and alternately unwrapping the long sections of linen that bound his neck. Next he moved to his waistcoat, carefully unbuttoning the cream-colored buttons that matched the fabric of the elaborately embroidered garment. Shrugging it off his shoulders, it fell in the growing pile of clothing pooling on the floor.

Genie still couldn't see anything beyond the elaborate ruffles of his linen shirtsleeves. Frustrated, she must have made a sound because he looked at her and chuckled.

His long, tanned fingers moved to the ties at his neck and stopped. Genie's breath caught. Her fear was temporarily forgotten. The anticipation of what was to come only increased the titillation of watching him undress. She felt warm and soft all over. From the smug smile on his face he knew what he was doing to her, seducing her by the slow tease of his performance.

Unable to turn away, she watched him, fascinated by the small vee of skin and smattering of brown hairs that the opening of his shirt had revealed at his neck. Finally, in one fell motion, he pulled the shirt over his head and tossed it on the pile at his feet.

A small choking sound emanated from somewhere deep in her throat. He resembled the Greek god that she'd once compared him to. The perfection of his too-handsome face was set off magnificently by the power of his tall, well-muscled form. His naked chest was even more impressive than she'd imagined. His shoulders were broad and strong, his chest and arms layered with heavy muscles, his stomach flat and hard. His tanned skin gleamed in the candlelight, smooth except for the small triangle of hair below his collar bone and a light trail that started below his navel and disappeared beneath the waist of his breeches.

He didn't get muscles like that from boxing and fencing. There was a raw virility to his form that suggested more strenuous pursuits. Perhaps he mined quarry in his spare time.

He kicked off his buckled shoes and yanked off the stockings he'd worn with the formal attire. His calves were as thickly muscled and well formed as the rest of him. But when he started to unbutton the fall front of his breeches, Genie stopped him. The embarrassment of her bold perusal had finally caught up with her.

"Please, the lights."

He looked like he might tease her, but instead he moved around the room to do her bidding—providing her the opportunity to notice that his back was every bit as powerfully sculpted as his chest. When he was done, only the fire and the flame from a single candle illuminated the large chamber.

He moved back to the side of the bed. Tore the bed coverings from her white-knuckled hold, pulled them aside and lowered himself to the bed so that he was lying half on top of her. She closed her eyes, savoring the familiar but nearly forgotten sensation of his weight on top of her. The primal feeling of protection.

She couldn't stop herself from touching him. She gasped at the sensation of his warm skin under her hands. He felt so smooth and yet so hard at the same time. Her fingers splayed over the powerful stacks of muscles, marveling at the way he flexed reflexively under her fingertips. There was a solidness to him that hadn't been there before. The boy had developed into a man. Her body responded to his undeniable strength. She never fathomed how potent an aphrodisiac a naked chest could be.

Her hand skimmed his stomach and she watched in wonder as narrow bands of muscles formed in parallel lines where she touched. Amazed, she traced the rigid bands with her fingertips, dipping lower and lower until the heel of her hand grazed the edge of his breeches. The unmistakable bulge of his erection gave her a moment's hesitation.

It was his turn to groan as she continued her bold exploration through the fine wool of his breeches, outlining the enormous dimensions with the palm of her hand. He was thick and long, straining against the fabric confines. His face darkened with exquisite torture as she molded him in her hand. The feeling of control excited her, never realizing that she could become so aroused just by sight and touch alone.

He grabbed her wrist. "Enough. You're killing me," he said through clenched teeth. "You'll have to save your explorations for later, my sweet. As it is, this is going to be over much too soon." He rolled over on one elbow to allow himself a better view. "Now it's my turn."

Boldly, his gaze traveled the length of her body, an unmistakable predatory gleam in his eye. He looked like he could ravish her with the heat of his stare. She hadn't been the only one aroused by what had just occurred.

His expression had turned fierce, hard planes and angles replacing the confident swagger. His jaw was clenched and restraint had caused the veins in his neck to stand out. He wanted her and he was fighting to control himself.

Genie felt a little of her panic return.

But he soothed her with the gentleness of his touch. Reverently, like the sculptor molding his clay, his hand skimmed the curve of her breast, the contours of her waist and hip and the long sleek muscles of her thigh and calf. "God, you're beautiful," he said hoarsely, more to himself than to her.

The heat of desire pooled again, low in her belly. His slow seduction was working, her body craved his touch. But would it be enough? She willed herself to not think about what was to come, but to surrender to the passion of the moment.

The moment was all she had.

She clasped her hands around the back of his neck and pulled him closer, welcoming the heavy press of his body against hers, all too aware of the way their bodies fit together perfectly.

Her lips parted as his mouth found hers in a hot, searing kiss.

Huntingdon was having a difficult time controlling the wave of desire that had crashed down upon him when she'd touched him. The burst of male pride he'd felt at her blatant admiration of his naked chest had been nothing compared to the sensation of her soft hands stroking his skin.

She'd never touched him like that before and the force of desire that hit him was entirely unexpected. And then her hand had moved lower. He'd held his breath, stomach clenched, trying not to explode. Trying not to think of how it would feel to have her hand curled tightly around his length, pumping him hard until he erupted.

Every little movement drove him mad. When her lips had parted in wonder, he'd imagined her mouth wrapped around the heavy head of his cock, running her tongue down his length, and sucking him dry as he came deep in her throat. A proper wife would never be expected to do such things, of course, but it didn't stop a red-blooded Englishman from dreaming.

It had been far too long since he had a woman, and Huntingdon was worried. Worried that it would be over too quickly. So he'd pulled her hand away from where he wanted it most, and tried to slow his raging lust.

But when she'd kissed him, he'd lost the ability to reason. He crushed her to him, deepening the kiss with his mouth and the press of his body into hers. He stroked her tongue with his, tasting the sweet honey of her lips. But it wasn't enough. He wanted it harder, faster, to devour her with the urgency of his need. He wanted it the way it used to be.

She met him stroke for stroke. Her mouth moved under his with equal desperation, equal hunger. Her nails bit into his back, deeper and deeper as the kiss intensified. The press of her hips against his groin drove him mad. He gripped her bottom and moved her higher against him, settling his fullness between her legs.

His skin was on fire.

Her breasts pressed against his chest, her taut nipples raked his bare skin. Through the soft silk of her dressing gown, he cupped her, weighing the incredible fullness in his hands. He ran the pad of his thumb back and forth against the hard tip, priming it for his mouth. She squirmed against his hand in frustration and he chuckled—a knowing masculine laugh. Deftly, he worked the ties of the gown, sliding it down her shoulders and arms. The chemise soon followed, leaving her half naked in his arms.

His eyes feasted on her wanton beauty. Her shimmering hair spilling out on the pillow behind her, her lips red and swollen from his kiss, her eyes half shuttered, and her gorgeous body flushed with passion. Her breasts were ripe perfection. Large and round, with tiny pink nipples, tight and puckered against the smooth ivory of her creamy skin. They begged to be kissed. He dipped his head and took the succulent tip between his teeth, nibbling and sucking gently. But it wasn't enough. He buried his nose between her breasts, inhaling the sweet floral scent of her skin, and took the tip in his mouth again, sucking and nibbling harder, until her back arched and soft moans of sensual delight filled the sultry chamber.

He smothered her moans with the force of his kiss, his hand stroking her breasts where his mouth had left off.

He'd exhausted his patience. The storm of desire swept over him, and all he could think about was finally making her his. Again. After all these years he'd have what he'd been searching for. His first love in his arms again. Laughing and teasing as they came together in nature's most powerful storm.

He'd known this was the right thing. Known not to let her put him off with vague excuses. The closeness they'd once shared would soon be theirs again.

He slid her gown and chemise down past her hips, hastily discarding them on the floor. His breeches quickly followed. He'd been waiting too long for this. He wanted to feel the slickness of her folds between his fingers, to sink his stiff cock deep inside her, to feel her tightness hold him as he plunged harder and harder, until the final clutch and pulse of orgasm freed him from the fever of desire that had taken hold of him.

His hand moved to the sweet crevice between her legs, he knew that he was only moments away from oblivion. Suddenly the tiny moans stopped. He thought he noticed her tense, but dismissing it as nerves, he forged on. She'd been so nervous that first time. No doubt this was the same. Soon her cheeks would flush and her eyes would sparkle. She'd gaze at him as if he was the most wonderful man in the world and he would feel complete.

Soon.

Genie flinched as his hand slid past the curve of her hip and down her thigh. Desire slipped away. Grasping wildly at the dwindling sensations, she fought to hold on, not ready to relinquish passion to fear. She thought it would work. She told herself to concentrate on the pleasure of his kiss, on the way his tongue stroked her mouth, on the heady taste of wine on his lips, on the silkiness of his hair tickling her skin as he nipped and sucked her breast. To not think about the hand that had moved between her legs.

No! She wanted to scream. No!

But it was too late. As quickly as desire had flamed, the magic fled, leaving her cold. Her body had deluded her into thinking that this time might be different. She'd felt so deliciously warm, so aroused. So safe. She'd wanted him, wanted to remember the sensation of him inside her, wanted to remember the closeness they'd once shared. But, despite their vows this morning, that closeness was gone forever. She wanted to trust him, but wanting to trust was very different from actually trusting.

His finger slid inside her and she had to bite her tongue to keep from crying out. The dampness that had surged between her legs when he'd kissed her earlier eased the pain that she would have otherwise felt. She couldn't look at him. She didn't want to see the haze of lust transform his face into the monster of her dreams. Where all men were the same. *Not him, too. Men only want one thing from a beautiful woman...*

Panic squeezed her chest. Terror rose in her throat, but she forced it back. She was in control. He wouldn't hurt her. He would stop if she asked. But she wouldn't. She could do this.

He murmured something, but she didn't hear.

She closed her eyes and willed herself away from the pain of her memories, remembering a time instead when she'd laughed and danced in the grass along a riverbank. She barely tensed at all when he slid his thick erection into her, inch by agonizing inch, barely noticed the rhythmic thrusting as he plunged inside her, barely hearing the growl of completion as he spilled his seed deep inside her.

Numb, she didn't feel anything at all—except perhaps for mild relief when it ended. She'd made it through the act, but it had been nothing like they'd shared before. The magic had disappeared. She felt hollow.

In that moment of utter emptiness, Genie realized that she wanted more from Huntingdon. She wanted him to see something more in her than a beautiful woman—an object of lust.

Once, she thought he had. But not anymore.

He rolled off of her and gazed up at the ceiling, silent save for the heavy sound of his breathing as it fought to return to normal.

Had he noticed her withdrawal? Would it matter?

Disappointment filtered through the emptiness. The night had begun with such promise. She'd dared to hope that Huntingdon could help her feel passion again. But it was useless. That part of her life was gone forever.

She'd made the right decision in sending the letter.

If he couldn't make her feel, no one could.

Unable to resist, she stole a quick glance at him lying beside her. His eyes were closed, though she could tell he did not sleep. His chest still rose and fell with the unevenness of his breath. A lock of hair had slipped across his face. Years ago she wouldn't have thought twice, but reached across to sweep it aside. But not today. Today such intimacies would feel awkward.

She turned away. Unable to look at him any longer. She didn't want to see the subtle reminders of all that she had lost.

But the dull ache in her chest, the longing for something just out of her reach, told her that she had not forgotten.

WHAT HAD HE DONE?

Huntingdon opened his eyes and stared at the ceiling,

trying to figure out what had just happened. His body had found release, but everything else felt terribly wrong. One minute she was nearly falling apart in his arms and the next she'd seemed a million miles away.

He didn't know what to say. He felt so bloody awkward. Like he'd failed her again.

Disappointment rocked him. He should be holding her in his arms, bathing in the aftermath of orgasmic bliss, but instead she lay stiffly next to him, every outward sign indicating not to touch her. So he didn't. Though he wanted to pull her into his arms and beg her forgiveness.

Never had he felt so inadequate. Even after their first time. The first time there was always pain. This time he had no excuse. He should have done everything to ensure that she joined him in release. But he'd fallen on her like some randy schoolboy.

He'd made a grave mistake. Rather than the closeness he wanted, she'd slipped even further away from him.

"Genie, I..."

Her gaze met his and he faltered. The disappointment in her eyes cut him to the quick. He'd let her down. "Genie, I'm sorry. I should have—"

She stopped him. "There is nothing to apologize for."

"But you didn't—"

"I was nervous."

Her words did not ring true. It had been more than nervousness. Something had made her withdraw from him and he was such a lust-driven fool he'd failed to heed the warnings her body had tried to give him.

Had there been more to her request than grounds for an annulment?

He'd sensed her pulling away that first time, too, but had attributed it to hesitation. Now he wondered if there was another reason—a far more nefarious reason. He knew where Edmund had found her, and the condition he'd found her in. She'd been beaten. But had there been more to it? Or had one of the men who frequented the brothel...

He couldn't finish the thought. Rage took hold of him.

Rage unlike anything he'd ever felt before. The thought of someone hurting her...

HE DIDN'T BELIEVE HER. GENIE could see it in his eyes. He blamed himself. And Genie feared that with how vulnerable she felt right now, if he pulled her in his arms and asked the right questions she could do something foolish and tell him everything.

Even worse than her shame would be his pity. Or would it be disgust? Her secrets were her protection, and she was scared that without them she would lose her strength. She would be weak—vulnerable—as before.

He stared at her long and hard, as if searching for an answer. A strange look crossed his face, like something had just occurred to him. His eyes flashed with a spark of anger.

He took her chin in his hand and looked deeply into her eyes. "Did somebody hurt you... intimately?"

Her heart fell to her feet. Her blood pounded with her increasing panic. How easily he'd guessed. Was her damage so obvious? Shame caused her to lash out. "Do you mean other than you?"

He flinched, but his hand didn't move from her face. "Were you raped?"

"No!" she snapped back honestly.

But he didn't believe her. She could feel the penetrating scrutiny of his gaze scanning every inch of her face, waiting for a crack. A crack that she wouldn't give him.

"If something happened you need to tell me."

She jerked her face away. She didn't need to tell him anything; he had no right to her secrets. "Why are you asking me these questions?"

"Something happened a few minutes ago, and I want to find out what it was."

"Nothing happened."

"I used to please you," he said softly.

She choked on the tears balling in her throat and blurted

out harshly, "I used to love you."

He jerked back as if she'd struck him. The force of the raw emotion that ravaged his face struck her cold. Her chest pinched with regret. He looked shocked, then destroyed, like a man who'd been beaten.

"I see," he said tightly. "If you'll excuse me, I'll leave you to your rest."

Genie stared in horror at his expression. She wanted to say something to explain, but the words stuck in her throat and he'd already turned his back on her. She hadn't meant to reject him so cruelly, she just wanted him to leave so she could nurse her wounds in privacy.

He rose from the bed and quickly moved to gather up his belongings, the clothes that not so long ago he'd teasingly stripped from his body.

A swatch of blue hanging from a pocket in his waistcoat caught her attention. He jerked around and she watched as it fluttered to the ground.

"Wait," she called after him, "you dropped—"

But her words were lost in the loud slam of the door. A knot of dread formed in her gut. She slipped out from under the covers and started toward the thin piece of blue fabric, the dread increasing with each step. In her heart, she knew what it was. And what it meant.

He hadn't forgotten her. He'd had her with him all this time.

She knelt on the ground and lovingly lifted the tattered and faded blue ribbon to her face. Tears streamed down her face. Dear God, what had she done?

CHAPTER TWENTY

THE RIBBON WAS STILL CLUTCHED in her fingers when she woke in the morning curled up in a ball on the floor, right where she'd collapsed in tears the night before. It felt like a dam had burst inside her. The discovery of the ribbon had shattered the protective wall she'd surrounded herself with since Edmund had found her at Madame Solange's.

The small, insignificant piece of trim had changed everything.

All this time, he'd kept the talisman of the time they'd first made love. She *had* meant something to him. He hadn't forgotten her. But the question that ate at her soul was what else it might mean? Could he possibly have cared for her all this time? Her cruel words from the night before echoed in her head and she knew she had to see him.

But not looking like this.

She rang for her maid and began the long process of her toilette, made longer by the damage she'd done to her eyes from the night of crying. Cold compresses helped with the swelling, and liniment with the blotchiness. By the time she made her way downstairs, it was midmorning.

His valet informed her that his grace had left the house on estate business before the sun had risen. As the manservant didn't know when he was expected to return, Genie waited for him in his private study.

Too emotionally drained to read, she passed the time by alternately staring out the window (as if that would make him appear faster) and inspecting the personal items scattered about the room. The two miniatures displayed prominently on his desk had to be his parents, though the cheery girl smiling back at her was barely recognizable as his mother. She chuckled at the charming portrait of him by his youngest sister, Penny, proudly hung above the sideboard next to a Gainsborough. Four or five books on husbandry and livestock were stacked on one side of his desk. Flipping through one on sheep, she noticed that he'd written extensive notes in the margins. Clearly he took his duties as duke seriously.

Without thinking, she picked up a few of the letters scattered across his desk and began to arrange them in a neat pile. Scanning the signatures, she noticed that most were progress reports from various local mines, mills, and factories. That surprised her. She knew he had numerous estates, but didn't realize that he had other sources of income. The discovery only made her realize just how little she knew of the man he'd become.

She sat down in the chair behind his desk and picked up one of the letters. She shouldn't be nosing around in his private things, but she admitted a certain amount of curiosity about his activities.

Intent on reading, she didn't hear the door open.

"What are you doing?"

She dropped the letter and looked up guiltily at the sound of his clipped voice. His dark expression gave no quarter. Genie's intentions faltered slightly under his hard stare. She'd laid down the gauntlet last night, setting the tone for their marriage, and he, apparently, had accepted. The boyish charm of the past few days had vanished.

She glanced down at one of the miniatures on the desk. He actually reminded her of his brother, Loudoun.

She drew a deep breath and lifted her chin. "I was waiting for you."

"In the future you may make an appointment with my secretary. If you have any questions about the managing of the household, please ask my mother. She has offered to train you in what is required."

The formality of his tone hurt more than she expected. "I didn't mean to look through your things, but I noticed the letterhead and I was curious."

He stared at her blankly. He wasn't going to make this easy.

"I didn't know that you owned mills and factories."

"Does my being in trade offend your refined sensibilities?"

"Of course not," she said, taken aback. "I think it shows an extreme amount of foresight."

He crossed his arms and leaned against the entry, interested despite his intention not to be. "How so?"

She shrugged. "I admit I'm no expert on the subject, but it doesn't take much to realize that industry will be an important part of England's future. And with landowners taxed so heavily with the war, it seems extremely prudent to diversify your sources of income."

She'd cracked his reserve. By his look he was unabashedly impressed. "Do not underrate your expertise, my dear. I'm afraid you have more insight into the subject than half of parliament. Which is one of the reasons a post in Perceval's government is so important to me."

For a moment Genie preened under his praise before the ramifications of what she had done hit her. He wouldn't have that post. Fearing that guilt was plain on her face, she stood up from behind the desk and moved to the window. He straightened from his lazy stance in the doorway and moved into the room, closing the door behind him.

"I'm sure you did not wait for me all this time to discuss my mills."

"No." She shifted uncomfortably, unsure how to explain.

"I'm afraid I'm very busy."

She gathered her courage and held out her hand. "I wanted to ask you about this." Her fingers opened to reveal the ribbon.

Something flickered across his face before his expression turned accusing. "Where did you get that?"

He obviously thought she'd been looking through his

things. Given what she'd just been doing, she didn't blame him. "It fell from your waistcoat last night."

He continued to stare at her wordlessly. It was impossible to guess what he might be thinking. She looked for a sign, any sign that he still cared for her.

Clearly, he wasn't going to explain, so she asked, "You kept it all this time?"

He shrugged noncommittally, perhaps embarrassed by the sentimentality.

"You remembered," she prodded.

"Of course I did," he said sharply. "I already told you as much."

"But I didn't believe you."

"And now you do?" He laughed harshly. "You trust a piece of ribbon and not my word."

"You'd given me your word before."

He flinched. "You've developed a rather keen ability to level a man with the blade of your tongue, Genie."

"If you mean I've grown stronger and I'm no longer a foolish girl to gamble everything on the word of a 'gentleman,' then yes I have changed."

"I never thought of you as someone I could take advantage of."

"That's not how it seemed from my perspective. I thought it was all a game to you."

"It wasn't a game. I cared for you." His voice grew thick. "Deeply."

He still cared. The knowledge of what they had lost cut through her. Her voice broke. "Then why did you abandon me?"

He sighed wearily. "I was a young fool. I won't excuse my conduct, but I never meant for things to happen the way they did. I never meant to make love to you. But it happened. And if you'll recall, I didn't have to force you."

"No, you didn't. But you promised to marry me. I trusted you."

"I wanted to marry you. When I spoke those words, I honestly believed my parents would not object to a match between us. You weren't the only one who was young and naïve. I should have fought harder, stood up to them, done the honorable thing. I know that. And if you had not disappeared, I would have. No matter what you think. I will accept most of the blame for what happened, but not all of it."

Stung, Genie recoiled. How dare he blame anything on her! She opened her mouth to argue, then she quickly slammed it shut again. What if he was right? For so many years she'd blamed him, she'd ignored her own part in what had happened. She'd been a willing participant, a very willing participant. He hadn't forced her. She'd known that what she was doing was wrong, but ignored it. *Two* people had made love on that riverbank. Shouldn't she bear some responsibility for her own decisions?

He'd made mistakes, but so had she.

But she wasn't ready to give up on all of that anger and resentment she'd harbored for so long. "You can hardly blame me for 'disappearing.' Your mother threatened to ruin my family, and when I wrote to you for help, you refused to come to me."

He took a few steps toward her, she thought he was going to pull her into his arms but at the last minute he stopped. Instead, he dragged his fingers through his hair. "That letter was the single biggest mistake of my life. I was being pressured from every direction and I was angry at you for forcing my hand. I came a few days later, but you'd already left." He reached out and took her chin in his hand, tipping her face back. Her heart twisted; stunned by the depth of emotion in his gaze. "Haven't you ever done something you regret, something that had consequences far beyond what you might have anticipated?"

Lizzie. Her sister immediately sprang to mind. Genie had never realized what leaving might do to her sister, just as Huntingdon could not have known the horrible chain of events that his letter would set in motion.

Suddenly Genie saw the events of the past in a very different light. He'd made mistakes, but he was not responsible for everything that had happened to her. Along the way, both of them had made choices. She could have stayed and forced him to marry her. At the time, when the duchess had approached her with her offer, she hadn't seen any other choice. She'd been naïve, innocent, and too intimidated by her position to defy her. But Genie realized if the same thing happened today, she would stay and fight.

She'd grown, why couldn't she accept that he might have as well?

"There are a lot of things I'd like to take back and do over again."

He smiled faintly at her words. "If I've learned anything over the past couple months, it's that we can't go back. All we can do is build for the future. I can't change what happened in the past. All I can do is swear that I will do my best to make sure it never happens again. If you give me your trust again, I swear I'll do everything in my power never to fail you again." He lowered his mouth so that it was only a few tantalizing inches from her own. "Trust me, Genie."

And then his mouth covered hers.

If last night he'd showed her his passion, with this kiss he showed her his heart. Slowly, his mouth moved over hers, brushing his lips against hers in a tender kiss that filled her with instant longing. A sweet, aching seduction that promised so much and ended far too soon. Giving her a long, piercing look he left her alone with his vow ringing in her ears.

Trust me. Words that had haunted her dreams. But this time they did not fuel her vengeance. Because this time, she wanted to believe him.

CHAPTER TWENTY-ONE

The weeks after the wedding passed quickly. In the beginning Genie was occupied with entertaining the hunting party and then, when the last guests had departed, with the difficult task of learning how to manage a household far larger than her girlhood training had ever contemplated. The duke had forty full-time servants at Donnington alone. Add the servants scattered about his other properties, and she was responsible for nearly one hundred people.

Bidding farewell to her friends had not been easy. Lady Hawkesbury and Caro's departure had been difficult, but by far the most painful leave taking was Edmund's. His departure had left a void that could not easily be filled. They'd been together for over a year and she'd come to rely more than she realized on the constancy of his friendship.

If only for necessity's sake, an unspoken truce had been forged between Genie and the dowager duchess. Huntingdon's mother was certainly a proficient instructor in the inner workings of the household, but Genie was surprised to find that behind the proud façade lurked a dry wit. She was a strong woman with a keen intellect and frank manner—not unlike Lady Hawkesbury. Under different circumstances, Genie might even have admired her. With all that had happened they would never be close, but by her willingness and patience to help Genie learn the intricacies of her duties, she'd earned Genie's grudging respect.

Of her husband, Genie didn't know what to think. Huntingdon confused and confounded her. Thankfully, he had chosen not to question her any further on what had caused her sudden loss of passion on their wedding night. At times she wondered whether he'd lost interest in that facet of their marriage. Though he danced attendance upon her during the day like the most ardent admirer, the door separating their rooms had remained firmly closed. At every opportunity, he stole kisses, but he kissed her with such sweet tenderness, Genie wondered whether his passion for her had tempered. The possibility that the savage urgency with which he usually kissed her might be gone bothered her more than she wanted to acknowledge.

Yet despite the unresolved issue of their marital bed, life in the country had brought Genie a sense of peace that had previously eluded her. Donnington Park was the country house she'd always dreamed of—and more. The house was as elegant as any palace with every modern convenience. The gardens and grounds were enchanting. The longer she spent at Donnington, the more she realized how much she could come to love it.

If it were possible.

With one last glance in the looking glass, Genie adjusted her emerald-green bonnet and made her way down to the stables. An invitation to join Huntingdon on his morning ride a few weeks ago had turned into a daily ritual. One that she enjoyed, far more than was prudent.

Ten minutes later she entered the stables.

"There you are." He flashed her that brilliant lopsided grin that never failed to tug at her heartstrings. "I was beginning to wonder whether I'd have to send someone up to wake you."

He took her hand to assist her in mounting her horse. Shockwaves of awareness tingled down her spine. Genie knew she was in trouble. Every day that she spent at Donnington, the deeper she fell under his spell. The relaxed charm was reminiscent of the youth, but far more devastating when set against the power of the man he had become. Whether conducting estate business, dealing with the mills and factories, or settling a dispute between two of his younger siblings, he exuded strength and capability in everything he did. And he'd put all of that strength and determination to work in trying to woo her. A patient seduction, but one that was not without substantial effect.

"I'm sorry, did I keep you waiting?" she asked innocently, well aware that she was late.

He brought her hand to his mouth. "It was well worth the wait, you look ravishing. Good enough to eat." Her cheeks pinkened, not from the pretty compliment but from the lazy suggestive look he gave her as he placed a lingering kiss on her hand before releasing it.

Ignoring the sudden racing of her heart, she asked, "Where are we riding today?" Usually they rode out to inspect the property, the livestock, or to attend to some business for the tenants. A few times he'd taken her to the mills and once to the mines at Ashby. One day last week he'd even taken her to the Huntingdon family's ruined ancestral seat—the Castle at Ashby-de-la-Zouch, slighted during the civil war. The castle that had inspired Sir Walter Scott's *Ivanhoe* was truly magical.

"Ah, no pressing business to attend to today, so I thought we'd go to the lake. Chef has packed a special surprise for you."

A picnic. She glanced up at the gray skies. Rather late in the season, but Genie did not mind the crisp temperature as long as the rain kept at bay. She tried not to think of other such outings long ago, but the similarities were impossible to ignore. Nor could she manage to rouse the anger that such memories usually entailed. Those people seemed so far away, and nearly unrecognizable from the people they were today. And for the first time, Genie allowed that perhaps that was not such a horrible thing.

They rode for a while, occasionally stopping to speak with a tenant or a worker, waving politely to others as they passed.

If she'd had any doubts about how seriously Huntingdon took his position as duke, they were dispelled soon after their first ride together. He immersed himself in every detail of the estate. That involvement was well rewarded with the unqualified respect of those around him.

Not that he didn't have his faults. He didn't like being told no, and stubbornly pressed on determined to find a solution often when there was none. He and Stewart butted heads often enough over some such matter.

She glanced over at him, noting the hard square jaw and haughty turn of his mouth. Now, however, Genie recognized that behind the superficial arrogance of his expression, lurked a man very willing to work with the lowest laborer. She'd not soon forget how surprised she'd been the first time he'd tossed off his jacket and joined in repairing a leaking roof or shearing an ornery lamb.

Her eyes lingered on the wide set of his shoulders. At least she'd cleared up one mystery. She no longer wondered where he got those muscles. They were well earned.

In Donnington, Huntingdon was in his element. She recalled what he'd once said about being a displaced farmer, though at the time she'd thought he wasn't serious. Watching the pride and calm in his expression, now she knew he'd spoken the truth—he didn't simply possess the land as a benevolent despot, he was part of the land.

"What are you thinking about? You've been unusually quiet," Huntingdon asked as they approached the lake from a spectacular vantage point high on a hill overlooking the water, surrounded by a wispy canopy of trees. The view was breathtaking. Even the bleak gray skies could not detract from the lush autumnal colors of Capability Brown's pastoral landscaping.

Genie thought for a moment before answering. "Do you remember what you once told me about being a farmer?"

He gave her a long, intense look. She rarely brought up anything about their past. "I remember everything about that time."

There was nothing suggestive in his tone, only honesty and perhaps a note of regret.

"At the time, I thought you were only trying to ease my embarrassment, but now I'm beginning to wonder whether you spoke the truth."

He chuckled, those brilliant blue eyes crinkling around the edges. He laughed so much easier these past few weeks. The resemblance to his humorless brother Loudoun had become fainter.

"Well, perhaps it was a bit of both. I must admit that being a duke has its advantages." His gaze swept over the wide expanse of land around them with no less supreme authority than a conqueror after the battle was won. "Though the life of a farmer is hard, there's something elegant in the simplicity of a life in such delicate harmony with the land, don't you think?"

"Perhaps a bit too much in harmony for my taste," Genie answered honestly. "You paint a pretty picture, but there is nothing romantic about hard work. Nor about blisters, a sore back, or an empty belly. Nor do I envy having the bread that I eat dependent upon the capricious nature of the weather."

She bit her tongue, knowing she'd said too much.

He gave her a hard, appraising look. Probably surprised by the rare glimpse into her past.

"Perhaps you are right. I did not mean to make light of the difficulties of such a position."

Genie turned her gaze, but he'd already seen enough.

His voice soothed over her like a mother's comforting caress. "I hope one day you will tell me what it was like for you, Genie. I can't imagine what it would be like to be left with no money, all alone in a strange country." His voice barely rose above the soft clop of their horses. "I admire your strength and bravery. Had I been in the same position, I doubt that I would have fared as well."

Her throat closed, overwhelmed by the respect in his voice. But he didn't know how weak she was. "I wasn't brave, I was scared." Her voice caught, thick with emotion.

"There is no shame in admitting fear, Genie. When I first inherited the dukedom, I was terrified."

She raised a brow as if she didn't believe him.

A small self-conscious smile lifted the corners of his mouth. "I assure you it's the truth. I didn't think I had what it took. The only time I'd ever faced real difficulty before, I'd failed." He looked deep into her eyes. "I failed you." He paused, allowing his words to penetrate. "But that failure made me realize that I didn't want to be that kind of man. The kind of man who lets people down. When my father and brother died I had a choice. I could rebel against the responsibility as everyone expected, or I could take the more difficult route and change. I chose the latter, and it wasn't easy. But fear is a very powerful motivator."

Touched by the little corner of his soul that he'd revealed to her, Genie didn't know what to say. She stared at the powerful, handsome man before her with new eyes. A man who on the outside appeared to have every confidence, but who on the inside was driven by a fear of failure. Though he obviously thought it was a weakness, to Genie the acknowledgment of vulnerability only made him seem stronger. When their eyes met, a shock surged through her, a deeper connection forged by understanding.

He'd fought to find his success—just as she had.

And she was going to topple him. She shivered, unease chilling her. That was what she wanted, wasn't it? She glanced sideways at him under her lashes and her chest squeezed. The more Genie learned about her new husband, the more she struggled with what she'd done. By now, the letter had surely found the hands of its recipient. The threat of pending doom was like a guillotine hanging over her future. Until it fell, she couldn't consider the alternatives.

But revenge no longer smelled quite as sweet. In fact, it had begun to stink.

HUNTINGDON HELPED GENIE DISMOUNT AND escorted her to a small stone bench beside the lake while the servants laid out the food and drink. Leaves littered the ground, providing all the excuse he needed to wrap his hand around that tiny waist ostensibly to prevent her from slipping. The smell of roses clung to her hair and instinctively he pulled her a little closer, inhaling the fresh scent.

A few weeks ago he would never have dreamed that he would be confiding his insecurities to Genie, but their relationship had changed. He'd changed. In an effort to win her affection, he'd rediscovered some of the lightheartedness that he'd lost. To earn a smile from those beautiful lips, he'd do just about anything. To wipe away unhappiness, he'd bare his soul.

And in spite of herself, she'd warmed to him. Ever since she'd discovered that piece of ribbon, she'd softened. He shook his head. If he'd known, he would have brought it to her attention a long time ago.

There were moments like last week when she'd frolicked about the ruins of Ashby Castle that he'd see flashes of the sweet innocent girl that he remembered, wide-eyed with excitement and wonder. But it wasn't that girl that made his heart feel as if it could explode. It was the contrast that intrigued him. Beneath the jaded exterior, she was still the girl he'd fallen in love with, only stronger—a harder edge, but she challenged him in ways that he never would have expected.

Yet, even as they drew closer, as the days went on, there were still many questions that had gone unanswered. Though the importance of the answer had diminished, he still wondered why she'd been at the brothel. And did it have anything to do with what had happened on their wedding night? A part of him was certain that something had happened to her, but another part of him wondered whether he was just looking for an excuse for her lack of response to him. *I used to love you.* Her words still haunted him—taunted him.

But he knew that until she trusted him, she would not confide anything about what had happened to her. He wanted the closeness back that they'd once shared. Their disastrous wedding night had showed him what a poor substitute passion was for intimacy. He wouldn't make that mistake again. It had taken the fear of a carriage accident to make him realize that he still cared for her, but these weeks had shown him just how much.

"Wait here," he said, seating her at the bench.

"Where are you going?"

"Patience, my sweet. I told you of a surprise. Now close your eyes."

She frowned, but did as instructed. He motioned to a groom to bring the basket forward. He opened it to reveal a banquet of mouth-watering confections, from tarts, to biscuits, to delicate chocolate cream puffs sprinkled with powdered sugar. Everything her heart could desire.

She sniffed in the air. Her tiny brows furrowed together.

"Keep those eyes closed," he ordered. Taking a chocolate cream puff, still warm from this morning's baking, he swept it under her nose. Her tongue darted out to wet her upper lip.

Heat surged in his crotch and he wondered who was teasing whom. She had the sensual, naughty mouth of a jade, and he could well imagine that tongue licking something else.

He cursed under his breath. Despite his vow not to ravage her until she was ready, the swift bolt of lust kicked him hard.

"Now open your mouth." His voice sounded rough.

When it looked like she was going to argue, he stopped her with a light kiss. She tasted of honey and it took everything he possessed to stop from deepening that kiss, from pressing the tight curve of her body against his in a crushing embrace. He spoke only inches from her mouth. "Open."

He popped the tiny ball into her mouth and she moaned. The deep, throaty sound of rapture only heightened the erotic images already swimming about his head.

"You devil," she said, but with a deliciously satisfied smile. "You know I don't eat sweets anymore."

"Chef and I thought we might change that."

Before she could argue, he plied her with a biscuit. His mouth salivated, whether from the smell of the warm caramel or from watching the obvious enjoyment she was getting from eating it. Genie chewed the tender confection as if every bite were pure heaven.

When she'd finished, she opened her eyes. Amusement twinkled back at him. "Perhaps you might."

With each tender morsel she devoured, Huntingdon watched her hard-wrought restraint crumble.

LATER THAT NIGHT, GENIE SUFFERED for her gluttony with a severely upset belly, but it was all worth it—every delicious bite. She never thought she'd be able to enjoy sweets again, but enjoy them she did—thanks to her husband.

She rose the next morning feeling substantially recovered and ready for another ride. A soft knock at the door interrupted her toilette.

"For you, Your Grace." The young housemaid bobbed and scooted out of the room before Genie could reply.

She quickly scanned the contents, then her heart lurched and the ability to breathe left her. The tersely worded note in the familiar scrawl paralyzed her with soul encompassing dread.

Distressing news from London prevents our morning ride. I await your immediate attendance in my private study. Huntingdon

The note fluttered to the floor. Stricken, she gazed out into nothingness.

The guillotine, it appeared, had fallen.

This was it. The moment she'd been waiting for. The moment of triumph for which she'd struggled. Genie would show him just how strong she was. That she was a woman who could not be forced, a woman not to be trifled with.

But it all felt wrong. The weight of what she'd done pressed down on her. She felt as if she was suffocating, not elated that revenge would soon be hers. Instead, it felt like her happiness had just come to a crashing, disastrous end.

She had everything she'd fought for: wealth, power, position... and now, revenge. The manor in Gloucestershire was hers, and she'd begun to implement her plan. She would never find herself at the mercy of a man again. But it wasn't enough. She'd also been given a glimpse of the life she'd dreamed of as a girl. A life with a beautiful home and a doting husband.

She tried to calm the race of her heart, tried to calm the wave of panic that threatened to overwhelm her. Her body felt tight, as if every bit of air had been sucked out of her.

Too late. It was too late to realize that revenge was not what she wanted.

Much too quickly, her maid finished arranging her hair in a soft knot secured at the back of her head with a jewel-encrusted comb. Gowned in a simple green morning gown instead of her riding habit, she made her way down the stairs and long hallways to Huntingdon. Each footfall felt heavier, like she was sinking deeper and deeper in mud with each step closer.

His back was to her as she entered the room.

Her hands clenched and unclenched in her skirts. "You asked to see me?" She couldn't control the slight wobble in her voice.

He turned and for a moment she froze, his visage was so severe. Her heart thumped loudly, waiting for the condemnation. At that moment, the magnitude of everything she'd forsaken struck her. The wait stretched beyond endurance, every muscle in her body clenched.

His handsome face broke out into a wide, easy grin, and a wave of pure relief washed over her. He wasn't angry with her. The news from London didn't concern her. Relieved, she exhaled loudly.

"Ah, there you are." He came toward her and took her hand, leading her to a chair. "Tea?"

"No, thank you." She didn't trust her stomach, it still churned with anxiety over what she'd narrowly avoided.

He lifted a tray too close to her nose. "Cream puff?" he

asked devilishly.

She grimaced, recalling her upset stomach last night and shook her head. "Beast," she muttered.

He laughed, setting down the plate of sweets on his desk. "I'm sorry we missed our morning ride, but I received some disturbing news from London."

"Yes?"

"I'm afraid we shall have to return to town sooner than expected. There is some unrest in Nottingham, a rebellion of sorts that must be put down before it spreads to Leicestershire."

"A rebellion?" she asked, suddenly alarmed.

He patted her hand. "Nothing to fret about, my sweet. A few workers calling themselves Luddites are upset with the modernization of the mills and factories and have destroyed some stocking frames. It began this past spring, but the unrest has spread. Something needs to be done before the rioting turns violent, and I fear that unless I'm there to sound caution, Perceval's reaction will be strong and swift."

Genie nodded, she'd heard some talk of these men—skilled croppers who resented the lower wages paid to unskilled workers who could operate the machines. With his mills and factories, it was only natural that Huntingdon was concerned.

"We will leave in a few days," he added.

Genie experienced a sharp twinge of disappointment. She would miss the quiet peace of the country.

Apparently, sharing the same thoughts, he squeezed her hand encouragingly. "We'll return as soon as we can. And I promise that it won't all be business. There will be plenty of entertainment. I believe the Duchess of Devonshire is holding a ball next week to welcome all those in town for the opening of parliament."

Genie forced herself to smile, but she knew it would not be the same.

She stood up. "I shall begin preparations immediately."

Before she could leave, he stopped her. Taking her in his arms, he tilted her chin back to meet his warm gaze. "I know you are disappointed, but we will be back at Donnington before you know it." He dipped his head, and placed a tender kiss on her lips.

An arrow shot straight to Genie's heart. The painful truth was that she might never return to Donnington. She had a reprieve, but for how long?

She started the long walk back to her chamber, lost in thought. Still shaken by what she'd narrowly avoided, Genie realized that she'd made a mistake in sending that letter to Fanny. Fanny had never been one to hold a secret. Genie's only hope was that Fanny would grasp the harm to Huntingdon if the news of Genie's sham marriage was discovered.

Perhaps London was the answer after all. Anxious to leave after the wedding, Fanny had traveled to London with Lady Hawkesbury. In London, Genie would convince Fanny not to disclose her scandalous secret.

Also in London, Genie could focus on her plans for the manor in Gloucestershire.

She reached her chamber and began instructing her lady's maid on the preparations for their trip. Resigned to leaving the happiness of the country behind her, Genie was determined that in London she would begin to make reparations.

CHAPTER TWENTY-TWO

DAMPNESS CLUNG TO THE DARKENED streets like a shroud of black pitch. Genie buried her nose in the heavy wool of her hooded cloak, trying to smother the overwhelming stench of bedpans that threatened to spill the contents of her stomach. This was a part of London that Genie was not supposed to know existed: the world of the underclass.

She jumped, startled by the sound of loud voices arguing across the windows above her. Besides the horrible stench, the noise was the first thing that struck her. Shrill voices raised in every perversion of the King's English imaginable pierced the night air. People who spent their days fading into the background made up for their silence at night with a raucous clamor. Yet oddly, despite the squalor, Genie found something comforting about all the activity.

Hugging the shadows, she wound her way through the narrow streets, her hand securely fastened on the gun in her reticule. Her neck prickled with apprehension. It felt as though someone was following her. She spun her head around, but no one was there.

She shivered and quickened her pace. She knew what she was doing was dangerous, but she'd put off her vow for too long.

Gravely injured from the vicious beating that she'd received at the hand of her employer, Genie wandered the streets of Boston's waterfront, finally collapsing at the door of a notorious brothel run by Madame Solange.

It was the first lucky thing to happen to her in a long

time.

The generous women scorned by polite society took pity on her, taking her in and gently nursing her back to health. With their bawdy humor and stoic acceptance of the brutal card that fate had dealt them, they gave Genie the strength to survive.

She vowed never to forget their kindness.

Genie knew that there was very little separating her from the "whores" at Madame Solange's. There were precious few choices available to a woman cast out, alone, without fortune. With beauty like hers, the choices were even fewer. Were it not for the timely arrival of Edmund, Genie knows she might well have found herself forced into a life of prostitution.

Luck in the form of Edmund had given her a choice they hadn't had. Genie wanted to do as much for other girls caught in the same trap. Her plan was simple: She offered employment and education at the manor in Gloucestershire. She didn't judge them if they refused her offer, her aim was to give them a choice—not make one for them. She'd already hired the small staff that had worked for the previous owner of the manor, but she would find space for as many additional girls as came to her.

In the week since they'd arrived in London, Genie had only had a few opportunities to escape the watchful eye of her husband. She'd visited a handful of notorious brothels passing out a card with the name and address of her solicitor, speaking to anyone who would listen. There weren't many. So far, two girls had contacted her solicitor. Not as many as she'd hoped, but it was a start. She squared her shoulders and raised her hand to knock on the door. At least she was doing something, not simply waiting around for scandal to hit. Fanny had avoided her thus far, but she was due to dine at Huntingdon House later that evening. Genie had to convince her to hold her silence.

Before the knocker fell, a large hand grabbed her arm.

THE LITTLE FOOL. THANK GOD he'd followed her. She'd disappeared so many times Huntingdon had grown suspicious. Now, to find her in the East End, standing at the door of a notorious brothel...

She'd better have one hell of an explanation.

He took her by the arm, intending to startle her—or perhaps shake some sense into her, he was so rattled. She gasped, turning on him as if she meant to fight him. Before recognition hit. Eyes that had been wide with terror only moments before narrowed angrily across her tiny nose.

"You frightened me," she accused.

"Good." Huntingdon tried to control his own burgeoning anger—his based on fear. "Don't you know how dangerous it is in this part of town?"

She jerked her arm away. "Of course I do. I'm not a fool."

He made a sharp sound, as if he would argue that point.

She squared her jaw defiantly. "I've taken precautions. I have a gun."

He couldn't believe this. "Aside from the obvious question of where you obtained the weapon, which I assume is in that reticule you were clutching so fiercely, I could point out—if I hadn't already so aptly demonstrated—that a gun is of limited value if you are grabbed from behind."

"Edmund gave me the gun." Her lips pressed together stubbornly. "And if you'll recall, I know how to defend myself."

Huntingdon didn't answer, but pulled her away from the door, practically dragging her to his carriage. Wisely, he kept her knee at a safe distance. He headed around the block, where he'd instructed his driver to wait.

Her eyes shot daggers at him. "I haven't finished my business," she argued, trying to shrug him off.

He lowered his voice and spoke in a tone that did not bode disagreement. "Yes," he breathed menacingly, "you have."

Genie remained stubbornly silent on the ride home, her

face carefully hidden in the shadows. When he thought of what could have happened, of the danger she had put herself in... he could throttle her. Or pull her into his arms and hold her so tight she could never put herself in danger again.

Alone in the most dangerous part of London. Without even a maid or footman. He felt sick. Anything could have happened. What could she have been thinking?

By the time they'd reached the sanctuary of his library, he'd managed to force his anger under some modicum of control. She refused to sit, so they stood facing each other across his wide desk. He crossed his arms and frowned, obviously forbiddingly because her hands twisted nervously in her skirts.

"Stop trying to intimidate me."

Despite the circumstances, he admired her spirit. "I hope you have some explanation for why I found my wife at the door of a place where no lady should be?"

Her hands clenched into tight fists. She visibly bristled at the word lady—as if he were personally disparaging her. She lifted her chin, some of the defiance returning. "I have been in such a place before—whether you choose to acknowledge it or not."

Although she'd meant it to shock him, her words had a very different effect. They made him think about why she would put herself in danger. There had to be a connection to her past. "Does this have something to do with the place where Hawk found you?"

Their eyes met. His heart clenched at the pain in her expression, for a moment he forgot his anger. She turned away. "You wouldn't understand."

Perhaps he was beginning to. "Try me."

She stared at him for a long time, apparently weighing her words carefully. She took a deep breath. "I want to give those girls a choice."

Thrilled that she'd chosen to confide in him, he forced the skepticism from his voice. "What kind of choice?"

"I've offered employment and an education to anyone who applies."

He couldn't hide his horror. She smiled wistfully at his expression. "Don't worry, at my manor in Gloucestershire."

Relief that she wasn't filling Huntingdon House with doxies gave way to sudden understanding. Whatever had happened to her in America, for whatever reason she'd found herself at a brothel, it had had a profound effect on her. Enough that she wanted to help girls in similar circumstances. He winced, suddenly embarrassed by his reaction in the face of her compassion. Something else occurred to him. "So that is why you wanted a house of your own," he said almost to himself.

She shrugged. "Partly, the other reasons are entirely selfish. I'm no saint. The ladies at Madame Solange's took care of me when I had no one. It might not make sense to you, but I want to repay their kindness."

There was something haunted in her expression. In that instant Huntingdon caught a glimpse of the forlorn girl left vulnerable and alone because of him. The image tore at his insides.

He was the fool.

How could he blame her for ending up in a brothel? If she was forced to sell herself it was because of *his* failures. Whatever had happened to her in America, whatever choices she'd had to make, he realized that it no longer mattered.

Something inside of him broke free. His heart opened and he knew acceptance.

He loved her, whatever her past. He should have realized what he was feeling when he'd reacted as he did from the thought of a carriage accident. Though he hadn't recognized it until now, he'd probably never stopped loving her.

His love had changed, just as he had. The youth had fallen in love at first sight with the sweet, innocent girl; the man loved the woman for her strength. She challenged him. She might not be as sweet or innocent, but the hard edge of the woman she'd become was even more enthralling and exciting. The love he had for her now was deeper, more real. It encompassed all of her virtues and all of her faults.

He wanted to shout his love from the rooftops. To sweep her into his embrace and cherish her forever.

He sobered, realizing the problem. He loved her, but could she ever forgive him enough to return his love?

"I'm sorry," he offered.

She shook her head. "I'm not blaming you. It's just something that I have to do."

"How many so far?"

Her cheeks reddened. "Two." She straightened her back. "But I've only just begun, when word gets around there will be more." There was true passion on her face when she spoke. In many ways she was still naïve. It would take more than an offer of employment and education to turn a hardened whore from her trade. But maybe she had a chance with some of the younger girls.

He made a precipitous decision. "If anyone discovers what you are doing you could be ruined. Even for a duchess, taking in whores is beyond mildly eccentric."

She gazed at him cautiously. "I know."

He nodded. "Very well, then. I'd like to help."

Clearly, he'd shocked her. She nearly choked. "Why?"

He circled the desk to stand before her. Taking her chin in his hand, he looked deep into her eyes.

"Because I love you, I've never stopped loving you. And I know that this is important to you."

"You love me?" she echoed. "But what about where Edmund found me—"

He put his fingers over her mouth to stop her. "It doesn't matter. Whatever you did, you did because I failed you."

Stunned, she gaped at him, as if she could not believe what he was saying. He chuckled, tilting her chin and dropping a soft kiss on her lips. "Whatever happens, I will stand beside you."

Her face broke out into a wide, blinding smile. As brilliant as the dawn of a new day.

HE LOVED HER?

Genie couldn't believe it. Was it possible?

He'd been so furious when he found her. She repressed a shiver, recalling his fierce expression. She'd expected him to forbid her from hiring any more women, not help her.

It was too much to take in, his willingness to help, his declaration of love... She felt stunned. But happy. Amazingly happy.

"You would do this for me?" she asked hesitantly.

"I would do anything for you."

Her heart swelled. Something wondrous surged inside her. Something that felt remarkably like hope. Hope for the future.

"I don't know what to say." Her voice sounded thick and husky. She stood up on her tiptoes and wrapped her hands around his neck. "Thank you," she whispered, placing a tentative kiss on his lips.

It was all the invitation he needed.

He groaned, enveloping her in his arms and deepening the kiss. His mouth moved over hers hungrily. The chaste kisses of the past few weeks were forgotten. She reveled in the sensations, drowned in the heat. Her heart fluttered excitedly in her chest, blood rushed to her ears, yet her body felt deliciously languid and soft.

Weaving her fingers through the thickness of his hair, she pulled him closer. But it wasn't enough. She pressed the softness of her breasts against the rock-hard muscles of his chest and opened her mouth to him, wanting more. His tongue plundered, with long deliberate strokes—both deeply sensual and wickedly carnal. He took his time, rousing her into a state of near frantic need, until her body throbbed and ached for more.

Suddenly, everything felt possible. With his love, perhaps she could begin to heal. And feel again. Genie surrendered to the magic.

The door crashed open, breaking the spell. He released her. Dazed, Genie blinked blindly. Her hand went to her mouth, her lips still burning. Genie turned to see the

Dowager Duchess of Huntingdon. That's odd. Huntingdon's mother in London?

Huntingdon recovered before she did. "Mother, what are you doing in town?" he asked, equally surprised that the duchess had broken her self-imposed exile.

"Trying to avert disaster. Obviously, you've not heard."

"Disaster? Heard what?" Huntingdon looked perplexed, but Genie's heart had stopped beating.

The duchess looked right at her, her expression grave.

And Genie knew. Her foolish dreams of happiness had been extinguished before they'd had a chance to flame. Hope had been a cruel, fleeting illusion. This time, there would be no reprieve from Madame Guillotine.

CHAPTER TWENTY-THREE

THE DOWAGER DUCHESS TURNED TO her son to explain what Genie already knew. "A rumor is circulating that Mrs. Preston was never married. The speculation is that she invented a husband to hide an illicit liaison."

Stunned, Huntingdon asked, "How?"

Genie clutched her stomach, feeling ill. She knew how. She hadn't reached Fanny in time. Dear God, what had she done?

"The particulars of how the rumor came to be are irrelevant," the dowager duchess said dismissively. "What matters is what we are going to do about it."

"What can we do?" Genie said tonelessly.

The dowager looked at her sharply. "I don't need to ask whether there is any truth to the rumor."

"No," Huntingdon said stonily. "You don't."

"I suspected as much. Well, we are fortunate in that the rumor has only just begun. Lady Davenport wrote me in the strictest confidence of a 'most disturbing story' that she'd overheard at a small supper. I left immediately in the hopes of reaching you before it was too late."

"You're overreacting, Mother. No one will believe it," Huntingdon said evenly.

Genie gazed at her husband enviously, wishing she could project such strength. He wore the same arrogant expression on his face as he always did; he stood with the same rock-hard stance. A scandal would be incredibly damaging to him personally, but you would never know it by looking at him.

He appeared perfectly calm and collected. Only the slight tick in his jaw betrayed his unease.

She, on the other hand, felt like her world was shattering all around her, and she was powerless to do anything about it. She had planned her revenge too well.

The dowager duchess shook her head. "The suspicion of impropriety is enough. Your position alone will not save you from scandal. We must do something." She tapped her jewel-encrusted walking stick on the floor. "We need proof."

"There is no proof," Genie said dully, despair weighing heavily upon her.

"There is nothing to do," Huntingdon said firmly. "Addressing the gossip in any way will make Genie appear guilty. I appreciate your concern, Mother, but we'll not even dignify the blasphemous story with a denial."

His mother remained unconvinced. "I hope you know what you are doing, son."

"I do." Huntingdon nestled Genie under his arm, as if he could protect her by his physical strength alone. "Don't worry, sweet. Everything will be fine."

Genie remained unconvinced. Not even six feet four inches of solid steel could shield her from the venom of the viper's tongue.

HUNTINGDON'S READY ASSURANCE RANG IN her ears two nights later as they alighted from the ducal carriage and made their way up the grand staircase of Devonshire House. Normally, Genie would be taking in every detail of her surroundings, marveling at the wonder of the lights and decorations. But not tonight. Tonight, there was too much at stake.

Her heart pounded furiously in her chest.

Her first ball as a duchess. Reason enough to be nervous, but there was so much more at stake than simply making a good impression. This was their first social engagement since the dowager duchess had arrived with news of the possible scandal. The first test.

Not surprisingly, soon after the dowager's arrival, Fanny had sent a note begging off dinner, claiming to be indisposed. If Genie had any doubts as to Fanny's involvement, her continued absence from her brother's house confirmed her fears. Not that Genie blamed her. It was Genie's fault for using Fanny so horribly.

The last two days had passed in a blur. With her secret exposed, Genie existed in a strange state of limbo, waiting for what she'd set in motion to come to fruition. Would the rumor be squashed or would it intensify, spreading like wildfire through the ton?

Tonight she would find out.

Huntingdon placed her hand in the crook of his elbow and leaned down to whisper encouragement in her ear. "Smile, sweetheart. You have nothing to be ashamed of. Remember, whatever happens, I love you."

Those three precious words ate like acid at her soul. She couldn't meet his gaze, the tenderness in his eyes was too painful.

She'd betrayed him. She yearned to run and hide so she wouldn't have to witness the humiliation on that proud, handsome face.

"The Duke and Duchess of Huntingdon." Too late to run. The announcement of their arrival rang out, reverberating like a pistol shot across the ballroom. The large, boisterous crowd quieted. Hundreds of faces turned in their direction.

The sudden appalled silence signaled society's condemnation.

The whispering and sly glances began almost immediately.

"Courage, love," Huntingdon said under his breath, but Genie could hear the strain in his voice. Clearly, it was worse than he'd expected.

She forced a brittle smile on her face and straightened her back. She'd survived worse. She owed it to Huntingdon to hold her head high. She'd made mistakes, done things of which she was not proud, but who were these people to spurn her? She didn't care what they thought of her.

Her heart sank.

But Huntingdon did. These were his peers. He'd fought hard to establish a name for himself after his father and brother died. With one misguided letter, she'd destroyed him.

The evening was more horrible than she could've imagined. Though not cut directly, the none-too-subtle looking the other way as they passed was just as effective. The only people who dared to venture into conversation with them were Edmund, Lady Hawkesbury, and the Davenports.

Their pity was nearly as difficult to take.

Huntingdon pretended as if he didn't notice, but Genie could tell that the rejection was killing him—especially that by his political cronies. People he considered his friends. Nonetheless, only one time did his expression slip and the rage and humiliation break through—when a gloating Percy mockingly saluted him from across the room.

Guilt suffocated her. Genie didn't know how much longer she could stand there at his side, feigning virtuousness, when the enormity of what she'd done hit her full force in the cut of every blank stare. Gazes slipped over them as if they weren't even there.

The night seemed endless. The torture of invisibility ended three agonizing hours later when they could finally take their leave.

HUNTINGDON WAS PAINFULLY QUIET ON the short carriage ride back to Huntingdon House. His silence only increased the weight of her guilt. Dread had swallowed her whole. Anxiously, Genie prepared herself for the worst. For his rejection.

This was what she'd wanted. To humiliate him in front of his peers, to exact the perfect revenge. An eye for an eye.

For forcing her to marry him, for the pain of his betrayal, she'd thought to ruin the precious social standing that had prevented him from marrying her all those years ago. Then he'd divorce her and she'd still have everything she wanted: wealth and property.

What had seemed so perfect when viewed through the dark blinders of vengeance now seemed petty and cruel. In her pain, she'd lashed out and hurt the man she loved. For tonight, at the very moment when she'd destroyed him, she realized the tragic truth. She loved him.

But it was too late. She'd ruined him. He would never forgive her.

If only she'd realized her feelings sooner. But her love felt so different. Before, she'd fallen in love with a handsome face and a fairy tale. This time, it had been more gradual. Not love at first sight, but a gentle awakening based on understanding. She loved him for the man he'd become: the duke who was responsible for seven estates and four younger siblings, the husband who had shown her nothing but thoughtfulness and kindness these past few weeks, who loved her despite the fact that he thought she'd sold herself, and the youth who'd not forgotten her—who'd searched for her for years and kept a small piece of ratty ribbon to remember the first day they made love. The enormity of her emotion stunned her.

But love wouldn't matter when he discovered her perfidy.

When the carriage finally pulled up to Huntingdon House, Genie was twisted into a tight bundle of nerves. Tension knit the muscles in her neck and back. Rigidly, she exited the carriage and followed Huntingdon into the townhouse.

In the entrance hall, Huntingdon finally looked at her. His face looked drained and tired. Tiny lines appeared around his mouth and eyes. The strain of tonight had seemingly aged him.

The dull ache in her chest twisted.

One side of his mouth lifted into some semblance of a

smile. "I think we could both use a drink."

She nodded and followed him into the drawing room. She sat stiffly on a velvet-cushioned sofa while he went to the sideboard to fix their drinks. "Here, something a little stronger than Madeira." Genie glanced at the snifter he'd handed her filled with an amber liquid. She took a sip and shuddered. Her throat burned. Whisky, not brandy. Grimacing, she forced herself to take another sip, allowing the smoky brew to work its dulling magic.

"I'm sorry," she said quietly.

Huntingdon sat beside her and took her hand in his. "Don't apologize. I don't blame you."

Emotion thickened her voice. "It was horrible."

His thumb gently massaged the top skin of her hand. "I never should have brought you tonight. It's my fault. I was arrogant. I thought I was above salacious gossip." He shook his head. "My mother was right, I should have listened to her."

Her chest burned with shame. He was trying to shoulder the blame when she was the one responsible. How could she have thought he lacked honor?

His gaze flickered over her face and his brows wrinkled with concern. He gathered her in his arms and gently kissed the top of her head. "Don't worry. The worst is over. We'll go to the country for a while until it blows over."

Genie felt like she was being torn apart. Her horror was complete. Again she'd presumed wrongly. He wasn't going to divorce her. He intended to stand by her.

She couldn't do this anymore. The emotion, the guilt that had been steadily building inside her all night finally exploded. "Stop it," she cried, shooting to her feet. "Stop it."

Shocked by the violence of her outburst, he gaped at her.

"You don't know what you're saying." Her voice shook.

He controlled his surprise. "Of course I do," he said calmly. "We'll leave for Donnington and wait for the gossip to die down. It always does. Eventually."

"I've ruined your political ambitions."

"I told you, it's not your fault. If I hadn't failed you long ago none of this—"

"But it *is* my fault," she choked, a hot ball of salty tears lodged in her throat. "Don't you see, *I was the one*."

His eyes narrowed. "The one?"

She braced herself, ready for the blow. "I started the rumor."

"You? But why would you—?" Comprehension dawned. He recoiled, his eyes widened with horror. "Of course, how could I be so thickheaded? Revenge."

She couldn't meet his gaze, couldn't bear to see the condemnation in his eyes that had once looked at her so tenderly. With love.

Please, take me in your arms. Hold me. Forgive me. But he did none of those things, just stared at her as if she'd ripped out his heart.

"When." His voice sounded harsh and empty. "When did you plan this?"

Her hands twisted as she fought to control her panic. "Some time ago. When you made your original marriage proposal. But it wasn't until you retracted your offer at Donnington and I thought that you were abandoning me again that I put my plan in motion. When I realized that I'd erred in judging your intentions, it was too late." Emotion strangled her voice.

"You planned your revenge well."

She flinched at the blow. Her control slipped. Her eyes burned with unshed tears. He was a cold, emotionless stranger again. "You must believe me. I would do anything to take it back," she pleaded, but to no effect. He'd apparently heard enough.

He stood. "If you'll excuse me, I believe I'm more tired than I realized. We will discuss what is to be done tomorrow."

The formality of his tone was pure agony.

Genie dared to look at him. It was a mistake. His eyes were haunted. He looked lost, like a man stripped of everything he cared about.

When he turned his back on her and walked out of the room, all hope went with him, shattering her fragile heart.

Her knees buckled and she crumpled to the floor. But she couldn't cry. The pain was too profound. She felt like an empty shell, devoid of sensation, except for the soul encompassing nothingness of despair.

What had she done?

She'd achieved her goals. She had her fortune and a beautiful house, but it was meaningless without Huntingdon. She loved him. But he would never forgive her treachery. With one fell swoop of her vengeful sword, she'd simultaneously ruined his social standing and his political ambitions. But worse, she'd humiliated him in the eyes of his peers. She curdled with shame.

She'd killed his love for her.

She picked herself off the floor and slowly made her way up the stairs and down the long corridors to her room. She knew what she had to do. She'd sever the connection as quickly as possible in the hope that it would lessen the burden on him. Perhaps then he could escape the destruction of scandal. The dull throb in her chest intensified. Divorce. Her entire being recoiled at the thought. But even if it killed her, she'd do it. She'd do anything to salvage what he had left of his pride.

She took out a small bag and began to pack. She had one more battle to face before she could retire into anonymity in the country. She knew where she had to go. To Thornbury. To her family.

CHAPTER TWENTY-FOUR

HER MAID HAD JUST FINISHED buttoning up the back of her morning gown when there was a soft knock at the door. A moment later, it opened to reveal her sister.

"Genie, Mother would like to see you in the drawing room." Lizzie smiled wanly in the open doorway, then turned to leave. A poor shadow of the vivacious, exuberant sister she remembered.

"Thank you, Lizzie, won't you—" Genie called after her, but Lizzie had already gone. Genie resisted the urge to go after her, realizing that Lizzie needed time. The shock of Genie's return was too fresh.

Genie had arrived on the doorstep of Kington House late last night. Unable to face Huntingdon, like a coward she'd fled before sunrise. She didn't bother to hide her destination; there was no need. Huntingdon wouldn't be following her. She'd left a note, all the explanation that was necessary under the circumstances.

My dearest Fitzwilliam, I hope my leaving will make it easier for you to return to your rightful place in society. I know that my actions have made it impossible for our marriage to continue. I will always love you. I pray that one day you will be able to forgive me.

Eugenia

The day-long journey from London to Thornbury had given Genie plenty of time to think about what she was going to say to her family, how she would explain her long absence, and her sudden arrival—alone—at their door, but it hadn't been necessary. Her mother had taken one look at Genie's wretched face and whisked her into her loving embrace. It was all she needed to burst out crying, finally releasing some of the heartbreak of losing love for the second time, the comforting arms of her mother.

Later, Genie had provided only the barest explanation. For the second time, she'd been forced to flee from scandal, but this one was of her own making. Her parents had been shocked, but thankfully hadn't asked many questions. At some point she would tell them everything, but right now it was enough to be home—and welcomed.

Genie gazed at her reflection in the looking glass propped up on a desk in her old bedchamber. Frowning, she patted her swollen eyes with a damp cloth and tidied her hair before starting down the stairs to her mother.

The narrow staircase creaked with each step. The house seemed so much smaller than she remembered. She smiled wistfully. It hadn't taken her long to grow accustomed to the grandeur of Huntingdon House and Donnington Park. In many ways she felt like a stranger here. She put her hand on the banister, feeling the familiar wiggle. She'd changed so much and Kington House so little.

Her parents had aged. There were quite a few more lines on her mother's face and her hair was now completely gray. Her father too had grayed, and was perhaps a bit rounder around the middle. With her brothers all moved away, only Lizzie remained. Fanny had not exaggerated. The quiet, reserved young woman was not the sister Genie remembered. Though Lizzie had greeted Genie warmly, she felt acutely the loss of their closeness. She vowed to do whatever it took to bring a smile back to her sister's face. Somehow she'd make it up to her.

To all of them.

A housemaid she didn't recognize opened the door to the drawing room and Genie faltered. Her heart skipped. Sitting on the sofa, opposite her parents, were her husband and his mother.

Genie blurted out, "What are you doing here?"

Huntingdon rose as she entered, his face bore such a look of relief that Genie felt something spark in her chest. But it was his mother who spoke first.

The dowager duchess lifted a brow. "Eugenia," she called her by her Christian name, which was a shock as she'd never even heard the Duchess call her son by his Christian name, "you have developed an appalling tendency to speak your mind." She turned to her son and lifted her eyes "America" as if that explained everything. She turned back to Genie. "A duchess must always remain unflappable," she instructed. "Even under the most strenuous of circumstances, isn't that so, son?"

What was going on here? Genie thought, confused. Her eyes fell to Huntingdon, the sight of his rumpled cravat and haggard face made her breath catch.

He spoke to his mother, but he didn't take his eyes of Genie's face. "Yes, indeed, Mother. I'm afraid we shall have to work on that."

The dowager duchess stood up and shook out her skirts, the black silk rustling. "Now, if you'll excuse us. I would like to speak with your parents alone." Her mother looked at her questioningly, but they quickly followed Huntingdon's mother out of the room.

Leaving her alone with her husband.

"I don't know whether to strangle you or to kiss you. How could you leave like that?"

Genie didn't allow herself hope at his words. "I thought it would be easier that way. With the divorce—"

He made a fierce noise and grabbed her arm. "There will be no divorce," he growled each word with superb finality.

Standing this close to him was torture. She yearned to curl against the warm shelter of his chest. "But after what I told you, I thought..."

"You were wrong," he said decisively. "I'm furious with what you did, but it doesn't change how I feel about you. You are my wife and I love you, whether we never attend another ball or not. But I have to know, did you mean what you said in your note?"

"Of course I'm terribly sorry for what I did. I hope someday you will forgive me."

He made another sound, this one of frustration. His arm tightened, pulling her close against the hard shield of his chest. "Not that." He cupped her chin. "You called me Fitzwilliam."

Her brows drew together. "It's your name."

He smiled at her confusion. "Do you love me?"

His mouth was only inches from hers. She trembled, overwhelmed. She couldn't believe it. He still loved her. Despite her treachery that could cost him the loss of his position, the very wedge that drove them apart years ago, he would stand by her. The unreliable young man of her past was truly gone. Her heart soared. "Yes," she said huskily, "I love you."

His mouth found hers in a tender kiss. "God, I thought I'd never hear you say those words again."

"I'd never thought to say them again."

He grinned and kissed her again. "I won't let you down this time."

"I know," she said. She trusted him completely. She'd learned to look at the past differently. He'd made mistakes, but so had she. "We've both changed." Her brow furrowed, someone else had changed—a fact that had been bothering her. "I'm surprised your mother is here."

"So am I, but she insisted. She blames herself for all of this. I believe she means to apologize to your parents for her part in your disappearance."

Genie was surprised. "I appreciate her support, but I'm afraid in this instance my letter did the damage."

"That's not entirely correct."

"What do you mean?"

He threaded his fingers through his hair. "We would have arrived sooner, but Fanny arrived at Huntingdon House with Lady Hawkesbury and Edmund. I know you sent the letter to Fanny, but it was not your letter that started the gossip."

"Don't blame Fanny, I knew she could not keep a secret—"

He stopped her. "It wasn't the letter, but it was Fanny."

"I don't understand."

"Both Fanny and I suspected that your marriage might not be on the up-and-up. Apparently, she unintentionally let something drop to Percy—before she received your letter. She blames herself."

"Poor Fanny! Of course it's not her fault."

Huntingdon's mouth fell in an uncompromising line. "She should know better than to voice her suspicions around Percy."

"I'm sure it was an accident."

He shrugged. "Perhaps. In any event, the damage is done."

"Is there anything that we can do?"

"My mother is working on something. But for now, we will return to Donnington Park. That is, if you still want to be my duchess."

More than anything in the entire world. Was this truly happening? Was she being given a second chance at happiness? This time, she'd never let go. "I've never cared about being a duchess, I just want to be with you." She smiled shyly and stroked his chest, her fingers dropping low on his stomach. She lifted up on her toes and ran feather kisses along his rigid jaw. She whispered in his ear, "But not Donnington Park, my manor is much closer."

His eyes sparked and a slow lazy grin spread across his face. "How soon can we leave?"

THEY'D SPENT THE DAY WITH her family and departed for her manor at dusk, promising to return the next day.

It was dark when they arrived, but the house was charming—everything she'd wished for. Genie turned to look at Huntingdon. Well, not everything. Her house could wait, Huntingdon could not. The staff had been alerted of their arrival. Too quickly she found herself alone with Huntingdon in the master's bedchamber. Despite her certainty that this was what she wanted, she couldn't hide her nervousness.

He took off his coat and helped her with her pelisse. Spinning her around, he began the long process of helping her remove her gown. She shivered at his touch.

"Tell me."

Her heart stopped. Fear prickled along the back of her neck. She knew what he wanted, but what would he think? Would he judge her? No. He loved her. Suddenly, she wanted to tell him. But she'd held on to the truth for so long, she didn't know where to begin.

So she started at the beginning with finding herself on the ship to America, pregnant. She explained her heartbreak at the loss of their child, the illness that had ravaged her, and the maid's perfidy. She told him of the kind sisters who'd nursed her, and of her early attempts to find work as a governess. Of the difficulties with her employers, how she'd tried to starve herself to appear sickly, and finally, of the man who had attacked her.

Huntingdon still stood at her back so she couldn't see his expression, but she felt his body tense when she spoke of her near rape, of the letter opener, her time at Madame Solange's and finally of Edmund's timely arrival—before she'd been forced to make a decision as to her future. When she was done, she felt as if an enormous burden had been lifted off of her shoulders.

Silently, Huntingdon picked her up in his arms and carried her to the bed. Without her realizing it, she was completely naked.

HUNTINGDON LISTENED TO HER STORY with a mixture of sorrow and rage. Sorrow for the difficulties she'd met and rage at the men who'd hurt her. No wonder she'd turned cold at his lovemaking.

Gently, he placed her on the bed and quickly removed the last of his own clothing. This time, damn his raging lust, she'd be in control. Even if it killed him.

He slid in next to her and nestled her body against his. "Thank you for telling me. You're an incredibly brave woman. I didn't think it was possible, but I love you even more after hearing about all that you went through and all you did to survive."

She looked surprised. "You're not repulsed?"

"Repulsed? Yes, of the vile bastard who attacked you, but certainly not of the strong, amazing woman who fought back. Of her, I'm incredibly proud."

His fingers skimmed the curve of her waist and hips, he fought to control his arousal at the sensation of her velvety skin. But when her hands splayed against his chest and her fingers slid across his chest, his control deteriorated. She stroked his stomach, exploring the way his muscles flexed under her fingertips. When the back of her hand brushed against the head of his erection she stopped. He waited, teeth clenched, for her to decide. Tentatively, seductively, she traveled the length of his cock with one finger, exclaiming with sweet little gasps as his erection grew under her fingertip. She traced the long, bulging vein and he groaned. Her thumb found the silky drop and rubbed it over the top of his head. By the time she'd circled him with her hands, his control was nearly gone.

"What do you want, Genie?" His voice sounded hoarse with desire.

"I-I," she stuttered. "I want you, but I don't know if I'll ever be able to experience pleasure again."

"Do you want me to go on?"

She nodded.

"If you want me to stop, I will."

She nodded again and he kissed her. Ravishing her mouth with his. She matched his urgency with her own. Her full breasts pressed sweetly against his chest, the firm, tiny nipples hard with desire. He lowered himself down the long length of her body, focusing all of his considerable attentions on her pleasure. He kissed her mouth, her breasts, every part of her body... except for one.

She might not know what she wanted, but her body did. She writhed in his arms, her skin hot and pink. He could smell the sweet honey of her arousal. He wanted to sink himself deep inside her and bring her to release, but he had to be sure.

So he continued his wicked onslaught. When he thought she was close, his mouth found the inside of her thigh and she stilled. He teased her, flicking his tongue agonizingly close to her slick little entry.

"Tell me you want me," he whispered. His hands slid up her sleek thighs and gripped her round bottom, lifting her hips to his mouth.

She didn't answer, but circled her hips, silently begging. "Tell me," he ordered.

"Your mouth."

He buried his head between her legs and gave her what she wanted.

GENIE COULDN'T BELIEVE WHAT HE was doing to her. The sheer intimacy stunned her—and thrilled her with naughty excitement. She nearly jumped off the bed at the first sweep of his tongue. He chuckled, but all she could think about was his mouth on her, the scratch of his beard on the inside of her thigh, the pressure of the burning sensation building inside her. He parted her with his fingers and flicked his tongue over her swollen flesh. The burning sensation intensified, lifting her body to the highest peak until his mouth closed over her and she exploded.

Boneless, it took her a moment to realize what had just happened. She'd found passion again. And now she wanted more. Their eyes met and something passed between them, a connection long broken now made stronger than ever. She could see that he was pleased to have brought her pleasure, but his fiery gaze still burned with unspent desire.

She reached for him, circling her hand around his stiff erection. He fell back on the pillow, his eyes closed and his head rolled back as she pumped him, finding his rhythm, until he strained under her hand. Tiny white drops beaded on its head.

She leaned down to flick her tongue over his sweetness and he cried out, a pained, guttural sound that flooded her with heat. Her mouth hovered over him, he was so tense with desire she couldn't believe the strength of his control. Remembering what he'd done to her, her tongue circled the thick head of his manhood. He made another sound, something that sounded like "please," and she took him deep into her mouth and sucked. Stroking him with her tongue, pumping him with her mouth. The swollen vein running down his length began to pulse and she knew he was achingly close.

She moved over him, reveling in the power of her position. She braced herself on his shoulders and slowly lowered her body down on him. He was agonizingly long and thick; her body did not take him easily. Every muscle in his body bulged, but still he did not move to help her. Finally, with considerable effort, he was inside her, filling her, stretching her. Making her complete.

She slid over him, easing him in and out, slowly at first then with increasing speed. She rode him hard, the burning sensation building inside her again. Faster and faster, her breasts bounced and his bollocks slapped hard against her bottom. She heard him grunt, felt him throb and pulse, and when the warmth of his seed shot inside her, she screamed, coming apart in the violent storm of a shattering orgasm.

Exhausted, she collapsed on top of him. More sated than she'd ever been in her entire life. Never had she felt so happy or so secure. This is where she belonged, in his arms, forever. "I love you," she whispered.

He took her chin and tipped her eyes up to meet hers. "I'll love you until the end of time."

EPILOGUE

Two months later

THE DUKE OF HUNTINGDON'S CARRIAGE rolled to a stop in front of Huntingdon House. Thanks to the Dowager Duchess of Huntingdon, they were back in London. A few weeks ago, a mysterious marriage license had materialized, attesting to the marriage between Miss Genie Prescott and Mr. Robert Preston. Nonetheless, despite the "proof" refuting the gossip, the duke and duchess decided to spend some time at Genie's manor to weather the storm of gossip. The past couple of months had been magical, but at the Dowager Duchess of Huntingdon's request, they had returned to London to face the fading scandal together.

Much had happened since he'd come to find her at the rectory. The most important was that Genie had begun to repair the relationship with Lizzie and her parents, confiding most of what had happened to her over the past five years.

Fanny was rusticating at one of Huntingdon's distant estates in some kind of self-imposed penance. No matter how Genie assured her otherwise, she blamed herself for what had happened. Huntingdon and Edmund seemed to reach some sort of accord, but it was Genie's mission to one day repair the damage she'd unwittingly done to their friendship.

But it was her relationship with Huntingdon that most astounded her. Each day was a miracle of discovery. The young love she'd experienced paled in comparison to the complex emotion she felt for him now. With his help, she'd finally erased the demons of her past. She smiled. Under his expert tutelage, her passion had bloomed.

The butler greeted them at the door. Genie noticed a spattering of cards on a tray on the sideboard. Certainly a good sign, but Genie knew that winning over the ton wasn't going to be easy.

Huntingdon sensed her disquiet. He eased the lines of worry from her forehead with his fingers. "What's wrong?"

"It's not going to be easy."

"No. But with time, they will forget."

"But you won't have a happy ending. Your plans, your ambitions..."

His finger stroked her cheek. "Don't you understand, my love? A happy ending doesn't mean everything is perfect. Life is fraught with difficulties. But as long as we have each other, we will survive whatever the future has in store. Together. This is only the beginning."

Genie's hand fell to her belly, a small knowing smile turned her lips. Huntingdon was right, perhaps the best ending was a beginning.

READ ON FOR ANOTHER REGENCY ADVENTURE FROM MONICA MCCARTY ...

They are known as the Rake Slayers... *Tired of the different standards applied to the men who flout society's rules, three young ladies seek a little primitive justice and hatch a plan to bring a few of London's most notorious rakes up to snuff before refusing them. But they soon learn exactly what it is that makes rakes so dangerous.*

Tasked with bringing down the most notorious rake of all, the always capable and efficient Lady Georgina "Gina" Beauclerk is determined to show the wicked Earl of Coventry just what she has to offer... by promptly turning his dissolute world on its ear. Instead she finds her own world spinning out of control. Because even after she has organized his household, rid his home of alcohol, and paid off his mistress, she can't help but see that there is more to the handsome earl than first she realized.

Forced into respectable society to escort his debuting sister, Coventry intends to find her a husband posthaste so he can return to the freedom and debauchery of his clubs. After the death of his unfaithful wife, the disillusioned Coventry has no intention of ever marrying again—especially not to an interfering busybody who won't take "no" for an answer. No matter how much she tempts him.

EXCERPT OF TAMING THE RAKE

Mayfair, Tuesday, 30 March, 1812

THEY WERE A SCURRILOUS BUNCH. THREE highly marriageable young ladies thoroughly dissatisfied with their lot—a veritable tempest of ennui waiting to explode in rebellion. Gina gazed fondly at her two companions. Cecelia's ink-black head was bent in apparent concentration over her tambour frame, and Claire, as fair-haired as her twin was dark, was fighting to keep her eyes open as she half read a salacious novel that had somehow escaped the watchful eyes of her mother. Gina shook her head. Looking at the three of them, who would have guessed what restless turmoil lurked below the deceptively placid surface?

Cecelia tossed her needlework aside with disgust. "I'm bored," she said, summing up the situation succinctly, if unimaginatively.

Claire smiled softly, her eyes still clouded with the vestiges of the afternoon nap she'd taken in her chair. "How can you be bored, dearest?" she asked. "The season has only just begun."

Cecelia ignored her younger (by ten minutes) sister and stood up.

"You could play the pianoforte," Gina suggested.

Cecelia put her hands on her hips, her mouth drawn in a tight line. "I *always* play the pianoforte."

"Then work on your watercolor," Gina countered

indifferently, knowing that when one of Cecelia's moods hit, she was virtually impossible to placate.

Cecelia gave her the evil eye.

Gina laid down her own needlework in a nice, neat pile. "Very well then, what would you like to do? You haven't alphabetized your offers in some time."

"Very funny."

"Do you really alphabetize?" Claire's eyes rounded. She thought for a moment then nodded her head in apparent understanding. "I suppose it would be helpful as there are so many to consider. Father and mother are forever losing track of who has actually proposed. Perhaps you should advise them of your method?"

Gina looked at Cecelia and shrugged as if to say, "What can you do?" Claire was hopeless when it came to sarcasm—or any kind of subtlety for that matter.

"I'm tired of the same parties, the same drawing rooms, the same callers," Cecelia lamented. "Nothing ever changes. Day in, day out, it's all the same."

Gina shook her head. Cecelia was only giving voice to what they all felt. Nevertheless, Gina felt it was her duty to rein in Cecelia before she did or said something outrageous. "What did you expect? That you would return from rusticating all winter in Staffordshire to an entirely new crop of suitors? The beau monde is rather limited in its members, Cece. As the daughter of a marquess, there are only so many suitable men to choose from." Gina grinned. "Though Prinny is rather appallingly fond of you: perhaps you could ask him to create a few more peers to expand your realm?"

Cecelia shot her a look of mild disgust. She wasn't too fond of her sobriquet, "The Queen of Broken Hearts."

"As the daughter of a duke, your choices are even *more* limited, Lady Georgina Beauclerk," she said tartly. "I see your barely concealed grimace when you are partnered by the same men dance after dance. And you've had two seasons to choose to our one, so don't pretend you don't know to what I am speaking."

"It's appalling," Gina mocked. "The dusty shelf of spinsterhood looms ever closer."

"Jest all you want, but there is talk. Five proposals, five rejections over two years is 'not the thing' at all. I would think you would be aware of this today of all days."

Gina grimaced, properly chastised. Today was her twentieth birthday, though she was doing her best to ignore it. Cecelia was right. Gina wasn't completely immune to the gossip. But she would not settle for a husband just to satisfy the likes of some narrow-minded dowager with nothing better to do than tally the numbers of proposals per debutante each season.

Satisfying her father, the Duke of St. Albans, however, was another matter. Gina knew her time to make a decision was running out, but having tasted freedom, she was reluctant to relinquish it. For years she had managed her father's many properties with little interference.

She bit back the feelings of bitterness. His recent marriage had changed all that. She didn't blame him for remarrying; her mother had been gone for almost ten years now, but did he have to choose Lady Louisa Manners—a woman not much older than herself? A young woman intent on staking her claim to the household. And usurping all the tasks that Gina took pride in. Left with little to do for the last few months, Gina had felt utterly rudderless.

She shook off the unhappiness caused by thinking about her new "mama" and turned back to Cecelia. "So what do they say about ten rejections in one season?"

"Twelve, counting the two in the country," Cecelia corrected automatically, scowling when Gina smirked.

"I feel utterly pathetic with only three," Claire chimed in.

"Chin up, love," Gina teased, patting Claire's hand. "Give it some time. You still have an entire year before you reach the lofty age of twenty."

"It's not just the men," Cecelia continued. "It's everything. Sometimes I feel like I'm being smothered by rules: 'That is just not done, Lady Cecelia' or 'You mustn't do that, Lady Cecelia,'" she mimicked in the haughty, slightly bored tone universally adopted by the ton's matrons. "My every movement, my every conversation is controlled by what is deemed proper for a well-born, fashionable young lady."

She was right. Society was a tough, unforgiving taskmaster. "But what is the alternative?" Gina asked. "Would you ignore society's dictates and end up like poor Lady Alice?"

All three girls fell silent, the unfortunate fate of their friend appallingly fresh in their minds.

Claire broke the silence. "There does seem to be something patently unfair between what is acceptable for a lady and what is acceptable for a gentleman. Lady Alice was forced to flee to the wilds of Scotland"—she shuddered dramatically at the very idea (who in their right mind would want to go to Scotland!)—"to escape scandal, yet Lord Coventry is welcomed at whatever ball or assembly he deigns to attend. Outwardly Lord Coventry is condemned as a rake, but the condemnation is tinged with admiration."

Gina and Cecelia's eyes met again, both struck by one of Claire's rare moments of insight. With her sweet disposition and innocent naïvety, it was sometimes easy to forget that Claire was a thoughtful young lady.

Cecelia's face darkened. "Rakes. Rakes. Rakes. If I hear that word one more time, I swear I'll—"

"Don't swear, darling," Gina chided. Turning to Claire, she whispered, "She's still not over 'The Incident.'"

Cecelia bristled. Her chin lifted haughtily. "I don't know to what you are referring, Lady Georgina."

"I think she's referring to the Duke of Beaufort, dearest," Claire said helpfully.

Gina giggled. Cecelia looked as if she could strangle

her sister.

"Come now, Cecelia," Gina said soothingly. "That was last year. You still cannot be—"

"Don't you dare lecture me, Gina. You were not made the laughingstock of the season."

"I'd hardly call you the laughingstock of the season," Claire said. "There was that other incident when Lady Penelope tripped down the stairs and landed at Prinny's feet with her skirts bunched around her ears and her bottom wide for everyone to see." She wrinkled her nose. "Or should I say her wide bottom for everyone to see?"

Cecelia threw her sister a venomous glare. "You aren't helping, Claire. Beaufort made a fool of me and I'll never forget it."

The vehemence in Cecelia's tone stopped Gina's teasing cold. She sobered. The Incident had obviously affected Cecelia much more than Gina had realized. Cecelia's pride had taken a vicious beating. As the reigning beauty, and an heiress to boot, Cecelia was not used to men who did not drop at her feet in besotted supplication.

The Duke of Beaufort—the leader of the Hellfire Rakes club and a man renowned for his exquisite taste—had taken her down a peg or two when he'd declared within perfect earshot of many a young buck, "Attractive enough if you like a chit right out of the schoolroom." But far worse was when he looked at his sensuous, well-endowed paramour in pointed comparison. He'd turned his quizzing glass on Cecelia's more modest bosom. "I confess I don't see what all the fuss is about." It was obvious that this arbiter of beauty found Cecelia's willowy figure sadly lacking.

"I'm sure everyone has forgotten," Gina offered optimistically, while knowing that it was unlikely. Not when the duke never missed an opportunity to remind the ton of his unique opinion of Lady Cecelia Leveson-Gower, cherished daughter of the Marquess of Stafford. Gina took

Cecelia's hand and gave it a comforting squeeze. "I know you were badly maligned, but it's nothing compared to what happened to dear Alice."

Cecelia's face lost some of its angry color. "You're right, of course. Poor Alice, caught in the wicked embrace of a notorious rake." Her voice turned suddenly impassioned. "Don't you ever get tired of the different standards? Why is certain conduct wrong for a lady, but not for a gentleman? There were *two* people caught in scandalous dishabille in Lady Wallingford's garden."

Even the normally forward-thinking Gina was shocked by the suggestion that the same standard might apply to men and women. The differences between what was permissible between girls and boys had been ingrained in her since childhood. Since the first time Gina was punished for tearing her dress climbing a tree and her male playmate was praised for his athleticism—though he hadn't climbed nearly as high as she had, she recalled smugly. On some level Gina had recognized the unfairness, but simply accepted it as a fact of life. Cecelia never accepted anything.

What Cecelia suggested was veritable societal heresy. But thought-provoking nonetheless. Not that she'd encourage Cecelia by admitting it. "Nonsense," Gina chided. "Don't be ridiculous. There are many benefits to being a young lady."

"Like what?" Cecelia challenged. "A young man can hunt, gamble, sport, drink, meander at will from club to club, keep a mistress or two. What can we do?"

"Ladies take pride in their many accomplishments. We sew, play music, paint, sing—"

"I'm sorry to disagree, dearest," Claire interrupted. "But I think Cecelia has the right of it. Having a paramour sounds infinitely more exciting than playing the pianoforte."

"Why shouldn't we have a bit of fun?" Cecelia prompted.

Gina immediately grew wary. She knew her friend too

well. "What kind of fun?"

"I don't know." Cecelia thought a minute before her frown lifted into a naughty grin. "We could play a little game."

Claire clapped her hands. "Oh, I love games."

"Let's hear the rules first, Claire," Gina cautioned.

"I think it's high time that Beaufort and his Hellfire cohorts get their due." Cecelia drummed her fingers on the top of the mahogany sideboard. When the tapping stopped and she saw the expression on Cecelia's face, Gina braced herself for what was coming next. "What's the worst thing that could happen to a rake?" Cecelia asked.

"Hmm. He could pass out on the road from too much drink and get run over by a carriage?" Claire posited.

"Or lose his estate in a hand of cards?" Gina suggested, but she could guess where Cecelia was headed.

Cecelia shook her head. "Worse. Much worse. He must fall in love. Become utterly and thoroughly besotted. We shall choose three of the most notorious rakes and see if we can bring them up to snuff."

"I may be nearing the shelf, but I could never marry—" Gina started.

"Of course we won't accept. The challenge is simply in procuring the proposal. Since we can't record it at White's we'll have to make our own betting book, with a wager befitting the importance of the challenge."

"But what if they find out?" Claire said.

"Leave it to me," Cecelia dismissed with a wave of her hand. "No man will know what we are about."

"It's not only the men I'm worried about."

Cecelia turned to her sister and frowned. "Stop worrying, Claire. You sound like Gina. We'll keep it a secret."

"Why?" Gina asked suspiciously. "Why should we do something so... mean-spirited?"

Cecelia's eyes fired. "Mean-spirited?" She huffed.

"Hardly. It's nothing compared to the sport these rakes make of us on a daily basis. I'm tired of hearing about the goings-on of the Hellfire Rakes. Think of it as a bit of feminine justice. We'll do it for all womankind."

Gina laughed. "That's a bit much, wouldn't you say?" Though she could not deny that there was a certain primitive justice in what Cecelia proposed.

Cecelia shrugged. "You want justice for Alice, don't you?"

"Certainly." But Gina hesitated. A tiny disloyal part of her wondered whether Alice hadn't gotten precisely what she'd bargained for. Coventry did not hide his character, if anything, he flaunted it. Involvement with Lord Coventry was a dangerous proposition.

Gina recalled the first time she'd seen the Earl of Coventry at the theater early in her first season. His dark, fallen-angel looks had sent her girlish heart racing in a fierce patter. Tall and broad-shouldered with dark, wavy hair, his features, even from a distance, were strong and classically handsome.

One look at his companion, however, was enough to erase any romantic notions she might have had about him. The bright-colored gown, the shocking décolletage, the heavy paint. The man escorted his paramour as openly as if she were the queen. Discreet inquiries had confirmed her first impression. Except when the gossip surrounding his wild escapades demanded her attention, Gina had barely given him another thought.

Even if Coventry had seduced Alice, she had to know the type of man he was. Even Claire knew the type of man Lord Coventry was. Gina shook off the disloyal thoughts. Alice had been wronged. "I don't know if this is the best way—"

"What other way can you think of? There's a certain poetic justice in beating a rake at his own game, don't you agree? These are men who play fast and loose with a woman's virtue without thought. Well, we shall give them something to think about the next time they are tempted to ruin a young lady." She turned to her sister. "Claire will do it, won't you Claire?" She didn't bother waiting for an answer, knowing full well Claire would agree to anything she suggested. To Gina she argued, "I know you are just as bored as I am with the men who frequent Almack's and the ton's ballrooms. You'll see. It will be fun." She smiled sweetly. "But if you're not up to the challenge…?"

Gina bristled. She was well aware that Cecelia was manipulating her, but it didn't make the ploy any less effective. Gina prided herself on proficiency. If she put her mind to it, not much would stand in her way. Certainly not a debauched roué. Cecelia was right. It was tempting to do something to avenge poor Alice. And though it had just begun, the season was already the same dull round of balls and assemblies.

Cecelia continued on as if they all were in agreement. "We shall form a club."

"A club?" Gina said, aghast. "Whatever for?"

"I thought we were going to keep it a secret," Claire added, but Cecelia paid her no mind.

"Men have clubs for everything, why shouldn't we? White's, Brooks's, Boodles, the Four-Horse, and this latest manifestation of the Hellfire Rakes club. I, for one, should like to know what goes on at Wycombe."

"Wycombe?" Claire asked.

Gina's eyes narrowed at Cecelia for bringing up such an inappropriate subject in front of her sister. She turned to Claire, answering with as little information as possible. "That's where the Hellfire Club has its meetings. Amongst other things," she mumbled vaguely. "We're not supposed to be aware of the caves at Wycombe." She turned on Cecelia. "You best not let anyone hear you talking about such things."

Cecelia wasn't listening. "There are so many of the

blasted creatures." Her nose wrinkled as if she'd caught a whiff of something foul. "We might need more recruits. And we shall need some help from the other ladies, of course."

Claire's eyes rounded. "I thought you said—"

"Trusted friends only." Cecelia cut her off, scowling at her as if she was ruining the game. "Never mind that for now. First things first, we must have a name."

"How about the ruined fools?" Gina suggested. "Or the spinster's folly?"

Cecelia shot her a hard glance. She tapped her chin. "I have it! We shall call ourselves The Society for the Hindrance of a Rake's Progress."

Claire giggled at the allusion to Hogarth's engravings. "Wonderful. But there's just one thing I don't understand, who qualifies as a rake?"

"Lord Coventry for one," Gina said.

"Beaufort for another," Cecelia snarled. "Certainly all the Hellfire members: Lord Percy, Lord Rockingham, Lord Petersham, Lord Ponsonby, Lord Ashley, Mr. Dashwood. But it is not simply enough to call oneself a rake. Rakes are also identified by their conduct."

"How so?" Claire asked.

"Well for one, you'll never see a rake willingly cross the threshold of Almack's. And if they do attend a ton function it is always with a new paramour."

Claire's eyes narrowed over her tiny nose. Something was obviously bothering her. "Are they handsome?"

Cecelia nodded, the grave expression on her face belied her gentle teasing. "Of course."

"By definition, a rake must be handsome," Gina agreed gamely.

Claire looked skeptical. "Are you sure?"

"Quite sure," Cecelia stated emphatically.

"Quite," Gina confirmed.

Claire appeared to be warming up to the idea. "What

else?" she asked.

"Hmm. Rakes are notorious gamblers; they drink bottles and bottles of port, and above all they are vile debauchers of women."

Claire grimaced. "That doesn't sound very promising. No wonder they don't marry, who'd want them?"

"Poor dears," Gina agreed, but the sarcasm was utterly lost on Claire.

Gina studied her naïve friend, suddenly concerned. In many ways this would be like sending a lamb out to a pack of wolves. "Rakes are very wicked and extremely devious," she warned. "You must be on your guard at all times. A rake will do his utmost to compromise you without marriage."

"Of course, we'll have to be on the watch for anything untoward." Cecelia said cheekily.

Gina threw her a quelling stare. Just because she'd been kissed three times to Gina's two, Cecelia thought herself the most experienced of the group. "It will do no good to allow the gentleman to sample the milk before he has purchased the cow," Gina said primly.

Claire muffled a giggle with the back of her hand.

"Careful, darling, your country roots are showing," Cecelia warned. To Claire she added, "One more thing. A rake avoids an unmarried debutante like the plague."

"Just so long as it's easy," Gina murmured dryly.

Cecelia raised her teacup high in the air. "To slaying dragons—or should I say, to slaying rakes."

Gina gazed at the amber contents of her cup as she raised it to the others. Somehow tea seemed inappropriate for the occasion. "Shouldn't we be drawing rapiers or something?" Gina asked wryly, but she knew Cecelia was right. A new challenge was just what Gina needed. By the time she was done with him, the poor blighter wouldn't know what had hit him.

"WELL, WHICH ONE *DO* YOU want?" Cecelia asked

Gina, the frustration evident in her voice. "How about Lord Ashley?"

They'd been going on like this for nearly an hour, suggesting names with no consensus. Gina had to pick somebody. Lord Ashley was handsome enough, but she knew him—and had witnessed his lechery for herself. "No." If she must woo someone, she might as well make it enjoyable. "No," she repeated firmly. "I think perhaps Lord Ponsonby?"

Cecelia pursed her lips, displeased. It was obvious she had come to a similar conclusion herself.

"Is he the outrageously handsome one?" Claire asked.

Gina and Cecelia both nodded.

"Oooh. I think I should like him too."

"I thought you might want Beaufort," Gina suggested to Cecelia. "An eye for an eye and all that?"

Her cheeks flushed. "No. Of course not. I want a challenge, not an impossibility."

If they kept going round and round like this it would take all night, and Gina had her party to get ready for. "I suppose the only fair thing would be to draw lots."

"But that seems so horribly random," Cecelia whined. "What if I choose someone I cannot abide?"

"This was your idea. Besides, you're the one who said you wanted a challenge," Gina pointed out. Deciding to limit their choices to the Hellfire Club, Cecelia rattled off a dozen of the worse offenders and Gina jotted the names on small bits of parchment and tossed them into Claire's straw bonnet.

Claire pulled out the papers and folded them again. Her eyes sparkled with mischief. To Gina's silent question she said, "We don't want anyone cheating." She glanced significantly to her sister who scowled, then asked, "Who gets to pick first?"

Gina groaned. If it was this difficult just to choose a name, it did not bode well for the rest of the game. "Wait a minute." She had an idea. She opened the doors to the drawing room and motioned to a housemaid who was sweeping the carpet in the adjoining hall. Grabbing the broom, she flipped it around and removed three pieces of straw of differing length. Handing the broom back to the baffled maid, she closed the doors behind her. "We shall draw straws. The longest shall have the first pick."

"But who should pick the first straw?"

Gina fought to contain her frustration. "Just pick, Claire."

Claire smiled and chose the middle straw from behind Gina's hand, pulling out the second-longest straw. Cecelia went next and picked the longest, leaving Gina with the shortest.

"I hope it's an omen," Cecelia said naughtily with a jaunty lift of her brow.

Gina pretended not to understand her ribald attempt at humor. She pushed the bonnet under Cecelia's nose and shook it. "You're first, so pick."

Cecelia closed her eyes and dipped her hand into the hat. She removed the paper. Opening her eyes, she carefully unfolded it. "Mr. Ryder," she said evenly.

Gina studied her expression carefully, but couldn't tell whether Cecelia was pleased. Ryder was something of a mystery, but he didn't seem a particularly bad sort— compared to his friends at least.

"My turn." Claire plunged her hand in the hat and playfully dug around for a moment.

Cecelia rolled her eyes. "Just pick one, Claire."

"I am." Claire fished around for another moment or two then slowly drew out a slip of paper and opened it. The excitement drained from her face.

"Who is it? Did you get Lord Coventry?" Gina asked consolingly, knowing he was the lowest of the low. The most depraved of the depraved.

Claire shook her head.

"Then who?" Cecelia asked impatiently.

Almost apologetically, Claire handed the scrap of paper to her sister. This time Cecelia could not control her expression, her lips curled and flames sparked in her dark blue eyes. She looked angry and something else—maybe a bit jealous. "Beaufort."

Gina winced. "My turn," she said, dipping her hand into the bowl of the bonnet. *Ponsonby, Ponsonby,* she prayed silently, drawing out the slip of paper. She nearly groaned when she read the name staring at her in her own bold handwriting.

"Well?" Cecelia asked.

Gina balled the paper in her hand and tossed it into the fire. "It seems it falls to me to avenge dear Alice. For I'm to tame the very devil himself."

ABOUT THE AUTHOR

Monica McCarty is the *New York Times and USA Today bestselling author* of fifteen (and a half!) Scottish Historical romances, including her current Highland Guard series (THE CHIEF, THE HAWK, THE RANGER, THE VIPER, THE SAINT, THE RECRUIT, THE HUNTER, THE KNIGHT (novella), THE RAIDER and THE ARROW), and two Regency Romances (THE UNTHINKABLE and TAMING THE RAKE). Her books have won and been nominated for numerous awards, including the Romance Writers of America's RITA® & Golden Heart®, RT Book Reviews Reviewers' Choice, the Bookseller's Best, and Amazon's Best Books of the Year. Known for her "torrid chemistry" and "lush and steamy romance" as well as her "believable historical situations" (Publishers Weekly), her books have been translated and published throughout the world. Monica's interest in the Scottish clan system began in the most unlikely of places: a comparative legal history course at Stanford Law School. After a short, but enjoyable, stint practicing law, she realized that mixing a legal career with her husband's transitory career as a professional baseball player was not exactly a match made in heaven. So she "traded" in her legal briefs for Historical Romances with sexy alpha heroes. When not trekking across the moors and rocky seascapes of Scotland or England, Monica can be found in Northern California with her husband and two children.

Visit Monica's website at: www.MonicaMcCarty.com
Find Monica on Facebook at:
https://www.facebook.com/AuthorMonicaMcCarty
Follow Monica on Twitter at:
https://twitter.com/monicamccarty
Sign up for Monica's Newsletter at:
http://monicamccarty.com/index.php

Made in the USA
Coppell, TX
04 September 2022

82597032R00204